Wings of the ▮▮▮▮▮▮ h
and When Satan Came to Town

TWO CLASSIC ADVENTURES OF

THE SPIDER™

by Norvell W. Page
writing as Grant Stockbridge

plus **historical essays by**
Will Murray and Ed Hulse

SANCTUM BOOKS

International Standard Book Number: 978-1-60877-148-6

First printing: July 2014

Series editor/publisher: Anthony Tollin
anthonytollin@shadowsanctum.com

Consulting editor: Will Murray

Copy editor: Joseph Wrzos

Proofreader: Carl Gafford

OCR text reconstruction: Rich Harvey

Cover restoration: Michael Piper

The editors gratefully acknowledge the contributions of Kirk Kimball, John Locke, Chris Kalb (www.spiderreturns.com) and Rebecca Searson.

Published by Sanctum Books
P.O. Box 761474, San Antonio, TX 78245-1474

THE SPIDER

MASTER OF MEN!

™

Volume 4

Thrilling Tales and Features

Cover art by Raphael de Soto

**Back cover art by John Newton Howitt
and Raphael de Soto**

**Interior illustrations by J. T. Fleming-Gould
and Joseph A. Farren**

ABOVE THE LAW ... SWORN ENEMY OF THE UNDERWORLD ... HATED BY BOTH ...

Wings of the Black Death

By

Grant Stockbridge

Like the consuming flames of a prairie fire the dread news spread: "The SPIDER has gone mad! He will massacre us all!" But Richard Wentworth, never more sane, was even then gambling life itself in one desperate effort to save the city which cursed his name— from the awful ravages of man-spread plague!

People died in the streets.
Thousands fled.

The Wings of the Black Death hovered over plague-stricken New York—and Richard Wentworth gambled life itself to save the city which cursed his name— fighting a desperate struggle against the vicious, twin attacks of the law and the underworld!

CHAPTER ONE
The Spider Returns

RICHARD WENTWORTH, immaculate in evening attire, wandered with swift, deceptive carelessness among the night blackened shrubs, stealing away from the police commissioner's stately mansion. Behind him rang the gay laughter of society at play, but in Wentworth's eyes was only grimness and an alert watchfulness.

If those revelers knew as he did the fearful skeleton that leered at their feast, their laughter would turn to screams of horror!

Suddenly Wentworth checked his advance, halted behind the spire of an arborvitae. He merged with its shadow, quick hands turning up satin lapels to hide the white glimmer of his shirt. Just beyond the tree loomed the pacing figure of a policeman swinging a nightstick. But without pause, or glance toward the arborvitae, the bluecoat plodded on with heavy, heedless feet. He would never know the *Spider* had passed in the night.

A wry smile twisted Wentworth's mouth as he catfooted on. This man was a guardian of the law. Because justice must wait on such men, Wentworth tonight had turned his back upon gaiety; leaving the side of the woman he loved to grope through the vicious underworld in hopes of grappling with that mocking skeleton at the feast; risking his life once more that the tentacles of crime might be kept from the throat of the city. Because of this, Wentworth tonight again became the *Spider*!

Silently as his namesake, the *Spider* sped on. A four foot wall of stone blocked his path. He rested his hands lightly on it and vaulted clear. A moment later he appeared beside a Lancia limousine parked at the curb. The chauffeur turned a turbaned head, and white teeth flashed in a dark face.

"*Sahib*," he murmured.

"To the address that you know, Ram Singh," Wentworth ordered and sprang into the back.

The auto muttered smoothly away and, drawing the curtain, Wentworth fingered a button under the left side of the seat. The entire section—cushioned back, seat and all—swung forward. The back revolved and a neatly hung rack of clothes was disclosed by a small shielded light.

Wentworth's movements were deft. Off came the tail coat, stiffly exact shirt, collar, tie. He quickly donned a dark tweed suit, set jauntily on his black hair a dark fedora whose brim shadowed his eyes. He strapped beneath his arm a compact kit of chrome steel tools. At another touch of the button, the seat swung back into place, and the *Spider* was ready.

Wentworth caught the speaking tube and spoke precisely in Hindustani to Ram Singh.

"It is now," said Wentworth, glancing at his watch, "half past ten. At exactly ten minutes of eleven, Ram Singh, phone the police and tell them that the jewels stolen in the Racine case are in the possession of John Harper, the pawnbroker. Tell them then that the back door will be unlocked when they get there and that without a search warrant they may invade his office and catch him with the stolen goods."

Jewels. They had led many to their doom.

But Wentworth had scant concern with them tonight. His wide information had brought him this knowledge, that Harper had the stolen goods. That bit of knowledge would serve to bring to justice a smooth criminal— and to prevent pursuit when the *Spider* had paid his visit.

Wentworth dropped the tube, seeing through the bulletproof glass that separated him and the Hindu, the slow single nod of the turbaned head. That was sufficient. Wentworth knew that Ram Singh would perform his task with time-clock precision. He relaxed into the cushioned luxury of the Lancia, drew out a cigarette and snapped flame to a lighter. He smiled thinly at its gleaming platinum sides.

Who would suspect that in this expensive toy reposed the seals of the *Spider*? Yet in a secret chamber in its base were those vermilion calling cards that had given him his name, that made the underworld cringe and the police rage in futile anger. Well, tonight he would need them again, would need once more to set police and criminals on his trail, united in their hatred of this master of men who set at naught the underworld's shrewdest plots; who snatched the criminal where police dared not go and left behind, to tell them he had struck, his mocking challenge—the seal of the *Spider*.

Wentworth snuffed the lighter, dropped it into his vest pocket and sat staring ahead with narrowed, burning eyes. Tonight was typical. In a bizarre combination of events too trivial for police to notice, the *Spider* had sensed the first outcreeping tentacle of a crime he scarcely dared to name, a crime that would blight city and nation for years to come. And because of that he went out quietly, with a smile, to battle with death.

It was the harder since the city, after drab years of Depression, was just beginning to shrug its powdered shoulders free of the dreary cloak of poverty, beginning to laugh again and to sing. That night the police commissioner, Stanley Kirkpatrick, had given the first really big, joyous ball of many seasons, never guessing the loathsome black wings of death that the *Spider* alone detected on the horizon.

On the surface, the crime which the *Spider* went tonight to rectify was a minor one. Virginia Doeg had been arrested for substituting forged bonds for genuine in the office of MacDonald Pugh, a Wall Street broker. She had cried out that she was innocent, that she had been framed. The *Spider*'s first casual investigation motivated by the fresh innocence of the girl's face, which showed even through the crude photographs of the newspapers, had convinced him this was so.

Ordinarily, as Richard Wentworth, an amateur in criminology, he would have gone to Stanley Kirkpatrick with his information, set in motion the girl's release; but—there on the horizon were those sinister black wings which none but he had seen.

Three days before the girl's arrest, he had noticed a small story on the front pages of the newspapers. It stated that a dog had died of the Black Death, the Bubonic Plague, which in years past had killed its hundreds of thousands—killed them horribly with screams of pain and awful strangling and blood gushing from their throats.

And that dog had belonged to Virginia Doeg, the same girl who now was accused of forgery!

Individually the two items meant nothing;

together they might mean—Wentworth's hand clutched into a cold fist upon his knee.

He flashed a look ahead, leaned forward and tapped sharply on the glass. The Lancia snubbed down its nose at the curb. Wentworth touched the automatic that weighted his pocket, unfolded his lean height to the sidewalk, and—the shadows swallowed the *Spider*.

CHAPTER TWO
"Spider, You Must Die!"

FIVE minutes later a passerby might have seen a black shadow slip into the entrance of a shabby tenement. Within the building, dim gas light scarcely dissipated the darkness through which the *Spider* slipped.

Wentworth went on soundless feet through the halls and out of a door that opened on a yard cluttered with cans and refuse. He crossed it at an angle, muscled himself to the top of a fence and vaulted over, then crouched, waiting.

From nearby tenements voices gabbled. A cheap radio dinned into the blackness, and a sick infant wailed. Wentworth glanced at the luminous dial of his watch. Five minutes had elapsed since he had left the limousine. In twelve more Ram Singh's voice would summon the police. He crept forward.

Never was there rest for the *Spider*. He had been back from Europe but one day, but already this injustice, this hint of impending horror called him forth.

Wentworth's smile was slightly mocking. Yes, injustice angered him. He flew to the protection of its victims with such anger as a man feels when he sees a dog kicked viciously, or a dray horse beaten senseless as it struggles against a heavy load.

His mind flicked back to the case in hand. Forgery of bonds—well, the *Spider* knew where that pointed. John Harper prospered by that racket. And John Harper's pawnshop lay just ahead of him, its back windows barred and forbidding, its heavy iron door a veritable Gibraltar.

The thin smile that the *Spider* perpetually wore in battle twisted his lips and he slipped forward across the shadow-blackened yard, threading a soundless way among tin cans and crates.

Before the iron door he paused a second, drew from the kit of chrome steel tools against his side a long, slender blade and ran this rapidly around the edge of the door until his sensitive fingers felt it contact the plates of the burglar alarm. Holding the metal grounded against that plate and the brick side of the building, he rapidly picked the lock and opened the door.

The *Spider* knew the secret of burglar alarms, knew that it was the break in the circuit formed by the plate on the door and the plate on the door-jamb—their separation by the door's opening—that caused the alarm to ring. So long as the connection was completed, grounded by that metal tool against the brick, it would not ring.

Swiftly the *Spider* slid into the blackness within and shut the door silently behind him. The tools went back into the kit against his side, and he drew from it a black silk mask that, fitting tightly across his eyes, hung limply down from there and concealed all of his face.

His left hand now held a small but powerful flashlight; his right the automatic.

Like his namesake, silently, the *Spider* drifted up old stairs that would have creaked aloud in protest against less able feet.

Beneath a door at their top a thread of light gleamed, but the *Spider* did not go directly to that door. Instead he moved silently along the hall, exploring it and the rooms that opened off it, and not until he found that they were empty did he glide back to the door where the light showed.

The flashlight vanished in his pocket, and with the gun held in his hand, he twisted the knob and thrust in the door.

There was a small squeak from the man who crouched behind the velvet-topped table, a tiny gasp of alarm, then silence. And the *Spider*, with the door kicked shut behind him, stood silently, his lips bitterly thin beneath the mask, and looked at John Harper.

The only light in the room was a lowswung greenshaded globe that focused straight down on the black velvet top of the table behind which the pawnbroker sat, shone queerly upon the man's prematurely bald head. A double handful of jewels glittered upon the velvet, and John Harper's fat fingers clutched them. His smooth, pink-cheeked face showed a mingling of greed and fear.

One of his hands moved slowly, slid along the velvet to the right.

"Keep your hand away from that button, Harper," Wentworth bit out.

Once more the quavering cry issued from the man, and he jerked his hand away from the spot toward which it had been traveling.

Wentworth's lip lifted in contempt. This man was a fence and a forger, to the *Spider* the lowest forms of all criminal life. He stood and stared at the man through the slits of his black silk mask. The edge of the light fell squarely on his hand, glittered on the leveled gun, and the two men were frozen into hostile statues.

Wentworth let the silence go on until it rang in his ears. He had time—ten minutes, perhaps. His eyes flickered to the huge safe at Harper's elbow. It was closed, locked, but such a safe would take only a few minutes for the *Spider*'s sensitive fingers to open.

He waited and finally Harper, gathering all his

courage, squeaked out, "What do you want? You know you can't do this to me. I am John Harper. When *they* find out about this they will make you pay!"

A short, sharp laugh came from the *Spider*'s concealed lips. Pay! *They had been trying to make him pay for years now*, and the *Spider* still lived, still nullified their cleverest plots, snatched from them their richest loot.

Wentworth took three short steps so that he stood only a yard from the table's edge.

"Listen to me," he said. "The bonds that were stolen from MacDonald Pugh's office, the ones for which you made forged copies. I want them."

Bewildered, embattled fear filled the fat sly face above the table. The high bald head wrinkled as John Harper strove to solve the puzzle as to why a crook with a gun should ask for bonds, when jewels sparkled beneath the bright electric light. But he dissembled swiftly.

"I don't know what you mean," he quavered. Wentworth's body crouched forward, the gun advanced an inch, and his masked face lowered slowly into the puddle of light.

"Don't lie to me, Harper," he said slowly.

"But I'm not lying," the man said rapidly. "Honest, I ain't got 'em."

"Don't lie, Harper," Wentworth repeated in the same voice. "Don't lie to the *Spider*."

At those two words, "The *Spider*," the pigjowled pawnbroker's eyes widened until the white showed completely around their evasive blue irises. His mouth opened and he swallowed audibly. But no sound came from his dry lips. He touched his tongue furtively to them, swallowed again.

"My God!"

There was grim amusement in Wentworth's voice. "Let me have those bonds—at once."

"But I haven't got them, I haven't!" the man cried.

The *Spider* allowed his eyes to flick to the safe, and the pawnbroker sprang into action, with an agility surprising for one of his weight. His fist shot into view with the ugly snout of a bulldog revolver. But even as he squeezed the trigger, the *Spider* flung himself aside and his own gun spat spitefully.

The crash of the pawnbroker's heavy revolver was deafening. Lead whined past Wentworth's ear and lodged futilely in the wall. But the *Spider*'s bullet had sped true. A round blue hole gaped in the forehead of John Harper.

For an instant he sat straight up in his chair, a surprised look upon his face. Then he slumped forward, his head spilling blood on the stolen jewels over which he had gloated. His life of greedy crime was ended.

The *Spider* whirled swiftly to the door, jerked it open. Outside all was deep, dark silence. No police whistles skirled in the streets; no sirens smote his ears; no one shouted. The acrid odor of gun powder drifted past his nostrils, and the *Spider* glanced swiftly at his watch.

He still had four minutes before Ram Singh would call the police. Four minutes before a radio alarm flashed out and swift two-seated cars sped through the crooked East Side to seize John Harper with his stolen jewels.

A swift smile crossed the *Spider*'s lips. No one would ever arrest John Harper now.

He closed the door and went swiftly to the safe, drawing on a pair of thin gray silk gloves. Then, with ear close-pressed against the face of the safe, he began to twirl the dial.

It took the *Spider* one minute to open the antiquated safe. It took him three more to ransack the compartments.

Dozens of documents were there that the police would be eager to see, but to the *Spider* they were unimportant. He skimmed rapidly through them, swiftly restoring to its place each document as he scanned it. He found no trace of the stolen bonds, but far down in a compartment in the lower left-hand corner of the safe, he came upon that which made his blood like ice in his veins. It was a glass vial upon the tiny label of which were printed two words:

"Hopkins' Solution."

The vial in his fist, Wentworth stared at the corpse of John Harper with eyes that held both fury and horror. Hopkins' Solution was the only efficient antitoxin for the Black Death!

He had been right. This man was involved in the framing of Virginia Doeg. Her dog had died of the Black Death, and in this man's possession was the plague serum. In Heaven's name, what diabolical crime was being hatched here?

Swiftly the *Spider* stooped again and reached more deeply into the compartment. Other tubes of the stuff were there, and also there was a card on which were two names—Virginia Doeg and that of another woman, Mrs. Henry Gainsborough, of Roslyn, Long Island.

Rapidly Wentworth slid the card into his pocket, glanced at his watch.

One minute left. Time for the *Spider* to go. Swiftly he drew out his cigarette lighter. Swiftly he detached its bottom and pressed the seal against the safe door, leaned over and pressed again on the arching dome of John Harper's head. And where he had pressed, the outline of an ugly spider showed in rich vermilion!

The seal of the *Spider*, his calling card! For a moment the *Spider* stared with his thin smile at the seals, then swiftly replaced the cigarette lighter in his pocket. A slight sound behind him whirled him swift as thought. A voice drawled into the tense silence of the room:

"Just keep your hands like that, Mr. *Spider*."

In the doorway stood a tall heavy man whose face, too, was covered with a black mask. In his right hand was a heavy gun, and its muzzle was pointed straight at the *Spider*'s heart!

CHAPTER THREE
Flight—and Challenge

FACING the gun in the hands of the masked man, Wentworth straightened slowly. His voice was entirely calm.

"You have me at a disadvantage. I'm afraid I don't know you."

The man chuckled behind his mask.

"You never will," he said. "It is unfortunately necessary for me to leave you here—dead."

"Really?"

There was mild amusement in the *Spider*'s tone, but there was none in his face beneath the shielding black silk. Death glared at him from the slits of the other man's mask, from the black muzzle of that leveled gun.

Somewhere not far away, Ram Singh was even then entering a telephone booth. Police would come. But they would bring no help to Wentworth. To the *Spider* the police meant death just as sure as that unwavering muzzle into which he looked. For there behind him in a huddled heap across the table was another who had paid the penalty for his sins. And the brilliant, small seal of the *Spider* glowed like a drop of blood upon his forehead!

Yet there was nothing of all this apprehension in the *Spider*'s voice. He must play for time and trust to his split-second reflexes, his keen mind, to yank him from the closing jaws of death.

"Curiosity," he told the masked man, "is an unpleasant thing to carry to one's grave. I don't know you, and I know most of the crooks of this world. Why do you seek my death?"

Once more the man chuckled.

"Simply because you have learned too much—"

Wentworth's eyes became pinpoints as he read the meaning behind those words. Then this man knew the secret of those vials in the safe, knew the horror at which they hinted.

"I don't know what you mean," he said. "Learned what?"

The man's laughter hissed into the silent room again.

"Guess, *Spider*," he rasped. "But guess fast. You have but a few moments left."

Wentworth raised a hand before him as though inspecting his fingernails, but his eyes shot to the face of his watch. Two minutes had elapsed now since Ram Singh had called the police. Any second would see them ascending the stairs. They might seize this man from behind, might interrupt this execution. But what would follow for the *Spider*?

Wentworth dreaded to think what might happen to the city should he himself be arrested now and placed on trial for murder. He might tell his suspicions to the police. But after all they were nothing but suspicions. And who would believe the *Spider*? Who would take his vague, unfounded charges seriously?

Wentworth's eyes caught the glint of electric light on moving metal and glanced quickly at the man who was his captor. The gun was rising slowly; he could see the increasing tension of the man's knuckles. The trigger was moving slowly back! And at the same instant, Wentworth's straining ears caught the cautious tread of feet upon the stair.

The police had arrived; it could be no one else. Wentworth's body tensed for the final desperate moment. Then in the blackness of the hall, a voice roared: "Hands up, there!"

The *Spider* himself could not have whirled more quickly than the tall man in the doorway. Whirl and shot were instantaneous, and in the hall a man cried out hoarsely.

With a single movement of his hand, the *Spider* extinguished the light. In two strides he reached the window, yanked down the top casement.

No fear now that the killer would get him. Guns roared and bellowed in the hallway; lead sang and whined. The *Spider* smiled thinly as he fled. The police would take care of his recent captor now.

With swift, lithe movements, Wentworth climbed out through the upper casement, planted his foot upon it as upon a ladder, and sprang upward. His hands closed upon the edge of the roof and for a moment he dangled there, clinging with aching fingers.

There were hoarse shouts below him in the yard, guns blazed, and lead plunked into the wood beside him. Wentworth flexed his arms, levered himself upward. In an instant he got a foot over the gutter, rolled and was safe.

More lead whistled by as he dodged away from the edge of the roof. He ran crouchingly across its narrow width, hurdled the barrier to the next house and, ducking beneath radio wires, proceeded swiftly across four buildings. Atop the fifth dwelling, he jerked up a roof scuttle and dropped through on light feet into the black upper hallway of another, smelly tenement.

It was the work of moments then to run swiftly down the stairs, jerking off the telltale mask and slipping it into the toolkit beneath his arm. And once more the *Spider* became a shadow, merged with the blackness of the lower hall. Casually he drifted out into the street and mingled with the excited crowd that was being pushed back by policemen from the danger zone about John Harper's pawnshop, where guns still blazed.

Richard Wentworth remained with that crowd until the police drove them away. Then, as if reluctantly, he moved off down the street.

Five minutes later, in a dank byway, he slid again into the Lancia with a brief nod to Ram Singh. Then, as the imperturbable Hindu slid the limousine into smooth purring speed, Wentworth's finger touched once more the button that revealed the wardrobe behind the seat and he quickly garbed himself again in evening dress.

As he alighted from the car at the police commissioner's house, he glanced again at his watch. Nearly an hour. Too long—he should have been back half an hour ago.

Swiftly he moved, dodging again the pacing policeman and entered the conservatory. Standing in the doorway, he drew out a cigarette and lighted it with a flick of the lighter that so recently had implanted the seal of the *Spider* upon a dead man's forehead.

A dangerous thing for any man to carry—the seal of the *Spider*. And so Wentworth had found it in the past; but now his old friend, Professor Brownlee, had made him a lighter which was practically proof against discovery. The seals were there in the base of the lighter, in a secret chamber, but even that secret chamber would be hard to find, for a thin coating of varnish which matched the lighter (and which Wentworth had reapplied on his trip back to Kirkpatrick's home) concealed the narrow crack that marked the opening of the secret chamber.

In addition to that, if anyone but Wentworth opened that compartment, the seals dissolved in thirty seconds, for it was necessary to press a small hidden button and to bring the seal swiftly in contact with a surface to which it would adhere to prevent its dissolution.

Wentworth's hand, as he held the flame, was rock steady; he smiled slightly to see it, and strolled out among the guests. Nita van Sloan, the one woman he trusted in all the world, was whirling in the stately measures of a waltz in the arms of police commissioner Stanley Kirkpatrick.

The men's eyes met, and a wintry smile lifted the small black pointed mustache of the commissioner of police. He turned slowly in the rhythm of the dance, and Nita's quick eyes flew to Wentworth's face. She smiled, but in the depths of her blue eyes was a haunting fear.

It was not that she did not rely on the keen mind of her sweetheart; it was only that she knew the desperate chances he took, and the knowledge that sooner or later every man must yield to the mathematics of chance.

Standing there in the doorway, carelessly smoking as if guns had never whined bullets past his head, as if his swift justice had never taken life,

Wentworth showed no evidence of his minutes-old tussle with death. What first impressed you about him was the remarkable physical alertness of the man. Five feet eleven, with the tapered body and light stride of an athlete, he had a keen, tanned face and the friendly interested eyes of a man who has long since learned the secret of enjoying life.

He smiled slowly, and even half across the room the magnetism of the man became apparent. He was so completely vital and alive. The music halted and he crossed swiftly, took Nita's hand and bowed over it, his gray-blue eyes smiling up beneath black brows that held always a hint of raillery.

"I have missed you," Kirkpatrick said.

Wentworth smiled lightly. "I have been communing with the stars. Libra, you know, is in the ascendant. That always brings luck—Libra, that is, in conjunction with Saturn—so I went out to watch my luck rise."

He turned smiling to the girl. His swift glance traveled over the bright turquoise of the simple dress that subtly emphasized the soft lines of her young body.

"Have I told you, my dear, how charming you are?" he asked. "A singularly trying color to wear, and you do it perfectly."

The girl blushed with pleasure, her face radiant beneath the clustering brown warmth of her curling hair.

"Really, Dick," she said, "and right out in public!" She turned to Kirkpatrick. "Isn't he simply impossible?" she asked lightly.

The commissioner's lips beneath the pointed black mustache were lifted by a slight smile.

"Dick Wentworth," he said, "is a man who does the impossible."

He took the cigarette Wentworth proffered in a platinum case.

"The stars have given me a message," Wentworth laughed. "I have a feeling that the *Spider*," he waved his hand and a thread of blue smoke from his cigarette wavered slightly, "I have an idea that the *Spider* will be with us again. I heard stories in Europe that he was returning."

The *Spider*!

The words seemed to hover over the three standing there in the brilliant ballroom. It was like an Arctic blast in the midst of warm comfort; like a window banged suddenly open into a quiet drawing room, the storm and the rain beating in.

The eyes of the two men met. Challenge was there, despite all the friendship between the two. Wentworth had once saved Kirkpatrick's life. There were bonds of admiration and respect between them, and yet in the police commissioner's mind was always a germ of suspicion. Many times now Wentworth and the *Spider* had been closely connected in circumstance and in simultaneous action. Always Wentworth had been able ultimately to turn aside that suspicion. But always it returned.

The girl's laughter at their side became strained and slightly uneasy, and the laughter was not in her blue eyes.

"Did the *Spider*, by any chance," asked Kirkpatrick softly, "come over on the boat with you?"

Wentworth threw back his head and laughed. "That man," he said, "he is so elusive. Who can say what boat he takes, what homes he will penetrate?" and he cast his gray-blue eyes over the rich assembly. "Why good Lord!" he exclaimed suddenly, "the man might even be here, in this room." He waved his hand again, and a tall man with forward-thrust bald head and eyes keen beneath heavy brows walked over and grasped it.

"What man is this that might be here, Dick?" he asked and laughed—and added, "Welcome home!"

Nita seized on the diversion.

"Really, Mac, it's been ages since we've seen you."

"MacDonald Pugh," greeted Wentworth, "the great fisherman! Tuna will be running soon, Mac, and we'll have to go for some."

Kirkpatrick bowed to the newcomer, bowed again to Nita. For an instant a third smile flickered over his lips. "It was the *Spider* we were talking about, Mac," he said, looking at Wentworth. "I trust the *Spider*'s presence, if he is here, will not cause you discomfort, Dick."

And Kirkpatrick, smiling suavely, moved away.

MacDonald Pugh looked after him with an amused smile.

"What's eating the old boy tonight?" he queried.

"Same old problem, Mac," Wentworth told him. "The *Spider*. I was teasing him about the fellow and, as usual, Stan rose to the bait. By the way, Mac, speaking of crime, you had a bit of an outbreak in your office recently."

Pugh's face lengthened so that creases diagonaled from his nose to mouth corners.

"A pity about Virginia Doeg," he said. "I'd have sworn she was honest. She was getting along nicely, too, engaged to marry a boy in the office, a James Handley. Intelligent lad, Handley, going places someday. And now— "

Pugh waved a hand.

"Goodbye to all that, eh?" Wentworth said musingly. "Usual thing, I know, that claim of frame-up. But I wonder if there isn't something to it in this case?"

MacDonald shook his bald head.

"Let's talk about something else," he growled. "Tuna fishing, for instance."

"I'll be by some weekend soon and make plans," Wentworth promised and Pugh nodded, smiled pleasantly and drifted off.

Nita's hand was quick on Wentworth's arm. "Oh, Dick, Dick, why must you always stir up Kirkpatrick? He's convinced already that you're the *Spider*. Why make him sure?"

Wentworth turned his head, smiled down at her with his gray-blue eyes beneath his mocking brows.

"But, my dear," he said, "there must be some zest to life."

"But to get it," cried the girl, "from hairbreadth danger, from laughing in the very face of death!"

Wentworth patted the small white hand upon his arm.

"Nita van Sloan," he said, "if I recall, has done a bit of laughing in the face of the gloomy old specter herself."

A pompous butler appeared in the doorway abruptly. Wentworth looked at him inquiringly.

"I was just looking, sir," he said, "For Mr. Kirkpatrick."

Wentworth glanced about. "There he is," he said, and at the butler's signal the police commissioner strode across.

"A phone call, sir, an important one, they say. Shall I attach the phone here?"

"Yes," said Kirkpatrick, and stood chatting carelessly with his two friends while the butler brought the instrument and plugged it into the wall.

The commissioner excused himself and spoke into the transmitter. Wentworth, watching him while apparently he listened to Nita's swift words, saw Kirkpatrick's tall body tighten, saw his hands clutch the telephone, heard his staccato words as he barked orders into the transmitter. Then he returned the phone to the butler and whirled. His striding across the room was like the charge of a lion. His eyes were hard as agates and his voice grated.

"The *Spider*," he said sharply, "has just killed two of my policemen!"

CHAPTER FOUR
"Shoot to Kill"

A THIN white scar on Wentworth's right temple, the relic of an old knife fight, turned red and began to throb. That was the only evidence of his excitement. His hands were steady; his eyes did not flinch from the stern regard of Kirkpatrick. Beside him he could feel the tightening of Nita's hand upon his arm, and knew that her blue eyes must be widened with horror.

Wentworth frowned slowly. "But that does not sound possible," he said. "I have never known the *Spider* to kill anyone except a crook."

"There is no mistake," said Kirkpatrick sternly. "That villainous red seal was printed on the foreheads of the dead men."

Wentworth's face stiffened with his effort at

self-control. Truly this new enemy was proving a worthy antagonist. For Wentworth could not doubt that it was he who had placed the seal upon the murdered policemen. The threat of the terrible Black Death, and now this. Anger rose slowly within him like a white-hot tide. He felt his brow flush with it, and he clenched his fists. It was too powerful an emotion for him to conceal. He stared into Kirkpatrick's eyes, and his own pupils were pinpoints of rage.

"Now I swear to you, Kirkpatrick," he said slowly, "I will help you bring to justice the murderer of your men."

The commissioner's face was set in harsh, commanding lines.

"Remember what you say, Wentworth!"

"So help me God," Wentworth repeated, "I will bring to book the murderer of those policemen."

"Will you trap the *Spider*?"

Wentworth's mouth went into a thin straight line. "If the *Spider* is the man who placed the seal upon their foreheads, the *Spider* shall pay."

For long moments the men's gaze locked, and the slow languorous strains of another waltz came like music from another world, so foreign was it to the tension of the two.

Nita van Sloan laughed uncertainly beside them.

"For heaven's sake, Dick," she said, "Don't look so grim. One might fancy you and Stanley were enemies."

Neither man replied; nor did their eyes shift from their rigid regard of one another.

"I'll say this to you," Kirkpatrick said presently, and there was strain in his voice, "in spite of the fact that the *Spider* is a criminal, I have admired him previously. Admired him because he struck down the criminals that I could not touch within the law; admired him because he was fair and just. But I tell you now that this is different. That hereafter it is war to the death between the *Spider* and the police. I shall order my men to shoot him on sight—if ever his true identity is disclosed to us."

A slow smile spread over Wentworth's face. He had got a grip on himself now, and the slow red throb of the wound on his temple had subsided.

"I don't know why you tell me all of this, Stanley, but I think you are entirely right. I too shall shoot on sight when I spot the man who placed the seal upon the foreheads of those dead police."

For a moment longer the men stood face to face. Then Kirkpatrick bowed swiftly.

"I must ask you to excuse me now; there is work to be done." He bowed a second time to Nita van Sloan, spun on his heel and stalked off.

Wentworth looked after him with a slight smile disturbing the equanimity of his lips, and mockery returning to his brow. He turned to Nita.

"Good old Stan seems to be a bit disturbed," he said. "Come, let's finish this dance; then we must go."

Nita van Sloan gave herself into his arms and they whirled slowly through the dancing throng. But her heart was not in it, and although Wentworth guided her skillfully and gracefully through the measures there was no pleasure in the waltz.

They took their leave then, and Wentworth, handing her into his car, said softly: "Will you go home with me for a while, Nita? I must talk to you."

"Of course, Dick," the girl said from the depths of the car and Wentworth, nodding briefly to Ram Singh, climbed in.

For a moment, while the car tooled through the traffic, he sat silently, the girl's white hand clinging to his arm. Finally the girl could stand the stillness no longer and broke out: "Oh, Dick—that awful seal. *Your* seal!"

"Yes," said Wentworth softly. "My seal. I think Nita, my dear, that I am entering the most deadly conflict of my life. This man is fiendish, utterly without heart. And he is clever." His fist struck suddenly on his knee. "Damnably clever."

In the darkness, Wentworth's breath came short and fast, and anger rose in him again. The girl's soft voice at his elbow called him back.

"But what are you talking about, Dick? I don't understand."

Wentworth then told her briefly what had happened that night, and that his enemy must have placed his seal on the policemen's foreheads.

"Do you know what that means, my darling? If any criminal has the courage to imitate the *Spider*, to try to pin his crimes on him, then that man must have an amazing and fiendish plot before him, for the underworld dreads the *Spider* and fears him."

Nita laughed amusedly at his side.

"For heaven's sake, Dick, you talk as though the *Spider* were someone else."

Wentworth laughed with her.

"Someone else! Child, sometimes when I get behind that mask and go out with a gun in my pocket, I feel that no such person as Richard Wentworth ever lived." His fist clenched. "Nita, something so fearful that it will rock the world is in progress here. I know it!"

Mentally he was visioning the shadow of the Black Death just below the horizon glow of the city's lights. But why, he asked himself, would any criminal deal with such a fearful thing? What could he hope to accomplish with it?

The car halted and a resplendent doorman opened the door of the limousine. Wentworth, with a smile on his lips, descended and handed Nita to the curb. Together they walked across the sidewalk and through the elaborate, tasteful lobby, a man of the world and his friend.

Who would think that here walked the *Spider* and the one woman in the world who knew his identity? Who could guess that this man was on the brink of battle with the most dangerous antagonist the world of crime had ever produced?

They entered the private elevator which lifted them silently to Wentworth's fifteen-room penthouse atop one of Fifth Avenue's most fashionable buildings. The ruddy-faced Jenkyns who opened the door bowed delightedly as he took his master's cape, gloves and cane; for Jenkyns, his hair silvering with age, looked forward to the day when Nita van Sloan would be mistress over the household, when the dread pall of mystery would cease to dominate the young master he adored. His ruddy face was wrinkled with smiles as he hurried on to his pantry, to put together with his inimitable skill supper for his master and the mistress-to-be.

Richard Wentworth did not pause in the drawing room, but led Nita directly to his thick-walled study. He seated her comfortably and gestured toward Ram Singh, who had followed them.

"A phone please," he said quietly.

Presently Ram Singh came back into the room with a portable phone and plugged it into the wall. Wentworth took it eagerly. "Have Jenkyns," he told Ram Singh, "get Mrs. Gainsborough on the phone. Mrs. Gainsborough in Roslyn, Long Island."

When the connection had gone through he asked quickly, "Mrs. Gainsborough? This is Richard Wentworth. Has anything unusual happened about your estate during the past week?"

As he listened to the woman's response, which grated so noisily that its rasping sound was audible to Nita van Sloan ten feet away, his hand tightened slowly about the phone, and his eyes took on an eager light.

"But Mrs. Gainsborough," he said swiftly, "you need not be afraid. I am not connected in any way with the police. I do a little criminal investigation work sometimes myself, and I ran across your name in that connection. Yes, yes, perhaps you are right. Certainly… I'll be out to see you tomorrow… Yes, until then. Goodbye."

He handed the phone back to Ram Singh and whirled on light feet toward Nita. "Darling, the battle is about to begin. I want you to call with me tomorrow on Mrs. Gainsborough. I think she holds the key that will start the fireworks."

The next afternoon was sullen beneath lowering clouds, and the wind that stirred in their faces as Wentworth drove his swift Hispana Suiza roadster over the Long Island roads was hot and oppressive.

They swept from the climbing highway into a broad stone-gated drive and went on their way through trees up to the colossal columns that marked the home of Mrs. Gainsborough. The whole mass seemed to have been built with the idea of making a showplace, and the result was slightly ludicrous. Wentworth's upflung glance, taking in the whole facade, was mildly amused, but when he entered the house and bowed before the stout matron who received him, his manner was deferential.

The woman was absurdly overdressed, stuffed like a sausage into a too tight dress that showed too much of her pudgy arms for afternoon wear, and too much of her ample bosom. But there was no laughter in Wentworth's eyes as he looked into her pudgy face; for grief and fear were there, and Wentworth was no man to mock at human misery.

So Wentworth smiled sympathetically, and the woman smothered his strong hand in both of hers.

"Oh, thank you, thank you for coming," she said. "I have been so afraid." She managed a smile and sank heavily into a chair in the over-decorated and over-furnished room where she received the two.

She poured out the story in a swift gush of words and Wentworth, standing silently before her, his eyes fixed in keen concentration on her face, listened with encouraging nods.

A letter had come, she said, demanding that she pay a million dollars to the writer lest her entire family be killed.

"A million dollars!" she exclaimed, and her hands flew in swift gestures. "A million dollars I have not got, or I would pay it willingly, to save my children."

She raised her voice and called out. "Marie! Marie! Bring Dave and Gertrude in!" She went on talking quickly. "This letter says if I don't pay they'll kill my children with—with the Black Death."

Wentworth started at the words. The Black Death. Then this was the answer to his fears, extortion under the threat of the Black Death! Good God! Who would not pay with that horror hanging over him? And this was only one case that had come to his attention. There must be hundreds of them. No man who could conceive using the terror of the Black Death would stop at one extortion. Wentworth felt the cold crawling touch of apprehension down his back.

Lord in Heaven! If one of the victims refused and the Black Death were loosed, what would turn its fearful stride from the city? What would prevent the murder of thousands? Wentworth spoke swiftly to the woman.

"Have you the letter?" he asked.

Mrs. Gainsborough lurched to her feet, moved awkwardly across the room on broken arches to a desk and returned with a crudely printed letter. It read:

Unless you pay us a million dollars, you and your children will be killed by the Black Death. If you agree, hang something red out of the upstairs window on the front. Remember: pay, or you all die by the Black Death.

Wentworth frowned at the thing. It was like any crank note, more than a little disappointing in its queer simplicity. But the Black Death—

A maid showed momentarily in the doorway, and two children came in. They were youngsters; the girl shy, with golden curly hair and eyes almost as blue as Nita's; the boy younger, with black hair and a chubby face that broke easily into smiles.

The woman's face softened as she turned and called them to her, and Wentworth felt a hand bite into his arm.

"Oh Dick, can't you do something for them?" Nita said softly.

Wentworth turned and smiled at her, and for a moment the alertness went from his eyes and they were very dark and tender. "I'll try, dear."

Somewhere in the house a bell pealed and the woman shuddered as she stood with an arm about each of her children. Fear came back into her face and her lips trembled.

"Oh," she said, "they called once before." Wentworth's eyes were narrow and hard. "Let me talk to them!"

The maid entered with a phone, plugged it into the wall. Wentworth picked it up.

"Hello," he said, and as he listened his eyes sparkled with anger, and his fists clenched. "You keep well informed," he murmured. "Very well! But since you know I'm on the case, let me warn you. If you attempt to harm any member of this household, you'll pay with your life. Understand?" and abruptly he snapped the phone away from his ear, whirled to Nita.

"The same man," he said. "It's the same man. I heard his laugh, the same fiendish chuckling laugh as if he were gloating over something horrible to come!"

He turned swiftly toward the woman. "I'd get guards here immediately. He knows in some way that I'm here, so there's no longer any use of pretense."

He jerked up the phone again, spat a number into it, and began barking out commands to the police—commands which he knew would be instantly obeyed.

The woman sent her children from the room, and Wentworth heard her laboring feet ascend the stairs. He turned to Nita.

"I think it best," he said, "that Ram Singh drive you back to town at once. The man who just phoned declared that he was about to loose the Black Death upon all of us!"

CHAPTER FIVE
The Black Death

WENTWORTH'S words seemed to hang visibly in the air. The Black Death! It called to mind the drab, narrow streets of medieval London, visions of direful axle-creaking carts drawn by scarecrow horses; callous drivers who called mournfully, "Bring out your dead!" and carried loads of corpses like stacked firewood to pyres that burned like the campfires of a besieging enemy about the city; a stench of death and decay; smoke of the corpse fires that beclouded even the sun.

Wentworth stared unseeingly with horror-widened eyes. Surely no human being could conceive so fiendish a crime. Visions of that terrible plague sweeping through the congested millions of New York rose before Wentworth's eyes. Abruptly he jerked himself out of the preoccupation into which he had fallen.

Motors of automobiles roared outside the door and he crossed the room with swift, long strides. A dozen police rolled from the cars and, in charge of a gruff-voiced, waddling sergeant, straggled up to the porch.

Wentworth conferred swiftly with their chief and found him intelligent and competent. Twenty-four-hour patrols about the house were organized, and two policemen who would alternate were selected to stand perpetual guard over the children. A vermin exterminator was called in to destroy all rats and mice which might bring in the disease.

No food was to enter the house without rigid inspection, nor would any stranger pass the police cordon. Finally, satisfied with the arrangements, Wentworth went back into the mansion to give further warning to Mrs. Gainsborough against even a momentary carelessness.

Had Wentworth's thoughtfully intent eyes spotted a figure that crouched on a distant hillside and watched him through binoculars as he entered the house, he might have felt some misgivings about the adequacy of the protection he had provided Mrs. Gainsborough.

But he did not see him. And on that distant hill a large-boned, skulking man with the brim of his black hat pulled far down over his eyes chuckled to himself.

Twenty feet away from the man was a small black satchel with a screen for ventilation opening in one end; such a satchel as small dogs and cats are carried in.

For more than an hour the man sat waiting, propped up against a tall tree, while he watched the distant house.

Finally he saw something which made him chuckle with a gloating satisfaction that was horrible to hear. For from a side entrance of the home a small golden-haired girl and a chubby boy came out, gazing big-eyed at the blue-coated policeman who stalked beside them. They stood close-clustered for a while in animated prattle with their big guardian.

Wentworth came out, too; gave some final swift instruction to the guard, then strode off on an inspection of police.

The children began to romp and play upon the lawn.

It was then that the sinister figure on the hill put the glasses into their case and stood erect. From his pocket he drew an antiseptic mask, such as surgeons wear in operating, and fastened it carefully over nostrils and mouth.

Onto his hands he drew thin rubber gloves, which he wet thoroughly with an evil-smelling germicide. Then he cut a long switch and walked with wary eyes toward the black satchel. He picked it up and, holding it well away from him, made his cautious way down the hillside until he came near the boundary of the Gainsborough estate.

Swiftly then he unfastened the satchel, opened it, and sprang back; and from the interior leaped a small, bright-eyed terrier. It wagged its tail furiously and, bent almost double in an ecstasy of pleasure over its escape from the confinement of the bag, flung toward the white-masked man.

He slashed at it sharply with the switch he had cut upon the hill; two, three, four times he hit the dog savagely. It yipped, turned tail, and fled into the Gainsborough estate.

The man turned and hurried rapidly back the way he had come, leaving the satchel and pouring strong germicide over his hands. He dropped the gloves and the antiseptic mask into a hollow tree stump, then continued his retreat up the hill. Once he had regained his vantage point he again used the glasses on the children romping upon the lawn.

He had not long to wait, for the dog, attracted by the happy cries of the children at play, penetrated to the lawn where they romped and, seeing them, ran eagerly forward.

It had been stolen from a home where there were children, and the monster on the hill, chuckling with sinister satisfaction, congratulated himself upon the thoroughness with which he had planned.

The policeman, he noticed, seemed completely unsuspicious. He patted the dog's head and allowed it to race and play with the children. Wentworth was a mile away, checking on the guards on the opposite side of the estate.

The man on the hill saw this through his glasses and he laughed aloud with a rasping harshness and, rising, vanished into the thickness of the woods.

Wentworth, striding swiftly forward toward the Gainsborough mansion, stopped suddenly and listened. The breeze brought him the excited, happy cries of the two children. But it brought him also another sound that made the blood chill in his veins.

Not a sound to exercise an ordinary man, but to Wentworth, in that moment, it suggested death in a most horrible form. The sound was the sharp barking of a dog.

Wentworth broke into a pounding run, sprinting across the smooth green lawns with furious speed. Nearing the two children, who were playing with the dog and the heedless policeman, he sent his shout ahead of him: "Kill that dog!"

The policeman whirled around and stared at him with gaping mouth. Running, Wentworth had drawn his own gun. But there was no opportunity for him to fire. The children tumbled upon the ground with the dog, and only for fractions of a second was the animal's small furry body visible.

After seconds that seemed like hours, Wentworth darted finally across the last yards of space, pocketing his gun and pulling on rubber gloves that he had carried with him since first he had sensed the threat of the Black Death. With these he snatched the boy away from his laughing struggle with the puppy. He jerked out his automatic and fired two shots in the dog's head; then, without pause, caught up the boy and, holding him at arm's length, rushed back toward the mansion.

He called back to the girl to follow and the policeman trailed in bewilderment after them.

"In the name of all that's holy, Mr. Wentworth, why ever did you kill the puppy?" He panted, half trotting to keep pace with Wentworth. But he got no answer.

Wentworth increased his speed, dashed into the house and shouted for Mrs. Gainsborough. "Get the doctor here immediately. Tell him it's life and death! Tell him to bring Hopkins' Solution with him, the antitoxin for the Bubonic Plague!"

Wentworth forced Nita to leave immediately. He ordered the children put to bed, made them gargle with germicide and washed them and himself with medicated soap. And he ordered the policeman to take similar precautions. He did the same. But for the others, who had been exposed for some time to the dog, the precautions proved futile.

Never before had Wentworth seen the dread Black Death work with such fearful swiftness. Within half an hour of the time he had shot the dog, the children's faces had gone gaunt and yellow with the feverish touch of the plague.

The boy tossed and moaned upon his bed in a half stupor, whimpering with pain. Upon his upper arms blue splotches appeared, the centers showing the spidery tracing of blood-red veins, that dread marking which is called the Flower of the Black Death. Beneath his armpits and thighs purplish egg-shaped swellings grew. Wentworth touched one with the tip of a gloved finger and a scream of wild agony tore from the boy's throat.

"It's the Bubonic Plague right enough," the doctor muttered. But the worry on his face was greater than even that dire announcement, with its threat to countless thousands, warranted. He shook his head, as he and Wentworth stared into each other's eyes with drawn countenances. "There is no record in history," the doctor said, "of the Black Death working this fast. The infection must have taken place four days ago."

Wentworth shook his head slowly. In the silence between them, broken only by the whimperings of the children, by the thudding of the mother's fists on the locked door, her broken pleadings that she be allowed to enter, horror raised its ugly head.

"I'm positive," he told the doctor, "that the dog brought the germ. This must be some new and as yet unknown form of the plague."

The little boy screamed out suddenly in anguish, straightened in the bed and doubled over its edge. Blood gushed from his mouth. The doctor went swiftly to work on him, and Wentworth made way for a trained nurse who had just arrived. Her skilled help would be of far greater assistance than his own. Somberly, he left the room, having almost to fight Mrs. Gainsborough to keep her out. He went directly to a bath where he stripped and literally bathed himself with germicide, syringing out mouth and nostrils. He burned the rubber gloves and, giving what small comfort he could to Mrs. Gainsborough, entered the car and drove away. There was nothing further he could do.

He had failed, and the Black Death had struck its first, horrible blow. Wentworth's eyes were bleak at the thought of the menace to the millions of the city; the thought of a thousand throats echoing with those screams of agony that seemed even now to ring in his own ears; of a thousand bodies tossing in beds that were racks of pain; of a city demoralized by fear.

And over the entire city brooded that masked figure that was the Black Death—a masked figure whose hands would be red with the blood of the innocents.

CHAPTER SIX
The Spider Unmasked

WITH those deaths at the home of Mrs. Gainsborough began the most amazing reign of terror the modern world had ever known. Newspaper headlines flung the ghastly news at their readers in letters two inches high. Wherever people gathered in frightened groups on street corners and public squares, they repeated over and over those three grim words: "The Black Death." They were shouted above the clatter and roar of the subways, whispered in awed tones over the family supper table. Mothers glanced with worried faces at their children; and men went about their work with drawn lips and haggard eyes.

For the dread Black Death that had swept England, that had wiped out whole cities, had laid its horrid skeleton hand upon New York. It was fortunate the panic-stricken multitudes did not know, as Wentworth did, that the deaths were of human agency, perpetrated by a monster whose fiendishness was almost beyond belief.

The Bubonic Plague had appeared in modern times before; it had killed its thousands in the East, but never had it been known in so virulent a form as now. For the present disease was almost instantaneous, killing within twenty-four hours. And the form doctors had known and studied had an incubation period of four days. They had devised two serums for it: one which gave a partial immunity immediately and was effective for five days; another which acted more slowly but which was effective over a longer period.

Both of these had been used in the present outbreak and both had proved futile. Doctors spent long hours over their test tubes; laboratories worked frantically turning out the serums. But it was slow work and nearly hopeless.

Wentworth, lean-faced and burning-eyed, blaming himself for the death of those innocents, flaming with a white-hot rage against the man who called himself tauntingly "The Black Death," was summoned into conference by Stanley Kirkpatrick, the commissioner of police.

There was a never-fading scowl upon Kirkpatrick's saturnine face as the two men, sitting across the desk from each other, sought to lay plans for the capture of the criminal. But what information Wentworth had he could not reveal lest he also betray the fact that he was the *Spider*, a man now sought vengefully by the police for the murder of two of their comrades.

He could not tell him of the connection between that battle in the pawnshop, of John Harper and the gloating laugh of a man over a wire foredooming two children and an entire household to the Black Death, threatening the city's millions.

It was midnight when Wentworth left police headquarters and, entering his Lancia limousine, drove uptown with unseeing eyes fixed upon the turbaned head of Ram Singh. The car snaked through traffic, turned west to the poorly lighted streets along the waterfront, and Wentworth pressed the button that opened the secret wardrobe behind the cushions.

He rapidly extracted and strapped beneath his shirt his compact kit of chrome steel tools, dropped into his pocket a small but deadly automatic, and closed the compartment.

At Seventy-Fourth Street the Lancia turned its nose east into a district of cheap lodging houses whose stingy light barely penetrated dust-filmed windows. Wentworth rapped sharply on the glass. Ram Singh glided smoothly to the curb and, with a few parting instructions, Wentworth (the *Spider* now) strode rapidly up the street, eyeing the dimly revealed numbers of the houses.

He spotted the one he sought near the corner and went deliberately up the steps. The door resisted his skilled use of the lock-pick only a few seconds, and the *Spider* entered.

But this time the *Spider* was bent on no errand of justice; nor was he out to exact the penalty for some crime. The girl whose cry that she had been framed for forgery had won his sympathy lived here, and he hoped she might give him some clue to the master of the plague. But this was an errand that Richard Wentworth could not perform in his true identity. It must be the *Spider* who interviewed the girl, lest later inquiries by the police link the two personalities and identify them as the same man.

Up two flights of steps he crept, and in the darkness of the third floor his hand slipped beneath his coat and once more a black silk mask hid the face of Richard Wentworth.

At each door on the third floor he listened carefully, but found nothing suspicious. Finally he knocked lightly at the one which opened into the girl's room.

A pregnant silence followed his tap. But a moment later he heard a hesitant step and a feminine voice quaver through the thin board panel.

"Who—who is it?"

"Your friend—" said Wentworth softly, "—the *Spider*."

There was a gasp and for a long moment more, silence. Then a key grated in the lock, and the door swung open. The *Spider* slipped in.

He shut the door swiftly behind him. Before his masked face the girl retreated with slow and fearful steps. Her face was pale beneath the glowing red of hair that showered about her shoulders. Her hands clutched about her a cheap negligee of green silk, to which the fresh youth of her body lent dignity. Her mouth was open and a scream had caught in her throat.

"Don't be alarmed, Miss Doeg," the *Spider* said. "It is necessary that I wear a mask, lest my enemies in some way learn who I am."

His words reassured the girl somewhat and she dropped to a seat on the side of the shoddy white-iron bed which, with a second hand dresser and chair, completed the furnishings of her small room.

The *Spider*, with one swift glance, took in every detail, noting the drawn shade. He drew a cigarette case from his pocket and offered it to her, but the girl shook her head with a small smile, and in turn offered him a box from the dresser beside her bed. A white box with gold letters and long gold-tipped Dimetrios cigarettes.

She laughed shyly. "My one luxury," she explained.

The *Spider* laughed, too. "Sorry I can't join you," he said. "But the mask—" He left the sentence in the air, and snapped a light for her.

When she had the cigarette going, Wentworth began his questioning.

"Do you know of any reason," he asked, "why anyone should try to frame you?"

The half-smile which had hovered about the girl's lips faded entirely. She shook her red head.

"Do you have any idea why you were framed?"

"Not unless someone merely wanted to steal the bonds, and I was the most convenient person to hang it on."

The *Spider* took an impatient turn up and down the room.

"You work in the office of MacDonald Pugh," he said. "Who, beside yourself, would have an opportunity to substitute the forged bonds for the genuine?"

The girl's face clouded and her eyes dropped. But in the brief moment before her lids veiled them, Wentworth glimpsed something very much like fear.

"Come," he said sharply, "what is it? This is important. If you want to be freed of the crime, if you want—"

The door knob rasped slightly. Wentworth turned toward it. But the movement was amazingly slow for the *Spider*, almost as if he wished to be too late. His hand did not even move toward his gun, and he stared calmly, a thin smile on his hidden lips, into the face of the man, masked like himself, who stood just inside the door with leveled gun.

A smothered scream burst out behind him. Wentworth, ignoring the girl, studied the slitted eyes that glittered at him through the slits of the mask.

The man advanced slowly, the gun in his right hand, his left hidden in his coat pocket.

"Over by the window, you," he ordered. Wentworth said "Certainly," in a casual tone, as if he granted a minor favor to an acquaintance, and moved slowly backward.

The girl came again into the range of his vision and he studied her. Was she the innocent victim she pretended, or was she in league with the Black Death? The *Spider* had been certain after their clash in the pawnshop that the criminal would seek to trap him. The only logical bait was the girl, and he had deliberately taken that bait, walked into the trap; for he knew of no other way to trace the man, and find him he must.

Otherwise the dread plague would stalk the streets; would lay its grisly hands upon man, woman and child—and the screams and meanings of the sufferers would rise to Heaven like an unanswered prayer.

Wentworth felt the white thin scar upon his temple throbbing angrily. He knew sudden fury at the thought that this man, or his master, was responsible for the death of that curly-haired boy he had snatched too late from his play with a plague-infested puppy. But the *Spider* forced himself to calmness, studied the girl narrowly.

She was standing tensely beside the bed, her hands clasped before her, shoulders hunched. Her red hair seemed to have drained all the color from her face. If she was actually in league with the Black Death and had deliberately betrayed Wentworth so that this man might trap him, she was as clever an actress as ever tricked a man.

Wentworth turned from her to the masked man again. The other's movements were wary, as he came forward toward the middle of the room now. The gun in his hand never wavered.

"Face the wall," he ordered Wentworth, "hoist your hands."

The *Spider* shrugged his shoulders slightly beneath the smooth fit of his dark tweeds, turned slowly and elevated his arms. A sharp cry from the girl, the sound of a blow whirled him about. But he was helpless. He only looked once more into the black muzzle of death.

The man bit out words, "I said 'Face the wall!'"

The girl was sprawled unconscious across the bed. From the man's left wrist dangled a blackjack.

"You filthy animal," the *Spider* rasped. "Why was that necessary?"

"Face the wall!" snarled the man, and the gun inched forward like the head of a poisonous viper.

The *Spider* hesitated. But once more he controlled himself, his muscles taut with anger. He longed to crush this beast, as he knew he could any moment he chose. But it was more important that he obtain a definite clue to the Black Death than that the injury to this girl be immediately avenged. He was convinced now that this man was not the arch criminal himself. Slowly he obeyed the order and faced the wall.

"Put your hands behind you," the man snapped and that, too, the *Spider* did. If he was to be bound, then at least his death was not intended now. He heard the man's heavy feet approach and—lights blazed suddenly in his brain as a blow crashed against his skull. The *Spider* reeled against the wall, slid along it and slipped to the floor.

The man's knees gouged into his back. His wrists were jerked together and ropes bit into them. Wentworth felt the pain of the bonds. The blow had been no more than a tap behind the ear with the blackjack. He felt dizzy and sick, but rapidly recovered. Swiftly then he forced himself back to full control of his senses, for the man raised a slow hand and jerked the mask from the *Spider's* face!

Then jarring laughter rang in the room. "So Richard Wentworth is the *Spider*!" his captor jeered.

CHAPTER SEVEN
Through the Flames

WENTWORTH'S eyes held an ugly light. But he smiled coldly into the slitted eyes of his captor, and his voice was silky.

"It was unfortunate that you did that," he said gently. "Now I must kill you."

The man started to laugh, but his mirth choked and died. He cursed and struck the *Spider* heavily in the face. A stiff smile twisted Wentworth's lips. His eyes did not falter.

He knew now that his suspicions were correct, that this fellow was merely a muscle-man of the Black Death. He knew, too, that he had been ordered not to kill the *Spider*, but to bring him alive before the Master of the Plague himself. Wentworth veiled his eyes with his lids lest they show his satisfaction. He would permit his captor to take him to the criminal's lair, and then— Wentworth's eyes grew bleak.

Somewhere in the darkness of the halls Ram Singh lurked. He would follow as Wentworth had ordered, and together they would bring this Black Death to account. If only Ram Singh did not interfere too soon. Wentworth flicked a glance to the door.

The masked man took Wentworth's gun, crossed the room and crumpled some newspapers on the floor. He laid a chair across them, thrust the entire mass into a wooden clothes-crowded closet and touched a match to the pile in a half dozen places.

Eager flames licked the paper, wrapped around the varnished wood of the chair; flimsy clothing in the closet caught up the sparks hungrily. Wentworth jerked to a sitting position, his head throbbing wildly. The man was calmly binding the girl's hands and feet with the obvious intention of leaving her to burn to death!

Wentworth's mouth closed in a tight, hard line. Even if it meant losing contact with the Black Death, he must save the girl. He got laboriously to his feet and inched forward.

The masked man spun with a curse, the blackjack ready. The *Spider* pretended to be dazed, wavering on his feet. The man struck— but the *Spider* was not there. Wentworth kicked out, caught the man in the abdomen and spilled him, writhing in pain, to the floor.

The *Spider* circled him, tugged open the door. "Ram Singh!" he called softly into the darkness.

No answer.

Once more Wentworth called his faithful servant, raising his voice. But his shout was absorbed into the blackness that gave forth no reply. The lurid glare of the flames tinted the shadows, but revealed no sign of the Hindu. The masked man struggled to his knees, beginning to recover from the blow Wentworth had struck. The *Spider* could have run down the stairs and gained safety in flight. Instead, he stared past the man to the girl. The hungry flames ate nearer, towered until the electric light was dimmed, clawed at the ceiling.

Wentworth sprang toward it, launching a kick at the man's jaw. The muscle-man blocked it fumblingly and snatched at the *Spider*'s foot. The grab missed. Wentworth skipped past him, turned his back to the fire and thrust his bound hands into a spire of flames!

His flesh scorched but he did not falter, did not flinch from the bite of the heat. Not until he felt the ropes give as they began to burn did he flinch away. His shoulders bulged as he strained against his bonds.

The masked man got laboriously to his feet, the black silk that covered his face gleaming redly from the flames. He reeled, recovered, roared an obscenity and charged. The *Spider* ducked under a slashing blow, and the man let out a shout of pain as he blundered too close to the fire and felt its singing heat.

He whirled, checked a rush at its start and began to weave in more cautiously, wary on wide- placed feet. Outlined against the leaping, smoke- thick flame, his hunched shoulders were like a giant ape's. Wentworth retreated before his advance, fighting the ropes until they tore the flesh of his wrists.

Black smoke drifted like fog between them, blew its hot breath in Wentworth's face and stung his nostrils. He coughed rackingly and sprang backward as a blow glanced at his face. Still the ropes would not yield. Desperately, he fumbled in his hip pocket, dragged out a cigarette case. He dropped it to the floor, set his heel upon it and crushed down heavily. The case shattered. Gray tear gas rose in a little cloud, scarcely visible amid the fire glare and smoke.

The other man's outstretched arms reached out to seize him, but the *Spider* ducked them, plunged across the room toward the cleared air near the window. An entire corner of the room was in flames now, but despite their leaping light the place was dark, blurred by smoke.

Behind him the muscle-man coughed and choked. Suddenly he tore off his mask and daubed at streaming eyes. But the tear gas Wentworth had released was not in sufficient quantity to put the man out of the fight entirely. The *Spider* had intended that cigarette case for use close to a man's face.

Shaking his head like a bedeviled dog, the other groped through the smoke toward where Wentworth crouched. His face was heavy, bestial, painted a lobster red by the flapping tongues of flame. Water streamed from his eyes. He blinked, gouging at them with his knuckles, finally spotted the *Spider*.

The man threw caution aside and charged, swinging the blackjack. Wentworth strained a final time at the ropes and a hand ripped loose with a tearing of flesh. He slashed out with his fist, burying

it to the wrist in his adversary's stomach. It turned the blow of the bludgeon from his head, but the weapon crashed down upon his shoulder. Wentworth's lips tightened with pain, and his arm dropped limp and useless to his side!

With a lumbering charge, the man was upon Wentworth again. The *Spider* smashed a fist into his face, leaped aside. With a bellow of rage the crook whirled and lunged again.

It was a one-sided battle, and only Wentworth's quick feet saved him from being instantly overpowered. The other was rapidly recovering from the small dose of tear gas, and all Wentworth's tricks could not overcome the handicap of that numbed left arm and shoulder. He could not block blows, could not feint. Instead he must retreat, duck and dodge, and get in a swift blow when he could.

Dense smoke and vagrant tear gas fumes smarted in his eyes, blurred his vision. The heat seemed to sear his lungs at every gasping breath. Good Lord! The girl! The *Spider* flung a quick glance toward the bed. A corner of the coverlet already smoldered, its slow fire creeping toward the helpless girl.

Abruptly, the muscle-man let out a shout of triumph. Wentworth's glance at the girl had cost him heavily. He was cornered! Fire licked out savage tongues to one side. Behind him, and to his right, walls hemmed him in.

Mouthing venomous curses, the man sprung forward and struck with the blackjack. No room to dodge. The *Spider* dropped to his knees. His right hand closed on something silken and hard in the corner. Gripping it, he lunged to his feet again, dived beneath another blow aimed at his head. He glanced down at the thing he had seized. Through smoke-bleared eyes he caught the gleam of crimson silk. A woman's parasol! Despite the shallow gasping of his breath, the menace of the flames and the crouching menace of the Black Death's hireling, Wentworth smiled—and it was a smile of triumph!

He now had a weapon. To any other man it would have been futile; to Wentworth it was perfect. He turned half to the left and faced his enemy along the line of his right shoulder. His feet were at right angles, the right pointed toward the crook, and his knees were flexed. He held the straight handle of the parasol across his palm like a sword, the ferrule raised slightly, pointed toward his enemy's eyes.

As the man charged in, the *Spider* thrust the parasol forward in a fencer's lunge, all his body thrown into the blow, his arm locked straight. The ferrule slid under the crook's chin, caught him squarely on the throat. The parasol doubled, snapped, but the charge was checked.

The weight of his own plunge hurled him backwards. He threw up his hands, staggered and thumped to the floor. The *Spider* sprang upon him, slammed home his fist. The head rolled limply over. Wentworth's hand went swiftly to the man's throat. The larynx had been crushed in, closing the windpipe and killing him instantly.

The flames' heat was fierce now. Long tongues of it crept across the floor. Smoke seeped up through the seams.

Wentworth sprang erect. Protecting his face with his arm, he plunged to the girl's side, slapped out the sparks that already had reached her negligee. He caught her up from the smoldering bed and put her by the window.

Back across the room he reeled, caught the dead gangster by the collar and dragged him to the sill. He balanced the body, then allowed it to topple to the ground, a cushion for the girl. From the kit beneath his arm then, he drew a thin cord of silk. Padding this, he knotted it about the girl's body and, snubbing it around a bed post to ease the strain on his one good hand, lowered her slowly to the ground. He tossed the line after her.

Smoke streaked with flame billowed around him, but Wentworth, instead of climbing out, groped across the room and yanked open the door. In the street fire sirens wailed, men raised excited cries. Somewhere an axe thudded on metal. The *Spider* ran through the halls looking for Ram Singh, who he felt sure had been overcome on his post of duty. Dark rooms and passageways yielded no trace of the Hindu.

Wentworth could wait no longer. At any instant now, police or firemen might crash into the building, find upon him the marks of battle and connect that with the man who lay dead in the yard. Kirkpatrick was sufficiently suspicious now. The *Spider* would do well not to direct the finger of guilt toward himself needlessly.

Wentworth darted to the back of the house and peered out. The girl was gone, but the crook's body still lay below. The *Spider* threw up the window and climbed out on the sill. Flame and smoke belched from the window directly overhead where he and the man had battled.

Feeling was slowly returning now to his left hand and arm. He still did not have full use of it, but he could steady himself as he reached out and caught hold with his right hand of a drain pipe. He stepped across the void and, taking a desperate chance, threw all his weight for an instant upon the grip of that one hand.

It was a terrific strain, but that hand had been strengthened by long hours with the foils. His hold slipped an inch but held until he could grip the pipe with his knees, then he let himself slide down, using his knees and his one good hand alternately.

When he reached the bottom, he leaned for an instant against the house, panting. But there was not time to rest. He crossed swiftly to the body on the ground and printed on its forehead the red seal of the *Spider*—a warning to the Black Death—and slipped away through the night.

He climbed a fence laboriously and, straddling it, suddenly was outlined in the bright beam of a flashlight. A gruff voice demanded, "Where the hell do you think you're going?"

Wentworth started to drop into the yard behind, but saw a second policeman bending over the corpse of the crook. The officer jerked erect, peered about. He spotted the *Spider* and a whistle shrilled between the man's lips. He grabbed for his gun.

Wentworth teetered to his feet atop the fence, crouched and sprang. Lead whistled through the air hungrily, but when it reached the spot, the *Spider* was gone. He had leaped high and wide and landed in the yard of the house next door. Another fence, running the length of the block, cut him off from the policeman whose light had found him.

Behind him a man's voice cried hoarsely into the night: "It's the *Spider*! The *Spider*! Get him! Death to the *Spider*!"

Heavy hands hit the fence, boots clawed at it. Wentworth ran at top speed. Necessity lent him new strength now. He swarmed over another fence, raced into a lodging house. In the street beyond more police whistles shrieked, and "The *Spider*! The *Spider*! Death to the *Spider*!" men cried.

No escape that way; no escape the way he had come. The roofs? That was too obvious. Already blue-coated men undoubtedly were scaling upward to snare him there. He might battle his way clear, but the *Spider* would not fight the forces of the law.

He raced up the stairs, ripping off coat and vest. On the top floor he tore collar and tie from his throat and piled all on the floor against a brick wall. He opened his lighter, spiced its highly inflammable liquid over the pile, set fire to it in a half dozen places. Flames leaped up. Smoke and the stench of burning cloth filled the hall. Small danger of it spreading against that brick wall, but it seemed real enough.

Wentworth raced down the hall, pounded at a door. "Fire! Fire!"

He ran to the next door, beat with his fist. "Fire!" he cried again. "Fire! Get out of here fast!"

Voices gabbled within. A door was opened a crack and a frightened, touseled head thrust out.

"Fire!" yelled Wentworth.

(Facing page) A corner of the coverlet already smoldered, as slow fire crept toward the helpless girl.

Other voices caught it up. Down the stairs he plunged and beat on more doors. The house was in a turmoil. People had been already awakened by the screaming sirens. The dread cry in their own building tumbled them out in panic.

Men with no coats, with trousers dragged on so hurriedly their suspender straps dangled; women in night clothes with kimonos caught across their breasts; young children laughing and shouting.

Wentworth tousled his own hair, let his suspender straps dangle, swiftly untied his shoes. He affected a limp in one leg. His smoke-swollen eyes seemed sleepy and his mouth drooped stupidly. In the midst of a jam of fleeing people, he ran to the street.

Police were clustered there, but the excited cry of "Fire!" broke their ranks and let the terrified mob through. Smoke was boiling out of the top floor window now. Police and firemen bounded into the building.

Wentworth stared stupidly up at the smoke, thumbed suspender straps over his shoulders. "Damnedest thing I ever saw," said the *Spider* with an atrocious accent to a man next to him. "Here I am sleeping sound and I hear the fire sirens making a fuss. 'Jeez!' I says to myself, 'Suppose that's this building?' Then they go on by and I goes back to sleep again. Then foist t'ing you knows here's this guy pounding on the door and yelling fire. Jeez! Was I scared!"

The other man shook his head glumly. "Me, too," he said, "And here I was having the first good sleep in a week."

Wentworth stared up at the building again, moved off grumbling. Nobody paid any attention to him and he eased into the darkened areaway of a building. The shadows absorbed him. He slipped a hand to the tool kit beneath his arm, and the iron grating yielded. It was the work of an instant then to penetrate the backyard, scale a fence and escape to the next street.

It was the heat of summer and a man without his coat was not conspicuous. Wentworth shambled with slouched shoulders, but he moved swiftly. His car was parked where he had instructed Ram Singh to place it. Just beyond it was a Buick coupé, spotlessly new except for a rear fender that had been crumpled as if in a vise.

The *Spider*'s eyes narrowed. He moved cautiously to the curb so that his own car interposed between himself and that other car. He stalked it cautiously. The Buick was empty.

But where was Ram Singh? A worried frown furrowed Wentworth's forehead. Never before had the faithful Hindu failed him in his need. Nothing short of injury or—Wentworth hesitated even at the thought—death could prevent him from coming to his master's aid.

With a dread that the prospect of death itself had not brought him, he went leaden-footed to the Lancia and tugged open its rear door. Two feet thrust out stiffly.

"Ram Singh!" Wentworth cried out.

No words answered him, but there was a muffled groan. The *Spider*'s hand was swift to the light. It revealed the Hindu prostrate on the floor, bound and gagged, a gash across his forehead but not— thank God—dead. An arm was twisted unnaturally and when Wentworth freed him, he found it was broken.

Wentworth sought no explanation, and Ram Singh volunteered none. Between them it was unnecessary.

"Did you see the man's face?" Wentworth asked.

Ram Singh shook his head slowly. Shame was on his face, but he met the *Spider*'s eye directly, then began to climb slowly, with dangling arm, into the chauffeur's seat. Wentworth laughed softly, stopped the Hindu affectionately. He made him as comfortable as possible in the rear, mounted the chauffeur's seat himself and drove rapidly to a doctor who was under obligations to him for a past and very secret service and who did not mind winking at the requirement of reporting to the police every suspicious injury he treated—if the man he treated was a friend of Richard Wentworth.

CHAPTER EIGHT
The Plague Again

WITH grim amusement, the *Spider* read next day in the newspapers of the adventures of the policeman who had fired at him. First he had found a murdered man and an unconscious girl beneath a window from which smoke rolled.

He had carried the girl away from danger and, returning, had found upon the brow of the murdered man the seal of the *Spider*! He had pursued the *Spider* and the man had vanished into thin air. Newspapers, putting the obvious inference on the rescue of the girl and the man's death, called the silken cord which had been found about the girl's waist a "piece of the *Spider*'s Web." They marveled over its strength, for in tests it had resisted a strain up to five hundred pounds.

Wentworth grinned at Ram Singh, standing silently beside him with his arm in a sling, a little pale, but refusing to be treated as an invalid. A broken arm? *Wah!* It was as nothing.

"That's what comes, Ram Singh," said Wentworth, "of using old silk. That bit of my 'web,' as they call it, should have tested up to seven hundred pounds."

But there was other news in the paper that brought not even grim amusement; that narrowed Wentworth's eyes with fury; that gripped his heart with cold fingers at the knowledge of his own failures to seize the Black Death.

For the Master of the Plague had not rested content with the toll at the Gainsborough estate. Once more the loathsome, strangling fingers of disease had clutched a family, and a millionaire's child had died with its nurse and mother. White-faced, Wentworth faced the conviction that daily, even hourly, the criminal was sending out his warnings, and where they failed, sending another message that carried with it death by diabolic torture.

And the *Spider*'s sole clue to the Black Death was now in police hands—Virginia Doeg.

The girl had finally admitted to police that the *Spider* had assisted her and they believed she knew much more about that mysterious avenger's identity than she had revealed. They had her under triple guard at an unnamed place.

Wentworth's gray-blue eyes glinted. That meant he would have to ask Commissioner Kirkpatrick to take him to her. He laughed shortly. Stanley would do it all right, hoping to trick the girl into some evidence of recognition. Once he had located her, Wentworth must in some way evade that triple guard, release her, and obtain the information he was sure she held which might point the way to the Black Death.

He first phoned Nita. "Darling," he said, "be very careful. The Master of the Plague is out for me. Now his bait is in the hands of the police. He might try to abduct you for that purpose." His voice dropped softly. "He knows, dearest, as anyone must who knows me at all, that life itself is not so dear to me as you."

He smiled slowly as he heard the girl's eager rush of words, her fears for his safety. He warned her again, and left with a smile for the ruddy, anxious face of old Jenkyns, the butler.

The door of Kirkpatrick's office opened to him instantly. A new grimness marked the commissioner's brown, saturnine face. The pointed black mustache, neat as always, seemed incongruous, like a butterfly on the face of a corpse.

He nodded without smiling, refusing to respond to this visitor's casual cheeriness as Wentworth offered one of his private brand of cigarettes and extended the lighter, which had always been a challenge between them since the day Kirkpatrick had searched the lighter in vain for the seal of the *Spider*.

"You have read the papers?" Kirkpatrick asked.

Wentworth nodded with a smile.

"The *Spider*, it seems," he said casually, "goes about his business as mysteriously as ever."

Kirkpatrick shook his head jerkily. "I mean the late editions of the afternoon papers," he explained.

"More of the Black Death?" Wentworth's mouth thinned.

"Yes," said Kirkpatrick slowly. "Old man Biltland himself has got it. Much good his millions will do him now. There are more of them every hour. Heaven only knows where this thing will end. Biltland came to me for protection after he got his letter, and now— "

"We must get this criminal, and get him quickly," Wentworth said savagely.

Kirkpatrick laid a clenched fist on the desk, his piercing eyes curiously steady on his friend's face.

"That seems to be the opinion of the papers, too," he said, "and they offer a clue."

Wentworth's quick question did not alter Kirkpatrick's curious stare. He spoke slowly: "They say, and with strong logic, that there is a connection between the *Spider* and the Black Death. They point out that the two came to the city together."

Wentworth's small smile still lingered about his mouth. But he felt the slow beginning of a throb in that thin scar masked by the hair upon his temple.

"That sounds ridiculous," he said calmly, "as ridiculous as newspaper theories usually do. The *Spider* kills only crooks, and he has never been known to do anything for the money in it."

Kirkpatrick leaned forward and put his elbows on the desk, drumming with the fingers on one lean hand, his eyes still unwavering.

"Granted," he said, "I, too, find it hard to believe. Yet the *Spider* killed two of my men."

The smile left Wentworth's face. He too, leaned forward tensely.

"For which I have sworn vengeance," he said sharply, "and that is why I am here. Take me to see this girl who last night saw the *Spider*. Perhaps I can get some useful information from her."

Kirkpatrick's fingers ceased to drum upon the desk. He stared fixedly into the lean, intent face of his friend.

"You ask me to let you talk to that girl?" His voice was muted.

"Precisely," said Wentworth.

For an instant the gaze of the two men continued locked. Then Kirkpatrick stood erect. A small smile twisted his mouth.

"Since you ask it," he said, "but in your place I would not have done so."

Wentworth's thin lips were mocking. "No, Stanley, I don't believe you would."

They went swiftly to the commissioner's dark, powerful car, and behind the wheel a blue-coated chauffeur whizzed through traffic. Kirkpatrick turned his head and fixed his eyes upon the imperturbable profile of his friend. "We have her at a hotel, the Marlborough."

Wentworth raised his brows in amusement. "Rather expensive, isn't it," he asked, "for a mere material witness?"

Kirkpatrick did not answer, and the men were silent while the car sped on. The Marlborough on South Central Park, home of the wealthy and the celebrated! The Black Death would think long before he found her there, Wentworth told himself. Yet there was an uneasiness behind his eyes as they slipped on up Seventh Avenue past a blue-coated policeman at Fifty-Seventh Street, who stopped all traffic to let them pass and saluted smartly.

There was an unchanging frown on Kirkpatrick's forehead; and abruptly, as the car whirled into Central Park South, he slid forward to the edge of his seat, bolt upright, his hand a clenched fist upon his knee.

"Good God," he cried hoarsely, "What can be the matter?"

Parked at the curb were three radio patrol cars. Two policemen stood guard at the door and a crowd boiled about the entrance.

Wentworth jerked open the door, leaped out with Kirkpatrick at his heels and together they pounded across the pavement, ploughing through the crowd like a charge of cavalry.

"What is it?" Kirkpatrick snapped at one of the guardians of the door.

The man saluted, his face grimly concerned. "The *Spider*, sir!" he said. "Three of our men dead, and the girl is gone!"

For an instant the news seemed to stun the two men, Kirkpatrick and Wentworth. They stared at each other, then ran into the lobby of the hotel, sprang into an elevator and were whisked to the tenth floor.

The hall swarmed with police, but a way was opened respectfully for the striding figures of the two men—opened to show them the bodies of two policemen on the floor, shot to death—and upon their foreheads glinted the blood-red seal of the *Spider*!

Wentworth stared fixedly at the seal. It was a clever imitation, faithful in almost every respect except that it was a little larger than the one he used. The two back legs of the *Spider* were curved a little too much also, but those trivial details would escape the attention of the police and indeed, if they were noticed, it would make no difference in their opinion of the guilt of the *Spider*.

A white-haired sergeant was in charge. His voice was bitter with anger.

"There's another of our boys in the room, sir," he reported, "and that makes five of them the *Spider* has killed. By God, sir, if ever I get my hands on him— "

Kirkpatrick nodded shortly, turned and stared for a moment fixedly into Wentworth's eyes.

He drew a hand wearily across his forehead, pushed on into the room where the girl had been held prisoner. The white-haired sergeant and Wentworth followed.

The commissioner prowled about the room, flinching from the *Spider*-branded body on the floor. "What happened?" he asked over his shoulder.

The sergeant's voice was still tight with hate. "No one seems to know exactly, sir. Nobody heard any shots. Nobody knew anything about the murders until someone rang for a bellboy and he came upstairs and found our men dead in the hall. They flashed an alarm to us and you got here almost as soon as we did."

"Then no one knows the time of the murders, exactly," said the commissioner, meeting Wentworth's eyes again. "That will make an alibi rather difficult."

Kirkpatrick took a short stride across to the window and peered out. The building dropped away for ten stories straight down. He shook his head, turned, and looked about the room.

"What I can't understand," the commissioner said, "is why the girl was taken away alive. Obviously this was done because, as I suspected all along, Virginia Doeg knew the identity of the *Spider*, and he was afraid she would betray him."

Wentworth slowly drew a cigarette and ignited it with a minute rasp of his lighter. He knew a different answer to this atrocity. He knew the Black Death had murdered the police and left the girl alive because Virginia Doeg was bait for the *Spider*, bait for a death trap into which he hoped to lure the one enemy he feared.

After hours of futile investigation, Wentworth took his leave of Kirkpatrick and at once set about starting a new search for the girl. She remained his one clue, his one hope of lifting the dread terror of the plague that hung over the city.

Probably the Black Death would communicate with him in some way to reveal the whereabouts of the girl. Wentworth did not wait for that, for then the trap would be set. It was better to strike before his enemy was prepared. The *Spider* had a clue that the criminal would not suspect; a slender thread, it was true, but it might prove fruitful.

Leaving Kirkpatrick, he first went home and got the tool kit he carried only when, as the *Spider*, he went forth to battle the underworld. He changed also to special high-topped shoes, light as a fencer's except that they had thick, soft rubber soles.

There was worry in Ram Singh's eyes. Time and again the fingers of his good hand touched gently his broken arm in its sling as his devoted eyes followed every move of the master he had failed in his last grave encounter with the Black Death.

Wentworth straightened from lacing his shoes, clapped Ram Singh on his shoulder and went out into the night. He took a taxi directly to the local distributors of Dimetrios cigarettes, the kind which he had noticed Virginia Doeg had smoked.

It was a brand not widely sold, and its distribution would be confined to the wealthy, for it was expensive.

From the distributor he quickly got a list of the stores which retailed the cigarette, and went systematically about the task of visiting them all. There were fourteen in all, and he visited ten without results.

It was near the closing hour when finally he strolled into a small tobacconist's shop on upper Madison Avenue, purchased a pack of Dimetrios himself and fell into casual conversation with the clerk.

"Not many people buy these, I suppose," he said.

The young man behind the counter talked with a slight lisp. "Yeth," he said, "that'th right. We keep them for a very thelect few. But you know, a little while ago, the motht unthpeakable ruffian came in and bought five packageth."

Excitement raced through Wentworth. Here, perhaps, was the clue he had been seeking. "Ever see the man before?" he asked.

"Never," shuddered the wavy-haired young clerk, "and I hope he never cometh back again."

Wentworth smiled slightly. "Tough guy, eh?"

"He wath," said the clerk. "He didn't even wear a collar, and had a mothst unthpeakable cap on his head and hith nothe—" He shuddered again, "Hith nothe had been mathed over on hith left cheek."

"Doubtless," said Wentworth, "a pugilist. And how long ago was this?"

"Jutht a few minuteth," the clerk said.

"You didn't happen to notice which way he went?"

The clerk stared at him. "Why?" he asked in a tense voice. "Ith he—are you—I mean—are you a politheman?"

Wentworth shook his head slowly. "No," he said. "I just don't want to go in the same direction the gentleman did. From your description I wouldn't want to meet him alone on a dark street this late in the evening."

"Oh!" cried the clerk. "Oh! Now I thall be afraid to leave at all." He moaned miserably, then he brightened. "Oh, but he wath in a car, that maketh it better."

"A car, eh? What kind?" Wentworth persisted.

The clerk frowned. "I'm quite thure it wath a Buick," he said. "But I didn't notithe the number."

Wentworth questioned him futilely a few minutes longer, then left, but with more confidence than when he had entered.

A ruffian who bought five packs of Dimetrios cigarettes. Wentworth felt a thrill of hope. He had not miscalculated, then. The vanity of the Black Death would lead him to make just such a gesture toward his prisoner, to supply the particular brand of cigarettes the prisoner liked; or perhaps— Wentworth's eyes narrowed—perhaps this was the thread with which the Master of the Plague hoped to draw the *Spider* into his trap.

Wentworth shook his head sharply. No, it was too slender for that. Something more obvious, more certain of detection would have been employed.

Butwhat to do now? He was in a fashionable neighborhood. Expensive and elaborate apartment houses raised their lofty crowns on every side. Where, in this habitat of the wealthy, would the Black Death hide a prisoner? In what sort of building could the ruffian he apparently employed find free and unchallenged entrance? How to trace any one Buick car among the city's thousands?

He strolled along inspecting the facades of luxurious buildings, many of their windows darkened now, showing untenanted apartments, since Depression days had cut into the higher bracket income.

And abruptly the *Spider* smiled. Of course, that was the answer. Some of the buildings were closed entirely, purchased by big corporations for conversion into handsome apartments. They had been stillborn by hard times. Boarded up, they awaited prosperity and meanwhile stood vacant—perfect hideouts for criminals.

He crossed double-laned Park Avenue with its drone of taxies and expensive motors, pushed on to Fifth Avenue, where apartments had been hardest hit.

Here in one block three such shuttered apartments stood. Wentworth had come directly from the tobacco shop to Fifth Avenue, probably the route a man searching for the cigarettes would have taken, and now, in the shadow of the wall that bounded Central Park, he stood and surveyed the looming buildings.

In front of a tenanted building next to a vacant one was parked a car that to Wentworth was vaguely familiar. He studied it and suddenly he remembered where he had seen it before. It was a Buick coupé, spotlessly new except for one rear fender that seemed to have been crumpled in a vise. That was the car that had been parked next to his Lancia the night he had killed one of the Black Death's men in the fire!

Hope warmed Wentworth. He started across the street, then caught a small gleam of light in the trade entrance of a building that was otherwise dark.

As he watched, a man with a cap ducked out and, walking with the heavy rolling swagger of those who live by physical competence alone, strode toward the Buick.

Wentworth watched intently. He wanted to catch a glimpse of that man's face. If his nose was broken as the tobacco clerk had described, if he was, in the language of that young gentleman, "a mostht unthpeakable ruffian"—a glimmer of a smile flickered across Wentworth's grim mouth—then the *Spider* would steal into that black-windowed building and deliberately enter the death trap the master criminal undoubtedly had baited for him.

Luck favored Wentworth. The man across the street entered the Buick with the crumpled fender and the dash lights showed the *Spider* the man's face. The nose was broken, mashed over on the left cheek!

Grimly Wentworth waited until the car had turned the corner, then strolled to the basement from which the man had come.

At a door he paused an instant, donned once more the black silk mask of the *Spider* and deftly picked the lock.

Quickly he entered and relocked the door. It made escape more difficult, but it prevented the alarm that an unlocked door might cause.

The *Spider* stole into the shadows, cat-footed to the stairs and mounted with the same sure competence. He went systematically about the tedious task of finding which of the many apartments concealed the Black Death and his prisoner, who, Wentworth was sure, must be hidden somewhere in this building.

He went from floor to floor, listening at doors, searching with minute gleams of his flashlight the dusty hallways for indications of recent passage.

Not until he reached the very top floor did he discover the trace he sought. There, mingling with the stuffy unventilated air, he caught the distinct odor of tobacco.

The *Spider* moved more tensely now, automatic in hand, every muscle, every sense, alert. The darkness was absolute. No vagrant gleam of street light could penetrate; no ray beneath a door betrayed the hiding place of the Black Death; no sound broke the tomblike silence.

Wentworth strained his ears, but there was no mutter of voices to guide him. The vast waiting stillness seemed to crowd close as if the very air were hostile.

Yet somewhere on this floor was human presence. Here, if anywhere in this building, the jaws of the Black Death's trap gaped open.

Softly the *Spider* went through the search that had become routine now, listening at each door. At last his ear caught the faint sound of movement within a room, and a thin smile twisted his lips beneath the mask.

The door to the trap was beneath his hand. Wentworth turned from it and stole to stairs that led upward, unfastened a door to the roof, and searched swiftly for other ingress to the apartment below.

Once more fortune—this time a fire escape ladder—favored him. And because it did, he was suspicious. Things were too easy.

Yet there was a chance the Plague Master was not yet ready, that the hair-trigger spring of the trap did not yet await his cautious foot.

Once more a grim smile played across his mouth. Others had trapped the *Spider* and found it a dangerous pastime. He descended the fire escape ladder that led down past the window of the apartment where lurked the Black Death.

Yet even in that he exercised care an ordinary man would not have thought of. He did not tread upon the rounds of the ladder but, taking his automatic between his teeth, gripped the sides of the iron stairway with knees and arms and glided down, lest an alarm had been connected with those rungs.

Wentworth's thick rubber soles made no sound on the iron grilling of the fire escape platform. He examined the windows. He could make out the shadow of heavy drapes, but no faint gleam of light escaped.

From the invaluable kit of tools beneath his arm he took out a small vial made of wax, and with a plunger attached to the stopper drew a semicircle on the glass above the window's fastening. Hydrofluoric acid, such as etchers use. Soft wax was impervious to it, yet it ate like fire through hardened glass.

Wentworth replaced the wax bottle and took out a rubber suction cup which he fastened to the pane. When the acid had eaten through, he removed the piece of glass, soundlessly.

For long moments Wentworth listened at the opening, and presently his straining ears made out the slow deep breathing of one who slept.

Was it possible that he had taken unaware the Black Death? Blood throbbed slowly in his temples. He had moved swiftly. Within a few hours of the girl's disappearance he had tracked the man down. Probably no such swift action had been expected. It was possible that within this room the Black Death slept!

Without a sound the *Spider* eased open the fastening, inched up the sash until it was high enough to admit his body.

He drew his revolver, caught up the small flashlight in his left hand, and smothering the light in his palms, stared fixedly at it for a few seconds until the pupils of his eyes became accustomed to the glare, lest bursting into a lighted room would dazzle him.

Silently he eased himself through the opening, stood erect upon the inner sill within the black drapes that covered it. Then, tearing them apart, he sprang into the room.

His gun was ready, but firing, he found, would have been futile. Behind a metal closet door peering through a peephole of bulletproof glass crouched a man, and the muzzle of his gun was trained on the *Spider's* breast.

Spring backward? No chance of that. The window was opened only narrowly; and before he could roll through, half a dozen steel-jacketed bullets could rip the life from his body.

Charge? The shield of the door completely protected the gunman. Swiftly the *Spider*'s eyes flickered over the room. It was barely furnished. On a bed nearby, her clothing disheveled, lay Virginia Doeg, eyes closed, her red hair a veil over her pillow. It was her deep breathing that had deceived him.

And now the man behind the shield chuckled gloatingly. "Welcome, *Spider*!" he jeered, "Welcome to the death trap!"

Wentworth straightened out of his crouch, his eyes calm.

"Better drop the gun, *Spider*," the criminal said softly. "I do not think that I care to deal with you while you are armed. You should not have waited so long after you opened the window. Those drapes permit no light to escape, but they are light and the slightest breath of air makes them quiver."

Wentworth let his gun fall.

"Now back three paces," the man ordered. And when the *Spider* had obeyed, the other came out from behind the metal door.

"It is not my intention," the man sneered, "to kill you at once. I would rather leave that to my amiable friends, the police. I think that even they will be able to capture the *Spider* if I put a bullet say, through his lung, and tell them where to find him.

"And you needn't fear that they will be unable to identify you as the *Spider*. I have a cigarette lighter myself, not half so clever as your own, which will readily yield up the secret of those little red seals to the police.

"If anything further is needed I shall murder the young lady who lies on the bed there—unfortunate that she is drugged and cannot hear us, eh?—place that ugly little *Spider* upon her forehead and let them assume that it was she who wounded you, and that then the *Spider*, in the excess of his fury, managed to strangle the life from his so beautiful betrayer."

The man chuckled once more, gloatingly, behind his mask.

"But already we have delayed too long. The Black Death must be about his work. And you must be accounted for first."

He lifted the pistol, leveled it at Wentworth's chest and slowly began to press the trigger.

CHAPTER NINE
The Voice on the Wire

IN her penthouse apartment, high up on Riverside Drive, overlooking the misty Hudson River which she loved to paint, Nita van Sloan sat upon a window seat and stared unseeingly out into the darkness of the night.

Far out on the bosom of the Hudson gleamed the pale yellow lights of passing boats. The black Jersey shore was shrouded in mist, a delicate problem for any artist's brush. But Nita van Sloan saw none of that. For all the deep cushioned comfort of the window seat, she sat tensely, chin resting on her palm. It was far past midnight, but sleep would not come to the troubled girl.

Lying beside her on the floor, the Great Dane dog that Dick Wentworth had given her as a puppy stared up at her with worshipping eyes, its nose outstretched upon its forepaws.

Nita sighed deeply, and the dog rose with a low whine in its throat and rested its head in the girl's lap.

The girl's blue eyes were tired as she turned them upon the dog. She smiled faintly.

"Are you worried, too, Apollo, about our Dick?" she asked.

The dog emitted a small coughing bark. It was his invariable response to the name of the master he loved.

The girl swung back her pajama-clad legs to the floor and strode nervously to a small table. She picked up a cigarette and ignited it. A moment later she tossed it away and moved restively about the room, changing the position of a picture, picking up a hair pin from the floor, doing a dozen things without thought.

For she knew that Richard Wentworth never before had crossed blades with so dangerous an antagonist as the Black Death. Swiftly Nita came to a decision. Phoning would be useless. He would only laugh at her fears, cajole her into remaining—and waiting—alone. And tonight she wanted warmer solace than that. She tore off the pajamas as if they strangled her, dressed with swift speed and, snapping a leash upon Apollo's collar, left the building.

In the pocket of her sport-suit she carried a small but deadly gun Dick had given her. She summoned a taxi, and entering it gave in a low voice the number of Wentworth's apartment house.

Her touch of the bell of his penthouse had hardly sounded the buzzer before the door swung open and the haggard face of gray-haired old Jenkyns stared out.

The smiles that usually wreathed his ruddy countenance were missing. Nita felt her heart contract.

"Then Dick—Dick isn't home?" she asked. Jenkyns shook his old head slowly, stepped aside for her to enter. Apollo, released, bounded ahead through the apartment, sniffing excitedly. But presently he returned and crowded close against Nita as she stood in the luxuriously furnished drawing room, looking about with vacant eyes.

"Ram Singh?" she asked.

Once more Jenkyns shook his head, and Nita's hopes sank again. "They didn't leave together, Miss Nita. Ram Singh went out a little while after the master." Ram Singh had a broken arm, and a man couldn't fight with his arm in splints, Nita thought. Listlessly she tugged her brown hat from her gleaming, curly head and walked slowly toward a window.

Abruptly she was tense again, for from the hall sounded the metallic buzz of the phone. She raced to it, snatched up the receiver.

"Richard Wentworth's apartment," she said, her words trembling with hope.

The voice that came over the wire was not Dick's. It had a soft sibilance that made Nita's hand tighten about the receiver, that made a chill of dread race down her spine.

"Ah, Miss van Sloan," said the voice on the wire, "I thought I could find you there after I called your own apartment vainly. Richard Wentworth—the *Spider*—is my prisoner."

A gasp shuddered from the girl. Someone had penetrated the secret that no one save those who battled for him knew. Someone had discovered that Richard Wentworth was the *Spider*! And that someone—she was suddenly sure—was the Black Death!

"What do you want?" she demanded, striving to drive the fear from her tone.

"Ah," said the voice, "I see that you are reasonable. That is fortunate. I was about to kill the *Spider*, but learning his identity I remembered that he was a wealthy man—and money is very dear to me. If you would care to ransom him—"

"Oh yes, yes!" Nita cried.

Evil laughter taunted her. "It will not be so simple as that. You cannot come with the police and liberate your... friend. For there is a little safety device which I have arranged to protect myself.

"In the *Spider's* pocket is a cigarette lighter that is a twin to his own in every respect save one. In this one the seal of the *Spider* will not dissolve when it is opened, and the secret chamber is so clumsily hidden that even the dull-witted police can discover it."

Nita heard that news with sinking heart. "You doubtless know," the Black Death went on, "where you can get hold of considerable money."

Yes, Nita did know. There was a safe in Dick's room where he always kept a large quantity of cash on hand against the possible necessity of flight that ever hung above his head.

"Get this money, then," the man ordered. "Come to the corner of Madison Avenue and Fifty-Seventh Street and walk uptown. Obey the man who meets you there."

Then reed-like over the phone; Nita caught a faint voice as if someone shouted from a distance, and she thrilled as she recognized the voice of Dick Wentworth.

"No, Nita! No! It—means—death!"

A curse snarled from the man at the phone. She heard a jar, silence, then the dread voice purred once more in her ear.

"It was unfortunately necessary for me to silence your... friend. He is unduly suspicious, and a trifle troublesome. It may be that unless you hurry I shall be forced to deal firmly with him before you can get here. In fact I can allow you only twenty minutes. Remember—" the man's voice rose suddenly in sharp warning—"if you bring the police, they will learn that Richard Wentworth is the *Spider*. They will not forget that the seal of the *Spider* has been printed on the brow of five of their dead comrades."

"Oh tell, tell me," cried Nita, "that Dick is all right. You haven't hurt him— "

Over the wires came only a sinister laugh. Nita put the telephone down with a listless hand. The anxious Jenkyns was at her elbow. "What is it, Miss Nita?"

She told him rapidly all that she knew, and the butler, too, begged her not to go.

"If Master Dick is captured," he reassured her, "you may be sure he wanted to be. And if he wanted to be, he has a way out. You'd only upset his plans."

The girl stared at Jenkyns. Dick Wentworth never went into danger unprepared, yet his cry over the wire: "It means death!"

She shook her head sharply. "Not this time, Jenkyns," she said. "You don't know what a terrible thing he is fighting, how clever the Black Death is!"

She turned swiftly to the task she had set for herself. The weight of the automatic in her pocket swayed against her side and lent a certain comfort. From the wall safe in Wentworth's room she took

NITA VAN SLOAN

two hundred and fifty thousand dollars, made a bundle of it under her arm. Apollo followed her every footstep, claws patting on the floor.

She looked down at him. Apollo had helped her in many a tight scrape. But how could she use the Great Dane now? Dick had taught the dog many tricks, had trained him to pretend hostility toward herself if she made a certain signal. It was an old smuggler's trick. Frequently their jewel-smuggling pets were captured by officers who then sought to identify the master through the dog. And the man trained the animals so that they would snarl even at the hand they loved if they received a certain signal from their master.

Perhaps it might serve her in good stead now. She spun toward Jenkyns, smiled at him.

"Jenkyns," she said, "we are going to do what we can to save Dick. I want you to help me."

"Anything, *anything*, Miss Nita! But I'm afraid these old hands have long since passed the time—"

Nita shook her head sharply. "No, not that," she said. "What I want you to do is this: I'm going to drive Dick's roadster uptown to the spot where they

want me to meet this man. I want you to get in a taxi with Apollo and follow me."

"When I meet someone, just let Apollo out. That is all. But in God's name, whatever happens, don't call the police."

Jenkyns smiled wanly. "Aye, I can do that, Miss Nita," he said. "But I hate to think of you putting yourself in the hands of that awful man."

Nita's hand strayed to her gun, and her sweet mouth compressed, became a straight line that was very much like the *Spider*'s own when he battled against odds.

She called the dog, fastened the leash and gave it into Jenkyns' hand. Together they left the building.

A newsboy dashed up as she crossed to the powerful Hispana Suiza.

"Extra!" he shouted in her ear. "Extra! Black Death kills twenty! *Spider* hunted! Extra!"

Nita almost flinched from the words. The Black Death. It meant a disease to the people, a plague that hung like a pestilential cloud over the city. To her it meant a sinister voice over the wire, a criminal genius who held her lover's life in vicious, tormenting hands.

She flung into the roadster, with the easy competence of experience touched the motor to deep-throated life. A glance at her watch. Fifteen minutes remained of the time the Black Death had allotted!

Her foot was heavy on the accelerator and the droning motor sped her uptown through nearly deserted streets. She parked at Fifty-Seventh and Madison and walked slowly up the avenue.

Behind her she glimpsed the taxi that contained Jenkyns and her faithful dog, but she dared not glance back again lest she arouse suspicions and foredoom her efforts to save Dick.

She heard the purr of auto tires, the metallic opening of a door, and a black sedan stood at the curb with motor running, its rear door open. Within, all was darkness.

With an effort Nita kept her hand away from the gun in her pocket. Her elbow clamped tight against the package of money beneath her arm. The chauffeur sat with his eyes rigidly front; no one else was visible, but a hateful voice that Nita recognized called softly, "Your car awaits, Miss van Sloan."

Nita forced her feet to carry her toward that yawning black interior and climbed stiffly in.

Not until then did she glimpse the man who had called. A faint glimmer of light seeped beneath a shade and revealed a large, broad shouldered man. There was no face, but eyes stabbed at her through the slits of a black mask.

The door slammed, and the car slid forward. Nita was very near despair. Of what use was her dog now? Of what use Jenkyns' faithful shadowing?

"Where is Dick?" she demanded. "I won't give you the money until—"

The man's soft laughter checked her words. She knew without explanation the meaning of that ugly mirth. To talk of giving him the money when she was in his power, in the power of a man so fiendish that he had loosed the Plague upon the city!

For a wild moment Nita considered snatching her gun, but even as she hesitated it was too late. The man's hand closed like a metal band about her wrist, took the revolver, then deliberately searched her entire person, for other weapons.

Nita's face burned with humiliation, but her angry protest earned only mocking laughter. One thought buoyed her, the hope that soon she would be with Dick. It might avail no more than that they should die together. But even so she went gladly.

It was fifteen minutes later, after many turnings, that the girl felt the car draw to a stop. The man with the mask held a gun so that she could see its glint and said softly:

"I would advise against any outcry. I would dis-like to put a bullet into your lovely body, but I should not hesitate to do so if the necessity arose."

He opened the door and Nita stepped out silently, found herself looking up at an elaborate apartment building.

Her heart beat wildly. Soon now she would see Dick. Sudden fear caught her by the throat. If—if this monster had kept his word and not harmed him.

A man walked on either side of her, and she got no opportunity to discover whether Jenkyns had followed, whether Apollo would be able to help if the need arose.

She was whisked into the building through the basement entrance, up many flights of stairs. The masked man roughly dismissed the chauffeur then and, with fingers clamped about Nita's arm, led her to a door. She heard the key grate. Light smote her eyes.

She started forward, eagerly, but the hand on her arm held her back, and the man's gloating laughter rang in her ears.

"In a hurry, Miss van Sloan? Sorry, but I must detain you a moment." And he held her while they walked slowly down a long hallway and entered a sparsely furnished room.

There Nita halted. A tremulous smile lifted her lips. Dick at last! But not the Dick she had always known. The man before her was plainly helpless— and there was a despairing droop to his shoulders that spoke clearer than words of lost hope.

CHAPTER TEN
Great Apollo

WENTWORTH'S wrists were handcuffed before him and another shackle about his ankles secured him to a steam pipe. His tool kit had been discovered by the Black Death and lay open upon the floor before him. Men had examined it. Tied to the bed lay Virginia Doeg, her red hair tousled, her face swollen, still in a stupor from the effects of drugs.

Wentworth smiled slowly, deepening the taut lines of his face. His eyes seemed to grow more haggard.

"Darling, darling," he said "why did you come?"

"Scarcely complimentary to the lady, my dear Mr. Wentworth," jeered the man behind the mask. "I marvel that she finds you so attractive."

Nita tugged against his restraining hand. "Oh, please, please," she said and, released, ran to Dick and threw her arms about him. For a moment she forgot all the evilness of her surroundings in the joy of being with him again. He buried his face in the softness of her hair, murmuring over and over, "Darling."

But Nita was not entirely absorbed in the greeting, happy as she was to be with Dick again. Her mind was working swiftly, seeking some way to help him escape. She put little credence in this man's promise to let her ransom Wentworth. But she turned to him with seeming confidence.

"Now turn him loose," she said, smiling. "You have the money."

The man regarded her steadily through the slits of his mask and made no answer. Nita walked toward him, her eyes pleading, her hands half outstretched.

"I have fulfilled my part of the bargain," she said. "It is your turn to do as you promised."

She was quite close to him now. The beginnings of laughter shook him. He chuckled in amusement, threw back his head and, like an uncoiling spring, Nita leaped forward, snatched for the gun she had seen him place in his pocket. The man snapped his arms about her. They were like steel bands and she was helpless. He laughed at her struggles, lifted her bodily from the floor and carried her well away from Wentworth.

"Almost caught me napping," he chuckled. "Ah, but I admire a brave and pretty woman." He took her hat from her head and ran his hand through her tangled curls, tilted up her face. He laughed again. "Only the necessity for wearing my mask," he said, "prevents me paying proper tribute to your beauty."

He turned toward the *Spider*, straining futilely against his shackles. "Perhaps," the masked man went on softly, "when we have disposed of your... friend—"

Wentworth forced himself to calmness. Showing agitation would merely be fuel to the flames of this man's love of torture. He laughed shortly.

"A petty criminal to the last," he jeered, "pulling petty little tricks. The Black Death? You haven't the brain to conceive such a thing."

Holding Nita helpless, the man turned the blank face of his mask to Wentworth.

"And the *Spider* gives evidence of human emotion," he mocked. "Imagine the *Spider*, the great altruist, being swayed by mere jealousy!"

Wentworth's face was disdainful, and in his eyes Nita caught a gleam that gave her hope. But it was only for a moment. Dick was courageous beyond all men she knew, but bravery could not break those gleaming shackles of steel that held him prisoner.

"Just a muscle-man," the *Spider* jeered, "a fool sleeping in the King's bed, pretending to be the Black Death. Why you—"

The masked man laughed!

"Give up, *Spider*," he said. "I'll admit you're clever. But when you try to goad me into talking, you're merely amusing. You've been trying now for two hours, excepting for the twenty minutes it took to collect your girl friend, and you've learned precisely nothing."

It was the *Spider*'s turn to laugh. The two men glared at each other fiercely.

"You think so?" Wentworth sneered.

Nita remained quiescent in the man's grasp. She could feel his anger mounting in the tightening grip of his fingers on her arms. They bit like the pinchers of the Inquisition, but she made no sound. Dick seemed to be trying to infuriate the man. If he would forget her for an instant, she might strike him from behind! She felt his fingers loosen, and relaxed her muscles for the test. A chuckle trickled from behind the mask. The steel fingers thrust Nita toward the bed, held her while he tied her.

"Yes, you are clever, *Spider*," the man said, "but not quite clever enough. It is a pity— "

He crouched and snarled suddenly, whirling toward Wentworth, helpless in his shackles of steel, "a pity you must die."

Slowly, while Nita watched with horror-widened eyes, he drew from his pocket the automatic she had tried to snatch.

"You were right, Wentworth," he said. "I only wanted the girl here so I could kill her with you. There was just the slightest chance that you might have struck some trail that pointed to me and confided your suspicions to her.

"But—" the gloating laughter cackled out, "—the Black Death leaves only dead behind. There will be no tales told."

He raised his gun.

"No, no!" Nita said, "No, not that! I'll do anything, anything, but please!"

The masked man did not even turn his head. The softness was gone from his voice now and it grated harshly like rusty iron.

"You are hardly in a position, my dear, to make promises. It is I who shall dictate, you who shall obey. But first— "

The gun snapped up. Wentworth dropped to the floor as lead whined past. He seized the shackle about his ankle, and it came loose in his hand!

He sprang toward his enemy. But in mid-leap he checked and twisted aside. Behind him, he heard the snarl of an animal raging.

The curtains before the window were whipped aside and a tawny shape hurtled across the room straight at the throat of the Black Death!

Wentworth rolled aside, shouting, "Get him, Apollo!" and Nita jerked to her feet, shouting excited encouragement to the great dog. But the masked man whirled like a flash, and the upswung movement of his gun and the crash of its explosion were almost simultaneous.

Apollo's leap sent him crashing against the man's chest, sent the crook reeling backward across the

Now Ram Singh burst into the room—knife gleaming in right hand, drawn back to throw.

room with arms waving frantically to recover his balance. But Apollo, great Apollo, plunged to the floor and lay quivering, helpless to move a muscle of his powerful body.

The Black Death brought up heavily against the wall, partly dazed. His gun came up slowly.

Now Ram Singh burst into the room, knife gleaming in his right hand, drawn back to throw. For a single instant the masked man wavered, then turned and fled.

Ram Singh's hand flashed forward, the knife glittered in the air. The door clapped shut, and the blade ground its point upon that metal barrier, and crashed futilely to the floor.

"A gun, Ram Singh!" Wentworth cried sharply.

The Hindu caught one from his pocket and tossed it to him. Miraculously, Wentworth's hands were free of the shackles, and he caught the weapon, raced across the room and snatched open the door.

CHAPTER ELEVEN
Virginia's Clue

GUN FLAME lanced at Wentworth. His answering shot was lightning fast and drew a curse of pain.

"The lights, Ram Singh," he shouted.

Darkness shut down like a lid. Gun din filled the hall, and lead chunked into the door at the *Spider*'s elbow. Suddenly then he groaned aloud, threw himself noisily to the floor and rolled silently toward the gunman.

He heard a muttered obscenity:

"Got the damned idiot!"

Wentworth grinned thinly and fired upward at the voice. A scream began and choked. A body slammed against the wall, slithered to the floor. The *Spider* rose. The pencil beam of his flash showed the broken-nosed man, shot through the mouth, dead.

The Black Death had fled, leaving his henchman to kill his foe!

Wentworth padded swiftly downstairs, then checked sharply, a curse of disappointment on his lips. Police whistles! Either the Black Death had given the alarm, or the shots had been heard.

Wentworth smiled and raced upward, almost slammed into Ram Singh coming down.

"Quick!" he snapped. "The police. Carry Apollo!"

He darted into the apartment where he had been held prisoner. Apollo stood on trembling legs in the middle of the floor, a bloody tear across his skull. Seeing Wentworth, he tried feebly to wag his tail.

"Stout fellah!" cried Wentworth, "Good dog!" He clapped the dog on the back, snatched out a knife and freed Nita and Virginia Doeg. He shook the drugged girl, fought to rouse her from her stupor. While they worked, Nita asked swift questions.

"How in the world, Dick," she demanded, "did you get those handcuffs off? How did Ram Singh find you and—"

Dick smiled grimly as he worked. "It's all your doing, darling," he said.

"But, I— "

"Shhh," the *Spider* silenced her. "You did it. I let drop a hint to the Black Death that you knew as much as I did about this business, and you did the rest. He called you up, and I pretended to be worried. Then, when he left to meet you, I used a file I had hidden in these shoes—" he pointed to the thick, soft rubber soles—"when I knew I had to walk into his trap. But the filing took so long that the Black Death's car was at the door before I was free. I just had time to phone Ram Singh—whom I had told to await my call near here—and to put the cuffs back on, when you entered. I was hoping to capture him. And I put off the showdown as long as possible, trying to learn something about his plans. But even when he thought he was going to kill me certainly, he was too cautious to talk."

He straightened and gazed down at the still stupified Doeg girl.

"No use working on her anymore," he said. "She can walk if she's led."

He turned toward Ram Singh and found the Hindu crouched behind the metal door. He spun toward the door, but found no danger threatening there. Frowning, he puzzled over Ram Singh's apparent fright.

Then he realized for the first time that Ram Singh was not wearing his turban, that his close-shaved head was bald! That, to a Hindu, was shameful.

The *Spider* found his own hat and gave it to Ram Singh, being careful to hide the laughter that lurked behind his eyes.

"How is it," he asked in Hindustani when Nita, leading Virginia Doeg, had started toward the door, "that thou hast lost thy turban, Ram Singh?"

The man answered with extreme dignity in the same language. "Oh, *Sahib*, it was in thy service. I feared to enter by the door lest the noise of it should cause thy captor to shoot. So disgraced one that I am, I used my turban to lower that unclean beast whom thou callest Apollo to the fire escape so that he might avert the tragedy which threatened here. That is why it was that beast which was first to enter the room and not thy servant, Ram Singh."

Wentworth placed his hand upon his man's shoulder. "Verily, oh Ram Singh," he said, "thou art a man, and through all India it shall be sung how Ram Singh bared his head that he might save his master."

Pride gleamed in Ram Singh's eyes and he stood no longer ashamed.

The sirens of police radio cars echoed in the streets now. There was need to hurry. Wentworth caught up the body of the man he had slain and, with it over his shoulder, led the way swiftly downward until they reached the first floor.

They heard then the shouts of policemen, the battering of axes on the door below. Wentworth laid the body of the man at the head of the steps, gun in hand. Then, smiling grimly, he affixed the seal of the *Spider* upon his forehead.

"That will stop them a while," he murmured to Nita. Quickly he unlocked an apartment and sped to a window which opened on the back.

Suddenly Nita quit the other girl and grasped his arm.

"The cigarette lighter, Dick, the one that man planted on you. Throw it away!"

Wentworth laughed softly as he raised the window.

"A souvenir of the Black Death!" he whispered. "I wouldn't lose it for the world!"

"But— " the girl started to protest.

The *Spider* kissed her swiftly on the lips, smothering the words, helped her over the sill and lowered her by her hands to the ground. It was a drop of only a few feet. Rapidly he lowered the others after her. Then he and the great dog sprang down themselves.

The *Spider* and those with him faded into the shadows.

The rising sun was red in the sky as Wentworth and his tired company threaded the city. But even at this early hour the streets resounded with the shouts of newsboys crying the toll of the Black Death. A hundred killed!

Wentworth's jaws locked. A hundred dead! The Black Death was striking more savagely. While Wentworth battled futilely against his traps, sought frantically for some clue to the man's identity, the black wings of the Plague were sweeping the city, as its purple flower of pain blossomed on scores of throats.

But Wentworth had the girl, Virginia Doeg, at least. When she had thrown off the drugs, he would question her. Desperately he hoped for a clue from her.

Later, when she had slept off the narcotic, safe in his apartment with Nita, he went to the girl.

Though his eyes were grim with the thought of the ravages of the Black Death ever at the back of his mind, he was gentle with Virginia Doeg as he insisted upon her answering the question that he had put to her a few hours ago. A smile twisted his lips—it seemed like years.

When last he had asked that question, fear had gleamed for a moment in her eyes. Then a man with a gun had interrupted their conversation. It was that fear which had led the *Spider* to believe that she might hold some clue to the identity of the Black Death.

"Who besides yourself," he asked again, "had the opportunity to substitute the forged bonds for the genuine?"

And once more the girl evaded his keenly questioning gaze. Wentworth frowned. "Surely now," he said, "you must realize the importance of answering that question. Your failure to answer it was the reason for all that has happened. Your kidnapping by that masked man."

"Oh," she shuddered, "that horrible *Spider*." Bewilderment clouded Wentworth's eyes. His sharp glance flicked to Nita, and he saw a sly smile about her mouth.

Then suddenly he understood. Nita had convinced the girl, whose drug-dazed memories were befuddled, that the man who had kidnapped her was the *Spider*.

Wentworth had believed it necessary to reveal to this girl that the *Spider* and Wentworth were one. And now Nita cleverly had kept the secret. His eyes gave her silent thanks as he picked up the thread of thought that the girl's cry of revulsion had revealed.

"Unless you want the *Spider* to come again," he said sternly, "you had better answer my question at once."

The frightened girl looked up at him, large-eyed and pale, beneath the glowing red shower of her hair. "Oh," she said, "he couldn't have done it. Not my Jimmy!"

"Jimmy?"

The girl spoke rapidly now. "Yes, Jimmy. He could have done it, but I know he didn't. He loves me. We are to be married. And he is not the only one. Any official of the firm could have done it."

"What's Jimmy's name?" Wentworth said softly.

"But he isn't guilty," the girl protested. "I know he isn't."

"Of course not," Wentworth reassured her, "but I would like to know the name of—" he smiled, "—the lucky man."

Virginia Doeg blushed, and dropped her eyes. "Jimmy Handley," she said.

"Ah, yes," said Wentworth, remembering then MacDonald Pugh's mention of the man. An intelligent youth, Pugh had said, one who was "going places." Was it possible that the girl was Handley's dupe, that he had substituted the forged bonds and given the germs to her dog, so that when the time came he could direct suspicion upon her by claiming that the bonds had been stolen to finance the start of this monstrous crime?

Wentworth nodded swiftly to Nita, signifying that the girl could go now, and left the room hurriedly. He glanced at his watch. It was late, nearly four o'clock.

He caught his hat and cane from Jenkyns' ready hand, strode into the hall, and a moment later a taxi was whisking him through the late afternoon traffic to the offices of Pugh & Works, Inc. on Wall Street.

Straight down Broadway they whirled until that famous thoroughfare became a narrow street that belied its name, until the graveyard that marked one end of Wall Street hove into view, and they whirled into the narrow canyon that was the money center of the world.

The taxi jerked to a halt. Wentworth tossed the driver a bill and climbed out. A two-seated green Ford with P.D. printed on its side, a radio patrol car of the police, was parked ahead of him.

The devil! Was he going to run into some new crime at every turn of the trail that the Black Death left? He told himself that he was foolish, that the police car had no connection with his errand. But when he thrust into the elaborate offices of the brokerage firm of Pugh & Works, he found the two policemen from the patrol car there before him.

And MacDonald Pugh himself, his high shoulders stooped, his forward-leaning bald head nodding emphasis to his words, was talking to them.

Wentworth caught the tag end of what he was saying. "There is no doubt about it," Pugh was declaring positively. "There is a shortage in his accounts. He left the office early yesterday and he has not returned."

"And what's his name, sir?" one of the officers demanded.

MacDonald Pugh looked up with dark eyes from beneath his almost white brows, saw Wentworth and raised a hand in affable salute. "Just a minute, Dick," he said, and turned back to the policeman.

"The man's name," he said, "is James Handley."

CHAPTER TWELVE
Wentworth Views the Plague

JAMES HANDLEY, the man Virginia had said could not be guilty! The man she was to marry! There was a shortage in his accounts—and he was missing!

Wentworth was keenly interested. But no hint of it showed in his face. He flicked ashes from his cigarette and lounged about the office, inspecting the oil paintings which hung upon its walls as if totally disinterested in the conversation between Pugh and the two policemen.

But the name apparently had been dismissal for the two officers. "We'll put out an alarm for him, sir," one of them told Pugh. "And you may depend, sir, that we'll pick him up very shortly. They can't escape our dragnet."

"Fine," said MacDonald Pugh heartily, and the policemen left.

"Good of you to call, Dick," Pugh said to him, and Wentworth turned smiling from the inspection of a portrait.

"You have atrocious taste in paintings, Mac," he said, "but you have managed to get one good piece here. Undoubtedly a Millet."

MacDonald Pugh smiled. "You didn't come here, Dick, to criticize my paintings, I'm sure."

"No," Wentworth told him. "I was down this way, thought of you, and recalled that promise of a fishing party some weekend. The tuna are running off Montauk, you know. A bit early, but I understand some large ones have been taken."

"That's damned nice of you," Pugh said, "but I don't see how I could possibly get away. The stock market is doing tricks these days, what with the NRA and Mr. Roosevelt's so-called controlled inflation."

Wentworth waved a hand negligently, tossing his cigarette into a smoking stand. "You business men," he sighed. "I wish I could find something in life that was half so interesting. Sure you can't make it, Mac?"

Pugh shook his bald head regretfully, smiling up from beneath those white brows. "No can do. But if you're out at your estate on Sunday, and decide finally not to go fishing, you might drop over. Bring Nita along. When the ticker stops Saturday noon, I have until the Stock Exchange opens Monday before I—"

A strangled cry rang through the office. Wentworth whirled, staring with narrowed eyes past Pugh to the door of an office marked "Private." The door swung haltingly open and a man staggered out, clutching at his throat.

"The Black Death!" he gasped. "I've got it!" His hand ripped his collar open, and on the corpse-like yellowness of his throat Wentworth saw the purple flower of the dread plague!

The man was Theodore Works, Pugh's partner, and there could be no doubt that he was dying. His stumbling entry had thrown the room into a panic. Stenographers sprang screaming from their tasks, and pale-faced men raced in panic for the street.

Even Pugh, with one terrified glance, joined in the pell-mell rush. And only Wentworth, jaw clenched and eyes aglint, remained.

The man collapsed into a seat, flung his arms across a desk top and leaned his chest against its edge, his breath coming hoarsely.

"You have been blackmailed?" Wentworth demanded.

The man stared at him unseeingly. Wentworth moved a step nearer and demanded again, "Were you blackmailed?"

This time the man's head nodded heavily. "Yes. And I paid."

His hoarse voice was scarcely human, the words mere mouthings. "I paid. And now— oh, God— I'm dying anyhow! Dying— the Black Plague— "

"Whom did you pay?" Wentworth snapped at him. Sympathy for the dying man touched him, but more than sympathy was at stake. Here was a man who had actually had contact with the dread master of the plague, had paid him blackmail. If he could obtain from him with his dying breath a clue that might save the countless millions of the city—

Works' head sagged forward. Breath rasped more harshly in his throat. He belched. Blood poured from his jaws. It tore a muffled scream of agony from him.

"Quick, man!" Wentworth shot at him. "Do you know who the blackmailer was?"

The sagging head raised an inch, wobbled slowly in negation.

"No—" Works got out, "but—voice on wire— thought I knew it."

Wentworth advanced two swift strides. Here was the Black Death in all its horror. Its contagion might strike him down. But here, too, might be the one clue that the *Spider* must have to track the plague master.

Suddenly Works convulsed, reared back in his chair with clutching hands digging into his throat.

"Speak, man, speak!" Wentworth cried. The purple lips opened, suffocation blackened his face. Blood gushed out. Sound issued from that ghastly mouth. But it was sound that was translatable into no word. It was the death rattle. And Works slumped forward upon the desk, his face dyed by the loathsome blush of the Black Death.

For an instant longer Wentworth stared at the body, his heart torn with compassion at the cruelty he had been forced to exert upon this dying man. Then he whirled and strode from the room with hard-pounding heels.

Gone was the airy nonchalance with which he had met MacDonald Pugh; gone the smile from his lips, and in its place was grim purpose.

From his path a man fled, running with a wobbling unaccustomed gait, a sloppy unpressed coat flapping in the wind, a dilapidated gray felt jammed down about his ears.

For an instant Wentworth pursued. But after two swift strides he checked himself. A grim twist that was only half a smile came to his lips.

He should know by now the earmarks of the gentlemen of the press, should know that no one but a careless, keen reporter would dare, as this man had, the curse of the Black Death for the comparatively trivial accomplishment of spreading first the news of a major story upon the front page of his paper.

Wentworth strode on to the curb and hailed a taxi, cried sharply, "Police headquarters!" Then he settled back upon the cushions and toyed with the head of his cane, looking down at its carved ivory handle with eyes that for once were unappreciative of its artistry.

It was time the news was spread abroad, time that the city learned that this Black Death was the work of a human agency. Then indeed would the whole world rise up to wipe out the sinister masked shadow that crouched with bloody hands over New York's millions.

But before his cab could traverse the mile between Wall Street and the headquarters of police, men were screaming extras on the streets, and black headlines blazoned forth the news that the Black Death was a blackmailer's plot.

Perhaps, Wentworth thought, that news would help bring in information from others who had been blackmailed—perhaps it would bring out a clue to the plague master himself. But though he doubted that the police would be able to find the man, there was a way in which they could help if they would. They could, in all probability, locate James Handley. If they would search in earnest for that man, putting their best men upon the case, it was at least possible that some definite lead might be uncovered.

But Wentworth entered the office of the commissioner with a feeling of futility. How could he convince Kirkpatrick of the necessity for that search, unless he revealed not only what Wentworth knew, but what the *Spider* had learned?

Kirkpatrick's face brought Wentworth to a stop just inside the door. It was the face of a living man who was dead, the face of a man haunted by a tragic fear, or tortured by a secret grief. He stared at Wentworth with eyes that were unblinking and utterly cold, deep-sunk beneath frowning brows. And for once his mustache was untidy and unpointed,

and his clothes, usually immaculate, were unpressed.

"Why do you come here?" he demanded harshly.

Wentworth stared at him without speech, and once more the commissioner rasped: "Why do you come here?"

Wentworth was unprepared for the attack. His lips moved stiffly in a smile that was without mirth. "I came to help—"

"I don't want your help," thundered Kirkpatrick. He smacked his fist on the desk and crouched over it like a man about to spring. His eyes were burning.

"In heaven's name, Stanley, what is the matter with you?" Wentworth demanded.

There was a sternness in his face and his eyes did not waver before the assault of Kirkpatrick's glare. For two full minutes the men stared so into each other's eyes, and then Kirkpatrick straightened slowly from his tense crouch, dragged a heavy hand across his furrowed brow.

He sank limply back into his chair, and Wentworth came forward until he stood just across the desk from the commissioner. He was smiling easily now, and offered his cigarette case to Kirkpatrick.

"You gave me quite a start, Stan," he said. "You must be under a terrific strain."

Kirkpatrick made no move to accept the proffered cigarette. He seemed infinitely tired, sagging in his seat like a man almost without life. But his hands upon the arms of the chair were white with the tension of his gripping fingers.

"Wentworth," he said slowly, in a voice that was as dull and empty as his eyes. "I have long suspected that you were the *Spider*. I have had no proof of it. God knows I didn't want proof of it, except as my duty drove me on. For the *Spider* to me was an admirable man, despite his crimes against the law. He struck down criminals that I could not touch because of the rigid regulations of the law. And he avenged the innocent. For that I revered him, respected him as I respected you."

Wentworth opened his mouth to speak, but Kirkpatrick's eyes stopped him. "I say respected," he went on, "but that is past now. And I'm warning you that any other commissioner of police, knowing what I know, would believe the *Spider*, believe *you*, guilty of the Black Death!"

Kirkpatrick stopped speaking and his chin sagged upon his chest. But still his burning eyes held those of his friend. He leaned toward him across the desk.

"This is—" Wentworth began. But once more the commissioner stopped him, this time with a tired lift of his hand.

"Knowing you, Wentworth," he said, "knowing the *Spider* of days past, I cannot believe a man of those humanitarian instincts could inflict the Black Death upon the city. If I did believe you capable of

STANLEY KIRKPATRICK

VIRGINIA DOEG

that—" Suddenly the commissioner snapped to his feet, stood rigidly, his fists clenched tightly at his sides. "If I believed that, Wentworth, *I'd shoot you down this minute in cold blood!*"

CHAPTER THIRTEEN
A Shot in the Dark

KIRKPATRICK'S intensity startled Wentworth for a moment, drove all thoughts of protest from him. The patent distress of his friend touched him.

He tried to smile, failed, tried again, and achieved a stiff travesty of mirth.

"And so you should, Stanley," he said, "shoot me down if I were the *Spider*— and if the *Spider* were guilty of the Black Death."

Krikpatrick's saturnine face did not lighten. "I think it wise that you go now," he said dully, "and do not return."

"But this is foolish," Wentworth protested. And now for the first time a thin smile lifted Kirkpatrick's lips.

"The foolish part of it," he said, "is that I do not arrest you, as my inspectors urge me to."

An almost perceptible start jerked at Wentworth's muscles. So Kirkpatrick was not alone in his suspicion! This was a thing that he had not realized before. He had thought the whole thing a figment of Kirkpatrick's tortured imagination. This revelation increased the seriousness of the situation.

"For God's sake, go!" Kirkpatrick ground out,

and the strain showed in the thinness of his voice. "Can't you understand?"

And now at last Wentworth did understand. He bowed with grave formality. "Very well," he said, turned on his heel and stalked to the door. And even while he was closing it he heard the commissioner's cracked voice rise madly:

"And—don't—come back!"

The uniformed clerk who stood outside the door stared at Wentworth with narrowed, suspicious eyes. But for once the glance remained unseen. Wentworth's keen senses were dulled by the enormity of the rift between him and his warmest friend.

He could see how Kirkpatrick was torn between duty and affection; between what his office urged and what his heart believed. Even the monstrous threat of the plague paled before this personal grief. It seemed like some nightmarish thing that could not actually exist.

Wentworth dazedly entered a taxi and gave his home address, hoping desperately that Nita would be there. He needed her warm understanding now, needed the consolation of her confidence and belief in him.

The taxi seemed to crawl. He was on fire to get home. He leaned forward and rapped on the glass. "Hurry, man, hurry!" he snapped. "Speed."

Tell a taxi driver to hurry in New York and you get the wildest ride that can be achieved by human ingenuity and mechanical power. Fender-brushing, brake-slamming, tire squealing speed!

Off slammed the taxi, weaving through traffic like a rabbit running through brambles. It whirled a corner on dry-skidding tires, dodged a head-on collision by a fraction of an inch, spurted between two encroaching trucks.

Wentworth, feverish-eyed, tense-muscled, leaned forward and rapped on the glass. "Faster," he cried, "Faster!"

The taxi driver whipped a frightened glance over his shoulder, the whites of his eyes showing, and suddenly Wentworth laughed. The man must think him utterly mad.

But the driver was trying desperately to fulfill the demand of this grim-faced passenger behind him, for when a passenger asks favors it means big tips. And even in taxi-riding New York, big tips are scarce nowadays.

He locked tires and skidded the last twenty-five feet to the curb before Wentworth's apartment house, and the violence of the stop almost flung his passenger forward upon his shoulders. Wentworth dropped to the pavement, tossed the man a twenty-dollar bill and, laughing with a cracked strain in his voice, went pounding into the house.

Behind him the taxi driver looked from the twenty-dollar bill to his retreating back, shook his head and muttered, "Jeez, the guy's nuts!"

Wentworth slammed into the elevator, and its express speed seemed infinitely slow. Key in the lock, he thrust open the door violently, strode into the center of the drawing room before he paused and stood stock still, staring about him. Nita wasn't there.

Wentworth's broad shoulders slumped. Jenkyns' staid old figure plodded into the room, took his

JAMES HANDLEY

THE BLACK DEATH

master's hat and cane from listless hands. Twice he opened his mouth to speak, and twice thought better of it. Finally he turned and plodded out again, his white old head shaking.

Wentworth moved on stumbling feet into the music room beyond. His fumbling hands brought out his violin case, picked up the instrument and thumbed slowly over the resonant strings. Their notes rang sweet and true, and he tucked the violin beneath his chin, touched bow to the strings.

Dirge-like the music rolled, funereal and slow. But as he played new animation seemed to come into his drooping figure, his fingers flicked more rapidly over the strings, his bow surged—and the music's tempo changed, became furious and wild.

It was mad, that music, as if all the devils of hell leaped in those flicking fingers. Jenkyns' frightened face showed in the doorway. He knew his master's habit of playing out his moods, but never before had he heard such wild notes torn from the straining strings.

The music spoke of a mind on the verge... the verge of—

Ram Singh appeared behind him, his dark face like carven stone with eyes glittering to the pulse of the music. But Wentworth was utterly unaware of the two faithful servitors at his back. All his being was centered on the vibrating instrument beneath his chin.

Gradually the wildness died, and in its place came a slow, limpid melody. But it was two hours after he had picked up the violin that he replaced it in its case and, exhausted, weary in every fiber, turned to find Ram Singh and Jenkyns standing transfixed in the doorway.

He smiled at them quickly. "My dinner clothes, Ram Singh. Jenkyns, phone Miss Nita that I shall call for her in half an hour."

"Yes, sir!" Jenkyns bobbed with bows, his ruddy face wreathed in smiles, and ducked away as fast as his old legs would carry him to perform his master's will.

Nita and Wentworth went forth gaily to dinner. And not until the meal was well underway did he mention, and then only casually, the afternoon scene with Kirkpatrick. He was callous about it, as if the friendship lost meant less than nothing, and Nita's quick blue eyes went to his face and searched it carefully.

She was a lovely girl, and in evening dress she was surprisingly beautiful. The low-cut gown of simple white left bare the exquisite slope of her shoulders. The gleam of her rich brown hair made a jewel-like setting for the perfect oval of her face.

The luxurious dining room was muted by the Depression, its usually crowded tables half empty, but not a man who passed but felt his pulses swiften, felt the dread curse of the plague lift a little for having glimpsed her and paid the tribute of admiring eyes.

But her gaze was solely upon Wentworth. Her eyes hovered now half between puzzlement and raillery. Well as she knew her Dick, she did not quite understand this new mood.

"But this is silly, Dick," she said.

Wentworth leaned forward across the spotless white and crystal of the table. "You have the dearest chin in the world," he said.

"Be serious, Dick," she urged.

"Oh, I really mean it," he said. She placed her small white hand upon his. "Dick, you're maddening sometimes," she said. "Tell me about this spat you had with Kirkpatrick."

"Spat?" Wentworth's eyebrows lifted, the hint of raillery that always lurked there emphasized. He laughed. He placed his other hand upon hers and leaned forward again. "Nita," he said, "I'm bored with the city. I think I shall go to the country for the weekend."

The girl looked at him with a faint frown disturbing her forehead. She did not speak.

"We have an invitation," he went on, "from MacDonald Pugh. A charming fellow, don't you think? And this constant business of the Black Death, this pursuit of shadows, grows irksome."

"Stop fooling, Dick," the girl pleaded, the frown deepening between her eyes. She smiled uncertainly. "What's the matter, boy?"

"I'm bored," he repeated.

She was completely serious now. "What are you trying to do?" she asked in level tones. "This isn't like you, Dick."

Wentworth's smile was crooked. "Can't I pick a quarrel with my only sweetheart?" he demanded.

"What are you up to, Dick?" she demanded again.

"Just this," he said in swift undertones. "I want everyone to believe that I have left the city. I wanted you to believe it, too. You are too honest, too lovely to be able to dissemble successfully. And everyone—absolutely everyone—must think that I have left."

"And so you tried to pick a quarrel with me?" the girl asked softly, reproachfully.

Wentworth's eyes kissed her.

"It was foolish, darling," he said, and abruptly his face went serious again. "Now, beautiful, get angry with me. Make a scene. Stand up and call me a coward. Say you don't see how I can leave the city when Kirkpatrick needs every man he has, and many more than he has, to track down the Black Death. Go on!"

"Is it really necessary?" the girl asked. Wentworth's nod was slow and completely serious.

"Very well," she mocked him, "but remember, I am too honest, too lovely, to be able to dissemble!"

She slapped her hand upon the table and her blue

eyes suddenly clouded. "I don't believe it," she said, and her tones were loud. Dick mumbled some words in a low voice.

Nita's tones rose even higher. "You couldn't do such a thing, Dick Wentworth," she said.

Faces turned at other tables. Startled eyes watched them. "You can't leave the city," she said vehemently in the same loud tone. "You can't. Commissioner Kirkpatrick is your friend. You can't desert him in his greatest need."

Wentworth leaned across the table as if urging her to speak in a lower tone of voice. Audibly he said, "For God's sake, Nita, don't make a scene." But under his breath he whispered, "You're doing splendidly! Keep it up."

Now the girl's voice turned pleading. "But, Dick, you must stay, and help Kirkpatrick catch the man behind this dreadful plague. Surely," she jeered at him now, "surely you are not afraid of the Black Death."

Absolute silence fell over the dining room. Her words "the Black Death" rang out stridently. They seemed to strike the room to silent terror. Not a person stirred. The girl was on her feet now, her chair thrust back so violently that it slammed to the floor.

Wentworth was on his feet, too. He moved around the table with imploring hands.

"Don't touch me, you coward!" Nita cried. She looked him contemptuously up and down. "To think that Dick Wentworth is a coward!"

She stooped and snatched her fur-edged cloak from the floor, flung it over her arm and half ran, half stumbled down the aisle among the crowded tables, among the staring faces, among the jabbering gossip, her face buried on her forearm as if she were too broken by tears to watch where she went. As she went she heard the murmured names: "Dick Wentworth—Nita van Sloan. Dick Wentworth—Nita van Sloan—Nita van Sloan—"

At his table, Wentworth stared like a stricken man after the girl's retreating figure, then sank into his chair, head hanging, one arm sprawled across the table.

For long minutes, Wentworth sat staring fixedly at the tablecloth. He too heard the excited jabbering about him, and behind his masking lids his eyes were amused. Mentally he cried, "Brava!" And I said she couldn't act, he thought. Be damned if I don't write a play for her—and he laughed at the conceit. As if Nita would ever desert her aristocratic solitude for the public spotlight of the stage!

Wentworth himself was no mean actor. When he got up from the table he was a grief-crazed man. His stumbling feet found no even path, and his head hung, and his shoulders drooped. But once in the street, away from curious eyes, his alertness returned.

He strode briskly along. Swiftly he returned to his apartment, donned the *Spider*'s dark tweeds, drew a black fedora down over his eyes, and with tool kit beneath his arm, automatic beneath his hand in his pocket, slipped out the servant's entrance and left by the servant's automatic elevator.

The *Spider* had work to do...

He rode the subway to Wall Street, and the *Spider* was but another moving shadow among shadows as he slipped into the building where Pugh & Works had offices. The watchman nodded in his chair, and so silent was the invader's tread, so inconspicuous his passage, that even had the man been awake he scarcely would have noticed.

Swiftly then the *Spider* stole up the stairway, picked the lock of the office door and, fastening it behind him, hurried into the private office of the partners, smelling strongly of disinfectant and germicides which had been spread to wipe out the threat of the Black Death in the room where Works had died.

The modern safe there resisted his skilled fingers and sensitive ear scarcely longer than had the old tin box in the pawnbroker's office. And in a few moments he had spread before him the firm's books, was skimming rapidly over double-entry bookkeeping and an auditor's report with the skilled ease of a practiced accountant.

His concentration was intense. So engrossed did he become in the frail thread that he followed, the key which involving Jimmy Handley might bring him to the identity of the Black Death, that he did not hear the opening of the outer door, did not look up until lights flashed on in the main office.

Like a flash then he extinguished his own minute gleaming flashlight by which he had examined the work. Like a shadow he moved across the room, crouched behind a door. And now a black mask concealed his features.

Slow and ponderous footsteps crossed the floor. A hand touched the knob and the door swung open, concealing Wentworth behind it. But the door had been thrust strongly; it struck Wentworth's feet and, shaking, bounded back. The indistinct figure in the doorway whirled suddenly in alarm. A hand darted up, and at almost point-blank range a pistol spurted its spear of powder flame at the crouching *Spider*!

Only Wentworth's split-second coordination of mind and muscle saved him then. He had seen the jerk of the man's hand and thrown himself to the floor so nearly in timing with the gun's discharge that it seemed he had been hurled there by the bullet.

He let the breath hiss from lungs in a half moan, and the crouching figure of the man who had fired straightened slowly. Wentworth's own gun was ready to his hand, but this was no battle with the underworld. In this case he was the interloper; the other man was in the right.

And the *Spider* never killed an innocent person.

On the other hand, in addition to Pugh, he knew a number of other members of the firm personally, and to be discovered in his present role with a black mask over his face would have spelled his doom.

He moaned again, his left hand pressed to his chest as if it covered a wound, and abruptly a white light glared into his masked face. The man with the gun moved cautiously nearer. Wentworth tossed on the floor as if in mortal pain, flung out his right arm convulsively.

The man came a step closer, gun ready, and Wentworth's outflung hand found his heel and jerked suddenly. The flashlight flung upward. The man cursed, fell heavily, and his gun blazed.

Glass crashed as a bullet screamed off into the darkness. Wentworth bounded from the floor, flung himself upon the man, and his right fist crashed home twice. The man jerked beneath him, straightened and went limp.

The *Spider* heard hoarse shouts, the first shrill blasts of a watchman's police whistle. He must make good his escape at once, or it would be too late. Already guards within the building must be rushing to the succor of the man he had knocked out.

Swiftly the *Spider* ripped out of his coat, flung it and his hat across the room. In them would be found no mark of identification. Swiftly he stooped over the unconscious man, tugged the coat from his body, flapped the other man's hat upon his head and, struggling into the coat, ran toward the outer door, ripping the mask from his face and thrusting it into his pocket as he sped across the room. He jerked open the door, as the first of the watchmen plunged up the stairs, gun up and ready.

CHAPTER FOURTEEN
Wholesale Death

THE *SPIDER* turned his head, staring back over his shoulder at the room he had just left, shouting hoarsely, "In there! He's in there!"

"Jeez, it's you, sir!" cried the watchman. "And I nearly shot you!"

"For God's sake, hurry," gasped the *Spider* hoarsely, and the man plunged past him with drawn gun. Wentworth hastened down the stairs. Behind him, he heard the guard shout a warning to his companions below. "Be careful, Bill. Mr. Robertson is coming down." And in the darkness another guard brushed past him with a muttered, "Pardon me, sir."

The *Spider* continued his dash to the front doors. But once there he cut his speed to a quiet stroll, left the building and walked briskly, but with no appearance of flight, through streets that shrieked now with the bedlam of approaching police sirens.

A subway entrance was near, and Wentworth descended unhurriedly, dropped a nickel into the clanking turnstile and walked slowly up the platform. A bum without hat or coat was stretched out sleeping heavily upon a bench. Grim humor twitched Wentworth's lips. What an evil trick he could play this derelict by the gift of a hat and coat!

He strode into the men's washroom and with powerful fingers shredded the coat he wore. With a knife blade he ripped the hat to fragments and flushed them into the sewer of the city.

After them he sent tie and collar, and slouched again out onto the platform with rumpled hair, a dissolute, half-starved bum. He smeared dirt from the platform upon his cheeks, beneath his eyes, so that they seemed sunken; rubbed his eyes violently so that they became bloodshot. And then it was that his genius for disguise became apparent.

The *Spider* was gone. Gone, too, was Richard Wentworth, the wealthy young clubman; and in their place, slack-jawed and slouch-shouldered, there lolled upon the bench beside that other slumbering bum another member of the vast army of the unemployed.

But before police could come pounding, searching down the subway stairs, the rumble of a train filled the hot place. Wentworth shambled aboard and slumped into a corner seat, to all appearances a weary, homeless man.

It was with difficulty that he entered his apartment house again, finally managing to slip into the rear entrance when for a moment the watchman walked away.

And in the morning, as if to mock him, the papers blazed forth with a new horror that transcended all previous perpetrations of that monstrous criminal, the Black Death. For the man had sent letters to every newspaper in town, stating demands that the banks of the city lend a billion dollars to the city government in cash. And that huge sum was to be paid to him! The club this super blackmailer held over the cringing multitude was the threat of the plague spread wholesale through the city!

The letter said:

If the city's millions knew me better, they would realize that I am no man of idle threats. But since it is unfortunately necessary that I conceal my identity, I shall deliver a free sample of my thoroughness. Even as you in the city read these lines, the Black Death will be among you. Oh, nothing to be alarmed about, for today I shall kill only a few hundred of your millions. Take heed, as these hundreds choke and die with the Black Death, that you do not provoke me by unnecessary delay, lest the next blow wipe out thousands.

And even as newsboys shouted the fearsome headlines, the plague had lifted its evil head.

Ambulances gonged their way through the streets to the Lower East Side area, where the Black Death had chosen first to strike. And people died in the streets. Thousands fled.

The news that the Black Death had fulfilled his warning threw the city into complete panic. Its people went absolutely mad with terror. Thousands fled. Trains and roads were jammed. It was like a wartime evacuation.

Wentworth, roaming the fringes of the area where the Black Death had struck, barred from nearer approach by a double ring of police who—with surgical masks upon their faces braved the plague—found the city about him dead. The usually crowded benches of Battery Park at the tip end of Lower Manhattan were deserted. Even the birds of the air seemed to have fled the Black Death. For the flock of pigeons that usually settled before the Custom House was missing.

Wentworth, plodding through deserted streets, past the closed doors of shops, of business offices, even of restaurants, saw their bodies in the streets. Good God, even the pigeons had fallen prey to the dread plague.

Wentworth did not approach the stilled birds, but went swiftly to a subway and, riding uptown until he reached a newspaper office, went in to insert a small ad.

The place was a hive of industry. Boys darted back and forth with bundles of paper under their arms. Trucks roared off with loads of the latest editions, their headlines still wet with ink, for the thousands who, unable to leave the city, remained behind locked doors or crept furtively through the streets with backward flung glances that seemed to fear the Black Death would spring upon them in the guise of a ravening beast.

A businesslike young woman took his ad crisply. It read:

Pigeons for sale. A large number of all varieties, fancy and homing.

And it gave an address on the upper West Side.

Wentworth made sure that the ad would appear that day, then hurried to the subway again, and sped uptown to the address he had given, where a druggist with whom he had dealt kept pigeons as a hobby.

Wentworth strode up the inner stairs to the man's house above the store, knocked, and when the bewhiskered little man with gold-rimmed glasses far down upon his nose opened the door, spoke swift.

"I want to board with you for a week. Here's fifty dollars in advance," and he thrust out two twenties and a ten-dollar bill.

The man's fingers closed on the money automatically. But he stared from the crisp new notes to Wentworth's entirely serious face in astonishment.

"I don't understand, Mr. Wentworth—you want to take board with me?"

"That's it."

"But I don't understand."

The pale watery eyes were bewildered. Wentworth smiled grimly. "It is not necessary that you should. You have the money. Do you agree?"

The man stared down at the green banknotes. His head wavered slowly from side to side. "I— I guess it's all right," he stammered. "I'll ask mother."

Wentworth heard his voice calling his wife and knew that when the woman saw the money it would be all right.

All that day, Wentworth sat in the small room that had been assigned to him, waiting. Waiting without action while the corpse fires burned on Riker's Island; while ambulances sirened through the streets, and people choked and died with the Black Death.

It was late when he let himself out of the lonely little apartment and hurried home to get a change of linen. He tarried only a few moments, then hurried back. Climbing the stairs, he heard excited voices raised within.

He knocked on the door and found the bewhiskered little druggist striding back and forth, gesticulating with stiffly waving arms. "They're gone!" he cried. "They're all gone—all my lovely pigeons."

Wentworth's eyes narrowed. "Not stolen?" he demanded.

The little man paused in his striding, peered at him above the gold-rimmed glasses far down upon his nose, peered and blinked and suddenly shouted, "You—you stole my pigeons!"

Wentworth cursed silently. Stolen! And he had expected that the Black Death would come and buy them legitimately. "I'm a dumb fool," he said. His hand reached into his pocket. "How much were the pigeons worth?" he asked.

At sight of the money the man ceased his jabbering. "I'm sorry, Mr. Wentworth," he said, his voice quavering, "I was half out of my head. I know you didn't steal the pigeons."

Wentworth said: "But I put the ad into the paper that caused them to be stolen."

He laid a thousand dollars on the table, whirled and strode from the room. He had been gone from the house scarcely half an hour, yet in that time the Black Death had struck. Was it luck? Or was the arch criminal even now upon his trail?

Wentworth flicked a glance over his shoulder. Hell, he was becoming as frightened as the rabbit-like people of the city, terrified by the plague, who ducked in and out of their doorways like hares out of a warren.

A taxi sped him home. He strode across the room to the phone without even pausing to remove his hat. Swiftly he called every pigeon fancier he knew, and all either had sold out their complete stocks of pigeons or had been robbed.

That clinched it. He dialed police headquarters, asked for Kirkpatrick, but giving his name was told the commissioner would not speak to him. Anger flared in Wentworth. This was no time for personal animosity. No time for foolish personal considerations. The entire city was in peril.

He left the house, and a cab sped with him to headquarters. He strode in, and policemen who would have objected stepped from his path, overawed by his blazing eyes. He stormed up to the door of the commissioner, and there the guard stood firm until the sharp voice from within bade the man step aside and let Richard Wentworth enter.

More worn than ever, commissioner Kirkpatrick crouched behind the desk. He did not speak until the door had closed behind Wentworth.

"I warned you," he said then, "not to come here again.

"But damn it, man, this is important. There is no time for personal considerations," Wentworth rapped out.

Kirkpatrick's face was grim, his lips so compressed that they showed only as a thin white line. When he spoke again, they opened and shut upon his words like slashing knives.

"I have but one question to ask you," he said. "Why did you steal the pigeons from that man?"

Wentworth stared at him. "Are you mad?" he demanded. "Have you been shadowing me?"

Kirkpatrick smiled grimly. "You leave me no choice, Richard. Give me your cigarette lighter."

Wentworth threw back his head and laughed. It was wild laughter.

"Stanley, in heaven's name, be sensible! I tell you I have the clue that will lead to the capture of the master of the plague."

Kirkpatrick had not moved since Wentworth had entered the room. He still crouched behind his desk, uttering words like bullets.

"Will you hand over the lighter, or must I summon help to take it from you forcibly?"

The gaze of the two men met, and locked. And Wentworth shook his head slowly. "If I do that, will you listen to me?"

The smile that just disturbed Kirkpatrick's lips was wintry. His mouth opened a fraction of an inch.

"Perhaps," he said.

Furiously Wentworth snatched the cigarette lighter from his pocket, the lighter that contained even now the damning seal of the *Spider* and flung it upon Kirkpatrick's desk. Even if it meant his death he was willing that it should be so, if by so

doing he could avert the doom that hung over the city.

Kirkpatrick leaned forward. Under the strong, shaded light upon his desk he examined the lighter. But he had done that futilely before. Now he took out a screwdriver and systematically took the thing apart. The white scar upon Wentworth's temple throbbed redly. Even though he was determined to sacrifice his life, if need be, to gain the hearing that was necessary to the salvation of the city, the sight of these lean, probing fingers ferreting nearer and nearer to the secret of the lighter sent the blood thrumming through his veins.

He waited tensely, and his breath came more swiftly. His eyes stared with a fearful intensity. Then, abruptly, it was over.

The screwdriver touched the hidden spring and the base of the lighter came loose in Kirkpatrick's hand. Wearily, with grief in his eyes, the commissioner looked up at Wentworth. And the seconds that their eyes met brought hope to the *Spider*. For he knew that each moment their eyes held the red seals were vanishing.

Kirkpatrick's eyes dropped at last to the lighter. He turned it curiously over in his hand, and Wentworth caught his breath as the commissioner held it under the light and peered into that secret chamber in its base.

Had the shrewd mechanics of the lighter functioned properly? Had the seals disappeared? With throbbing pulses, Wentworth waited. Kirkpatrick's face revealed nothing. It was as if made of steel, its lines drawn so taut it seemed no emotion would ever stir them again.

Then slowly Kirkpatrick looked up.

"I am glad, Richard," he said slowly, "that there are no seals of the *Spider* to add to the damning evidence my men have piled up against you. This secret chamber in the base of your lighter is enough without that.

"Richard," he said, "I hate to do this, but I have no choice. Any other man in my position would have arrested you days ago. I still cannot believe it, but— "

His hand moved heavily to a row of buttons at the end of his desk and pressed upon one. Behind Wentworth a door opened, and with the sudden feeling of a trapped animal he whirled and stared into the muzzles of two police pistols, held in the brawny hands of two grim-faced officers.

"Richard Wentworth," Kirkpatrick intoned. He might have been a judge in his black robes with a black cap upon his head, pronouncing doom upon a convicted man. Almost Wentworth could imagine he heard the words, "Dead—dead—dead," that would terminate such a sentence.

"Richard Wentworth, I arrest you on suspicion of homicide," he said. "Take him away."

CHAPTER FIFTEEN
"Is That a Confession?"

WENTWORTH whirled back, staring into Stanley Kirkpatrick's wooden face. The man looked like a sleepwalker, his eyes staring straight ahead, as if they were looking into infinity.

Wentworth started forward, and strong hands gripped his arms.

"In God's name, Stanley, hear me first! Hear me— "

"Take him away."

"—hear me, Stanley!"

"Take—him—away—" Kirkpatrick's voice rose to a shriek.

"Stanley, those pigeons—"

"Shut up!" snarled a voice in Wentworth's ear. He was lifted forcibly, dragged backward.

"Stanley!" he cried.

But the doors slammed between them, and a heavy fist thudded against the base of his skull. Lights danced in his brain, his head sagged, and only half conscious he was dragged with feet that thumped on every stair up a long flight of steps. A cell door clanged metallically and Wentworth was flung inside. He tripped, collapsed upon the concrete floor.

Once more the steel rang. Wentworth thrust his body up from the floor, head dangling. "Stanley," he called. "Stanley!" He caught the bars, dragged himself to his feet. "Stanley!" he cried again, and his voice rang down the steel-barred alleys. He beat upon the iron, shouted, but only the echoes answered him. And from the next cell a man snarled, "Fer cripes' sake, dry up and go to sleep."

Another man muttered, "Youse damned dopes give me a pain. Yuh can't take it."

Wentworth took his hands from the bars, clenched them at his sides until the nails bit into the palms, and forced himself to calmness. In some way he must force Stanley Kirkpatrick to listen to him.

Swiftly he stripped off his belt, climbed upon the iron bed that constituted the cell's sole furniture. He fastened one end to the bars, put the loop about his throat, and let himself sag upon it, sustaining his weight with his hands on the bars so that he could still breathe. Then he beat against the steel as if he kicked in his death agony.

The man in the next cell rolled over and cursed, saw the dangling body and shrieked. "Hey, the damned dope's killing himself!"

"God Almighty!" another man cried.

The entire cell block suddenly went mad, cursed, screamed, shouted, beat upon the bars, cried out like a menagerie in a blasting thunder storm. Guards came running, and lights flashed into the cells. Wentworth still hung on by his hands, waiting until the light bathed him. Then he released his hold and dangled in the noose.

Now he actually choked. His tongue thrust up in his throat. His eyes seemed to be starting from their sockets. Blood drummed in his ears. The guard cursed, keys rattled and the door swung open. Powerful hands grabbed Wentworth. He felt himself lifted, the noose jerked free, and he slumped to the floor, almost unconscious.

And now Kirkpatrick came striding, long-legged and somber along the echoing tiles. He came into the cell where Wentworth lay upon his back on the cot.

Kirkpatrick's face was more drawn than ever. His eyes had a haunted look. "In God's name, Dick," he said, "why have you done this thing?"

Wentworth could not speak above a whisper. His throat had been torn by the metal of his belt buckle. "I must talk to you," he articulated. "Those pigeons— "

Abruptly Kirkpatrick straightened above Wentworth's prostrate body. "Carry this man to my office," he ordered harshly. And Wentworth was lifted bodily and borne away through the still clamoring cells.

In Kirkpatrick's office he was allowed to slump into a chair and the commissioner stood before him, a gaunt skeleton of his former self, with eyes that glared in near madness.

"Outside," he said abruptly, gesturing to the officers who had brought Wentworth into the room.

One of the men ventured a protest.

"Outside!" Kirkpatrick roared, and the men bolted for the door. Kirkpatrick's eyes still had not left Wentworth's. "Now speak," he croaked hoarsely.

"In God's name, Stanley," Wentworth whispered, his words wide-spaced and painful. "In God's name let me out. I'm the only one in the world who can keep this plague from killing every mortal soul in the city."

The commissioner's face went pale as death.

"Is that—is that—a confession?" he asked, and his voice sank to a whisper that was as rasping, as painful, as Wentworth's own.

Wentworth, slumped in the chair, stared up at him with sick eyes and with mouth twisted awry in a bitter smile.

"Is that a confession?" Kirkpatrick rasped again, and his voice rose. Suddenly his hand darted beneath his coat. A long-barreled revolver gleamed. Wentworth's eyes did not waver, nor did the twisted smile leave his lips. He continued to stare into Kirkpatrick's face.

But the commissioner made no move to shoot. He reversed the gun, thrust it toward Wentworth.

"Either kill me or kill yourself," he said. "For, God help me, if you are guilty! But how could you be guilty? I can't believe it." He broke off, panting. "If you are guilty," he said again, "I have failed in my duty to the city." And once more he thrust the gun toward Wentworth.

Slowly his prisoner shook his head. "No man can accuse you of that, Stanley." Wentworth's mind was racing swiftly. He realized now that he could not tell Kirkpatrick the information he had; that he dared not tell him what he had discovered, since to the man's now distraught mind it would seem an additional link in the evidence against him. And Wentworth knew he must get free.

True, he had a clue, but it was a clue that no one but himself could follow to its end; that no one but himself could turn into a weapon against the sinister master of the plague. He must take a long chance— one that would involve his own possible death and that of Stanley Kirkpatrick. But that chance alone would give him his liberty; would in the end enable him to save the city. And he knew that no other hand than his could triumph.

Wentworth stared into Kirkpatrick's eyes. "Take me out of here," he said, "and I will lead you and your men to the master of the plague."

Kirkpatrick shook his head heavily. He turned his back on Wentworth and strode across the room and back again, pressing his temples with his palms, but no words squeezed from his lips.

"The master of the plague," Wentworth whispered, "I'll take you to him!"

Kirkpatrick's hands dropped. His eyes were dull. "The city is under martial law," he said. "Troops patrol the streets. Any person who leaves his house after dark is shot on sight. Mobs howl about the doors to the City Hall, pound at the doors of the banks, demanding that the Black Death's ransom be paid. And you—you confess at least to complicity in these things, and I let you live!"

He raised a clenched, shaking hand above his head.

"It isn't so, Wentworth," his eyes were pleading. "Dick, it isn't so. You're not guilty! I know you're not guilty! You *can't* be. Why, man—"

For moments the men's eyes met, then abruptly Kirkpatrick crossed to his desk and touched a button. A man sprang into the room. Kirkpatrick looked at him as if he were some strange apparition, but presently he got out words:

"Order out my car. Get a squad of men. Take charge of this prisoner and wait for me. If he tries to escape—kill him."

The man saluted. Others entered the room. Obviously they had been listening. They caught up Wentworth, dragged him from the office. Actually he had recovered most of his strength, but he feigned weakness and let the men carry him.

He had lied to Kirkpatrick. He did not know the hiding place of the Black Death. But a reckless smile twisted his lips. All his money on one spin of the wheel. His life was forfeit anyway. He must gamble the lives of these men, the life of his dearest friend, for the salvation of the city.

Surrounded by police, he was roughed out of the building into the commissioner's car. He was placed on one of the small, collapsible seats in the tonneau with a man on either side, and two more behind. The commissioner climbed stiffly into the forward seat. He twisted and stared into Wentworth's face.

"Well?" It was a question.

Wentworth apparently was scarcely able to hold himself erect. "Over Brooklyn Bridge," he whispered, "and hurry. In God's name, hurry!"

The car sprang forward, its deep-throated motor roaring. Its siren began to wail, and it ripped through city traffic at forty, fifty, fifty-five miles an hour. Ahead of them police whistles skirled, traffic cops sprang forward to block traffic, and the commissioner's car slammed through, spun on to Brooklyn Bridge, and wove a rapid way among other, slower moving cars.

Wentworth sagged forward, his arms upon the back of the seat ahead, his head upon his arms. They raced out into the middle of the span. Ahead of them the roadway was clear. Suddenly Wentworth lunged forward, both his hands grasped the right hand side of the steering wheel and with a savage wrench he sent the car crashing through the rail, hurtling out into space, somersaulting to the river far below.

The top ripped off with the force of the plunge, but Wentworth gripped the wheel and hung on.

Then the car struck and plunged beneath the surface of the East River.

In falling they had just missed the stern of a tug. Men shouted on its decks, ropes snaked out, and one by one the commissioner and all of his men were hauled to safety. They stared out over the roiled waters of the river. Not a head bobbed in the swift current. Not a ripple except the wash of the boat broke the surface.

Wentworth, the *Spider*, had vanished.

CHAPTER SIXTEEN
Nita Cries Vengeance

SPIDER ARRESTED FOR PLAGUE. KILLS SELF IN BRIDGE LEAP

Those black headlines screamed at Nita van Sloan when, with the morning sun warm in her face, she walked briskly along the drive with Apollo, joying in the fresh breezes that swept in from over the Hudson.

"*Spider* Arrested!" A boy shouted. "Extra! Paper!"

With hands that trembled despite her every effort at control, Nita bought one of the smeary papers, gasped at the headlines, skimmed through the story. Her eyes caught on two sentences and she breathed hope deeply through her nostrils.

Everyone else in the car was saved by the men on the tug, but the *Spider* was drowned. The body has not been recovered.

The body has not been recovered. Hope. Hope. But why in the name of Heaven had Stanley Kirkpatrick ordered the arrest of his friend? Knowing Wentworth innocent as she did, knowing Kirkpatrick's friendship for him, she could not understand how he could have been driven to such a step.

She saw that Kirkpatrick had been plunged into the river with Wentworth. Surely from him, then, she could learn the truth. She flagged a taxi, sat with whitely clasped hands while it twisted into the express highway which, elevated on stilts, shot motor traffic down the bank of the Hudson. Once she threw back her head and laughed. But it was as if hands closed on her throat and the laughter stopped. Dead? Dick could not be dead. He could not be! He must not be—

Her name won her instant admittance to the office of the commissioner, and Kirkpatrick, gray-faced and sleepless, rose to greet her. As the door clicked shut behind her, Nita van Sloan stopped in her tracks, staring at this apparition of the man she had known as gay, debonair, perpetually smiling.

Then she hurried forward, and suddenly her lips were tremulous.

"Tell me! Tell me!" she commanded.

The wintry smile that was Kirkpatrick's only mirth these days stirred his lips, but his deep-sunken eyes remained dull, without life.

"I hope," he said slowly, "and it's for your sake as well as his, that he is dead."

The girl fell back a little staggering half pace, her wrist against her mouth smothering the cry that rose there. But suddenly in those words, too, she found hope.

"You don't know!" she cried at him. "You don't know!"

He drooped into his chair. "No, I don't know," and a gag seemed taken from his mouth. He began to talk as he had not spoken for days, pouring out words. "You don't know the evidence against him, Nita. It was overwhelming," and he recited the long list of circumstances that pointed to Wentworth as the *Spider*, and to the *Spider* as the perpetrator of the Black Death. He seemed suddenly obsessed with the necessity for convincing this girl, perhaps of proving to himself, that he had acted rightly.

"—And there in the base of his lighter was a secret compartment," he finished. He spread his hands, palms upward. "I ordered his arrest."

"And you—you," the girl's scorn rang in the room, "—you called yourself his friend."

"But, Nita—"

The girl leaned across the desk and her eyes were burning in a dead white face.

"You know that Dick Wentworth could not do the things you accused him of."

Kirkpatrick eyed her shrewdly. "Yet you yourself quarreled with him, and I do not believe it was for the reason that the gossip columns of the newspapers reported. I believe it was because he could not explain—"

Nita laughed wildly.

"We quarreled. Dear Lord, we quarreled! Dick said that if we pretended to, over his leaving town, it would help convince his enemies that he had left. In which case he would be able to help you better to track down the Black Death. That was what he said!"

The girl paused, her breasts rising and falling, straining against her dress with the quickness of her breath. She went on more slowly. "Yes, that was what he told me, but I see now that his real reason was to protect me. He knew that he was going into terrible danger. Yes, Dick Wentworth did that, and you think that such a man could—"

Kirkpatrick jerked to his feet. His voice rose and cracked.

"Don't you suppose I know what kind of man Dick Wentworth is? Why do you suppose—"

He stretched out both his hands and they were trembling. "It was the pigeons that clinched the case against him. Whether I believed or not did not matter. I was forced to act."

"The pigeons?"

"Dick offered to take us to the place where the plague master was hidden, where he had concealed the pigeons that, Dick says, bring the plague of the Black Death to the city."

Nita straightened slowly. Pigeons. She shook her head slowly, and all at once she was weary. Her head throbbed. She pressed the back of her hand to her forehead, and the Great Dane pressed against her legs to comfort her.

"Nita—" Kirkpatrick began, moving about the desk.

But the girl shook her head. "No! No!" she cried, and turned and left the office in a stumbling run. And Kirkpatrick watched her go with haunted eyes. The Great Dane turned its head and looked back at him and its lips lifted in a soundless snarl that showed gleaming white fangs.

Nita fled to Wentworth's home, hoping against hope that she might find reassurance there. But Jenkyns' old eyes were swollen with weeping, and Ram Singh had already left for Dick's Long Island estate, there to gather his belongings and leave for India.

With a savage wrench he sent it crashing through the rail—hurtling out into space.

Nita, still refusing to believe, went to her home, with Apollo pressing ever close to her side. In her apartment, the girl threw herself down on her knees, caught the dog's great head between her hands and looked with brimming eyes into his face.

"But we don't believe it, do we, Apollo? Do we, boy?"

The dog whined low in its throat, licked out its pink tongue. Nita got slowly to her feet. She would not believe. She began feverishly to pack a small overnight bag, stopped a moment to repair the damage emotion had wrought on her face, and hurried out. She took a taxi to a garage and wheeled out the compact but powerful Renault that Dick had helped her select.

She sent it skimming over the roads, Apollo on the seat beside her, thrusting his head out from behind the windshield into the push of the wind. The swift drive over the Queensborough Bridge and out onto Long Island roads cleared her head.

Wasn't it possible that Wentworth had escaped? He was a superb swimmer and, unless he had been stunned in the plunge, unless he had wanted to die—Dick want to die? She laughed, and actual gaiety crept into her voice. He would risk his life gladly in any just cause, but it was because he loved so to live that he got pleasure in thus defying death.

It was an hour and a half later that she swung into the drive that twined, through trees, up to the

home Dick had built on the hill for the day, he had explained to Nita with a twisted smile, when some other man, stronger than himself and with an equal oneness of purpose, could take up his battle against the forces of evil. The day when Dick and Nita—

She choked on the thought, saw the old caretaker running toward her, a man with a face the weather and sun had thickened like leather and seamed with good nature.

"Is Dick here?" she called gaily.

The man came smiling up to her, a battered straw hat in his hands, his overall knees smudged with dirt from his labors among the flowers.

"Ain't seen him this month, Miss Nita," he said. "And I've been wantin' to show him his peonies. They're gorgeous, ma'am. And that cross he worked out that I says wouldn't do a thing—Miss Nita, it's the loveliest flower you ever saw."

Nita's hope died. She had hoped that Ram Singh's coming here meant Dick had set up a secret domicile in this place.

"Then Ram Singh isn't here, either?"

The man frowned a little in bewilderment. "If the master ain't here, ma'am, why would—"

Nita nodded jerkily, her throat too choked for words. She moved a hand in farewell, spun the wheel and shot the Renault down the drive again with gravel-spurting tires. This place was too full of memories.

She turned back toward town. Perhaps she might run into Ram Singh on the road. Evidently, he had not yet had time to reach the estate. She forced herself to drive slowly and, passing brick columns beside the road, saw the name of MacDonald Pugh on a mailbox. On an impulse, she spun the wheel and drove in. This was where Dick had mentioned coming for the weekend. Perhaps in this part of the country he expected to find some clue to the Black Death. Perhaps she—

Grimly, Nita van Sloan decided that if Dick had died, then she would devote the rest of her life, if necessary, to clearing his name of the besmirching charge that he was the Master of the Black Death. For his identification as the *Spider*, she had no apologies.

Nita had been nearer collapse than she had realized. But the determination strengthened her. She drew up before the house, and MacDonald Pugh, seeing her from the porch, hurried out to greet her. He was dressed in tennis flannels. His face and great bald head were redly sunburned. Even his big hands, clasping hers, were red.

"I'm damned glad you came, Nita. Of course this whole business about Dick is preposterous."

The girl smiled bravely with lips that quivered a little in spite of her. It was good to find someone who believed.

"Dick told me the other day you had asked us out for the weekend," she said. "I know he'd want me to carry on."

"Exactly," Pugh agreed. He caught up her grip himself and carried it into the house, walking beside her with his heavy, forward-thrust head bent attentively. "If you give way to grief, people might think you gave some credence to those ridiculous charges. The late papers practically refute them anyway. Have you seen them?"

Nita stopped, whirled toward him. Her lips dared not frame the question. Pugh's wide mouth turned down wryly.

"The newspapers got another letter signed the Black Death. Even if the *Spider* is dead, the letter said, the plague will go on unless the money is delivered. Good Lord," Pugh growled, striding on into the house. "As if the banks could shell out a billion dollars like so many rolls of pennies and not feel it. But they'll do it." His face went grim. "They'll have to, or else—"

Nita's shoulders sagged slightly. She had been hoping against hope that there might be some new information about Dick.

"But they haven't—" she hesitated, walking into the cool dimness of the hall, "they haven't—"

"They've found no trace of Dick's body, no," Pugh said kindly.

A maid came then and took over Nita's case and showed her up winding stairs to a coolly bright room. She dismissed the servant instantly and stood in the middle of the floor staring about her while the Great Dane prowled around, sniffing at everything and finally standing before Nita, peering up with lolling tongue.

Nita forced herself from the lethargy that kept dropping back upon her, opened her case and swiftly dressed in riding clothes. The clue she believed Dick sought might lie in the country about here, or it might lie among the weekend guests. But the guests could wait until night. She would have to do any exploring she was to accomplish at once.

A short while later, she went alertly down the stairs, wearing khaki jodhpurs, a silk blouse that, open at the neck, showed the sweet curve of her throat and, drawn down over her rebellious curls, a soft brown felt. Pugh sprang to his feet as she came to the porch. He was alone there.

"The others took a spin down to the town for drinks," he said. "Katherine said she was damned sick of rye all the time and longed to taste some real bathtub gin again." He made a face, and Nita saw gratefully that he was religiously avoiding the subject of Dick, deliberately treating her as though tragedy had not a few hours before sought to tear her heart in two.

"Your wife has small cause to complain of your rye, Mac." She smiled up at him, then glanced down at her riding clothes. "I know it's the wrong time of day, but I wanted to take a ramble through the woods on one of those excellent riding horses of yours."

Pugh nodded instantly.

"I'm only sorry I can't accompany you," he said, "but I'm expecting someone from town. Business," he wrinkled his reddened face wryly. "Otherwise Dick and I would be trolling for tuna off Montauk.

"I'll go have a horse saddled for you," he broke off, turned and strode long-legged off toward the stable.

He was gone a considerable while, and Nita began to stroll down toward the red-painted barn herself before he came out of its dimness frowning.

"Something seems to have happened to all my good horses," he said angrily. "It looks as if that new groom has gotten poisoned weeds in with their hay. I've only got one to offer you, Nita, and he won't be very spirited. It's an old one I got for Katherine. She doesn't like them lively."

Nita nodded carelessly. "I'm sorry about your horses," she said. "If it wasn't that I'd set my heart on a ride—"

"Quite all right," said Pugh, and the stable boy led out a dappled gray horse to whose back he assisted Nita. Apollo threw up his head and frisked about like a puppy.

Suddenly the horse reared on its hind legs,

pawing the air, whinnied shrilly and flopped flat on its back. Only Nita's long experience and her swift leap saved her. She sprawled as her feet hit the ground, but she was up instantly.

The horse jerked up its head from the ground, tried to maneuver its legs, flopped back and, breathing hoarsely a few times, died. Nita stared at it with startled eyes, then walked about its head, cried out and pointed at the gray forehead.

"A bullet hole!" she gasped. "Someone shot the horse!"

CHAPTER SEVENTEEN
The Cave of the Pigeons

MACDONALD PUGH was stunned for a moment. Then he crossed to Nita's side and stared down at the horse's head. Fury seized him, and his clenched teeth showed between his lips. But mingled with his anger was bewilderment.

"But why in the devil—"

Nita knew the answer, but could not tell him. She knew now that the clue she sought was in the country about Pugh's place. She did not know by what devious means Wentworth had fathomed the secret, but following in his intended footsteps, she had found danger. And that explained anew why he had asked her to feign a quarrel. It had been, too, at the same time he had announced his intention of coming to this place. And now, coming here, she found the horses poisoned. When she tried to ride the one that remained, it was shot! Could anything be clearer than that?

"I'll get the police on the trail of whoever dared to do that!" Pugh swore. "It's damnable, shooting down a dumb beast like that. And he might very well have killed you, too!"

Nita laughed a little shakily.

"That thought has just this minute occurred to me," she said.

She walked slowly away toward the house, frowning thoughtfully down at the grass. Death had brushed her, but she was the more determined to investigate. She knew a thrill of excitement. This was how Dick had dared!

While Pugh stormed into the house, she had her Renault wheeled out and, climbing in, summoned Apollo to join her. It was only a few miles to Dick's estate, and he kept a stable there.

A half hour later, mounted on a thoroughbred that paced exuberantly across the fields, Nita loped off into the woods toward Pugh's place. Evidently his house was watched and near there she might pick up the trail of the man who had shot the horse. She wondered if it was because she, revealed now as the sweetheart of the *Spider*, was at the house that it was watched. She hoped fiercely that it was

so. In the pocket of her jodhpurs rested the weight of an automatic. In the woods somewhere lay danger. But there also lay the trail to the man who had placed the onus of the Black Death upon the *Spider*.

Her excitement communicated itself to her horse. Its stride lengthened with the shaken reins and she whisked through the woods. Then abruptly she hauled back on the bit, brought the animal curveting to a halt.

On the opposite hill, perhaps a mile away, she had seen the brown flanks of another horse. She urged her own mount into the shrubbery and, rising in the stirrups, peered beneath a shading palm at that distant hill. The late afternoon sun probed its rays into the foliage of the hill opposite, and once more she saw movement there, saw a horse with a man upon its back move across a small clearing.

Excitement raced through her veins and she felt her breath quicken. As she had told Pugh, this was no time for riding. It was late. Besides, the land ahead was on Wentworth's own estate and beyond was Pugh's. There was no stable nearby from which the horse might come. The man must be a trespasser, and that meant—

Softly Nita called Apollo to her side and, keeping him close, pushed down the shadowed hillside toward the trail the mounted man followed.

All about her was the sunset beauty of Summer woods. An oriole's evening warble was soft in the hollow. A faint breeze fanned her nostrils with the damp sweet odor of the rich earth. Somewhere near at hand a red squirrel chattered. But Nita noticed none of these things. Low upon her horse's neck, ready to clamp a hand upon its nose if, approaching the other animal, it sought to whinny, she urged forward upon the trail she hoped would lead her to the lair of the Black Death.

When she reached the spot where she had seen the mounted man, there was no trace of him except the hoofprints of his mount in the soft mold. Calling Apollo softly, she dismounted and indicated the trail. Then she stripped a silk neckerchief, tied it to make a long leash and, fastening it to the dog's collar, remounted and urged him on the hunt.

Apollo tugged at the restraining silk, sniffed the ground and loped off through the woods. Nita was hard put to follow, but the hoofs of the thoroughbred were nearly soundless on the damp earth. She laid low upon its neck, and branches whipped past with the speed of her passage.

Small, bending trees switched her arms and brambles scratched her. She scarcely felt them, for Apollo strained steadily on the leash, dragging forward upon the hunt, his tawny body a perfect, powerful machine, running silently as he had been trained. Not until he sighted his quarry would he give tongue.

Many times Nita had ridden to the hounds, raced beside Dick for the honor of the brush. She had taken the hurdles with courage, but never had the chase been over such terrain as this. Uphill and down, a striding leap across a ravine, a choppy jump over a log, a poise and a twist sideways about a tree. Finally the frail leash parted in her hand and Apollo was off, a tawny flash.

Then, indeed, the race became furious. She shook out the reins, and the gallant hunter beneath her responded. She could feel the marvelous power of his stretch and recover. Wind sang in her ears. The branches became whips now. They stung her shoulders, ripped at the silk of her blouse. She jammed her hat tighter about her ears, crouched lower and let the horse run.

She spotted Apollo only occasionally now, but dared not call him back. At this furious pace, they must be rapidly overtaking the man ahead. Then suddenly she pulled strongly on the reins, brought her horse to a sliding halt. There it was, the deep rich bay of Apollo giving tongue. He had sighted the quarry!

Nita's breath was quick, her face intent, the lovely blue eyes narrowed with an expression of hate that would have shocked many of the friends who knew her in their conventional drawing rooms. Here was no society girl out for a canter. Here was a woman whose lover had been torn from her in disgrace, a woman upon the trail of her lover's foes!

Nita swung to the ground and led the horse into a dense clump of birches where the shadows were gathering swiftly She loosened its cinches and, touching the gun in her pocket, moved swiftly off through the dusk of the woods.

Above, red sunset still tinged the treetops. But here below the dying light filtered through but dimly. Nita's blouse was torn. The right sleeve had been ripped loose at the shoulder and slit half its length. There was a scratch across the smooth white flesh, and the stinging red slash of a branch had marred her cheek. But there was a smile on her twisted lips and her eyes were bright and keen.

Ahead of her Apollo still gave tongue. Suddenly his deep bay broke off in snarling anger, then all was silent. The Great Dane was never noisy when he fought.

Nita broke into a run. The gun was in her hand now, clenched ready in a white fist. She sprang across a narrow stream, stumbled, recovered and raced on. The grade ahead was steep. Her run slowed to a rapid walk, and even that became difficult to maintain.

Footing was uncertain now, and the light was almost gone. Nita tripped over a vine, sprang up silently and hurried on. Her lips were open and her lungs panted for air. Ahead, through the trunks of the trees, she could see the crest of the hill against the sky, and it was empty of life. A great rocky eminence thrust upward just below its top and its jagged peak was like the masked face of a man.

Nita halted, tried to still her laboring breath, to listen. The evening hush had fallen upon the woods. The birds were silent. The insects had not yet taken up the orchestration of the night. Faint wind rustled through the leaves with a sound like men whispering. That was all. Yet somewhere near here, Apollo had bayed, had snarled in anger and charged.

More cautiously now, her eyes questing through the blackening night, Nita advanced. Had the great dog triumphed, bowled over the man she trailed? Or had her faithful Apollo been killed? Was that man even now lying in ambush for her among the shrubs and great fragments of rocks that tumbled from that peak which was near at hand now and were strewn across her path?

The pulsing of her blood was a throbbing excitement in Nita's ears. She thrust the gun ahead of her and pushed on, then jerked to a sudden halt. *What was that sound?*

It was soft and gentle, yet seemed to have strong volume. Hearing it, Nita wondered why she had not detected it before. It was such a sound as a church full of people might make whispering a prayer together. Each one made little sound but, together, the volume filled the vast vault of the building. But this was without sibilance. It was all round vowels in two tones, a—a *cooing!*

And in a flash, Nita knew. Somewhere near her, together in the blackness, were vast numbers of pigeons! Kirkpatrick had spoken of pigeons in connection with the Black Death. Wentworth had sought a clue here, and she had followed a suspicious man to a hiding place that was filled with pigeons!

There could be only one answer to this. she had stumbled on the secret spot from which the Plague Master loosed the dread Black Death upon the city, sending the doom of thousands on the homing wings of flocks of pigeons.

A strong shudder shook Nita. Here all about her was probably the contagion of this terrible new form of the Bubonic Plague which killed so horribly. But Nita did not turn and flee from the terror of that discovery as another woman might have done—as indeed many men would. Instead, her face became drawn with the intensity of her determination. Holding the gun ready, she moved forward again— toward the cooing of the pigeons, toward the lair of the Black Death!

As she advanced, the soft, gentle sound grew louder. It was fantastic that their muted voices meant a horrible death. Yet she realized how efficient was the plan this monster had devised. For who would suspect that death hovered on their wings? Who but the *Spider*!

And who—discovering how the Master of the Plague operated—could turn aside the swift, homing flight of a flock. May as well try to shut the air from the city! A few might be killed; a flock might be turned aside for a while. But ultimately even their dying wings would speed them to their habitation in the city, and the Black Plague would stride grimly through the streets, touching this man and that, clutching its strangling fingers about a baby's throat.

Grimly Nita resolved that if she died in doing it, she would destroy these messengers of death, checkmate the Black Death. It was for the *Spider*.

"Dick," the girl murmured. "Dick."

And as if that word had been a magic talisman, it gave her strength. She moved on.

Then the shadow of a rock seemed to come to life! Nita fired as quick as thought, and a man cursed. Footsteps sounded behind her. She whirled, gun ready, too late!

Steel bands seemed to clamp about her arms from behind. Her wrists were pinioned at her sides. The automatic was wrenched from her hand. On the back of her neck was the panting of a man's hot breath.

"I've got the little hell-cat!" a hoarse voice grated in her ear.

"The she-devil!" cursed another voice. "She got me in the arm."

Footsteps approached, and a shadow loomed before her. A hand slapped her face violently, and she gasped at the pain.

"Lay off that!" the man behind her rasped. Another blow. Nita kicked out with her riding boot, and a man howled in agony. The shadow danced before her.

"Good for you, baby," said the man who gripped her.

She struck backward at him with her boot. But her heel thumped against a rock and the man laughed—then snarled.

"Cut it out, Bill," he ordered. "Served you right. Now lay off that and help me tie her up."

Ropes bit into her wrists then. The man she had kicked yanked them savagely tight, cursing at the pain his arm caused him.

"Hurt you bad, Bill?" asked the man who still held her from behind.

"Not as bad as I thought," the man grumbled, trapping her kicking feet and tying those, too. "Bullet just burned my arm."

He finished binding her and the two men, one at her feet, one with his hands beneath her arms, carried her through the darkness toward the sound of the pigeons, until the cooing became like the washing of soft waves that blurred all other sound.

Echoes clapped back the footsteps of the men then. They rang hollowly, and she realized that she had been carried into a cave. Her feet were dropped, she heard a match scratch, and an end of a candle flickered into yellow light.

She stared about her. The walls were lined with coops of pigeons. The stench was sickening. The men who had captured her were roughly dressed, and handkerchiefs hid their faces. One had blood on his left sleeve, and he glared at her hatefully.

Nita was suddenly aware of her torn blouse, of the low V of the collar which had been ripped. Suddenly the other man strode across to the one he called Bill.

"None of that," he snapped. "We gotta wait and see what the boss says to do. You get out and make sure that dog is dead. You hit him an awful wallop, but them things are tough to kill."

Bill glared at him. "And leave you in here with her, huh? I ain't quite that big a fool!"

The two men glowered at each other. Then the larger man, the one who had captured Nita, shrugged his shoulders.

"Okay," he said, "We'll both go."

They clumped off together, first blowing out the candle, and the echoing cave brought back their voices to her.

"Damn!" said one, "I'll be glad when we don't have to hear these damned pigeons all the time."

"It won't be long," the other muttered. "We'll turn them loose before long. Then we'll see about the girl."

"How long?"

"The plane with the money takes off at dawn. And about three hours after that— "

The man's voice trailed off into the distance, but there floated back to Nita's ears, as she lay helplessly straining at her bonds, the coarse laughter of the two men. It was lewd, suggestive.

Nita's eyes were wide with fear, and her face burned.

CHAPTER EIGHTEEN
Doom of The Plague

RANSOM PLANE TO FLY AT DAWN

In New York City, miles from where Nita van Sloan struggled in terror against her bonds, thousands read the headlines and sighed with relief. It meant that the city had been forced by the threat of the Black Death to borrow a billion dollars from the banks, to place that money in a plane and start it off along the line the Black Death had charted.

If any other plane took the air, the Plague Master proclaimed, he would loose death upon the city.

So at Floyd Bennett Field, out on what had been barren filled land beyond Brooklyn, men who moved like stooped gnomes in the weird, searchlight-cast shadows fueled a black plane with silver wings. Suddenly the men whirled, staring off toward the long straight road that stretched to the city.

Sirens were purring there. One-eyed motorcycles droned, and behind them came swiftly a long line of armored cars. Troops patrolled the field, bayonets gleaming on rifles aslant their shoulders. One by one the armored cars rolled up to the black plane with its silver wings. The doors clanged open, and while men stood with drawn pistols, bundles of currency were transferred to the plane.

A billion dollars that would fly into the dawn sky to ransom a city from man-inflicted plague! The false dawn already showed in the East. In an hour would come the takeoff.

And back in the cavern where the plague pigeons kept up their everlasting murmur, Nita van Sloan—who alone knew the secret of the cave struggled futilely with her bonds.

Masked in shrubbery, on a field not far from the entrance to that dread cavern, waited another plane: a ship that, mockingly, was painted all black, the plane the Black Death would fly. It was fueled and ready, a few moments of warming up, and it would bear the monster into the sky.

A billion dollars ransom.

In the close, murmurous darkness, Nita was suddenly still, straining listening ears. Was she overwrought from long waiting in the blackness, or was that a furtive footfall in the shadows? She scarcely dared to breathe. It would not be death that crept upon her. Death she could face, but those men—

More frantically than ever she sawed upon her bonds, tugging and straining. On came the footsteps. They had entered the main chamber of the cavern where she lay now and still they came on, softly and steadily. If the walls had not caught up and magnified the sound, if her ears had not become accustomed to the pigeons, learned to hear through their cooing, she would not have detected it.

But, hearing it, there was nothing she could do but lie helplessly and wait. The footsteps were quite near now, almost beside her. In a few moments she would know. A scream rose in her throat, but she choked it down. A foot struck her leg.

Abruptly white light slapped her in the face. Her eyes flinched shut from the glare. From above came a gasp, and—

"Nita, Nita darling!"

The girl caught her breath. That voice. It couldn't be! It was!

"Dick! Oh, Dick!" she sobbed.

Strong arms caught her up in the dark, a kiss brushed her lips, competent, swift fingers worked on the ropes that bound her. Loosed were her wrists, her feet.

"Dick," babbled the girl. "A light, I must have a light. Let me see you."

In the darkness Richard Wentworth laughed softly, and a match flared. A candle took slow flame and he crossed back to where she still huddled on the floor.

"I'm sorry, darling," he murmured into her hair, holding her close against him. "I'm sorry, but there was no other way. I was afraid, was sure the police would be watching you in case they were not convinced of my death. Even the newspapers did not prove anything. Kirkpatrick might have told the reporters he knew I was dead so that he could capture me again."

Nita was sobbing unrestrainedly now. She had no words but his name.

"Shh! Stop now, dear," he soothed her. "You must get out of here at once."

Slowly she stifled her tears of happiness, smiled at him tremulously with wet eyes. She got up on numb feet, rubbing her rope-chafed wrists.

"I'm ready," she said. "Come on."

The *Spider*'s smile was still on his face, but it fled from his eyes. "I can't go, dearest. There's work to do." He touched a black valise that stood beside his feet, which she had not noticed before. "But you must. Hurry, now. The Black Death and his men will be here any minute."

Slowly the girl crossed to him. She put a hand upon each of his shoulders.

"Dick," she said, "I'll never leave your side again until this Black Death is beaten, or until—until we die together."

Wentworth peered deeply into her blue eyes. There was no fear there, only a great love and a vast determination. He did not argue with her any longer, for he knew it would be useless.

"Very well then," he said. "Help me turn loose these pigeons."

He strode toward the nearest coop. Nita hung onto his arm.

"But the Black Death!" she gasped.

Wentworth turned and stared at her, then laughed softly.

"They haven't been given the germs yet," he told her swiftly. "The plague acts on them much more quickly than on humans. They will be infected only just before they are freed."

The pigeons were stirring restively in the light of the candle. Outside, the night was still pitch black. But already, distantly, a rooster was crowing, and there was a sleepy first twittering of birds. Wentworth picked up a coop, shouldered it and carried it out of the circle of light to the open, tore off the door and hurried back. Nita, at his side, told him how she had happened to be captured.

Wentworth nodded. "That explains the rifle shot

I heard in the woods this afternoon," he said. "I couldn't figure what the man was firing at. But I followed him and found this place. I went back home to get this valise."

"We must have passed in the woods!" Nita cried.

Wentworth stopped on his way back for the third coop of pigeons, placed his hands on her shoulders.

"Darling, won't you go?" he pleaded. "Believe me there is more danger here than there was when I sent the car diving off Brooklyn Bridge, hung onto the wheel and let it drag me down."

Nita smiled at him, made a little moue. "You know damned well I won't," she said quietly.

Wentworth shook his head, still smiling, but there was grave fear in his eyes. He knew that at any moment the super-criminal would come, and he must remain. He turned and strode into the cave again, Nita beside him.

"How far did you swim underwater?" she demanded. "That was terribly dangerous, Dick."

"Dangerous?" A thin smile twisted his lips. "Yes, of course. Well, the current helped, dear. But if Kirkpatrick or his men had thought to investigate a crate that was floating downstream about fifty yards from them, they'd have found the *Spider*'s head on the other side. I was lucky, Nita."

As he lifted another coop of pigeons, a grating laugh broke out behind them. It echoed horribly in the cave and Wentworth, dropping the coop before him as a guard, whirled, but he saw at once that the shield was useless, for the masked man held a high-powered rifle that would drill through that frail covering like a sword through cheesecloth.

The man was high-shouldered, and a black hat drooped over his forehead. When he spoke it was with the evil, taunting politeness of the Black Death.

"You used the right tense, Wentworth—or do you prefer to be called the *Spider*?—I refer to your last sentence. You *were* lucky, but that—" he laughed horribly—"that is all over now."

Wentworth let the coop slide to the floor. He straightened, with his arms hanging at his side and his right foot pressed against the side of the valise that lay on the floor. Nita saw and hoped there was a weapon there—some new device of Dick's clever friend, Professor Brownlee.

But nothing happened, nothing except that Dick, speaking sharply, in a voice Nita hardly recognized because of its harsh vehemence, snapped out: "Why do you continue to hide behind that mask? Do you think I am a complete fool? Can you imagine that the *Spider* doesn't know that the name of his enemy is—" Wentworth paused, laughed shortly—"is MacDonald Pugh?"

The man snarled behind his mask.

"That knowledge will do you no good, Mr. *Spider*. I do not intend to leave any witnesses to accuse me of the Black Death."

Slowly he raised his left hand and took off his black hat, ripped off the mask. Nita expected Dick to fling himself forward then, during the instant the man's eyes were covered. But Wentworth made no move; only stood with his gleaming eyes fixed on the face of his erstwhile friend.

Wentworth smiled calmly.

"I know all about you, Pugh," he said in his harsh, accusing voice. "Know how you framed that girl, Virginia Doeg. Know how you involved young Jim Handley. Know why you—"

"Brilliant, positively," sneered the man behind his rifle, and his usually pleasant face was twisted into a mask of hate. "You astound me, *Spider*. You've learned much since we met in Harper's office."

Wentworth laughed tauntingly. "And I fooled you there. Have you figured yet how I called the police and escaped?"

Pugh flung back his laughter at him. The sound was abnormally loud in the enclosed space. "Have you figured yet, how I managed to get away after putting your ridiculous *Spider* seal on the foreheads of those police?"

Nita stared from one of the men to the other. Why in Heaven's name was Dick standing here bandying words with this criminal? Was he playing for time? Was help on the way? She felt a small thrill of hope.

Wentworth's revelation that Pugh was the Black Death had startled her, but now she saw the entire trail plainly. The forgery had been committed in Pugh's office. The earlier conflicts had centered about the girl, Virginia Doeg. And when the *Spider* finally had wrested her from the super criminal, there had been another trail from the same spot, the trail of Jimmy Handley.

"...Jimmy Handley," Wentworth was saying. "I know that you framed him lest I should suspect you when I traced Virginia Doeg. But what I don't see is how you managed to kidnap that girl from the Marlborough, killing those three policemen."

"It is enough that I did it," MacDonald Pugh snapped. "Enough of this talking! I have work to do." He raised his voice. "Bill! Dan!"

The two ruffians who had overpowered Nita came in now and at Pugh's orders rapidly bound Nita and Wentworth to a huge rock. Pugh placed an empty coop in the middle of the cave, and from each of the other crates against the wall extracted two birds which he placed inside this one wired cage.

(Overleaf) The two ruffians who had overpowered Nita came in now and at Pugh's orders rapidly bound Nita and Wentworth to a huge rock.

He was in high glee, chuckling as he went about his work. As soon as he had taken two birds from a coop, the men dragged it outside. It was still dark there, and the pigeons moved restively but did not take wing.

"You get the idea, don't you, *Spider*?" he jeered. "Surely your brilliant mind can follow me. From each flock I take two pigeons, the others I turn free. But when these two fly to join them— " he stroked the head of one of the pigeons in his hand, "they will carry with them the virus of the Black Death. What a welcome they will get!"

Finally the work was completed, and Pugh came to gloat over his two helpless captives. He smiled at them gently.

"Ah, love," he said, and laughed like a fiend. "I want to leave you with something to occupy your minds, lest you grow weary with waiting for death. When I fly to collect the ransom money, I shall carry with me the pigeons from each flock. And when I have the billion dollars, I shall release them!

"I am afraid the city will be too busy fighting the plague to give much thought to pursuing me." He snarled suddenly. "America, bah!" he spat out. "How I hate it. But this plague will help to humble it and, in the end, when my own land whistles, America will come to heel."

"Your country?" Wentworth asked slowly. "And what is that?"

The man threw back his head and laughed. "America will learn," he said.

Nita shuddered at the sound of his mirth. It was unholy.

"But surely," she said, "Surely, you would not doom an entire city—"

Her voice trailed off. She knew he would. Pugh turned his vulture-like head toward her.

"There is another pleasant thought for you to wait with," he snarled. "Your dog is not dead. He recovered consciousness, but rather than kill him, I drugged him. Any moment now, he will wake up. He will be very thirsty. But see what an humanitarian I am! I have left water for him, a full pan of it!"

Wentworth frowned up at the tall, shoulder-hunched figure. What was the madman driving at?

"Ah, but I see I puzzle you, *Spider*," Pugh said, smiling terribly. "Very well, I will explain. Primer English for primer minds. When the dog wakes up the dog will be thirsty. The dog will drink the water which the man has left for him. And when he has drunk the water he will look for his master. And he will come to his master and lick the master's face. The dog will not know that the water he has drunk has in it— "

Pugh paused, gloating over the two. Wentworth's eyes widened slowly with horror. Words struggled to his throat.

"Not that," he pleaded. "Or kill me that way if you will, but not, not— "

"Not the lady?" Pugh supplied. "Ah, but you would deprive yourself of her company for many hours. Once more I must point out to you, *Spider*, that you are scarcely complimentary to the young lady. The Black Death, you know, takes about twenty-four hours to kill."

Nita cried out, "The Black Death!"

"Yes," smiled Pugh. "The dog will not know that the water has in it the germs of the Black Death."

He turned and strode from the cavern, laughing, and the walls echoed with the horrid sound. It rang in the ears of the two who lay waiting for the Black Death.

Outside the paean of the birds increased. The mouth of the cavern faced the East; and Wentworth, raising his head, could see the first gray edge of the day thrusting palely above the horizon. He saw something else, too, saw the huge, hunched body of a great dog, of Apollo, reel up with drooping head.

Wentworth turned to Nita, looked at her with eyes that smiled tenderly.

"Darling," he said, "I begged you to go. You refused, even, you said, if it meant your death."

The girl met his gaze bravely.

"Yes, Dick."

Wentworth's smile grew twisted.

"The time has come," he said with slow words, "for the *Spider* to die. Apollo has wakened. He must be drinking the germs now. You know that if I order Apollo to stay away, he will do it. And presently he will crawl off to die, and eventually you and I would go free."

"Yes, Dick, I know that." The girl's voice was grave. A courageous smile was on her lips.

"You know, too, dear, that if I call Apollo here, his sharp teeth will soon sever these ropes, that then you and I can get my plane, kill Pugh and save the city from the Black Plague."

"Yes, Dick, I know that." There was no break in Nita's words.

It was Wentworth's own voice that cracked, not for himself, but at the thought of this dear loved face dyed with the horrid blush of the Black Death.

"Darling," said the *Spider*, "shall I call Apollo— or order him away?"

The girl's smile never faltered. She puckered her lips and whistled.

"Here, Apollo!" she called. "To me, Apollo," and even the *Spider*, who knew and loved her, who understood her as no one else in the world, marveled at the clear courage of her voice. Her voice was as soft, as gentle, as if she called a child to her lap, instead of summoning the dread specter of the Black Death.

Wentworth, raising his head again, saw the dog throw up its head, spin drunkenly and come at a stumbling run into the cavern. He plunged toward them with lolling tongue, the tongue that so recently had lapped up the germs of the Black Death!

"Down, Apollo!" Wentworth ordered sharply. The dog stopped, stared at Dick and crouched slowly. Wentworth tugged as far away from Nita as their short bonds would permit, held out his bound hands behind him toward the dog.

"Apollo," he called sharply. He waved his bound hands the few inches the ropes permitted.

It was a game to the dog. They had played it before against some such emergency as this. But Wentworth had never thought that those sharp fangs, gnawing at the thongs, might mean death to him as well as freedom.

The instant his hands were free, he ordered the dog sharply away, bent and untied his ankles. Then, snatching up the valise, he turned and smiled at Nita, across the width of the cave.

"Goodbye, darling," he said.

"Dick!" the girl cried wildly. Wentworth shook his head slowly. "I have risked your dear life as much as I will," he said. "If I unbound you, I could not keep you from coming. I will send Ram Singh to free you."

He turned and stumbled from the cave, tears blinding him. He could not even kiss Nita goodbye, lest already the loathsome contagion was at work within his blood, lest he pass on to her the Black Death.

Apollo quickly ran past Wentworth.

And then, in the entrance of the cavern, he paused, staring at an upset tin pan, at sand that had soaked up water, at Apollo far down the hill lapping eagerly from a creek. Carefully Wentworth examined the ground. The sand had almost dried again. There were no dog tracks beside it as there would have been if Apollo had stopped to drink water there. But there was the heavy print of a man's shoe and scuffed sand!

One of the men in leaving, either deliberately to torture the animal, or blindly in the dark, had kicked over the carefully set pan of water, and Pugh had left without noticing! Probably he had given that spot of contagion a wide berth as he had gone toward his plane to fly for the ransom money.

Wentworth leaped to his feet and raced back into the cave. Nita, sobbing, cried out to him.

"I knew you couldn't leave me. I knew you couldn't!"

Rapidly untying her bonds, Wentworth explained what had happened, that they were saved from the danger of the Black Death. Together, then they raced from the cave, down the hill, hurrying toward Wentworth's place. In the hollow there was a crude cabin. As they crashed heedlessly through underbrush, they heard a man's voice cry out and Wentworth, hurrying forward, found a young man bound hand and foot beside a small coop of pigeons.

Wentworth knew what that portended. Another fiendish trap of MacDonald Pugh. He caught the man under the arms, dragged him to the open and freed him, asking meantime who he was.

"Handley," said the man, "James Handley." Wentworth smiled grimly. That explained it. This was the fiancé of Virginia Doeg, the man who had been framed by Pugh to throw the trail away from himself.

As he worked on the ropes, he spoke swiftly. "When I have freed you, I'm going to run like hell. I've got to overtake Pugh before he can release pigeons and turn loose the Black Death on the city. As soon as you can move about, kill those pigeons in there and burn the shack. My home is a little over a mile due east of here. Head for that, and I'll leave word for you to be taken care of."

As he finished speaking, he unfastened the last thong about the man's wrists, sprang up and ran off to where Nita was toiling up the hill. The man shouted thanks after him. Wentworth waved a hand and saw Nita plunge into a thicket of birches, heard the whinny of a horse and gave a great cry of hope. He had been afraid the mile of woods between the cave and his home would doom their chances of saving the city. But with the horse—

Nita already had tightened the cinches when he raced up to her. He sprang to the saddle, caught her up behind him and gave the thoroughbred his head. The animal had suffered no great discomfort except a lack of water, but there was no time to wait for that now.

Crashing through shrubbery, ducking under swooping tree branches, they raced back to Wentworth's home, the tawny form of Apollo a flash in the distance ahead of them, the black valise still clutched in Wentworth's hand.

Straight to the hangar that housed his always ready plane, Wentworth galloped the horse. He sprang to the ground and with Nita close behind him, darted to the wide, sliding doors, threw his weight against them. While Nita completed their opening, he vaulted into the cockpit, touched the starter button.

Compression whined, the propeller moved slowly, and suddenly the motor caught with a coughing roar. The girl clambered up the wing, the slipstream whipping her hair about her face, completing the ruin of her blouse. Wentworth jerked the throttle, and the ship trundled out onto the field. He whirled it into the wind and, chancing the danger of a cold engine, sent the ship racing down the runway, took to the air like a bird.

It was a speedy Northrup, a special plane with an adjustable pitch propeller, and it glittered as scarlet as one of the *Spider*'s own seals as it swept in a steady climb upward, banked sharply and streaked off on the trail of the Black Death.

Wentworth knew the course that the money plane was scheduled to follow and guessed that Pugh planned to attack it. Pugh had ordered all planes from the sky on pain of releasing the Black Death. And Wentworth, turning the controls over to Nita— it was a dual control plane for long flights— swept the sky with glasses.

For long moments as they raced toward the city, he could see nothing. The haze of smoke above Manhattan's towers intervened. But once the scarlet streak had dipped through that and the course swung westward and north along the Hudson, he tried again with the binoculars.

The early sun was behind them, and suddenly Wentworth caught a flash of light. He focused the glasses more sharply and made out the silver wings of the ransom plane. Even as he watched, a small black plane swooped out of the clouds above it.

Wentworth's hands tensed upon his glasses. His eyes glinted. There before him was the plane of the Black Death!

Far up the river he saw the two planes slant downward together. They disappeared behind trees. The scarlet Northrup droned on. It was equipped with no machine gun, but in a compartment beside him Wentworth had a "Tommy," a Thompson submachine gun that would be wonderfully effective at relatively close range.

Grimly now, as the plane swept on, he unfastened the straps that held it and drew the gun up past his chest and above the cowling. He fastened it down with another strap, then wriggled into a parachute. After which he took the controls while Nita availed herself of similar protection.

Wentworth was ready for the battle. They were near at hand now, only a mile or two from the spot where the two planes had settled. And even as he watched, the black craft of Pugh shot above the treetops and began to climb steeply. A moment later they flashed over the field and Wentworth, peering down, made out the inert bodies of three men stretched beside the silver-winged ransom plane.

Wentworth's mouth went grim. He unstrapped the machine gun and held it ready in his hands. Only a few hundred yards separated him now from the Black Death. Suddenly the plane ahead vaulted upward in an inhuman turn and shot back to meet him, with a flicker of flame behind its propeller that he recognized with mounting anger was a double machine gun. Where in Heaven's name had Pugh got a military plane?

But there was no time to speculate on that. He must destroy the man. Wentworth had been watching keenly, and he had seen no pigeons winging back toward the city. He was positive the dread harbingers of the plague were still aboard.

He raised a hand to signal Nita to give him the controls, but the girl had already thrown the ship into a twisting spiral, dodging from the line of Pugh's fire. Pugh veered to meet them, and she whipped the nose back the other way. And now the black ship was within range of Wentworth's lighter gun.

Pugh was still struggling for altitude.

– RICHARD WENTWORTH

Abruptly Nita let him have it. Instead of climbing, she put the Northrup into a steep dive, swishing down across the black ship's nose before Pugh could bring his guns to bear.

The killer flipped up the tail of his ship, but it was too late. The scarlet Northrup had darted under, and a stream of .45 caliber bullets ripped into the motor and underside of the black ship.

Nita zoomed, Immelmanned and flashed back upon the tail of the black plane. But there was no need of further firing. Black smoke and a burst of flame ripped from the engine of Pugh's ship. Wentworth saw the Plague Master pumping frantically with a fire extinguisher.

The flames blossomed into full flower, flicked back at Pugh. He threw up his arms. The motors drowned the sound of his shriek. He reared for an instant in the cockpit, then leaped far out, clear of the flaming black plane. His parachute whipped open.

Without an instant's hesitation, Wentworth

leaped, too, dropping the gun back into the cockpit, depending on the automatic in his pocket. But instead of jerking his ripcord immediately, Wentworth let his body hurtle downward unchecked. He shot past Pugh like a bullet and fancied he heard a strangled cry of rage from the man.

A thousand feet from the rolling farm land beneath him, Wentworth yanked the rip cord. His parachute snapped open and he drifted downward, seeming scarcely to move. He could not see Pugh now. The man was hidden by the open bell of Wentworth's own parachute. But the Black Death would not escape him.

Already the plague had perished in the flames of the ship, burning fiercely in a nearby field. And Wentworth would reach the ground first. He would be free of his parachute and ready, when Pugh landed, to exact vengeance for the hundreds who had died.

The ground sprang up beneath him and, flexing his knees, Wentworth spilled down on the soft earth, tugging at the windblown parachute. In a few moments he was free of it and, peering upward, spotted Pugh. He was sideslipping his parachute, putting as much distance as possible between himself and the vengeful *Spider*.

But Wentworth paced him easily. He saw Pugh's automatic flame in his hand, but he still pursued, dodging the hail of bullets that spat viciously into the dust of the field. He put his hand into his pocket for his gun. It was gone!

Somewhere in that frantic tumble through the air, it had spilled from his pocket. For an instant Wentworth checked, then he ran on more swiftly than before. Counting shots on Pugh, he estimated that at the present rate the man would exhaust his bullets about fifty feet above the ground, would be unable to reload in time.

But Pugh was canny: he held one shot. His parachute was only forty feet from the ground, now thirty, now—Pugh bent his knees and took the landing perfectly, whirled with raised gun as Wentworth raced at him.

But Pugh had figured without the wind in his parachute. Even as he leveled the gun, the collapsing sail was caught by a gust.

Wentworth had crowded him too closely. He had not had time to free himself from the harness, and the tugging parachute jerked him nearly off his feet. Before he could recover his balance and fire, the *Spider* was upon him.

His fist struck the wrist of Pugh's gun hand, knocked the weapon fifteen feet away. And then began a grim battle for life, the Black Death and the *Spider*, grim-faced and bleak-eyed, in the warm bath of the morning sunshine.

"The end, Pugh! The end for you!" Wentworth cried. And there was laughter on his lips—fighting, angry laughter. "Remember the dog? Even if you overcome me, you—"

Pugh's face blanched. "Good God!" he cried in frantic terror. "You've got the Black Death!"

Wentworth laughed again tauntingly. And suddenly Pugh turned and ran.

The *Spider* let him run a little way, dragging the parachute, working with desperate hands on the harness. And just as Pugh was almost free, Wentworth jumped on the parachute with both feet. The man was yanked to the ground.

He scrambled up, tore off the last of the harness, and the *Spider* sprang upon him, seized him by the throat. Pugh struck in a frenzy of fear with his fists, but his blows were weak.

In the end, the Black Death was a coward and died a coward's death, with terror in his eyes, with the *Spider*'s fingers crushing the life slowly out of him.

Wentworth rose from the body of the man with disgust mingling with the ferocity of his hate. He brushed his hands, reached into his trouser pocket and brought out the crude imitation of his own cigarette lighter with which Pugh had sought to incriminate him.

With it he printed upon the great bald head the vermilion death seal of the *Spider*.

Then abruptly he shot a glance upward, hearing the whistle of wind on a swooping plane. The scarlet Northrup glided in to a perfect landing, its wing slots cutting its terrific landing speed to a mere forty-five miles an hour. The slots were still in an experimental stage. But Wentworth had contrived to have them installed on his plane, and they worked perfectly.

Wentworth glanced once more at the man who had paid the penalty at last for his crimes, then turned and loped toward the plane. But Nita did not wait for him. She whirled the ship and taxied swiftly in his direction, pointing toward the woods a few hundred yards distant with an outflung hand.

Then Wentworth saw that Nita had maneuvered the lever which hid the plane's license number on wing and tail with a thin layer of cloth on which a fictitious number had been painted, and he sprang to the wing.

Even as his feet touched, Nita jerked open the throttle, and the ship's wheels left the ground before Wentworth was settled into the cockpit. Then, peering over the side of the swiftly rising plane, he saw the need for haste. Bluecoated policemen were rushing onto the field from the woods, and guns glinted in their hands.

The seal of the *Spider* they would find, but—Wentworth threw back his head and laughed, turned and blew a kiss to Nita—*the Spider was gone.*

CHAPTER NINETEEN
Kirkpatrick Is Generous

THE *SPIDER* was gone, yes. But that seal would tell the world that the *Spider* was not dead, that he had escaped the grave that had threatened in the river. And once more police, now that the Black Death was finished, would be able to turn their attentions to catching him.

Wentworth dared not go to his home, lest they be waiting for him there. Nevertheless when Nita and he drove back to the city in her speedy little Renault, the *Spider*, having sent Ram Singh on ahead with the small black valise and some private instructions in Hindustani, turned downtown and headed directly for police headquarters.

"Dick!" cried Nita, grabbing his arm, "Are you crazy? Have you forgotten—"

Wentworth smiled at her, stopped the car before police headquarters and kissed Nita for all the world to see.

"No, darling," he said, "It is you who have forgotten."

And he led the puzzled and still reluctant girl to the office of the police commissioner. An officer sprang up smartly and swung open the door, ushering into the presence of Stanley Kirkpatrick, the *Spider* and Nita van Sloan.

Nita stared in bewilderment at the three persons she saw there. Virginia Doeg, a young man she didn't know, but whom Wentworth bowed to and addressed as Handley, and commissioner Kirkpatrick.

Kirkpatrick's face was grave, but years seemed to have dropped from him. His clothing was immaculate again, his black mustache was waxed to needle points, and he bowed with a gallant gesture to Nita.

"I have already communicated with the newspapermen," he said gravely. "They will be here in a few minutes."

"But I don't understand," Nita whispered to Wentworth. "What is this all about?"

Wentworth smiled down at her.

"Let Kirkpatrick have his fun," he said. The door opened again and the newsmen filtered in, a keen-faced dilapidated lot.

Kirkpatrick greeted them somberly. One of the newspapermen nudged another.

"The *Spider*," he whispered, and all eyes riveted on Wentworth.

He pretended not to hear, but Nita's hands gripped his arm until her fingers ached.

"I called you gentlemen in," Kirkpatrick said, "to hear a dictagraph record which was delivered to me today by the *Spider*—" Kirkpatrick looked up at the newsmen with a slight smile —"though not

in person. But he called me up in advance and told me it was coming, and a taxi driver brought it."

He stooped and lifted to the table a rusty valise. He opened it, and gleaming metal showed inside.

"If you press the side of this bag," Kirkpatrick said, "it starts the machinery going, and a magnifying device which is the cleverest bit of work I've ever heard of, picks up any sound within a radius of ten or fifteen feet perfectly. I want you to hear the record."

He pressed the side of the bag at the point he had indicated, and suddenly a harshly vehement voice spoke from the bag with a tone so lifelike that Nita started: "Why do you continue to hide behind that mask? Do you think I am a complete fool? Can you imagine that the *Spider* doesn't know that the name of his enemy is—" a short laugh barked from the instrument— "is MacDonald Pugh."

Then another voice snarled out, the voice of a man they all knew to be dead, the voice of MacDonald Pugh.

"That knowledge will do you no good, Mr. *Spider*. I do not intend to leave any witness to accuse me of the Black Death."

And Nita, her heart singing, recalled that long talk she had not been able to understand in the cavern and remembered that it cleared her Dick in every particular, of every crime that the police laid at his door. She smiled gaily.

"Why didn't you tell me?" she whispered into Dick's ear.

"When?" He merely framed the word with his lips, and Nita, remembering, laughed. When would he have had a moment to tell her before they had landed again at his estate and started back over the road to town? And really this was much nicer than being told.

She heard, as in a dream, Wentworth's voice grating as it never naturally did and realized that he had been disguising his tones there in the cavern. Then Kirkpatrick stopped the machine and turned toward Wentworth.

"It's very obvious, Dick," he said, "that the *Spider*'s voice is not yours. But that eccentric gentleman left nothing to chance. He told me over the phone— " He smiled and drew toward him a slip of paper. "I think I have the exact words. 'I do not appreciate your confusing me with that numbskull, Wentworth. He's all right, but he hasn't the brain for this type of work!'"

Wentworth was angry.

"That's all very well for the *Spider* to brag," he said vehemently. "I was on the right trail, though. He just beat me to it."

"That's right, Wentworth," jeered a reporter. "He just beat you to it."

Then the newspaper men made a concerted dash for the door to phone in the biggest story since five hours ago when the Master of the Plague had died.

Virginia Doeg and Jimmy Handley were the next to go. Handley stopping to shake Wentworth's hand and say again the "Thank you," he had shouted when Wentworth had saved him. Then only Kirkpatrick and Nita and the *Spider* were left.

Wentworth crossed to the desk and held out his hand. Kirkpatrick gripped it fiercely, and the men's eyes locked affectionately. Nita, who could understand, slipped from the office, a soft smile on her lips. Finally the two men dropped their hands, a little embarrassed by their show of emotion.

The *Spider* cleared his throat. "That was generous of you, Stanley," he said, "making it as public as all that."

His fist struck the wrist of the other's gun hand.

"Forget it," said Kirkpatrick shortly. "You have much more to forgive than I."

And he proffered his cigarette case. Wentworth accepted one and, with a quick gleam in his eyes, dug from his pocket the clumsy lighter that Pugh had made, the lighter which even now bore the seals of the *Spider*—seals that would not dissolve in an unknowing hand.

"I wonder," said Wentworth slowly, his tip-tilted brows mocking, "if you'd let me have that dictating machine as a souvenir of a case on which the *Spider* beat me to the kill?"

He flicked flame to the clumsy lighter with its *Spider*'s seals and touched it to Kirkpatrick's cigarette.

THE END

Coming soon in *THE SPIDER* Volume 5

Uncanny, unbelievable—more deadly and more horrible than open bloody warfare—a new terror assails the nerve-centers of American life in . . .

THE CITY DESTROYER

A powerful, gripping novel featuring the SPIDER, lone-wolf champion of humanity, in his greatest crusade against the greed and blood-hunger of the underworld.

Quietly, subtly, like an army of voracious rodents hungrily devouring the substance of the land, the new enemy was destroying the nation. The strong steel skeletons of the skyscrapers, bulwarks against wind, decay, and time, were eaten away mysteriously and rapidly, toppling the edifices and crushing countless thousands! Firearms, bayonets, all weapons to protect the land, turned to a dusty powder in the hands of the men who tried to use them. Cities from coast to coast were laid waste, pillaged by the sly organization of the *Master*, the criminal who was wrecking a nation, taunting the SPIDER at his helplessness. Commerce was ruined, families wiped out—as men and women fled in terror from the wrecked shambles which had once been proud homes and offices. And the criminal behind all this devastation, cunning and vicious, escaped every trap the SPIDER laid, avoided every tentacle of suspicion!

How can Richard Wentworth, working hand in hand with the organized forces of law and order against overwhelming doom, strike at the hidden master-brain?

How can the SPIDER outwit the enemy, when at every turn he himself is hunted and persecuted?

How can the nation survive when Terror and Death walk the highways, arm in arm, and the government rests in the hands of unnerved, exhausted men?

plus

Cunning, vicious, a new menace, deadly and horrible, strikes America in . . .

THE PAIN EMPEROR

A gripping, powerful feature-length novel of the SPIDER, lone-wolf champion of humanity, who carries on his greatest battle against a wily foe risen from the ranks of the underworld!

The woman was preparing for bed. She sat at her boudoir table and spread a thick unguent over her face. She smoothed it over her facial muscles, patted it on evenly. She picked up a soft tissue to remove it, and at that moment, her agonized screams broke the quiet silence of the night! She tore at her face with frenzied, long-nailed fingers; she staggered from the low chair, screamed once more as she clawed her cheeks, and fell dead. . . . Throughout the land, this scene was being repeated, nor was it confined to women alone. Men, even children, were stricken down by a dread acid which assailed them in many forms. . . . And the SPIDER, who strove ever to protect his countrymen, was embroiled in a colossal battle which threatened his love, his life, his friends, and his honor. For a new public avenger—one who was cunning and cruel; one who was mulcting the innocent to line his own pockets—was determined to crucify the SPIDER for his own vain honor!

With one of his faithful servants already victim of the vicious Avenger—with the others imperiled, and his own case almost helpless—what can the SPIDER do?

When Richard Wentworth is offered a chance to return to the placid tranquility of private life, will he do it? His identity for all time hidden, his seeming innocence established, will he seek personal safety and happiness—while thousands of others die horribly, in agony!

OF ALL THE SPIDER'S COURAGEOUS CRUSADES AGAINST THE MASTER-BRAINS OF THE UNDERWORLD, THIS IS THE MOST STARKLY REAL AND GRIPPING! A COMPLETE, BREATH-TAKING NOVEL OF THE MASTER OF MEN.

THE WEB by Will Murray

For this fourth *Spider* volume, we span the length and breadth of the 10-year-long series.

Popular Publications launched *The Spider* magazine in the Autumn of 1933 amid a swirl of mystery. The initial issue showcased *The Spider Strikes,* bylined R.T.M. Scott. Scott was a famous novelist and short story writer who created Secret Service Smith, a template for Richard Wentworth and The *Spider*'s dramatic cast of characters.

Readers picking up that first issue, dated October, 1933, may well have recognized the famous byline. Although Scott had not published a novel in several years, his remained a name to conjured with.

Eighty years later, the byline attached to the first two *Spider* novels remains enigmatic. For there were *two* R.T.M. Scotts: the famous father, and his more obscure son, who also wrote pulp fiction under the byline "Maitland Scott." Both were named Reginald, but the son was familiarly known as "Robert."

The abrupt disappearance of the Scott byline after only two issues suggests something unusual was going on, for with the third issue the byline became the house name of "Grant Stockbridge," in obvious emulation of "Maxwell Grant," mythical author of The Shadow, and Scott vanished from the series forever.

Stockbridge, of course, initially concealed the identity of moonlighting newspaperman Norvell W. Page. We'll get to Page shortly.

One question that has remained unanswered over the last eight decades: which Scott, father or son, wrote *The Spider Strikes* and its sequel, *The Wheel of Death*? The answer may not be very simple. It's entirely possible that the first installment was the work of the father, while the second was the work of the son. This is only a theory, however.

Adding to the mystery is the fact that a 1934 *Terror Tales* story called "Shadows of Desire" which featured a sinister character named Ram Singh. The story was attributed to Maitland Scott. This certainly suggests that the son was the R.T.M. Scott of the *Spider* series. So it may be that the father objected to seeing his famous byline duplicated on a trashy pulp magazine, albeit legitimately so. The son was formally known as Reginald Thomas Maitland Scott II.

I first asked Popular Publications founder Harry Steeger about Scott back in 1977, and he replied:

I don't remember anything about R.T.M. Scott. My dealings with him were very brief since he was handled by Rogers Terrill.

Harry Steeger

Years later, I learned of Scott's son, and went back to Steeger to see if he recalled either one. His response this second time was more illuminating:

I did see your discovery about R.T.M. Scott. I completely forgot that there were two Scotts connected with the office, because by the time they arrived on the scene I was no longer the day to day editor. Rogers Terrill was, I believe, the editor who dealt with the Scotts. Since you have mentioned it, I remember very well the name Maitland Scott. He, indeed, would have been the *Spider* author. I have been trying very hard to remember who it was wrote those original novels, and your discovery really rings a familiar bell in my memory. My recollection is that it was Robert, the son, who wrote that additional *Spider* novels [*sic*] because I remember the author as a rather young man. I do remember that.

If Steeger's memory was reliable, that would seem to settle that. However, he once claimed that later *Spider* ghost Emile C. Tepperman was really a woman! There, he had apparently misremembered Mary Dale Buckner, who wrote for the same magazines as "Donald Dale." So the matter can be called only partly resolved.

Whatever was going on behind the scenes of Popular Publications, Scott was out, and Norvell Page stepped in to fill the vacancy. It was a stroke of luck that Page was available for this work, since he had just sold his first story to Rogers Terrill of Popular Publications.

Fortunately, we know exactly how Page came into the Popular fold. For he told us so.

R.T.M. Scott

Norvell Wordsworth Page was a rising star in the pulp firmament. He had broken into print only three years before, with the short story, "Corralled," for *Western Trails*, October, 1930, followed by a steady stream of gangster stuff for Harry Widmer at *Detective-Dragnet,* shifting over to detection-action type stories when gangster fiction faded and that magazine became *Ten Detective Aces* early in the fateful year of 1933. During this transition, he dropped his contrived pseudonym of "N. Wooten Poge" for his real name. At the same time, he broke into the prestigious *Black Mask* magazine. His career was heating up.

Page was still holding down his day job with the New York *Evening Telegraph* when destiny tapped him on the shoulder. Or was it the other way around? You decide.

Here is an except from "How I Write," *The Writer's Year Book 1934*, telling the tale of how Norv Page crashed the editorial gate at Popular Publications:

Norvell W. Page

> That story is titled "Dance of the Skeletons," and it's of the pulp type called "Mystery-Horror"; that is, it's about foul deeds which are to make the reader's blood run cold and to keep him guessing as to who actually committed those deeds.

> The history of this particular story began one evening when I climbed three steep flights to a Greenwich Village attic and invited a writer friend to visit a new speakeasy with me. My friend was depressed. He sat before a table on which sheets of manuscript were scattered. "The editor wants me to cut my sixty-thousand word novel to thirty-six thousand," he said bitterly, "and get it in by next Monday. I've only written ten thousand and I like the plot as it is." My friend decided he wouldn't cut his story and that he couldn't plot and write another in seven days.

> "Mind if I have a shot at it?" I asked. "I've never written for that editor, but I can give him thirty-five thousand words in a week, if that's what he wants."

> My friend said morosely, "Go ahead," and the drinks were on me.

"Dance of the Skeletons" appeared in *Dime Mystery Magazine*, October, 1933, which hit the newsstands the same month as the first issue of *The Spider.* By that time, the second *Spider* manuscript would have been in production. As for the third....

Page was known as a speed demon of the pulps. A deadline emergency may have caused Rogers Terrill to turn to him, begging for a fast *Spider* novel. Whatever the case may have been, Page banged out a white-hot tale he titled "Web of Murder," which was retitled *Wings of the Black Death* for the December 1933 issue of *The Spider*, which went on sale November 5th. Things were moving very fast for Norvell Page.

The novel was an auspicious start, full of Page's fevered stylistics, and he immediately made the series and its cast of characters his own. However, it's only a foretaste of what was to come.

Over the following decade, with only one break ascribed to overwork, and supplemented by the occasional pinch hitter, Norvell Page produced an estimated 93 *Spider* novels.

Our second story was the last lead novel ever to appear in the pages of *The Spider* magazine, which went on sale November 3rd, 1943—almost exactly a decade after *Wings of the Black Death* was published. The magazine had enjoyed a solid ten-year run, but changes were in the wind. World War II and its paper shortages were causing companies like Popular Publications to winnow their mighty pulp lines down to just the top sellers. While *The Spider* had a loyal following, ten years is a long time for one hero to run in the pages of a single magazine. Perhaps there was dissatisfaction with Page's work. What had been pulpy and current in 1933 was considered dated and out of style by 1943. It is known that some of the final *Spider* novels were rewritten in-house by writers like Robert Turner, who was one of its last editors.

The final issue of *The Spider* was edited by W. Ryerson Johnson, who was primarily a Western writer but was shifting over to detective stories at that time, and had ghosted popular characters like the Phantom Detective and Doc Savage in the past. He may have heavily edited or even revised the manuscript, as Turner had with the previous *Spider* stories.

Johnson remembered little of his brief tenure:

> On that occasion when I went to work for Popular Publications for a few months, they put me to editing *Detective Tales* and *Dime Mystery*. And for a little while *The Spider*. You wrote them fast. They edited fast, too. I worked under good old Mike Tilden. In his stable were also Harry Widmer and Damon Knight.

> I had never read an issue of *The Spider* in my life and was only faintly aware that it was one of the couple of hundred pulp titles. I did a bit of editing on the mag. I was so disinterested, though, that I don't remember a thing about it....

> They stopped publishing it just after I went to work there.

It's not certain that *When Satan Came to Town* was revised, but the prose shows some signs of this. The authorship of the story has always been murky: the check to Page was countersigned by Laura Winchell, wife of Prentice Winchell, who also wrote as Stewart Sterling for *Black Mask* and other titles. This led some to conclude that Sterling actually ghosted the story. However, an earlier *Spider* check was countersigned by Page's good friend, Theodore Tinsley, whose widow insisted that it was simply a financial transaction having nothing to do with authorship, and that they had simply helped Page cash his *Spider* check while he was vacationing in Florida. Since the Winchells also wintered in the Sunshine State, it's likely that they too occasionally cashed checks for visiting writers.

Another reason to assume that Page was the original writer on *When Satan Came to Town* was a simple fact that the opening situation is virtually identical to the opening situation of a 1938 Shadow story called *The Fifth Napoleon,* which was written by Tinsley. It's unlikely that Sterling would be copying a Ted Tinsley Shadow opening, although the three men were the closest of friends. "Winch" was best man at Tinsley's wedding, and Page was also in attendance.

The story, which was submitted as "The *Spider*'s Raid" in August of 1943, also features Page's sometimes bizarre renamings of actual places—in this case, Garago, Michigario seems to be a stand-in for Chicago, Illinois. Or perhaps an amalgam of Chicago and Detroit, Michigan. The story was written in August, two months prior to the time that Norvell Page's first wife, Audrey, tragically passed away. So her death is not a factor here.

What is certain is that *When Satan Came to Town* was the final *Spider* story to be published for many decades. With it, Norvell Page and Popular Publications rang down the curtain on one of the most memorable pulp heroes ever created.

After this, both Page and Ted Tinsley went off to Washington D.C. to work for the Office of War Information, having been orphaned by the shrinking pulp magazine industry, which was being hammered by changing tastes and constant reductions in the amount of paper to which publishers had access. Between Tinsley's loss of his regular markets at Street & Smith after *The Shadow* went monthly and editor John L. Nanovic left in the wake of the cancellation of most of his mystery magazines, as well as *The Spider* going bimonthly the Spring before its suspension, both pulp veterans understood they had to seek greener pastures in order to survive.

Now turn the page and enjoy The *Spider*'s last hurrah. Although he has been revived by other writers in the decades since, no one does the Master of Men better than Norvell W. Page! •

When Satan Came To Town

118th Novel Based on The Case Notebook of The Spider

By Grant Stockbridge

When the CONQUEROR and his hordes from hell tried to blast their bloody way through America to the Nation's Capital, only an ex-inmate of Alcatraz stood in their way. The madman's hirelings knew him as Number 347. You know him as Richard Wentworth—The SPIDER.

CHAPTER ONE
Dead Man

THEY call Alcatraz The Rock. It was built for the incorrigible among the criminal horde and it's as hard as its name. When a man's last day is served, they walk him down to the ferry and put him aboard. Guards go with him to the mainland slip and that's where he finally steps out, a free man. Free, at least, in his body.

Case Brent was one of the men for whom Alcatraz was built. Hard, incorrigible, too slick to burn, too vicious for ordinary pens. His last day was up. The ferry slip was ahead.

He sneered at the guards. "Me, I was too tough for you. Me, I'm Case Brent. I crack rocks. I'll take care of you later."

The guards looked at him impersonally. One of them said, "Over here, three-forty-seven. This is your way out."

Case Brent obeyed the authority in the man's voice before he thought to sneer. He'd been trained that way, on The Rock. He was out of the ferry slip before it really occurred to him to be tough. He swaggered and looked belligerent, but deep inside of him he was afraid. All these years of being 347, until you got so you answered to a number instead of your own name—the name you'd made feared and respected—had got him down.

Things looked different. There weren't many cars on the streets and there were a lot of guys in uniform. Case Brent looked about him pretty carefully. You couldn't tell how long some punks would bear a grudge. One of them might be on hand to take a shot at him. Case Brent wet his lips and didn't swagger quite so much. He slipped up a side street away from the waterfront.

When the car slid up along side of him, Case Brent's mouth ripped open in a silent scream and he leaped for the cover of a doorway. The car opened. A voice spoke to him: "In here, three-forty-seven," it ordered.

There was authority in the voice and it checked Case Brent in mid-flight. He faced the door and looked into the car. His face drained of color. It turned pasty yellow and he began to breathe through his mouth, noisily. He had never known such terror as this before, and there was a reason. The shadowed face that peered at him from within the car was stern as justice and as remorseless. The eyes that bored into him were eyes of command, the eyes of the Master of Men! That black-draped figure, that face beneath the broad brim of a black hat—yes, Case Brent knew him well, knew him for an avenger, a human sword of justice beyond reach of the law, inevitable as death itself.

"You don't want me," Case Brent whispered. "You don't want me. Cripes, I done seven years on The Rock. I ain't no good anymore. You don't want me!"

The man inside the car did not answer. He made no threatening gesture but Case Brent moved toward him, still whimpering, still protesting, but obeying because he must.

"You don't want me," he whispered again. "Don't kill me, *Spider!*"

So the man known to Alcatraz as 347 disappeared from the general knowledge of men, and nobody cared except a few hoods who had at sometime double-crossed him. They worried and kept a gun handy. The government didn't worry. When a man finally left Alcatraz, they knew they didn't need to worry about him.

THE young policeman, walking his beat along Dacey Street in Garago, didn't even remember the name of Case Brent. Brent had been sent up in the days before Frank Kelly had started reading the newspapers. Patrolman Frank Kelly was still on his first beat. It was a job and it took care of his mother and the kids, and he was proud of the uniform and the badge. There are many cops like that.

He turned from Dacey into Fifth Street, heard a man cry out and then a shuddering moan. He heard the sound of heavy blows, the crash of a glass window. He whipped out his police whistle and made excited noises on it. He gripped his club and revolver, ran toward the small fruit store from which the noises came. It was night and the street was dim, but he could see the big car parked in front of Tony Domenico's shop.

Just before he got to the shop, two men came swaggering out. One of them took the time to dump over a stall of piled fruit. There were still groans sounding from inside, and a woman weeping. The two men saw Patrolman Frank Kelly, but didn't pay much attention to him. They looked at each other and grinned and climbed into the car.

Patrolman Kelly ran up to them. "Okay, you two," he said, his voice a little high. "You're under arrest."

ONE of the men was behind the wheel. The other was just getting into the car beside him. He looked at the cop. "Shove off, copper," he said, flatly. "We're Harpo's boys."

Kelly said, "I don't give a damn who you are! You can't beat up guys on my beat! Get out of that car." He waved the gun. He was excited.

The crook spat on the sidewalk by Kelly's feet. He said, "Don't get me riled, copper. Come on, Pinky, let's go."

Frank Kelly pulled the trigger, sent a bullet straight up into the air. "I can shoot straight," he said. "Give me the keys of that car, and no stalling."

The two men looked at each other. Their eyes acknowledged their conspiracy. The man nearest the cop turned toward him fully and leaned forward, spreading out his body to hide the movements of the driver who was furtively drawing his gun.

"Now listen, copper," the thug spoke placatingly, "you don't want any trouble with us. Harpo wouldn't like it if you arrested us. You might find yourself suspended for a couple of months. You wouldn't want to skip pay for two months, would you?"

The driver tapped his friend between the shoulders, which meant that he was ready with the gun. He was to duck out of the way now while the driver put two or three slugs through the copper. They were ready, and... a car slewed around the corner behind them. It came around fast, tires screaming. It swung wildly, straightened out. The driver of the crook-car yelled. He batted at his door. He was a moment too late.

The second car slammed into the rear of the crooks' sedan at high speed. It leaped from a stationary stand to fast movement in that split-second of time, but the inertia of the crooks' bodies was not so swiftly overcome. They were hurled backward against the seat, over the seat. One of them fell limply into the rear, with his head twisted flat on his shoulder. The second man was caught under the wheel. He hung there, screaming, and couldn't move his legs.

Patrolman Frank Kelly stood on the curb, his mouth open, the gun dangling from his hand. The second car stopped beside him and the man behind the wheel leaned toward him.

"Some of Harpo's boys?" he asked.

Kelly gulped. "They were going to kill me!"

The man nodded. "Sure," he said, "but things are going to be different now. I'm moving in on Harpo. Name of Case Brent. I don't like cops, but I don't let my boys kill 'em."

He nodded and drove off. Patrolman Frank Kelly stood on the curb and called, weakly, "Hey!"

The car with the man who called himself Case Brent turned the corner and was gone. The crook trapped under the wheel of his own car had stopped screaming now. The street was very peaceful.

Patrolman Frank Kelly said, "Hey—hey!" He reeled around and ran into Tony Domenico's store and grabbed for the telephone.

CHAPTER TWO
The Second Lesson

IT MADE big news in police headquarters and in certain underworld circles, but the general public knew nothing about the man named Case Brent who was moving in on Harpo. They knew about Harpo all right. They groaned under his dominion but somehow couldn't do anything about it. Everything in Garago cost half again as much as it should. Those who thought knew that Harpo took the difference. But witnesses against Harpo didn't live to testify in court. The police made a big bluster— and accomplished nothing. Even if people had heard of Case Brent it would have meant little to them—a change of masters.

The man they would have welcomed, had they known his true purpose, was the *Spider*. Where he walked, criminals perished and the reign of law and order was reestablished.

It meant nothing to any of them that, at a downtown hotel, two persons had registered the night before. One of them signed the record as Richard Wentworth, the other as Nita van Sloan.

Wentworth was a man of lean purpose whose careless air was a mask. There was a smile on his chiseled lips now as he spoke easily to the girl who sat across the dinner table from him.

"I understand," he said casually, "that a man named Case Brent is going to pay a visit to the Jive Parlor tonight."

Nita van Sloan tried to keep smiling, but her violet eyes had sudden depths that were shadowed by fear. She said, slowly, "The Jive Parlor is Harpo's headquarters."

"So I understand," Wentworth said.

They sat smiling at each other… and no one except themselves knew that, with those words, the *Spider* was announcing the opening attack of his campaign against the criminal overlords of the city. Few knew that Wentworth and the *Spider* were the same man—for that knowledge in hostile hands would mean Wentworth's death!

Nita reached casually across the table, touched Wentworth's lean fingers lightly. "Could this man have a friend with him tonight?"

Wentworth leaned toward her, his smile just showing the even white line of his teeth. He nodded, "A moll named Nita van Sloan," he said. They laughed together. It sounded lighthearted.

But there was a deeper, more somber tone under the surface.

The Jive Parlor spilled colors as jumbled as the echo of its music into the darkness of Mayfair Avenue. Staggered letters spelled out a name and around about the words neon figures of dancers reeled and whirled. Against all that brilliance, the entrance itself seemed inconspicuous. The doors were frosted glass and, when they were opened, air-conditioned coolness gushed out into the heat.

The interior was as dim as the outside was brilliant. All the lights were shaded and rosy. They made nooks of shadow among the dancers' tables. They hid the doors that led to other less reputable floors, and to the gambling hall below street level. In Garago, all things ran wide open, but they kept up a pretense of secrecy because it appealed more to the victims. And the same people who groaned at the gang and racket dominion of the city nevertheless freely patronized the Jive Parlor, were pleasantly thrilled that the proprietor was responsible for many of the frequent killings in and about Garago. It added to his stature that the police never even took him in for questioning.

People in general had said that the old days of the rackets and the gangs were finished forever. But whenever restrictions are put upon the public— even for the best of possible reasons, as in wartime rationing—there are those who want their own way regardless of the cost to themselves or to others.

Such people, patronizing black markets, harkening to whispers of, "I can get it for you, but it will cost you more," make it possible for the gangs to come back—for the rackets to return—for the deadliest enemies of democracy to flourish.

So it was in Garago… and the public was thrilled.

Garago lies on the shores of Lake Michigario. It has four-hundred-thousand people in its rows on rows of streets. Its weekly payroll runs well over two million dollars. Fat pickings for crooks in a town like that. Fat pickings for crooked police. When the combination gets together, it's hard to break, because the legitimate agencies of the people are strangled.

One man was moving to combat all that—one man—the *Spider*, risking death in a selfless cause. And he chose to fight in the disguise of a criminal from the Rock: Case Brent—

When Wentworth walked into the Jive Parlor, with Nita van Sloan beside him, he was Case Brent to the last brazen swagger. Nita was the typical, overdressed, over-painted moll. They strutted past the doorman, and it was to the cold-eyed thug lounging beside the entrance to the main dance floor that Wentworth first spoke.

He went toward him and stood two yards away, his coat swinging loose, his right hand carelessly buffing nails against his lapel in obvious readiness to draw a gun.

"Tell Harpo that the new boss of Garago is here for a bit of fun," he said, harshly. "The new boss—Case Brent."

HE SAW the man's eyes widen with shock, then narrow in fear. Wentworth didn't wait for an answer. He turned and offered his arm to Nita van Sloan. Together they went across the floor, toward the table Wentworth had selected. Nita giggled.

"My, big boy!" She made her voice loud. "You sure told him!"

Wentworth's genius for disguise consisted of the fact that, when he altered his appearance, he altered even his mode of thinking. He was the old Case Brent, showing off for a woman.

He stopped beside the table he had chosen, and it was occupied by a boy and girl. "Shove off, punk," he ordered contemptuously. "This is my table. Didn't you see the reserved sign?"

Nita giggled.

The boy stammered, started to his feet and, intimidated, moved off with the flouncing and angry girl whom he escorted. Wentworth seated Nita elaborately, settled himself beside her. His eyes shuttled over the dance hall secretly and spotted the assemblage of the gunsels of Harpo. They had no concerted plan, as yet. That was plain in their indecisive movements.

"They're waiting for their orders." Wentworth leaned toward Nita, as if he were telling a joke. "As soon as they receive them, I have an idea the lights will be put out, probably with the excuse of a spotlight dance. If that's it—there's a man alone at the next table."

Nita laughed. Her eyes were very serious. She understood what Wentworth wished her to do. "Is that all?" she asked.

"It's enough," Wentworth assured her quietly, "and don't worry."

Nita glanced carelessly about the hall and saw one man hurrying toward the gunsels grouped at the main entrance. Before he reached them, the master of ceremonies caught up a microphone.

"All out for the spotlight dance!" he called. "Everybody out, folks! All holds barred and catch as catch can. Dat old debbil moon will keep an evil eye on you!"

There was laughter about the room. Nita smiled into Wentworth's eyes, and the lights went out—

HARPO was not disturbed. He knew Case Brent by reputation, but he knew also what the Rock did to men. They might still talk tough, but they were softened up plenty when they came out. It was a spot that Harpo intended to keep away from. He was thinking more about that than about Case Brent.

Harpo had been sitting on top of things for five years, and each year had found him stronger, more solid. He looked that way, square-built, ponderous, immovable. His face had the immobility of a pan of dough beneath a bush of faded red hair.

Thoughtfully, he reached into a drawer of his desk and took out a special radio-type phone. He held it to his lips and compressed a buzzer on the handle with a thick finger. He did that three times and then waited. There was no heat in this wood-paneled office. The window was closed and coolness eddied out of concealed registers. The desk was in a corner and the windows were at its right end. Harpo wasn't looking out the window. He blinked impassively at the door. That was why he didn't see a hand move to a corner of the glass pane, and then withdraw, leaving a black suction disc attached to the glass.

A voice came out of the desk drawer.

"Yes?"

"Case Brent showed up here tonight," Harpo spoke into the phone. "He talks big. I'm taking him. You want him?"

"No, but keep it quiet. I don't like the smell of things. Somebody is behind Brent."

Harpo blinked slowly, "He's got a dame with him. One of them will sing."

"Keep it quiet."

Harpo put the phone back into the drawer and closed it. Something that might have been an enormous black bat hovered outside the window for an instant. Harpo caught a glimpse of the movement. He came out of his seat and clawed at the drawer of his desk for a gun. The glass smashed inward then, and the thing leaped into the office—and it wasn't a bat. It was a man from whose shoulders a long cape swirled with an effect of black wings.

For Harpo, the sound that came from his own throat was like a scream. "*Spider!*" he whispered. "*Spider!*" He got his hand on his gun—

WHEN Harpo's men moved in on the table where Case Brent had sat, no one was there. But the door was covered; all exits were covered. Their eyes turned toward the dance floor. One of the men hurried off in answer to a whispered order, and after that the spotlight moved with more deliberation, purposefully. It fixed presently on a girl in a bright red dress, held an instant, and then skipped on. Its movements became erratic again. Harpo's men moved out on the dance floor, quietly, deftly.

One of them tapped the shoulder of the man who was dancing with the girl in red. "Cut in, pal?" he said.

The man turned his head, and suddenly pain shot through his skull. Two men caught him as he fell, and the man who had tapped him on the shoulder was dancing with the girl in red.

"Don't make any noise," he whispered, between motionless lips, "or you're a dead duck. We're moving out of here."

Nita widened her eyes in a pretense of terror, breathed through her mouth. "Don't hurt me!" she whispered. "I ain't done a thing!"

THEY were on the edge of the dance floor. The man's hand clamped with bruising force on her arm, thrust her roughly through the empty tables toward the alleyway that led to Harpo's office. Nita van Sloan didn't resist. She was following orders, but her heart beat with a slow heavy pound in her throat. Dick Wentworth had said, "Don't worry." This was something he would have foreseen. She didn't know his plans.

They were in front of a heavy door now. It had no knob. Beside them were two other men, supporting the unconscious body of the man whom she had asked to dance with her. There wasn't much light here, but she could hear their whispers. They were waiting. Abruptly, the door in front of them slid aside. Light dazzled their eyes. The lamp on the desk was tilted so that its naked bulb threw a barrage of brilliance into their faces. The men blinked and moved forward uncertainly. Behind the light, it was possible to make out the bulky loom of a figure with bushy hair.

As they stepped inside, the door slid shut again, clicked solidly into its groove.

"Here they are, boss," said the man who held Nita's arm.

Somewhere in the room, a man laughed. It was boastful and triumphant laughter. It didn't come from the squat and motionless figure behind the light.

"That's swell," a voice said, and Nita recognized the jeering tones of Case Brent. "Just swell! I'm the boss, all right, and Harpo ain't interested. *Harpo is dead.*"

Nita turned her head quickly. She could feel the stiff tension of the three men with her as they turned their eyes toward the sound of that voice.

Wentworth stood in the corner of the room behind them. There was a gun in each of his fists and Nita had to remind herself that it was really Wentworth, for everything about him so perfectly resembled Case Brent.

"Harpo is dead," he said again. "I killed him. I'm perfectly willing to rub you punks out, too, but you can work for me if you want to. I'm your new boss."

He moved toward them, two swaggering strides. "Get that? *I'm the new boss!*" His words struck with the brutality of thrown rocks.

Nita caught Wentworth's eye. He jerked his head toward the desk. Nita walked over and moved the lamp shade, so that the brilliance washed over the hunched body of Harpo. They could see then how he had died, with a bullet through his face.

Wentworth laughed, harshly, "I told Harpo I was the new boss. He didn't seem to believe me. You punks can go now. And tell anyone who doesn't believe me that he can come and argue it out with me. Maybe I can convince him—*like I did Harpo!*"

The door whirred open again and the three men stumbled out, leaving unconscious on the floor the man with whom Nita had danced. She moved toward him.

"I'm sorry he was hurt," she said. "He seemed embarrassed when I asked him to dance—but not half as embarrassed as I was!" Her laughter broke off with a gasp. "A badge! He's a detective," she said. "A city detective!"

Wentworth was completing his swift inspection of papers in Harpo's desk, interrupted by the entrance of the men. "A fine place for a cop," he said dryly. "Everyone knows this is Harpo's headquarters. What's his name? He must have some identification."

"He danced very politely," Nita said defensively. "His name is Whitney Small."

"Small?" Wentworth repeated absently. "Yes, here he is. Down for fifty dollars a week. On Harpo's pay-off list."

Nita shoved the cop's wallet back into his pocket with distaste. She bit her lip. In her code, there was no worse criminal than the man who, sworn to defend the public, took protection money from their victimizers.

Above the door, a subdued light glowed. Nita stared at it, and then backed slowly toward a corner of the room. She slipped a small automatic out of a garter holster.

Across the room, Wentworth laughed lightly. He folded up the paper in his hand, and crossed to the broken window. He whistled softly, piercingly, and the signal was answered. He tossed the paper out the window, watched it disappear. "We mustn't keep them waiting," he said dryly. "I do believe that some of Harpo's men still are not convinced I'm their new boss!" He tumbled Harpo's body to the floor, dropped into the chair. He opened the drawer and caught up the radiophone, squeezed the button three times.

He had an automatic in his left hand, and with its butt he depressed a button on the desk. The door slid open and gun-armed men crowded across the sill.

CHAPTER THREE
Death Drives

WENTWORTH saluted the three men in the doorway with a slow sweep of his automatic muzzle. "There's a gun behind you, too," he mentioned casually. "Now be good children while I talk to papa." It was Case Brent's jeering voice again.

Out of the drawer came the answer to his radio signal. "Yes?"

"Harpo tried to take Case Brent and got taken," Wentworth said into the phone. "This is Case Brent. You want to see me?"

"Yes."

"Good," Wentworth said. "Me and the boys will be right over."

He replaced the radiophone in the drawer and grinned at the three gunsels in the doorway. "A regular yes-man," he said, happily. "Which of you three is top man?"

The gunsel in front said, curtly, "Me!"

He frowned when he said it, drew his stiff black hair almost down to his smooth black brows. His eyes were pale.

"Name?"

"Cottrell." The man gathered confidence through speaking. His crouch was less stiff.

Wentworth said, "Cottrell, we're taking your ex-boss, Harpo, with us. Come and get him." The command cracked.

Cottrell started. He hesitated, but nothing else was said. The pressure of Wentworth's eyes was upon him. The black eye of the automatic looked at him. He took a step forward, then stopped. His gun hand stiffened.

"To hell with it," he said. "You ain't my boss!"

Wentworth squeezed the trigger of the gun. The bullet took the man between the eyes. He wrenched backward, twisted awkwardly on bent knees, pitched down on his face.

"Next?" Wentworth's voice was soft. "Now, who's the top man?"

The other two men stood like statues. One of them swallowed noisily, but it was the other who spoke. "You're the top man," he whined.

Wentworth nodded equably. "Okay, that's better. Come and get Harpo. I don't want anybody but the boys to see him. Take care of that. We're going to see—him." He pointed toward the drawer that held the radiophone. He looked at Nita. "You stay here, babe, and sit on the lid."

That was what his lips said, but his eyes went to the window, and he pursed his lips as if whistling. Nita said, "Whatever you say, big boy! You're the boss!"

When the two men had picked up Harpo's body and carried it toward the door, Wentworth heaved Cottrell across the sill into the corridor.

"We'll take him along, too," he said. He was swaggering, with Case Brent's fat smile on his lips.

Nita watched him go, watched the door slide shut behind him. A shiver jerked at her shoulders. No matter how many times she walked with death, that cold always touched her. And now Wentworth, alone, with only his superb courage, his keen intellect to support him, was going into the power of the man who ruled the city.

Nita closed her eyes and her lips moved. She pulled in a slow breath and then, steadied, moved toward the window. She whistled softly. The signal was answered from outside. Something sailed out of the darkness and flipped against her. She caught it, and knew then what Wentworth's plan for her was. This was the silken rope that was the *Spider*'s web. This was her signal to make a swift and secret exit.

Nita looped the silken rope about the desk, twisted the doubled line about her arm and stepped onto the sill. As she stood there, she heard a sound behind her.

"Wait a minute, sister," a man's voice said hoarsely. "You ain't walking out on this!"

She twisted her head around. The detective had recovered consciousness. He was propped up on one elbow and he held a revolver very steadily in his right hand. His eyes squinted painfully. There was anger in the line of his mouth.

"All right," Nita said quietly. "Just a minute until I undo this."

She loosened the silken rope about her arm, and caught it lower down. She moved as if to come back into the room. Her foot slipped with a gasped cry of fright and she pitched backward out into space. The cop swore, staggered to his feet. He reeled and pressed the heel of his fist to his swelling head, but kept going. He saw that the silken rope was taut.

Suddenly, it was lax, and then it was snaked out through the window with the speed of a sliding reptile. He reached the sill an instant later, gun in his fist, sent flame and lead crashing down into the darkness. Nothing answered him. He squinted his aching eyes to see into the black channel of the alley below. There was no movement that he could discern.

He swung away from the window and reached

the door with big strides. He was swearing. He was scared—not of his job, but of Harpo. He would catch hell for this. He had let that girl suck him into some play against Harpo. Nobody but Harpo's men would dare pull any rough stuff here. He bore no resentment for that crack on the skull. He had that coming to him for playing dumb. But if he didn't straighten this out, then—

He whipped open the door and two guns blasted him at the same time. He was caught in the cross-fire. The bullets jerked at him and shook him first one way then the other. When they stopped he slid down the jamb of the door, hit and rolled, was spread-eagled on the floor of the corridor. In the distance, the band music thumped and howled. It had swallowed all gun sound.

The two men who had killed him came up and looked down at him. One of them swore in a harsh monotone. He looked into the office, empty now. "It ain't funny, bumping a cop, even in this town," he said, thickly. "I don't like it, brother."

"The boss can fix it." The other man sounded nervous, unsure.

The first man said, "To hell with that. I'm getting out of town, and fast!" He turned and walked away. He began to run. The other man followed him....

A BLOCK away from the Jive Parlor, Nita climbed into a coupé and let herself relax against the cushions. The man who slid under the wheel was big in the shoulders, heavily bearded. His head was wrapped in a tight turban.

"Do we attack the men with the *sahib*?" he asked. His voice was eager.

"Follow the car," Nita ordered, "and don't let them know it, Ram Singh."

The Sikh's voice rumbled with disappointment, *"Han, missie sahib."* The coupé slid smoothly forward. It was a dilapidated looking vehicle, but there was enough power under the hood to satisfy even Ram Singh.

Presently, he spoke again. "Perhaps, later, we may attack?"

Nita laughed. "There will be fighting enough for you before we're through with this, thou bloody one!"

Ram Singh's teeth gleamed white in the thicket of his beard. "Nay, *missie sahib*." His voice deepened with pleasure. "Never yet was there enough fighting for any Sikh! And I—I am a Singh among Sikhs! A mighty lion among Singhs!" It was the beginning of a chant—a battle chant.

Nita said, gently, "We must be quiet, Ram Singh."

"Ah! I am a fool!" the Sikh rumbled. "There is not yet anything to boast about!"

He drove with the skill and the powerful reckless ease of a pursuit pilot, but the car ahead was moving with equal speed. "Perhaps," he said, "they, too, are in a hurry for a fight!"

Wentworth, himself, was under no illusions about the conditions under which he was going to meet the man whose cold voice over the radio bespoke an emotionless and analytical mind. That voice, and the calmness with which the man had accepted the elimination of his lieutenant, was like a trumpet call to the *Spider*. So far, in his campaign to free Garago from its criminal dominance, he had been successful. So far—but he had come no distance at all.

For years, the *Spider* had fought against the various manifestations of underworld viciousness. He had destroyed, one after another, those whose overlordship had threatened the people and the orderly processes of law. A faint and characteristic smile touched for an instant the lips of Case Brent. It was paradoxical that he, the greatest force for law enforcement in the world, worked outside the law.

When Wentworth looked about him, it was with the swagger and the bullying hostility of Case Brent. He was alone in the tonneau of the car... alone with the bodies of Harpo and Cottrell. The two gunsels were in the front seat. Case Brent looked confident, triumphant. Wentworth, behind that mask, was acutely watchful. He had overridden the first obstacles, and he was, presumably, on the way to see the city's real boss.

Wentworth leaned forward, drove his words flatly at the two gunsels. "Just remember this, punks," he said. "If anything should happen, you're too close for me to miss with the first shot!"

The man beside the driver twisted about with a violence of fright. "We ain't trying nothing!" he protested.

"No," Wentworth said, softly. "No, you ain't!"

It was when he leaned back against the cushions again that he suddenly saw the shape of the trap that awaited him. The street was dark and tree-shadowed. It was also narrow. Before it had been empty of traffic and now it was suddenly becoming crowded. Coming toward them were two cars, one behind the other. It would require a maneuver as simple as swinging out to pass in order to block the entire street. Behind, there was another car, a big one that would carry six or seven men, and it was coming very fast.

Even as Wentworth spotted the build-up of the trap, the cars ahead executed their maneuver and parked side by side, blocked the street. Their headlights reached out with dazzling strength. Other headlights, behind, drenched Wentworth's car in brilliance.

The death trap was snapping shut upon the *Spider*!

THERE is one characteristic possessed in common by all those who seek tyrannical power. It is a ruthless and irresponsible ferocity. It is a bitter fanaticism of self. The boss was such an man.

He examined, now, the thin knife-line of his mouth, the arrogance of his thrusting chin, the fanatical cruelty of his staring eyes, in his mirror, before he went to hear the reports of his underlings. He gave himself a thin, approving smile, then pivoted away and punched out the lights. He was a small man. He moved with a limp.

He moved through darkness without hesitation except for the faint drag of his left foot. He was proud of such a small thing as moving unerringly through the dark. Even if he were blind, he told himself, he would move with the same unfaltering courage. He seated himself in a chair that had no back. He sat bolt upright. He scorned comforts and, habitually, he denied himself whatever his body craved. That was strength, to him.

Beside him, a small green light glowed. A man's voice whispered into the darkness: "We're closing in on him now," the voice said. "Two cars coming from straight ahead, one from behind, according to plan. The two cars move up abreast and stop. Their headlights make everything as bright as day. The car with Brent in it is caught like a plane by the searchlights. It swings uncertainly. The driver is blinded.

"The car suddenly swings broadside. It is going fast, to the right. Everyone in it is plainly visible. In the front seat, there are two men—in the back, three men. The one nearest, on the left, is Harpo. His head hangs. I cannot identify the other two men. Our guns open fire. They deluge the car with bullets. The tires explode. But the car keeps going, fast. It strikes the curbstone and bounces. It is over the curbstone and plowing through a hedge. Our cars close in, still firing. The car is burning now. Just a little flame at first, but spreading rapidly. It explodes!"

Over the air came the rumbling burst of the explosion. The man called the Conqueror made no sound. His eyes stared wide into the darkness. There was a drunkenness in him like hot wine. Power. The voice on the radio ran on: "Our men are out of the cars now, closing in, shooting into the flaming wreck."

Suddenly the announcer's voice was speaking rapidly, slurred, a little frightened: "There is something wrong," he said. "I cannot see what it is, but while the shooting goes on, three of our men have fallen to the street! Another one falls! Apparently, someone escaped from the wreck and is shooting. It must be that, or else our men are killing each other by mistake. Our men are taking cover, and their machine guns are sweeping every inch of cover.

"Around us, there are lights going on in various houses. People look out the windows, and then turn and run away. The lights go out. They are afraid. They know it is death to look on when the Conqueror's men strike!"

There was a muffled sound, like a blow, and then a strange voice cut in on the radio. "This has been a nice little shindig, boss," the voice said. It was the brash and mocking voice of Case Brent! "I thought you'd want to give me a little workout before you took me into partnership. Me and the punk that drives the car will be along to see you in a little while. Case Brent signing off!"

In the dark room, the Conqueror reached out and switched off the radio. There was a cold smile on his mouth.

Suddenly, there was light in the room. It came from a single brilliant focus just behind and above his head. It showed his small, shining head, utterly bald. It emphasized the breadth of his shoulders. It showed nothing at all of his face.

A door opened on the far side of the room and two men came in. They were naked to the waist, muscled like titans. They kept their eyes on the floor and rumbled, "Hail, Conqueror!"

The Conqueror's voice was contemptuous. "A man is coming here soon," he said. "He is a fool, but he is cleverer than some who serve me. I do not want him hurt. Disarm him. Bind him. Bring him before me—*on his knees.*"

The two men repeated, "Hail! To hear is to obey!"

They backed toward the door, and the Conqueror spoke once more, thoughtfully. "We will kill him, of course—later!"

The men closed the door silently. The light went out and the Conqueror sat in silence, in darkness, waiting. Such men know no true laughter, but there was an expansive feeling within him. It was a sense of absolute power.

He did not yet know that the *Spider* had come to challenge that power.

CHAPTER FOUR
For the Kill

WHEN the last man in the Conqueror's ambuscade had been destroyed, Ram Singh and Nita van Sloan came out of the shadows and joined Wentworth. Ram Singh's forehead was knotted in a scowl.

"Wah, sahib," he complained, "that was not fighting! Thy servant's knife never left its sheath! Yet the missie sahib—"

"It was an order," Wentworth told him quietly. "The missie sahib did well! Thou also have done well, warrior!"

Ram Singh grumbled, but there was a pleased light in his eyes. Wentworth signed him toward the car. "A man unconscious there. Keep him so. I need him."

In the black shadows beneath a tree, Wentworth stood with Nita van Sloan and talked swiftly, telling her of the radio arrangements, and the way in which the announcer had addressed his boss.

Nita shivered slightly. "He sounds like a madman," she whispered, and was glad of Wentworth's arm about her.

"So did Hitler," Wentworth said grimly. "This man is dangerous. And we cannot destroy him, yet."

"We could all three attack!" Nita said eagerly. "We could trap him, and—"

"And the organization would go on," Wentworth said quietly. "It will go on until the situation which allowed the organization to arise is eliminated. Surely, in the years the *Spider* has labored, peace would have been restored if destruction alone could accomplish it!"

Nita put her forehead against Wentworth's shoulder, felt his arm tighten about her shoulders, his cheek against her hair. "...*The years the Spider has labored*..." were before her in a whirling kaleidoscopic pattern, death and torment and pillage, slaughter and catastrophe, and those brief hours of respite when they could savor triumph and peace. Even those seemed feverish, with the memory of what lay behind, and what surely would come again. Crime was like a great and turbulent sea that beat against the dikes of civilization.

"What can we do, Dick?" Nita asked.

Wentworth laughed shortly. "Eliminate the conditions that cause these uprisings. In this case, it's a weak police force, based on a crooked political regime."

Nita jerked up her head. "But, heavens, Dick!" she cried.

"It has to be done." Wentworth was quiet. "Otherwise, the destruction of this one man would give only a breathing space, and then the terror would come back in a new guise."

Ram Singh's bulky body loomed out of the darkness. "The man began to come to," he reported. "I hit him again, gently."

Wentworth nodded. "That's what I've been doing for years," he told Nita. "Knocking crime on the head. Now, we change the pattern. This time, there must be a strong guardian of peace, like Ram Singh here, to keep crime knocked on the head. Do that long enough, and perhaps it will die!"

Ram Singh said, "*Han, sahib!* He will die when you wish!"

Wentworth laughed, lightly. "Orders!" he said, his voice becoming crisp. "I go on alone. Case Brent is going to become the lieutenant of this madman. I have here a list of police officers taken from Harpo's office. It gives the amounts of money that have been paid to them as graft. Make three copies and conceal them variously. Then get all the personal history you can on certain key men... without making inquiries which will get back to the involved. Ram Singh will go with you. Ram Singh, give me that paper I threw out the window. This list is a lodestar for trouble. You'll need a guard."

There was a moment when Nita was locked breathlessly close in his arms, when his lips burned on hers, and then Wentworth was striding toward the car where the radio announcer lay unconscious. And it was no longer Wentworth, but the swaggerer, Case Brent.

Nita van Sloan watched him drive away, and then turned toward her own car with Ram Singh grumbling beside her. Only when they were underway did she hear the first faint whimper of the police sirens, and a bitter smile edged her lips. The very slowness with which they answered the alarm to stop what must appear to be a gang battle showed the truth of Wentworth's estimate of the situation.

The task of straightening out the police force, of bringing honesty into the city's politics, was greater than merely eliminating the criminals... and equally fraught with death! Nita shuddered. She held one key in her hands—the list of grafters. Police or underworld would murder to regain it. She felt a wild urgency to do the necessary copying and get it out of her hands. She was not yet aware that, among the criminals, there was a standing rule—complete the job given you, successfully, or else! And the order had gone out that Case Brent's moll was to be captured!

WENTWORTH drove for several minutes and then, pulling to the curb, set about reviving the one criminal who was left alive after the ambuscade. His radio broadcast had been quite professional. Wentworth hazarded a shrewd guess that the man actually was a radio announcer who had been bought in by this criminal overlord.

Under Wentworth's ministrations, the prisoner began to regain consciousness. As his eyes blinked open, Wentworth shook him angrily.

"Get up and work this radio!" he demanded. "We're wiped out and we have to report to the chief!"

Since Wentworth had put the transmitter out of commission, the man struggled futilely with it. His hands shook. Wentworth bullied him, finally thrust him behind the wheel, violently.

"Drive!" he ordered. "We could get there while you fiddle with the damned thing."

The radio man, face pale with pain, rolled the sedan. He protested, weakly, "I'm an announcer, not an engineer."

Wentworth grunted at him and bent over the transmitter. "I know something about these gadgets," he said.

Occasionally, he touched disconnected wires together so that the lights glowed. He would wait to make the repairs. This had been cleverly contrived so that his prisoner would drive him directly to headquarters without realizing that Wentworth was completely ignorant of its whereabouts.

When the car finally jerked to a halt, the announcer leaned his head on the wheel and moaned. "I can't go in!"

Wentworth yanked him out of the car by his collar. "Trying to weasel out of explaining to the chief!" he demanded. "You're going right in, pal!"

He shoved the man forward. The announcer stumbled blindly, head down, along the treeshadowed sidewalk. Wentworth's eyes darted keenly about him. This was a residential neighborhood and lights were generally extinguished for the night. Ahead of him, the Conqueror's radio man stumbled dejectedly.

Abruptly, the radio man turned through a break in the high hedges beside which they walked. Wentworth was just behind him, every sense alert. The night was dead still. A few crickets chirped in the grass and somewhere a cat yowled. A block away a car's motor droned and faded. They moved beside a line hedge between two lots, where the grass was rank, the house untenanted. In its back yard there was a garage and on its door, the radio man thumped twice, kicked once, thumped again. The hollow sounds seemed loud in the night.

The door opened silently and Wentworth crowded his unaware prisoner into the inner darkness. He thrust the man strongly forward, stepped to the right. The sweep of his arm found the guard. He whipped the doorman into a left hook that snapped out his consciousness. Instantly, he squeezed light from a pocket torch and swept the garage. The radio man had stumbled to his knees. There was no other foe except the stunned guard.

"Get the door open!" Wentworth commanded.

The radio man's face was frightened as he screwed about. "Who are you?" he stammered.

"I killed Harpo," Wentworth snapped. "Maybe you want it, too?" He flipped out an automatic and cocked it with a click that sounded loud in the empty garage.

The radio man shivered. His hands fumbled, but finally effected the release of the trapdoor's catch. A slab of concrete hinged upward on counter balances and Wentworth was over the kneeling man. He had knocked out the guard because he could not afford to have enemies between himself and liberty along this thin line of retreat. He must protect his back-trail.

Now, for the same reason, he jabbed rigid fingers into his prisoner's throat. The compression on certain nerves knocked the man cold. He was no longer of any value. Wentworth's lips drew out thinly in a grim smile. He was under no delusion concerning the nature of the reception that would be tendered Case Brent. And that's where he finally steps out, a free man. Free, at least, in his body. He was expected.

Thoughtfully, he holstered his automatic. His light probed into the darkness below. An empty corridor would be reached by a vertical iron ladder from the trapdoor. He leaped the distance to the corridor's floor, landed lightly in a crouch. He spent a few seconds learning how to operate the trapdoor from within and closed it before he went forward. The very soles of his feet seemed alert for danger, testing the solidity of the floor over which he advanced. These close walls would megaphone a loud breath into a snake-hiss of warning. The *Spider*'s swift progress was soundless—but not unobserved!

THE probing of his light caught a flicker of movement at its extreme range. He identified it as the lifting of some barrier that had blocked the corridor. That opened door might mean a trap.

Wentworth's light, questing over the walls, caught an almost imperceptible break in their smoothness. But he did not even hesitate beside it. He kept on.

Two strides past the opening in the wall, he checked and waited. There was still no sound but, suddenly, he clicked off his torch. When a man is in a closed space, any break in its walls becomes as abruptly apparent to him as if his brain encased a radar which could spot the distance of any object toward which it was directed. He knew that a door in the wall against which he pressed had been opened and that the enemy was prepared to attack.

The laughter of the *Spider* whispered within him, but he stopped it in his throat. It was always thus when he went into battle against odds. These men who came against him were less quiet than he. There was the whisper of a footfall and the sound of tense breathing. Only two of them! But then, they didn't know they moved against the *Spider*! They expected only Case Brent.

RICHARD WENTWORTH

The memory of that fact was like a douse of cold water in his face. He must not fight too well! The battle thrill faded from him. His guns were still in their holsters. The two men were almost upon him. Their breathing was ridiculously loud. Wentworth's eyes narrowed. The sound of that breathing was above the level of his head! The men who hunted him were well over six feet tall, and probably big in proportion.

Wentworth crouched close to the floor and, with the suddenness of a tiger's charge, he sprang to the attack. He drove between the two men and his arms hooked about their legs. He had not left his feet but, like a football linesman, he kept his body, weight and strength surging forward. His arms locked like vises about the knees of the men. Their bulk was apparent for those knees were like the knotty trunks of trees. As he went past and behind the two men, Wentworth straightened and lifted.

There was a confused shout in the darkness as the men pitched forward. Wentworth pivoted and leaped like a leopard upon the back of the man on his left. The assailant had caught himself on hands and knees. Straddling the man's torso, Wentworth felt the muscles bunch and writhe between his knees. Wentworth's hands flashed out. One of his arms, levering over a swelling shoulder, heaved up the man's head. The other struck like a snake at the throat. With a gasp, the man collapsed to the floor. Wentworth dove straight forward over his head, balled, landed silently on his feet. He waited, breath light and shallow, soundless.

In the darkness, there was scrambling and a whisper: "Bo?" Then there was a great coarse oath. The other killer had found Bo's body. Wentworth heard the man blunder forward, careless, furious. It was easily possible to tell within inches where the other was. He checked, turned and charged the other way. He pivoted—the rasp of his shoe leather told that—and was suddenly quiet. He thought he was quiet. An insect walking made more noise than the *Spider* as once more he glided to the attack.

He reached out and slapped the man across the mouth!

Bellowing, the killer charged—empty air! For Wentworth had leaped back, kept just ahead of the man. Once more, Wentworth slapped him. The other's charge was like a bull's—and this time, Wentworth let him rip past in the darkness. He tripped him, kicked him as he fell, slapped his face as he rolled. Then from a distance of twenty swiftly covered feet, he laughed.

It was not *Spider* laughter, but the sound of it was blood-chilling, senseless and mad. In an instant he was beside the fallen man again. In the darkness, he used his pocket knife—and drew the dull back of the blade across the man's throat.

That finished the fight. The man leaped to his feet with a scream of sheer panic. He raced down the corridor and off at right angles through the side passage. His screams kept on.

"My throat's cut! My throat's cut!"

Ten feet behind him, the *Spider* kept pace, knowing that in his blindness, the man would spring any traps—and lead him to his master! Suddenly, the fugitive burst into a room that was all blackness save for a single focus of brilliant light that silhouetted a massive head, the rigid shoulders of the Conqueror!

The fugitive hurled himself to his knees and babbled that he was dying, that his throat was cut.

Behind him, Wentworth closed the door and leaned his shoulders against it carelessly, gazing straight at the Conqueror across the quivering and defeated killer's prostrate form. It was as Case Brent that he spoke: "All your men are fools, Chief," he swaggered. "You really need my brains and guts around here! Me, Case Brent!"

CHAPTER FIVE
Jaws of Hell

THE Conqueror made no move at all. There was utterly no fear in the man, only a vast contempt for these puppets who were under his domination. His voice, when it issued, was a thin whisper of drawn steel.

"Kill the fool!"

Case Brent said, "Sure, chief!"

The man on the floor rolled and came to his feet with the smoothness of a cat. He was turned so that the light washed across his chest and made black valleys between the swell of his muscles. Hate glittered palely from his eyes. He took a sharp stride forward and, as he moved, his hand flashed to his belt and he was driving a wide bladed knife at Wentworth's middle.

The *Spider* would have evaded that knife, broken the man's arm with a deft snap and hurled him across the room to death against the wall. But this was not the *Spider*. It was Case Brent. He jumped backward a yard, brought up against the wall and pulled out an automatic. He began pumping bullets of execution into the body of this giant killer. They were heavy bullets, with a high shocking power. They shook the killer, stopped him, drove him back a step, hammered him into extinction upon the floor. It was a gangster-type killing, not the clean swift execution of the *Spider*.

Still it was justice. Within minutes, this man had been intent upon a stab-in-the-back murder of Wentworth!

As the giant fell, Wentworth sprang toward him. His face, mimicking Case Brent, was contorted with fury. Curses dripped from his mouth in a piercing whisper, but his lips did not move. That was the way men spoke in prison, and he was just freed of seven years in Alcatraz!

"The yellow-back!" he hissed. "There was a screw just like you on the Rock." He kicked him again, and rage mounted. "A man ain't a man to you. He ain't got no name. He—" He checked himself abruptly, shrugged and forced out a strained laugh. "Sorry, chief," he said. "Those screws at the Rock—"

"*Three-forty-seven!*" the Conqueror's voice was flat, emotionless.

Wentworth snapped to attention, then snarled and relaxed. His heart gave a leap of exultation. He had, by his words, hoped to suggest such a test of identity to this criminal overlord, and the man had accepted his bait.

"Don't do that to me, chief!" he whined, but there was an undertone of threat in his voice. "I had seven years of that, and it's plenty. I—"

"Shut up, Brent!" There was the same flat tonelessness, but the impact of his contempt was like a blow.

Wentworth held his breath to make his face flush. He had a very careful role to play. He must convince this man absolutely of his identity. To do that, he must play a double, even a triple part. He must be swaggering and efficient. He must indicate his sly purpose to seize control as Case Brent. And yet, as Case Brent, he must manage to suggest to this brilliant and powerful mind that he could be controlled and, at need, removed.

So now he let hatred show in his eyes and he let his glance steal secretly toward his flanks to indicate fear of attack. He opened his mouth to speak, and then didn't. It was the Conqueror who broke the silence.

"It is possible I can use you," he said flatly. "You have cost me a number of valuable men, and for that you will be fined. If you prove yourself half as good as you say you are, I'll allow you to take over Harpo's rackets. But—at the first treachery, I'll destroy you!" Again that whisper of drawn steel. It cut.

Wentworth permitted himself to shudder faintly, immediately hid that with a weak swagger. "Hell, chief," he said, "I came to you because I knowed you was smart, and would appreciate a smart guy like me. I want to play your game, that's all. Just tell me what to do and I'll show you I'm the man who can do it for you. Me, Case Brent!"

The contempt of the Conqueror's voice increased. "You will remain here until I send for you."

The light went out and Wentworth knew suddenly that he was alone. But he would be under observation, no doubt of that. He could not, for one instant, forget that he was Case Brent. He did now as Case

Brent would have done. He waited for a while in silence, called out questioningly and in fear. He turned on his pocket torch and cursed to find himself alone in an empty room, except for the guard he had slain. He tested the door, found it locked and, after that, he moved restlessly about the room for what seemed a long time. Finally, he sat down uncomfortably against the wall and lit a cigarette, waiting.

Exultation burned within him. He had passed the first test. It would have been very easy—he thought it would have been easy—to kill this overlord. It might have had some value, but in the end only one thing would straighten out this city and end the reign of criminal terror—the rebirth of honesty among officials.

First, he must learn the workings of this organization and trace out its tentacles. By now, Nita should have mailed the list of grafting police to Alexander Height and Morris Dutton, the two civic leaders whose help would be invaluable in the *Spider*'s plans.

He had won the first exchange. The next move was up to the Conqueror!

IN ANOTHER room, the Conqueror sat in the darkness which he seemed to prefer and spoke into a phone-mike. "You have done well," he said. "No, I will not question the woman tonight. Bring her in the morning. Meantime, tell her nothing."

He released the button which closed the mike off and, in his black sanctum, he allowed himself to smile faintly. It was not perhaps too important that he would have the woman of Case Brent his prisoner. Such men rated women at no value, which was wisdom, but they told them things, and that was insanity. He would be able to check on Case Brent a bit more fully. Afterward, he would decide whether to hold the woman prisoner or to kill her. It was not of much importance, one way or the other.

Meanwhile, he would sleep for three hours. It was all he allowed himself, all he required. He was very proud of his ability to do with little sleep. To him, it was only another indication of his superiority to all other human beings.

He threw a switch and heard Case Brent talking to himself. Men got that habit in prison.

"I'll play along with this high and mighty bird," Case Brent was mumbling. "Sure, I'll play his game, and take his guff until I get everything in my hands, and then—" The voice broke off, and the Conqueror knew the sublime pictures of murder Case Brent would be forming.

The Conqueror smiled once more, in contempt. He had gauged his man correctly. Yes, he could use Brent. The Conqueror almost chuckled. The

"Three-forty-seven!" The Conqueror's voice was flat, emotionless.

end would be not very different from the one Case Brent was picturing now, but Case Brent would be on the receiving end.

The Conqueror threw off all the switches except those that connected with the electric guards about his chamber. He closed his lids over his eyes and allowed sleep to claim him.

Hunted men do not sleep as other men sleep. They live in eternal vigilance. Two hours of sleep, and they awake, to smoke a cigarette, to prowl about and peer into blackness—then back to sleep again. In the space of a few hours they again awake and once more feel out their surroundings.

On this night and day, Wentworth slept like that. Even in such matters as this, he followed out the character he portrayed. It was in the light sleep following such a period that he became aware of men entering the room where he rested. He sprang to his feet at once, gun in his fist.

The three men who had come in looked at him curiously and kept well away from him. They did not speak even by nodding their heads. Their eyes were hostile, reserved, waiting. Wentworth slowly holstered his automatic and let a sneer crawl across his lips. He, too, waited. His manner showed that, when the time came, he'd show them who was boss.

Once more the Conqueror was suddenly in the room, under the blaze of the light that silhouetted the powerful line of his head and shoulders and gave no other hint of his appearance.

"Your orders for tonight," he began abruptly, "are simple. Brent here will be in charge. A disturbance will be created at the meeting tonight of Height's fools. There are three men who are to be beaten up and put in the hospital. Brent, I'll supply you with a fingerman. You'll do the rest. That's all."

Wentworth showed a scowling frown. "Hell, chief, that's two-cent stuff," he protested. "Me, I'm Case Brent. I—"

"You will obey!" the Conqueror stated. "There is no discussion of my orders. You obey, and you succeed, or *you will be destroyed!*"

Once more, Wentworth made a flush swell into his face by holding his breath. He finally spoke, thickly, "Okay, chief."

Behind his angry face, his thoughts were racing. Alexander Height had seemed to him a wrong-headed but sincere man, with mistaken ideas about the city, its politics and its police force. But Height, from the standpoint of criminals, would seem to be valuable since he urged the people to cease to doubt their local government and to trust their police force... which Wentworth knew to be crooked. Yet the Conqueror was deliberately fomenting trouble at such a meeting and, moreover, was ordering assault upon certain adherents.

It didn't fit. Wentworth was suspicious of anything that scouted logic in the behavior of such a man as the Conqueror. They were alone in the room now—the Conqueror had withdrawn and the three men still eyed Wentworth like hostile dogs. He had to swagger over them and bully them, and he did it while his thoughts paced steadily on. He watched them for signs of mockery, but there were none. They plainly accepted their orders at face value. It had not escaped Wentworth that the whole setup might be planned deliberately to destroy Case Brent. But, if it had, he was reasonably sure these men knew nothing about that fact.

BELOW, in his other chamber, the Conqueror was allowing the weight of his anger to fall upon the Chief of Police of the city of Garago. That official sat in red-faced anger and absorbed the punishment that was meted out.

"You will endeavor to use your brain power a bit more effectively," the Conqueror bit out, "or I shall be forced to replace you with a cleverer man. In the first place, you have allowed your men to grow careless about accepting graft. In the second place, you have allowed evidence of those payments to accumulate, so that the list which was placed in Alexander Height's hands can be substantiated. In the third place—"

Chief Poland shifted uncomfortably. "Wait a minute, now," he protested. "I can't keep track of all my men. I didn't do any of that. If some of the fools get caught, to hell with them. I—"

"*Silence!*" The word was like a slap in the face. Chief Poland gasped, and was silent. His face was blanched with fear. "I'm not interested in a catalogue of your failures," the Conqueror said flatly. "You will turn them into successes." He did not threaten, but threat was implicit in his tones. "Tonight, Height will be killed. The fool has outlived his usefulness. Morris Dutton and several of his Law-and-Order Men will be present by arrangement. Dutton will not be killed, but two others of his men will be. We are arranging evidence that Dutton prompted the murder of Height. You will find this evidence and the city will be reassured as to the efficiency of its police department, operating without fear or favor against even those highly placed persons who consider themselves above the law." There was a rich flavor of irony in the Conqueror's words. He was enjoying himself.

Chief Poland was ashy pale. "Good Heavens, man," he whispered. "You're asking me to become an accessory to murder and a frame-up!"

The Conqueror ignored him and pressed on. "Present at this meeting also will be one Case Brent, late of Alcatraz. He will not be captured, but you will arrange it so that he is publicized as a possible employee of Morris Dutton, with a full record of his past crimes. You will say he is wanted."

Chief Poland squirmed, opened his mouth... was silenced by the continued cold words of the Conqueror.

"We will continue to build up Case Brent as a master criminal," he said. "I intend to give him considerable power. He will be a fall guy for us. If the public presently becomes too aroused, we will throw him to the wolves. You, Poland, are supposed to be a wolf. You will gain considerable prestige by killing him personally. If we need another such fool presently, we will find one."

Chief Poland staggered to his feet. "I can't do this," he whispered. "I can't. I don't mind a little honest graft. It goes on everywhere all the time, but murder and accessory, frame-up—" His voice trickled off.

The Conqueror rose to his feet. "Fool," his voice was toneless. "Why must I always be served by cowards and fools? But I'll put steel into you! Listen, Poland, I can just as easily arrange for you to be blamed for Height's murder tonight. Would you prefer that?"

Poland shivered. His mouth was loose. The cold driving force of the man before him left him no will, no strength. "No," he whispered. "No. Of course not. I'll obey."

He fumbled his way out of the room and the Conqueror lifted a clenched fist above his head. The tension of that fist was terrible. He brought it down, and there was a cracking of a wooden table beneath its impact. Afterward, he was completely motionless.

He flipped a tumbler on the annunciator beside him. "Notify Deputy Craig of the police that I wish to see him, at once. Our emergency has arisen sooner than I expected. And add another name to the list of those to be killed tonight. Chief Poland."

He closed the cam and presently his lips smiled again. After all, it would build up the prestige of the police if their chief died heroically. And the police would be more firmly in his hands than ever before. He had known that sooner or later he would have to remove Poland.

He flicked another annunciator cam.

"Send to me the men who are going to set fire to Height's Hall tonight," he said. "I have some final instructions for them."

Panic, he decided. A few jammed escape doors to increase the death list. There must be a plentiful smoke screen to hide the real purpose, the real perpetrators of the murders. Besides, it was time to start putting the squeeze on the insurance companies. His organization was expensive, as all good organizations must be.

For a time, waiting for his arson squad, the Conqueror was a little depressed. He must always depend upon fools and weaklings! If only he had a few men from the home country who knew how to obey the orders of a master without question, and efficiency. Here in this damnable country, even the criminals were independent. But he had to have this country in his power. It was the hub of the world. When he had conquered here... he shook his head, impatient at any dream. First this city, then the state, the nation. Today, the city—tomorrow, the world!

He did not, at this point, even think of Case Brent or the woman he held in his power. They were unimportant pawns. And the stage was set for big happenings. After tonight, he would be in a three-times stronger position. There were only a few more moves on the chessboard and the city would be completely his.

The door opened and the three arsonists came in.

CHAPTER SIX
Murder Hall

ALTHOUGH the meeting this night in Height Hall had been called in the name of the Civic League, it was in reality a political rally. A portion of the general public came, those whose party ruled City Hall—the rest were party workers rounded up by energetic wheel horses—made an impressive mass as they slowly filled the auditorium which the Conqueror, with impartial murder in his heart, had elected as a funeral pyre for many of their number.

At the hour appointed for the rally to begin, a man came out and announced there would be music. A small orchestra filed in and began to play. A girl sang some songs. It was necessary to wait because the hall was still only partly filled and Alexander Height could scarcely address so small a meeting as this one.

In a little room off the stage where rostrum and chairs had been placed, Alexander Height sat and looked with deliberate austerity over the typed papers which contained the text of his speech. He published the *Garago Globe*—"First with the news, first with sound views."

Soundness was the keynote of his character, and of his appearance. He looked solid, like the facade of a bank. His frequently barbered head had a solid, squarish set with the scalp showing pinkly through cropped silver hair. He had senatorial aspirations—from the Senate to the White House was a not impossible step.

He looked up at the satellite assistants and was immediately a center of attentive faces.

"I have decided," he said, "that up to the time of my speech, everything will proceed according to schedule. You will talk, as usual, about trusting our city officials. Our theme, as usual, will be, 'support

your officials while they are in office. If you don't like them, kick them out, but while they are your officials, stand behind them.'"

All the men in the room were solid citizens, propertied gentlemen. One of them, Laskar Deeping, cleared his throat to answer Alexander Height. "Are you sure, Height," he asked, "that you are doing the right thing in exploding this bombshell of yours publicly? After all, Chief Poland is a reliable man, a sound man. If these facts were put before him, he would go about adjusting the situation quietly. There would be no scandal, no weakening of public support."

Height's smile was superior. "This cleanup will do more to make the people support us than anything else!" he said. "You don't understand public opinion as a publicist must. The public undoubtedly is aware of crookedness. A thorough housecleaning by the party in power, not forced from outside but done voluntarily by that party, with full publicity, will do more to confirm the public in its support of us than any other thing!"

He did not add that also it would establish Alexander Height in their minds as an honest man who put the public before his party—always a popular slant. He was well pleased with himself, and with his arrangements. His papers headlining his speech would hit the streets within minutes after he began to talk. He glanced at his watch. He must start soon.

"The auditorium is pretty well filled now," a man stuck in his head to report. "We can start, if you wish, Mr. Height."

There were close to a thousand people present now. The Conqueror thought of them as fools, whom presently he would rule as slaves, or twist into the chosen channel that would raise him to dominion. The *Spider* alone thought of them as human beings, as struggling working men and women, strong and independent in their opinions, fit to rule. Inasmuch as it was possible for one man to do so, he hoped to give them that opportunity.

The *Spider* was there as Case Brent and with him were four men. The finger who would point out the individuals whom the Conqueror wanted beaten into insensibility was beside him. Wentworth heard a whisper among the men at his back.

"There's the Sniper," it said. "Guess the chief has some other work going on here, too."

A grunt answered him. "Keep your nose out of it, Morgan, and keep your health."

Wentworth's eyes narrowed slightly over that intelligence. He had guessed that there would be more at stake than a mere beat-up. The man called Sniper must be an expert shot. That sounded like murder—

Below the auditorium there were many corridors and many storerooms. It was a fine place to start a fire, a big, blazing fire that would burst out with explosive suddenness and sweep under the entire building in a flash. It would be possible to have the whole building aflame in minutes by a judicious use of gasoline and time bombs. The arsonists had those instruments of arson.

Wentworth was aware of increasing tension in his breast. Height certainly had, by this time, the police graft list which also had been sent to the head of the Law-and-Order League. Wentworth's questing glance raked about the hall. There were the usual number of police guards and fire-watchers. Up front was a man he identified as Chief Poland. As he watched, the Chief mopped the back of his neck with his handkerchief. There was a perceptible tremor in the hand—and the hall was not hot. Did Poland have an inkling of what was to happen tonight?

A faint smile stirred Wentworth's eyes, and his plan of action sprang, fully formed, into his mind. He needed more information about Height and this was his opportunity to acquire it. It was possible also he could force into the open exact knowledge of the night's plans.

Wentworth spoke to the fingerman, without moving his lips, without turning his head. "The punks in sight yet?"

"Not yet."

WENTWORTH grunted. "Go down and tell Chief Poland that Case Brent wants to talk to him. And tell him to come to the men's room alone, or else! Get it?"

The fingerman's head whipped about and there was shock in his eyes. "You carrying out orders, or doing something extra?" he demanded.

Wentworth thrust his face close to the man's. "The chief said I was in charge, didn't he? What do you think? Hop to it!" He walked, swaggering, up the side aisle toward the back of the auditorium to the rest room. From a phone booth there, he put in a call to Nita's hotel. Presently Ram Singh answered.

"Sahib," his voice was subdued. "The missie sahib sent me on an errand. When I returned, she was not here. That was this morning. I did not know how to reach you, sahib, and—"

"In disguise?" Wentworth cut in, sharply.

"Sahib, I do not know!"

Wentworth stepped out of the booth with a cold readiness that amounted almost to rage. If the enemy had identified him, they had moved with more swiftness than seemed possible. If Nita van Sloan had been captured, in disguise as Case Brent's friend, he had reason to walk carefully.

Wentworth loved Nita van Sloan. The knowledge that she was undoubtedly in criminal hands was like a hot knife in his breast. But this was the torment through which he must live. It was their proved understanding that the service to which they were dedicated must always come first. Their own lives were secondary in their battle.

Despite his super-human accomplishments, the *Spider* was a man, and Nita was the woman he loved. Though he did not waver in his decision, there was an extra vehemence in his every movement, and anger smouldered just under the steel of his control.

When Chief Poland strode into the rest room, it was apparent that the Chief, also, was angry, because he was uncertain. As the Chief, he did not do things at the behest of criminals, but he knew that Case Brent was one of the Conqueror's men, even though foredoomed. He came and, inside the door, he called out cautiously, impatiently.

"*Brent!*"

There was a whisper of laughter behind him, and Poland jerked about awkwardly on his short legs. His breath sucked in and his head wrenched up with shock. The crouched, menacing figure behind the door was swathed from neck to heels in a black cape. A remorseless face was shadowed under the brim of a broad black slouch hat.

The Chief cried: "The *Spider!*"

"Brent is—indisposed, Poland," the *Spider* said softly. "I am happy to greet you in his place!"

Poland took a sidling step toward the door. The *Spider's* hand reached out and clamped about his throat, not in strangulation, but in grim and silent warning.

"Listen, Poland," his voice was almost gentle, but the touch of his fingers was like steel. "Listen, Poland, you are a type I hate above all others. You are a public official who has betrayed his trust. You have allowed your men to become grafters. I suspect much more that that. I suspect that you receive money, and orders, from the underworld ruler of this city!" He shook Poland slightly. "I should hate to have that knowledge confirmed, Poland, wouldn't you?"

Poland tried to get out words and couldn't. His face was livid.

The *Spider's* lips drew back thinly from his teeth. "There is only one thing that would save you, should my suspicions be confirmed: if, in the meantime, you had made every effort to straighten out your affairs and eliminate crime from Garago. As a first step, I suggest that you should call on Alexander Height, now, and tell him about the graft in the force and what you are going to do to correct it!" There was a breath of laughter, cold as the wind of death. "I leave this to your free will, Poland. Should you decide not to accept my advice, I will have to apply *other* measures!"

He shook Poland again and his fingers clamped lightly on nerve centers in the Chief's throat. The room reeled before Poland's eyes. He staggered back, struck the wall, and darkness swam in his brain. When he could see and think again, he was alone in the rest room. The *Spider* had vanished!

There was a terrible compression in Chief Poland's chest, as if he were strangling. He staggered out of the room, and leaned against the wall. His hands shook as he tried to light a cigarette, but fear would not let him stand there. He had to do what the *Spider* ordered. It would not conflict with the Conqueror's plan. He could tell the Conqueror that he had merely wanted to make sure that Height intended exposure. He threw down the unlighted cigarette and almost trotted out of the hallway.

At the back of Height Hall, there was a corridor that led from a small outside door to the speakers' chambers off the stage. Into that dimness, a shadowy figure in black robes stole. Swiftly, the *Spider's* eyes cast about the passage. There was a door under a narrow stairway that led upward, another that would open into the auditorium, and a third into the speakers' chambers.

The *Spider* chose the door under the stairs. It would be a closet, or a basement entrance. There was no sound as he reached that door. He whipped it open with soft violence. There were two men crouched in the darkness. They had guns in their hands. Those weapons jerked into line on the *Spider's* breast.

CHAPTER SEVEN
The Hour Strikes

THE *SPIDER* made no perceptible pause

between the opening of the door and the moment he struck. His life many times had hinged upon his instantaneous response to emergency. He saw an emergency, and as quickly as jerking a hand away from heat, he reacted—and attacked!

Feet first, he drove into those two men crouched on the steps. The door clapped shut as he went through. One heel drove against the jaw of a gunman. He looped an iron-hard arm under the chin of the second. They went down the stairs into darkness that way. The unconscious body of the first gunman was a cushion for the fall. Wentworth took occasion to knock the head of his second captive against the wall. There was some noise, but not much. The stairs were concrete and so was the floor. Swiftly, the *Spider* searched his two prisoners.

There was nothing in their pockets except money. No papers—not even any keys. There were guns and ammunition. But there was something else that made Wentworth draw up as tautly as a tow cable. There was an odor of *gasoline!*

For an instant, Wentworth hesitated. He had come here to see Alexander Height, to test him and to warn him. Gasoline on these men's clothes could spell but one thing—arson! A firetrap was set for the hundreds in the auditorium!

Wentworth swore, and the sound was rasping, bitter. He tossed the one gunman who remained alive to his shoulder and went up the stairs in swift, effortless bounds. Behind him, he left a criminal who would prey no more upon the public—a criminal marked with the *Spider* seal—a crimson sprawling figure of menace upon his forehead.

At the door of the speakers' room, the *Spider* paused for a heartbeat and heard the heavy timber of a man's voice.

"I know I am right," the voice was saying. "There is no other way. This thing must be smashed into the people's face. Never mind Chief Poland. He's in on this, and he has to go. I tell you we will gain more prestige—"

The *Spider* opened the door and threw the unconscious body he carried upon the desk in front of Alexander Height. Men saw the threat of the twin guns in his fists. They stood, rigid statues of fright, of bewilderment. Height's face paled, then flushed angrily. Before he could speak, the *Spider* was talking. His voice was low. His words struck like bullets.

"I sent you that list of grafters, Height," he said. "Tell your friends to remain quiet a moment and listen. Chief Poland and these others are only pawns in this battle. There is a criminal behind them, a man of the type you gentlemen do not believe exists. A ruthless killer. A megalomaniac Hitler of Crime! He doesn't want those grafters

publicized. He has planted murderers in your auditorium. This man and another were planted in the back entrance way, possibly to kill you, Height. Do you notice the odor on that man's clothing? Gasoline! Do you guess what that means? It means fire! Arson! Perhaps massacre—as a cover-up for the murderers. There's only one possible course—clear the hall until the firetrap has been uncovered. Up on your feet, Height! Get moving!"

Height's face had a stubborn set, but his gaze was fixed on the *Spider*'s eyes, and his brain was receiving the swift words thrown at him. He pushed to his feet.

"They wouldn't dare!" he gasped. "*They wouldn't dare!*"

The *Spider* had timed things perfectly. At that moment the door opened and Chief Poland, of the police, stepped into the room.

In a leap, the *Spider* had him by the shoulder, had whipped him inside the room. Holding him pinned on the point to his gun muzzle, Wentworth threw his swift words at Height.

"Ask Poland!" he said. "Ask him if the man who secretly rules Garago would dare to murder you and set this building afire!"

Poland's mouth popped open and sweat beaded his pallid forehead. Guilt was etched like burning letters upon his face. Height roared: "You grafter! So you'd conspire to murder me?"

Chief Poland whispered, "No, no! I came to tell you I couldn't go through with it. You've got to believe me, Height. I never dreamed—I'm an honest man—I wouldn't—"

The *Spider* whipped out of the room, clapped the door shut and was speeding toward the entrance to the auditorium. Height would act now! As he moved, he swept off the cape, the steel mask that disguised his features, and the broad hat. He thrust them into a dark corner and stepped through the door once again disguised as Case Brent.

There was a speaker on the platform now, just getting warmed up, a preliminary to the main bout when Alexander Height would deliver his startling news of graft—a secret until then.

"...how can the police operate efficiently to protect you," he was saying, "when you, the people, do not treat them with confidence? You must go to them with your knowledge and enable them to gather evidence against the criminals. Only in that way can you have a police force that actually polices. Support your city—"

As Wentworth slid in beside his men again, the fingerman nodded at him: the speaker, Lacker Deeping, was one of those Case Brent was to beat

Terror shook them... and in that moment the *Spider* turned the corner behind them....

up and put in the hospital. Another man came hurriedly to the platform, whispered to the speaker. Immediately, he swung into his peroration, and gave the introduction for Alexander Height's appearance. Applause clattered through the house.

Wentworth said, "Hell, we can't do nothing in here. We'll have to wait until the meeting's over. I'm going where I can breathe better."

Once more in the robes of the *Spider*, he raced down the steps and into the dim corridors of the basement. Here there was an awful confirmation of his deduction. The odor of gasoline was rank. So thick were the fumes that he knew the spark of a gun might set off the entire roaring inferno. And then he saw two men at the far end of the corridor. They saw the shadow of his passage, the sweeping bell of the cape like the black wings of death.

Terror caught them by the throat. They flung up their weapons and fired.

The bullets screamed down the corridor, ricocheted off the walls... and the *Spider* could not fire back. Here death waited, not only for him, but for all those hundreds above, if this firetrap was touched off. He raced on, twisting, bent double, charging into the mouths of those guns. The menacing laughter of the *Spider* whispered from his lips.

The sound of that laughter, the revelation of the identity of the man at whom they fired, worked its fearful magic. The swift vengeance of the *Spider* was the one thing which lawless killers dreaded. It disconcerted their aim. What use was it to fire on the *Spider*? Their bullets seemed to take no effect. He did not even trouble to return their fire.

Terror shook them and they turned and fled from

that soundless charge, from the whisper of eerie laughter that beat in their ears. The *Spider* pivoted the corner behind them, and was clear of the fumes of gasoline. The twin guns were suddenly in his hands, twin wasps of death. They spoke their piece, and the peremptory echoes of their voice never reached the ears of the fleeing men. The lead was swifter. It cut off their hearing and their lives.

The two men went down into bulky, awkward heaps of clothing upon the floor. Over them, the *Spider* crouched briefly. His seal burned their foreheads. His swift hands searched them and found nothing to identify them, or to link them with the man who had sent them out to loose massacre upon the helpless hundreds in the hall.

The *Spider* whirled to race back along that corridor to find and root out any infernal machines, possibly already planted, and he heard a hissing violence of sound. It was not loud, but it was fierce and bitter with energy. He knew the sound of burning thermite. He was already too late. Already, the four-thousand degree heat of that flame was slashing out into gasoline laden rooms!

The *Spider* hurled himself prone between the bodies of the slain, whipped his cape close about him, ground his face into the floor. Heat swept over him. It was flaring, terrible heat. His clothing was ignited in an instant.

The flash of the initial blast died down and in its wake came the low mutter of flames, already beginning to roar. The *Spider* rolled swiftly on the concrete, blotting out the flames that touched him. He careened to his feet and raced for the stairs. He was staggering. The heat was mounting swiftly. Within instants, the wooden beams overhead would ignite spontaneously. He made the stairs, reeled up them. He could hear the tramp of feet now, of stumbling, panic-driven feet. He could hear the screams of women and the hoarse shouts of men.

As he ran, he also heard a sudden fury of gunshots.

The assassins had struck. The *Spider* raced on, into the face of death, into the challenge of hostile guns, intent upon only one thing—the salvation of the trapped humans whose screams spoke already of despair, and death, and doom.

CHAPTER EIGHT
The Conqueror's Way

CALMLY certain of the success of his plans, the Conqueror had turned his mind to other matters. From the flare of light that left his face in darkness, he looked toward the woman who, cringingly, sat upon a chair across the room from him.

"I don't know nothing about Case Brent," she protested violently. "He said he was a big shot and he threw away dough like he was. He says he's going to take over this town, and if I stick with him, I'll dress in diamonds. What the hell!" She shrugged spasmodically. "I like diamonds."

But in spite of her harsh words, Nita van Sloan's violet eyes looked glazed with fear and she was enough of an actress to be able to create lines of strain by the expression of her mouth, by the movements of her hands. So far, she was certain, the Conqueror had no idea that Case Brent was anything but what he seemed.

She made her voice shrill, "He ain't nothing to me! A meal ticket is all. But I ain't had no diamonds yet."

The Conqueror considered through a minute of silence that ticked into eternity. Nita wet her lips and made her expression sly. "I don't know nothing about him, but I might could find out. He talks an awful lot."

Men who depended on women were fools—men who used them must be careful. They were not trustworthy fools—especially women of this stamp. They had no compunctions, no scruples, no morals. Properly handled, told nothing, this ottoman might have her use. Her only loyalty was to herself, money, possessions, fear. She was smiling now.

"Come here," the Conqueror commanded.

Triumph flickered in the woman's eyes. In her red, tight dress, she came swaying toward him. The light glare was blinding. She blinked, trying to see through it. Suddenly, she was caught and forced to her knees. Her dress ripped back from her shoulder and something agonizingly hot burned into her shoulder. She staggered back, gasping at the pain. On the floor, at her feet, the Conqueror contemptuously flung a packet of money.

The Conqueror's voice rang coldly. "That was a promise," he said. "The money is yours. Pick it up."

Nita van Sloan throttled her fury and her impulse to destroy this egocentric brute. She picked up the money and pretended she wanted it. The Conqueror's voice ran on, suavely, murderously gentle.

"For service, I pay well," he said. "For failure—I have other payments. *Go!*"

It was not as simple as that to leave the Conqueror's domain. A man with ugly eyes gave her information as to how she could get in touch with a man who would relay her reports. She was blindfolded and driven for an indeterminate distance at a leisurely pace. Nita van Sloan forced herself into an appearance of patience. Each second of delay was a torment. It had been hours since she had been taken prisoner, and it had happened just after she had mailed to Height and to Morris Dutton the lists of grafters as Dick Wentworth had told her. The aching question in her mind was whether the Conqueror knew about Height and Dutton.

That was the idea she tried to keep in the forefront of her mind, because it was in accordance with Wentworth's dictum that service to the public came before service to self. But, under the surface of her thoughts, fear ran like a molten river. Her capture by the Conqueror, and the slight questioning, indicated doubts of Case Brent. The Conqueror

was not a man who needed certainty for action. At the first doubt, he would destroy.

Nita suppressed a shudder and her hand went unconsciously to the torn shoulder of her dress where the burn throbbed in her flesh. Apparently, she had succeeded in fooling the Conqueror. Nita van Sloan's teeth were set on her lip. From now on, she would be watched day and night and even an attempt to shake off her shadowers would arouse suspicions. How fortunate it was that she had been in disguise when she was captured. The mere discovery of the fact that she played a double role would be fatal.

Resolutely, Nita thrust fear out of her mind. Fear always had the effect of preventing clear thought. She had need of all her clarity of reason now. Her first duty was plain. She must reach Alexander Height and Morris Dutton and warn them that the enemy probably was aware that they had received lists of grafters from her—that they must take all steps to protect themselves from *murder!*

"Where are you taking me?" she demanded abruptly of the driver beside her.

The man said, flatly, "Where we got you from. Keep your trap shut."

THE leisurely crawl of the car continued and, after an eternity, the blindfold was whipped from her eyes. Her dazzled gaze presently made out the main street of Garago. She leaned over to look in the rearvision mirror, set her hat and hair to rights. When the car presently stopped, she got out with a studied sneer at the driver.

"I'll know you next time," she said, angrily. "My big shot will take care of you!"

The man gave no answer. His face remained impassive but ugly laughter flared in his eyes. Nita swung away and hurried down the street. It was a quarter before nine, she saw by a clock in a jeweler's window. How much time did she have? The killers might already have struck! She could not search out the shadowers she was sure were behind her. She must keep her actions natural. She spotted a barroom where there was a mixed crowd, and swung abruptly through the doors.

She waited for her drink while impatience burned through her. Did Dick Wentworth know she had vanished? Probably, if he had called Ram Singh as was his plan. She nursed her drink, letting her eyes search the room by looking into the bar mirror. No one had entered the place after her. She looked at the drink with distaste. She didn't want it, but she had to keep in character. She tossed it off, and then looked about, casually, spotted the women's room and went to it. As she had expected, there was a phone booth in there. Height wasn't home. Dutton wasn't home.

"This is urgent," she told Dutton's secretary. "Mr. Dutton received certain information by mail today. I have had reason since then to think that certain criminals know that fact. That information was of such a nature that Mr. Dutton's life probably is in danger—serious, immediate danger. It is absolutely imperative that he be warned of this, and that he make very sure of the authenticity of all messages or phone calls he may receive. They might be intended to lead him into a murder trap!"

The voice of the man who answered grew sharp. "I don't know you. I can't give you any information about Mr. Dutton's movements."

Nita said urgently, "I can understand that. But I place upon you the responsibility of getting my message to him at the first possible moment. Any delay may cause his death. I am completely certain of this."

The man's voice sounded worried as he answered, "Mr. Dutton received a phone call a while ago. I know where he has gone. I'll do my best."

He hung up and Nita van Sloan sucked in a breath of relief. She had done all that was possible at this time, but in Height's case, she had got no satisfaction at all. The man who had answered was plainly a butler, and had been able to give no help. Something more must be done about Height. For a moment she hesitated over phoning the *Garago Globe*, which he owned. It was when she was going back toward the bar that she saw a printed placard announcing a meeting of the Civic League, to be addressed this night by Alexander Height.

Even as the significance of that fact thrilled through her, Nita became aware that a man was watching her. He had not been at the bar when she entered. Nita turned abruptly and moved toward the side door. The man hurriedly slapped money on the bar and tossed his drink; came after her. But Nita did not go out the side door. Instead, she sat down at a table, as if to wait for somebody. She looked up at the clock, shrugged irritably and signaled to a waiter.

The watcher did not know whether he had been observed, but having made that fast start for the side door, he could not check his exit now without attracting attention. He went past Nita's table without a glance and, as soon as he had gone out, Nita returned to the women's room. It would have been an amusing game of cat-and-mouse but for the need for haste. Alexander Height's life hung in the balance!

Out of sight, Nita nevertheless could peer into the barroom occasionally. The man came back in the front door, looked sharply about, then hurried to speak to a waiter and pointed toward her table. The waiter shrugged and jerked his head toward the side door and the front door, shrugged again. The man went hurriedly back out the door.

Two minutes later, her follower shaken, Nita entered a cab a block away and sent it racing toward Height Hall.

Two blocks from the auditorium, Nita became aware of the stench of burning gasoline upon the air. It startled her. She leaned sharply forward in the seat, stared toward the hall. Against the street lights was a thickening brown haze of smoke.

A few people burst, running, from the doors of the auditorium!

The taxi jerked to a halt. "Height Hall's on fire!" the driver said wonderingly.

"Turn in a fire alarm!" Nita snapped. She flung a bill at the man and jumped out to the pavement. There was no hesitation about her now. Gasoline could mean only one thing—arson. And arson meant that the Conqueror had murder plans against Height. It could, in view of her knowledge, mean nothing else.

She raced toward the building, her heels clicking out a frenzied machine gun beat of speed. A glance showed her that the front door was an impossible entrance. It was jammed with people who fought to escape from the threat of fiery death within. She wheeled and raced along the building's side, seeking another entrance. There were doors here, fire doors. They were shut fast, and within Nita could hear the screams and the beating fists of men and women as they sought to dislodge the barrier that separated them from safety.

Nita ran to the doors and sought some handle, something by which she could aid those struggling people inside. The outer surface of the fire doors was blank, but at the bottom and top, thin wedges of steel had been driven in to secure them. Criminals had sealed the doors of escape so that human beings would perish horribly! Nita choked with horror, whirled from that door. On the opposite walk, three men stared openmouthed at her. Nita gestured to them imperatively.

"Get crowbars!" she shouted. "Axes! Any tools you can think of to release these doors! They've been wedged at the top and bottom. Hurry! People are dying!"

TWO OF the men looked at each other and then turned and ran in different directions. The third man came toward her. As he reached beneath his coat, Nita saw a badge. He was a city detective. No matter. He would not interfere. No man was crooked enough to turn his back on people dying by fire!

"See," Nita pointed to the wedges, "someone has deliberately fastened these doors. I think that if you hold your gun here, and shoot at the side of the wedge, that you will loosen it." She demonstrated the proper position.

The detective looked at her with puzzled eyes, then stared speculatively at the wedges. The screams within hurried him. He lifted the revolver, fired. The pressure on the door drove it outward and the wedge was freed. People screamed their way into the open. The slam of the door caught the detective and spun him backward. He looked around for the girl in the red dress who had gauged the action of gunfire so accurately. He saw Nita just ducking into a rear door of the auditorium.

He looked at his gun, holstered it and then, deliberately, he walked after the girl. The Chief had warned him to look out for funny stuff tonight. But there were plenty of uniformed men to look after the people inside. And the fire boys would be here in a shake. Detective Faile took up the trail of the girl in red.

Inside, in the dimness of a black hall, Nita van Sloan hesitated. It was insufferably hot here. Black smoke seeped out around a door under a flight of narrow steps. There were other doors. She moved toward them, and beyond one, she heard the screams of trapped people. There was the deep subdued roaring sound of the fire. Nita opened the door, and was in the auditorium. As she stepped into sight, people suddenly rushed toward her. They had not known about that door until she showed in it, bright in her red dress. Nita jumped hurriedly aside from their charge.

Detective Faile was caught in the rush of fleeing people. He was driven back into the street, where he fought frantically against the stream of fugitives. Detective Faile was a man of single-track mentality. He had started to go in, and he was going in. For the present, the crowd stopped him. But not for long.

In the auditorium, Nita van Sloan became aware of one voice raised dynamically above the bedlam of panic. She worked her way into the dark auditorium until she could see the stage. On the speakers' rostrum, in a focus of flashlights, a solid looking man, scalp red through thin-cropped, silver hair, was shouting out admonitions to the people to be calm, to take their time—that help was on the way. They would be saved. He, Alexander Height, gave them his solemn promise. The lights were out in the auditorium. Aside from the flashlights, the only illumination came from a red flicker of fire that had thrust through the floor and licked out its ugly tongue at the terror-driven crowd. Against that red glare, Nita saw the silhouettes of two men crouched together. They did not seem frightened. They were facing toward the speaker. She saw a glitter of steel in the hand of one of them.

Terror caught Nita by the throat then. She had

been right in her surmise. They were about to assassinate Alexander Height. Nita cried out a shrill warning: "Mr. Height! Assassins! Guns! Hide!"

She ripped off a high-heeled slipper and flung it with all her strength at the face of the gunman twenty feet away. Her aim was true. The whirling slipper caught him below the eye. He shouted, stumbled backward. His gun lanced flame through the dimness, but the bullet sped wide.

At the same instant, a gun crashed from the opposite side of the auditorium. This time the scarlet flicker of powder flame was not directed toward the stage, but toward the dark rows of seats.

Nita heard a man scream, and saw him pitch backward over the seats. There had been two groups of assassins, and a friendly gun had knocked over one of them. Nita had foiled the others. She dared not hope that the friendly gun was grasped in the hand of Dick Wentworth. She dared not—but she did.

Alexander Height had dodged out of sight, was safe for the moment, but the two gunman at whom Nita had thrown her slipper were still very much in evidence. Their curses were fierce. They clattered over the seats toward her, and their guns caught the ugly glint of the fire.

Nita crouched low, darted between the seats. She clasped her other slipper in her hand. The heel would make a feeble weapon, but it was all she had. Under her feet the floor was hot. She dropped flat and wriggled between the legs of two seats, was in another row, repeated that maneuver.

Two rows behind her, a gun blasted out. She heard the bullet scream through the spot where, a few moments before, she had crouched. She made the central aisle and, keeping low, ran toward the stage. She stumbled suddenly, pitched headlong, and landed with a clatter among chairs and music racks in the orchestra pit in front of the lip of the stage. Instantly, with triumphant shouts, the gunmen raced toward her!

Nita lay, half-stunned, among the wreckage of the chairs among which she had fallen. She heard the slap of pursuing feet and the eager cries of the killers. She tried, desperately, to gather herself together, even to move, and could not. All breath was knocked out of her.

Suddenly, she was aware of a man's figure standing above her. She summoned all of her will, all her control, but still could not move. A hand touched her shoulder gently.

"Take it easy, Nita," the voice was as gentle as the touch. It was Dick Wentworth!

Even as he spoke, the two pursuing gunmen reached the lip of the orchestra pit. A flashlight in the killer's hand lashed out with a sword of light—

Then there was laughter, bitter-edged—the mocking, sinister laughter of the *Spider*!

Screams of terror sounded then, punctuated by the frantic blasting of guns. Over and above that bedlam of panic, the guns of the *Spider* spoke with fierce authority. They spoke twice—and after that there was no sound at all, except slamming echoes. The two killers made no sound, no movement after they fell.

Nita pushed herself up feebly and saw the robed silhouette of the *Spider* as he reached over the verge of the pit to imprint his seal upon the foreheads of the dead. Let the men of the Conqueror take warning, for where the *Spider* walked, justice would be served. Criminals would pay for their inhumanities!

Nita got shakily to her feet, and her hand reached out for the *Spider*. His arm closed about her, and his lips crushed hers. "I was worried about you," he murmured. "I should have learned by now that you can take care of yourself."

Nita wanted only to relax in the warm security of his embrace, but she stirred herself to spill out swift words about her capture and what had happened— how she had been sent to spy upon Case Brent.

The *Spider* said grimly, "Case Brent has to put in an appearance right away, or it may be unhealthy for him when he reports to the Conqueror."

"But, Dick—" Nita shuddered. "You don't have to. It's dangerous!"

She had been unnerved by recent events, or she would not have said such a thing. Danger never deterred the *Spider* by a hair's breadth from the course he deemed necessary. He did not answer Nita, and she went on talking. The Conqueror was worse than inhuman. There was death and bitter greed in him, and a wanton disregard of any being who might stand in his way. If he even suspected her—and she had been trailed—Case Brent would be destroyed on sight.

"It's my job, Nita," Wentworth said quietly. "Come now. If Case Brent doesn't appear in about two minutes—"

"*All right!*" A voice cut in harshly. "It's the law! Get those hands up, you two, or I'll cut you in half with bullets!"

Brilliant light from a flash reached out and spotted the *Spider*, with Nita in the curve of his arms. It showed the glitter of the gun leveled by the man who held the light. And the *Spider* did not fight the men of the law!

Detective Faile was a man of single-track mind, and he had continued his quest. He swore harshly, now, as he saw his catch. "All right, Gerigan, Johnson," he said, his voice rising. "Put them on the girl, too.

"I've... by Hell! *I've caught me the Spider!*"

CHAPTER NINE
Men Must Sometimes Fail

THE *SPIDER* met that triumphant shout with a burst of mocking laughter. He could not use his guns against the men of the law, but though his guns were an important part of his armament, it was the flashingly keen brain of the *Spider* that was his chief weapon! So now he laughed... but before that, he had whispered to Nita, one word: *"Drop!"*

As he laughed, he flung high his arms. His cape clung to them like bat wings, and he made a frightening silhouette of black. He seemed to take off in flight. Nita dropped limply as a corpse to the floor. The *Spider* dove forward across her.

It was a wild and frightening moment. His shadow, caught in the flashlights, leaped high across the vault of the walls as if a vampire bat swooped toward them. The guns crashed, thundered a frantic protest of fear. But the *Spider*'s leap had been a shrewdly calculated thing. It carried him forward over Nita, protecting her. It carried him forward so that the lip of the orchestra pit interposed between him and the guns.

In that instant, Nita rolled also to the protection of the pit's front wall. Then the *Spider* attacked. He was balling even as he dove. His feet whipped over and he landed lightly, surely. As he came to the floor, his hand stabbed out to seize a musician's chair. His momentum, his weight whipped it upward as lightly as a baton and he hurled it, tumbling, at the clustered group of police.

They shouted, tried to duck aside. The flashlight beam streaked toward the ceiling as Detective Faile flung up a protective arm. In that blank moment of darkness, Wentworth's voice reached, soft as a sigh, to Nita's ears: *"This way!"*

In a single silent surge, she sprang to him, and his arm caught her up. She felt herself hurtling through space. Then they were through the narrow doorway that led beneath the stage—the musicians' exit from their pit. It was a momentary advantage, but the *Spider* needed no more. Carrying Nita in his arms, he ran easily, his pace and voice effortless.

"The last people are escaping from the auditorium by the back door," he said quietly. "Join them. The fact that you have no shoes on will attract no attention under the circumstances. As soon as possible, phone Ram Singh and have him bring you clothing. He is to avoid or eliminate all trailers. Together, go to Dutton's home. Insist on seeing him personally. You have information. Tell him all you know. I'll join you at the first possible moment. Remind Dutton that men tried to kill him tonight, and that he was saved by gunshots from a man he did not see."

Nita's hand reached up to Wentworth's face, shrank a little from the cold steel of the mask that covered his handsome features. "Dick," she said. "Oh, Dick, when did anyone ever need you that you failed to arrive in time?"

Wentworth's voice was grim. "Many times," he said flatly. "These steps lead to the hall. Up you go."

He was stripping off the mask and garments of the *Spider*. He thrust them into a dark corner, gathered Nita once more into his arms. Behind them, they could hear the blundering of the police as they clattered through fallen chairs, seeking the exit by which they had fled.

Nita tightened her arms about Wentworth's neck, then turned blindly up the stairs. She had had only a glimpse of Wentworth's face when a spire of flame taunted them for a moment, but it had been enough. He was returning to his role of Case Brent!

Nita fled up the stairs and, behind her, she heard the laughter of the *Spider* mock his pursuers as he led them aside from her path of flight. There was a sob in her throat. She was a woman, with a woman's dreams, and a woman's need of security and love. Yet she had chosen this path of her own free will—blood and danger and death—because she loved the *Spider*. No, it was not the *Spider* she loved, it was not even Dick Wentworth—it was the inflexible and generous man beneath all those exteriors, by whatever name he was known.

Nita shook all such thoughts from her head, and rushed in among the last fleeing people from the auditorium. She must weaken herself now by no thoughts of love, for with them ran thoughts also of fear. She had chosen her path. She would walk it!

It was good to hear Ram Singh's deep voice over the phone and to catch the echoes of his happiness that she was safe. It was even better when, presently, she sat beside him in the coupé he drove, and to relax for the contest that lay ahead.

Thoughts of the Conqueror made her feel strangely weak. The man was a monster. Ram Singh's brawn and the strong angry profile of his jutting beard was reassuring. He was angry now because there had been a battle in which he had been denied a part.

"Better if thy servant had stayed among his own kind, in his own hills," he rumbled his insincere protest. "There, at least, are enemies with whom a man can fight once in a while. Here—*Wah*, here, I sit and wait!"

"There was no fighting," Nita smiled at him, "only trickery and running away. Where there is real battle, we always need you, Ram Singh. There will be fighting enough before this is finished!" There was a shudder behind her words as she said that. She, too, could be an efficient fighting machine, but she was a woman.

Dutton's home blazed with lights and she left Ram Singh outside, to keep watch, to await Dick Wentworth's arrival.

"There is danger," Nita said curtly. "Once before, men tried to kill this man. Those men are our enemies. They may try again."

Ram Singh's teeth flashed whitely through his beard. "May Kali grant me that favor!" His bulk faded skillfully into the shadows.

MORRIS DUTTON was in his shirtsleeves and his shoulders were crossed by black suspenders, ornamented with small dancing silver nymphs. His scanty hair was rumpled and he had shrewd humorous eyes above a generous mouth that laughed easily. He was a courtroom lawyer, a shrewd and successful man.

His eyes searched Nita van Sloan now and formed their estimate of her integrity and her character.

"As a matter of fact," he drawled, "I have already asked Height to come here, along with Lasker Deeping and a couple of my own friends to keep the balance more even. Schneider here convinced me that there is a criminal element operating in the city which is trying to keep us divided. *Divide et impere.*"

Nita glanced toward Schneider. Glittering gold-rimmed glasses gave him a worried air which was emphasized by the sleekness of his appearance—as if he sought, by strict self-polish, to eliminate a gnawing uncertainty. The glasses distorted his eyes and made them owlish.

"It is an old trick," Schneider said, disclaiming brilliance. "A trick we have learned painfully in the Fatherland. Dissension among us, friend against friend, race against race, clique against party. It is easy then for a minority to rule, a minority governed by strict discipline."

Dutton laughed easily. "Schneider hates the Nazis but admires the brilliance of their technique."

"They are copyists, improvisers," Schneider's tones were deep, contemptuous. "They are taking a sure path to defeat. They seek to divide the conquered peoples, and by their very greed and brutality, they are uniting them! Stupid fools!"

There was a polite tap at the door, then Schneider hurried out of the room while Dutton turned his attention more completely to Nita.

"What do you think of my secretary?" he asked innocently.

Nita shot him a smiling glance. "You can't question the soundness of his views," she said.

Dutton chuckled. "There is something about the average Nazi that infuriates all American women," he said. "I think it's the *kinder, kuchen, kirchen* philosophy."

Before Nita could answer, Schneider opened the door again. "I have taken the liberty of bringing Mr. Wentworth in without permission," he said formally.

Because Dutton had made her self-conscious, Nita was aware of how warmly her eyes reached out to Dick Wentworth. She was defiant, even happy, about it. In any company, Dick's vitality, his sharp intelligence, his warmth of heart made him instantly outstanding. He dominated this room easily now, precisely because he made no attempt to do so. Dutton told him briefly that a meeting already had been arranged—that he would be glad to have Wentworth present.

"Height is coming?" Wentworth asked. "Has he arranged for police protection, or is he depending upon private guards? Have you taken adequate precautions?"

Dutton's jaw set, "This isn't the gangster era. Even if it—"

Wentworth said, "Pardon me. Are you under the impression that what happened at Height Hall tonight was accidental?"

Innocence was drawn over Dutton's face like a shade. "Tell me about it," he invited humbly. It was a courtroom trick which Wentworth brushed impatiently aside.

"For years, Mr. Dutton," he said quietly, "I have worked in cooperation with the police in New York City. I know whereof I speak. When organized crime is profitable, men of large caliber move into that field. We are in such a time now, because restrictions upon things which the people demand have been instituted as a necessity of war. There are always those who will evade any restriction. We have a large share of such people in this city. Crime is profitable here. You have such a gangsterism as Prohibition produced. If I tell you that I believe you and Height have been needled into opposition to each other so that concerted action is difficult, you will probably deny it."

Dutton was slumped down in his chair. He lifted a long arm and rumpled his hair. It made him look boyish and innocuous... hence more dangerous.

"I'm known as a confused liberal," he murmured. "Height is not confused—and not liberal."

Wentworth said, "If he is murdered tonight, you'll probably be arrested and indicted for the crime."

Dutton's eyes went blank, the reaction of a man accustomed to hiding his emotions when startled.

"It's the logical path for a divide-and-rule plotter," Wentworth said. "You are threatening to form a united front. Such an accusation, even if it failed, would cause wide hostility between your two camps. The police can be—manipulated."

Dutton swore mildly, apologized to Nita. "Schneider, try to reach Height. We'll find out about his protective arrangements, and then—"

The blast of gunfire was devastatingly loud, but it was not within the house. It came from the automobile drive. A man's voice lifted in a hoarse and inarticulate cry, and then there was the sound of fighting. Gunshots, curses, crashing shrubbery, stamping feet.

Wentworth was at the door in a bound, and Schneider and Dutton were right behind him. As he whipped it open, the front entrance became visible. Through its glass panel it was possible to see the sprawled body of a solid, powerfully built man. His hands were straining against the porch, pressing him upward. He got his head up, and there was blood on it. The effort was too much for him. He collapsed.

The man was Alexander Height.

"We're a little late, Mr. Dutton!" Wentworth's voice rang like clashing swords.

CHAPTER TEN
Hell's Gambit

RAM SINGH was in his glory. He had discovered the presence of the criminals, already lying in wait, an instant before their ambush exploded. He saw their crouching figures, silhouetted against the brilliance of the victim's headlights.

With swift, soundless strides, he bounded to the attack. He was still fifty feet away when he made his first kill. His knife flew from his hand like a silvery bullet, thudded to its hilt in a killer's back. Almost as quickly as that, Ram Singh was among them.

To an observer, his attack seemed a blind, courageous rush into certain death, but Ram Singh fought always shrewdly and vigilantly. If he had a fault, it was his eagerness to come to grips with his enemy.

His thrown knife destroyed the rearmost of a wedge of three men. Instants after the thud of death into that man's back, Ram Singh reached out his beamlike arms and seized the remaining two gunmen. He was aware, even as he did it, that there were other killers across the drive. Two guns were still firing there. One man ducked out of the sedan and—crouched low, hands pressed into his belly—stumbled toward the door of the house.

Lead reached after him, stung him, felled him, but he wrenched to his feet again, more slowly, more laboriously, and reeled on. Ram Singh saw these things in a glance out of his eye corners.

His lips were drawn back from his teeth, and there was a vast exultation in him—a happiness he knew truly at no other time except in the thick of battle. His fingers bit into the necks of the two crouching men, and he whipped his powerful arms together. The men were yanked bodily from the earth. Their heads struck together with the force of full-swung mallets.

Ram Singh's lips began to shape the first words of his battle chant. He dropped one of the bodies, seized his remaining victim with both hands. As he heaved the corpse before him, those hidden guns across the road centered on him. Their impact was such that the body he held for protection shivered and jerked in his grasp.

Ram Singh was in mid-swing, and the threat of bullets did not check him. He heaved the body upward, as an athlete might swing a hammer for the throw. His shoulders creaked with the abrupt strain, his powerful back and thighs were bent like a bow. Then he unleashed that savage force, and the body lifted and hurtled toward the ambuscade.

Cries burst from the shrubbery, which threshed violently and cracked as the two men hidden there sought to avoid the crushing missile the Sikh had launched. Ram Singh's song was in full-swing now. It roared from his lips jubilantly, strange staccato bursts of sound, like mysterious curses.

It was a very simple song, for Ram Singh was a simple man, hugely delighted in the violence of his great body and savage temperament. War, he sang, was glorious, and he, Ram Singh, was a lion among lions, a Sikh among Sikhs, *Ahie!* A Singh of all Singhs! Ram Singh, the destroyer!

Ram Singh was charging once more, with the ferocity of an angry elephant. Once more, his gigantic bounds took him into reach of his enemies almost before his missile had landed. The hurtling corpse caught one of the escaping men and slammed him to earth. Ram Singh, a moment later, leaped into the air and landed with both driving heels upon the fallen man's neck. He used that as a springboard to hurl himself headlong through the air at the last killer of all.

Ram Singh's hands reached out and his great shoulder drove into the man's back. Together they crashed to the earth. The Sikh's right hand fastened on the gunwrist of this last man and, as he fell, Ram Singh rolled over in a gargantuan somersault, taking the killer's arm with him.

The man screamed terribly, but he was still alive and Ram Singh was not through with him. As the Sikh landed, he was facing back toward his enemy, and he threw his weight, his momentum, into a heave on that arm which ripped the man from the earth.

Ram Singh whirled on close-placed, lightly pivoting feet. He whirled the man three times about his head, and then let him fly from his hands.

The scream ended when the man crashed against the stationary sedan which he had helped ambush. After that, broken, he slumped to the earth. Ram Singh stood with bowed arms, his arched chest swelling impatiently. His fierce eyes sought about him for more victims.

HE MISSED the sixth man in the ambush—a man who now rose from the darkness behind a shrub who took deliberate aim at Ram Singh and squeezed the trigger. Ram Singh's head jarred forward, but even after that, he wheeled and took two prodigious strides toward the gunman. Then his legs went numb under him and, with a deep oath rasping between his teeth, Ram Singh fell.

From the porch of the house, Wentworth saw only shadowy movement beyond the screen of blazing headlights. He shouted to Ram Singh, and heard no answer. He leaped from the porch and raced across the broad, even expanse of the lawn. It was while he was still fifty feet away that the sedan leaped into sudden violent movement. The gravel spewed from under its tires like bullets. It skidded on a curve and flashed out of sight.

Wentworth threw up his revolver, hesitated, and it was too late. He plunged then into the shadows. He saw the carnage that Ram Singh had wrought, but of the Sikh himself there was no trace. He flung his probing light about in the bushes, and then he stopped. His lips grew grim and thin.

On the earth was the close-wrapped turban of Ram Singh, drenched with blood. That told the whole story in a single brief tragic word. Without his turban, the Sikh would never have moved from this spot of his own volition. Wentworth's brief thought that perhaps Ram Singh was driving the car in pursuit of some fugitive was smashed in the instant. Ram Singh was in the car beyond a doubt, but he had not gone voluntarily. He was wounded, probably not dead, since they had bothered to take him. But he was a prisoner of the Conqueror!

Wentworth pivoted and raced back toward the house. On the porch, Dutton was bending over Height's fallen body. Nita stood in the doorway, behind Schneider, and Wentworth saw that she had a gun in the hand that nestled in the folds of her skirt.

"My Sikh chauffeur," Wentworth said swiftly, "attempted to break up the ambuscade. He accounted for a number of men who are over there in the shrubbery, but in the end he was shot and, for some reason I don't understand, they have carried him away with them. I am going after them. Miss van Sloan knows all that I know of this case, and can give you the information. Is Height dead?"

Dutton said, "He is!" His voice was thick with anger. The mask he habitually wore was stripped aside. His eyes blazed. "They'll pay for this. By the heavens, they'll pay for this!"

Wentworth wheeled and raced away across the lawn toward his parked car and Nita, watching him

go, knew as if he had spoken to her exactly what his plan was. Wentworth knew, with fierce certainty, who was responsible for this attack, and he had ingress to its perpetrator—as Case Brent. Wentworth would press his attack in that guise.

Dutton was striding toward her. "Turn off those lights, Schneider," he said roughly. "I'm calling the police."

He reached into his library with long strides, snapped up the telephone. Within seconds, his call went through.

"I want Chief Poland, and I want him fast," he snapped. "No evasions, damn it! Put Chief Poland on! This is Morris Dutton, and—" He stopped then, said, "What?" His voice sounded incredulous. "Dead? Murdered at the hall? Good Lord, man, then who's in charge? All right, put on Deputy Craig."

His eyes stared past the transmitter to Nita van Sloan in the doorway. "Chief Poland murdered!" he said. "Good Lord, what next? *Who* next?"

Nita nodded at him. "How about you?" she formed the words, but Dutton poured out his story into the telephone. Finally, he said, "All right, wait."

He turned brusquely toward Nita. "I'll ask you to wait outside, Miss van Sloan," he said. "Schneider, come in here!"

Nita moved back from the doorway and Schneider went past her abruptly, with a muttered apology. Nita's mind refused at first to accept the significance of Dutton's attitude toward her. But it was unmistakable. He had a logical, lawyer's mind. Wentworth was the one who had warned him of danger to Height—but Wentworth himself had fled immediately afterward. For that matter, Dutton was not even certain of Wentworth's identity. Dutton expected to point suspicion toward Wentworth.

NITA VAN SLOAN pivoted and started toward the door of Dutton's library… and stopped herself. No protest she made would swerve him from his purpose. Why, Dutton himself might be the guilty man! He might be the Conqueror! Nita closed her eyes in an effort to bring up the memory of the head-and-shoulders silhouette which was all she had seen of the Conqueror. Could Dutton be the same man? There was no surety. Her light-dazzled eyes had seen only a blurred silhouette.

Another impulse beat upon Nita—to follow and warn Dick Wentworth. But she knew in the same instant that he must have analyzed all this in a flash. He had known how Dutton's suspicions would point as soon as he had a chance to think. And he had left Nita van Sloan here—as a hostage, perhaps—certainly to carry out the role he had specifically assigned her. That was the one best way to turn suspicion from him.

NITA VAN SLOAN'S head lifted proudly. Resolution was strong in her heart. Dick Wentworth had trusted her with a very difficult role, estimating the situation with his invariable accuracy and speed. She would prove to him that he had not misplaced his trust. She would see this through.

Nita smiled to herself at the melodrama with which she made her resolution. She moved slowly into the living room. It was as she crossed the threshold that the lights suddenly went out. Rough hands seized her. It was an entirely unexpected assault and Nita's arms were bound to her sides by the powerful grasp of the man's embrace. She was bent backward, even lifted from the floor as brutal lips ground down upon hers. She felt hands upon her shoulders. The silk of her dress tore, and she winced as cruel fingers bit into the brand that the Conqueror had inflicted upon her shoulder.

Then, before she could do more than grope for the gun she had thrust into its garter holster, she was alone again, leaning weakly against the wall.

Nita's senses reeled from the unexpectedness of the attack.

This had been no lecherous attack. The man who had seized her had an entirely different purpose, and he had fulfilled it. Undercover of that mauling, he had managed to ascertain that she had a burn upon her shoulder.

That could mean only one thing. It meant that a representative of the Conqueror, at least, was here in this house—that he had suspected that she and the moll of Case Brent were one and the same. She saw now another reason for the Conqueror's branding of her, for his releasing her. He had intended some such trick as this, and now he was sure. Now he knew that Case Brent's moll was in reality— Nita van Sloan!

He knew more than that. He could make a shrewd guess that Case Brent was in reality Richard Wentworth. Even if he didn't make the latter assumption, the fact that she had masqueraded as Case Brent's moll was enough to doom Case Brent. And Wentworth had just left her to resume that identity, in order to rescue Ram Singh.

With fierce energy of action, Nita van Sloan rushed down the hallway to the door of Morris Dutton's library. She whipped it open and went inside, gun masked behind her skirt.

Behind the desk, John Schneider looked at her in bewilderment. Morris Dutton was just coming through another door into the room, and as he came, he was carefully wiping his mouth with a handkerchief.

Nita presented the gun. Her voice cut like a lash, "I'd like to see that handkerchief, Mr. Dutton," she said. "Spread it out, please."

Dutton raised his brows and spread the handkerchief with deliberate hands. It contained no lipstick stains, as Nita had thought it would. But that might have been a very clever dodge. He'd had ample time to remove the stains, and this would be used as an alibi.

Dutton said, "Really, Miss van Sloan. Was the gun necessary?"

Nita van Sloan let herself sway. Her head slumped forward. The gun dropped from her hand and she flung out an arm to catch herself, rolled to the floor. She was playing a desperate gamble to try to tie these men up with the Conqueror—perhaps to identify Dutton. Dick Wentworth's life was at stake, for if the knowledge that she was really Case Brent's moll was flashed to the Conqueror, Dick Wentworth was doomed. One of these men need only take up his phone and say into it, "She has a burn on her right shoulder."

Nita had dropped her gun, but it was close to her hand as she had intended. Impulsive though her action seemed, she realized to the full the implications of her position. If one—or both—of these men were the Conqueror's associates, or even the Conqueror himself, she had placed herself completely in their power. She ignored that. If one of these men made such a phone call as she anticipated—Nita set her resolution hard. She had never shot down a man in cold blood, but she would do it in order to save the man she loved.

CHAPTER ELEVEN
While Murder Waits

FOR moments after Nita van Sloan slumped to the floor, neither of the men moved. Then Morris Dutton moved impatiently around the desk toward her. He was still a dozen feet away when the imperative peal of the doorbell sounded.

He said, curtly, "I'll go."

He went past Nita to the door of the library and left it open when he walked down the hall. John Schneider smiled contemptuously toward Nita.

"I must confess," he said smoothly, "that I do not understand the full implications of your behavior, but you must be rather uncomfortable on the floor. Don't you think you'd better get up and take a chair?"

There were sharp voices at the door, and then the vehement chop of heels as a man came impatiently, even angrily, toward the library. The man who came in through the door was not above middle height, and he had an aggressive thrust to his shoulders, to the abrupt turn of his head as he looked down at Nita.

"This is the woman, Craig," Dutton said dryly. "As I phoned you, the man, Wentworth, chased off. His excuse seemed legitimate, but under the circumstances, I thought you should know all details."

Deputy Craig, of the police, kept his eyes on Nita. She felt the prod of his gaze as he took in the torn shoulder of her dress—she had contrived to draw it so that the burn was invisible—and his speech was staccato, abrupt.

"I'll put her under arrest, of course," he said. "There are certain questions I'd like to ask. Who was with you when Height was shot?"

Dutton had started to move forward into the room, but at that question, he turned with a rather studied slowness to confront Deputy Craig. "Would it be impertinent to ask you, Craig, just where that question is expected to lead?" he asked.

Craig pivoted toward him now, a jerky swing of his forward thrust shoulders. "No, it would not," he said, "and to keep it legal, I'll warn you that what you say may be used as evidence."

Dutton flushed, "This is utter nonsense, you know."

Craig made no answer to that. It was Schneider who interposed. "Mr. Dutton was in the front room with myself, this woman, and Wentworth at the time the shooting occurred."

"By your own admission," Craig said crisply, "you suspected Wentworth, even though he was with you. Height was your political enemy. Some men of your Law-and-Order organization, so called, started riots at Height's meeting tonight, during the course of which shots were fired at Height. Then, you invite Height here, making overtures of peace, and on your doorstep Height is killed."

Dutton's eyes were narrowed. There was a tautness through his somewhat pallid face. "Besides, as you pointed out, I am of the opposing political party."

Craig's mouth made an ugly line when he smiled. "Politics will never influence the police department under my direction, Mr. Dutton. On instructions from the state's attorney, I am placing you under arrest on charges of suspicion of murder. We have at least a prima facie case against you, so habeas corpus action will get you nowhere." He lifted his voice. "In here, sergeant!"

A uniformed sergeant, flanked by two patrolmen, appeared in the doorway. Craig's voice had grown harsh with authority. "Place everyone here under arrest," he said. "I'll swear out the warrants on our return. The woman is probably shamming. Get that gun first of all."

They were swiftly and efficiently herded to a car and Nita van Sloan found herself bewildered by this twist of events. She had assumed that, if Chief Poland had been murdered, his deputy would also be a servitor of the Conqueror. She had been equally certain that either Dutton or Schneider, perhaps both, were the Conqueror's men.

Morris Dutton seemed stunned by the swift course of events. He had said only one thing to Schneider, who was thrust in beside him. "They can't make it stick, and they know it," he said. "It's purely a political trick."

The car, containing Nita and the other two prisoners, plus the sergeant and his two men, rolled swiftly through the dimmed streets of Garago. The siren whined occasionally at a busy crossing. Out of her eye corners, Nita considered her situation. Regardless of Craig's connections, there were police who were in the pay of the Conqueror. Supposing she had been entirely wrong about the attack on her and its cause. It would be easily possible for the police to report to the Conqueror the burn which identified her as Case Brent's moll—if that were necessary. Someone, she felt sure, must already have sent him that information. And Dick Wentworth was walking into the trap. She had to get away. Somehow she had to be free to warn him.

NITA regarded the driver beside her, the policeman on her other side who, gun in hand, was twisted about the rear seat. If she managed to overcome them by a swift trick, there was still the policeman in the back. She could expect no concerted action on the part of Schneider or Dutton—unless they were the Conqueror's men. In which case, she would be safer in the hands of the police.

Still, Nita sought a way out. It was because of her alertness that she was the first to spot the fact that the truck which blundered into their path and slowed was deliberately blocking the road—and to the cars which raced to overtake them, notice the men streaming out of the shadowed lawns on each side of the street. It was a concerted, well-planned and swift attack. No need to wonder about who had organized it.

As they charged forward, there was a single crack of a gun. The driver of the police car was driven over against Nita. The sedan suddenly swerved in a wide circle, jounced over the curb and slammed into a tree.

The sergeant leaned forward, drawing his gun. Dutton's voice sounded suddenly frightened. "Don't shoot, man," he urged. "They'll riddle the whole car. We haven't got a chance!"

The sergeant hesitated and, in that moment, the car was overwhelmed. Nita slid to the floor as one of the assailants, his face wild and angry, reached in to slug the guard beside her. The sergeant, covered by a half dozen guns, lifted reluctant hands and allowed the gun to drop to the floor.

The man who had slugged the guard was shouting angrily at the sergeant. "You damned cops think you run the town!" he shouted. "Bunch of crooks, that's what you are! Think you can hang Height's murder on our boss—you got another thought coming!"

Dutton protested, "This will get you nowhere, men. I've told you that the law must be upheld. If you set me free, I'll only surrender to the authorities. I'll have to disown any responsibility for such actions."

The man laughed, reached out and slugged the sergeant. The three policemen were all out of the picture now. The leader of the mob continued to laugh exultantly while they carried off Dutton and Schneider. Nita, apparently, escaped observation, or else they were not interested in her. She lay, passive, on the floor until the mob had shouted and howled its way off down a side street. Hurriedly, then, she opened the door and slipped to the pavement. She began to walk swiftly away along the street, keeping to the shadows. In her hand, close against her side, she carried a revolver taken from one of the unconscious policemen.

There were two possible explanations of what

NITA VAN SLOAN

had happened. One was that the men were just what they said, members of the association which Morris Dutton headed, angry over what they considered the operations of crooked police. The other was that Dutton—or Schneider—was a hireling of the Conqueror and this mob attack was a clever arrangement of that master criminal to arrange for Dutton, or Schneider, to go free. Either might be true.

Nita turned a corner and began to feel easier about her safety. In the shelter of a narrow alleyway between two buildings she tucked the revolver into her garter holster, and set about repairing the tear to her dress. She had no set way to get in touch with Wentworth, under these circumstances, but she had been told how she could communicate with the Conqueror, indirectly.

The stealthy sound of a footfall just behind her made Nita gasp. She flung herself away, snatched for the revolver. It caught in the too small holster, but she would not have had time to use it anyway. Men rushed her from both sides of the narrow alley. They were powerful men, silent and fierce of purpose. In an instant, she was gripped helplessly in their arms. Nita opened her lips to scream, but a hand clapped savagely over her mouth. A man glared close into her eyes.

"Keep your trap shut, or I'll brain you," he said. "I ain't got any orders to hurt you, and I won't if you behave. The boss, he says he wants to see you."

The boss—Nita repressed a shudder. There wasn't any doubt at all that he meant the Conqueror! But still she did not know who had arranged for the release of Dutton and Schneider. She only knew that the men of the Conqueror had been nearby—and that she was once more a helpless prisoner of his brutal slaves.

Nita strangled a sob as her captors hustled her along the alleyway and into a car. The damage was done now. Even her escape would accomplish nothing, unless she could carry a warning to Richard Wentworth. She could do that best by submitting to captivity, by allowing these men to think she had given up; then, when they reached the Conqueror's headquarters, she might perhaps make a break, reach Dick Wentworth—

As they entered the car, one of the men slugged her in the jaw. Her senses blanked out.

CHAPTER TWELVE
Jaws of The Trap

RICHARD WENTWORTH paused only to disguise himself as Case Brent before rushing to the headquarters of the Conqueror. There was disquieting news on the radio—about Case Brent, and Wentworth's eyes narrowed as he heard it. That was a matter to take up with the Conqueror.

He had no difficulty entering the headquarters, but once there he found himself shunted to a large soundproofed room used as a pistol range. There were a dozen or more men waiting there, amusing themselves at cards or by firing at vanishing silhouettes on the range. Some looked at Wentworth. A few nodded. He was Case Brent, but he was outside their close fellowship. And they were a little afraid of him. He had killed Harpo.

Wentworth walked directly to a card table where three of the men he had commanded at Height Hall and two others were playing blackjack. Wentworth put his foot against the table and sent it crashing over into the laps of the two men he did not know. He had his gun in his hand before they hit the floor.

"All right, you cheap punks," he snarled at them. "Which one of you is trying to frame me?"

Rage distorted the faces of the men, but under the threat of Wentworth's gun, none of them stirred. His back was to a wall. The whole room was under the muzzle of his revolver, and his voice lashed out like the crack of a whip.

"Speak up, damn you!" he rasped at them. "You know who's talking! It's me, Case Brent! I'm the boss' right hand man, and any guy that tries to doublecross me gets it the hard way. I said, *speak up!*"

One of the men whined up at Wentworth.

"Hell, Case, nobody is trying—"

Wentworth reached over and gave him the back of his left hand across the mouth. "Don't come that stuff with me!" he shouted. "You know damned well you're in on it. The radio is after my scalp, and the cops, too. Saying that I murdered Chief Poland! Saying I tried to kill that fat slug, Height! Who framed that up? Who split on me and squealed a lie to the cops? By God, you'll talk, or I'll blow your guts apart!"

He took a step toward the men and they cringed, their faces white. The man he had hit whined up at him. "I'll swear we didn't, Case!" he protested. "We don't talk to cops! Somebody must have spotted you, that's all. The cops are always looking for a fall guy to—"

Wentworth's voice was suddenly completely savage, unbridled. "So that's the frame! I'm going to be the fall guy."

The sound of his voice struck utter silence to the whole room, that and the sweep of his ruthless gaze.

"Only I ain't," Wentworth told them. His tones grew confidential. "I don't play fall guy for nobody. Frame me for murder, and I may do a few, just to make sure the picture is right. Maybe I ought to start with a few of you punks." The hammer clicked back under his thumb.

A door opened on the far side of the room.

"Boss wants Brent," a voice said. "Over here."

For moments Wentworth seemed to hesitate, then, reluctantly, he let down the hammer on his revolver and holstered it. With a contemptuous swagger, he turned his back on the men and sauntered toward the door where the messenger from the Conqueror stood.

Wentworth's walk underlined his claim that he was cock-of-the-walk, second only to the Conqueror himself. The men were thoroughly cowed—which meant that if it came to a pitched battle, they would murder him very happily. But Wentworth knew no halfway measures in his game. He played it to the hilt.

He could not guess that Nita van Sloan had been identified.

Abruptly, he was alone in a dark room. The door had been closed behind him by the messenger and now, from the blackness, the Conqueror's voice spoke to him.

"Wait here, Brent," it said. "I'm not yet ready for you, but I will not have my organization disrupted by you. One more such display, and you are finished."

There was silence then, silence and darkness. Wentworth smiled faintly. Of course, the Conqueror would keep him under surveillance as much as possible. And Wentworth knew now exactly what part in the play the Conqueror had allotted to Case Brent. He was indeed to be the fall guy, to take the rap for all the major crimes of the Conqueror when he had outlived his usefulness.

The radio news he had heard on the way to the Conqueror's headquarters had quoted the police as saying that they had witnesses to the assassination of Chief Poland, and that they were looking for Case Brent. It also stated that police were certain that Brent had murdered Poland and attempted to kill Height.

The news of Height's actual death had not yet been broadcast at the time. Wentworth listened to the report. But what he knew had given him a lever to use on the Conqueror, who would want to keep him satisfied for a while.

WENTWORTH put thoughts of the coming encounter out of his mind and tried to estimate when Ram Singh could be expected to arrive at the headquarters. He was forced presently to acknowledge, reluctantly, that the Sikh probably had arrived before him. It would take a little maneuvering to find out, from hostile gunmen, the whereabouts of the prisoner...And first he must face the Conqueror. Wentworth flicked his thoughts back to Nita van Sloan. He had deliberately left her in such a position that she would be arrested by the police. She would be safer that way during the crisis which Wentworth sensed was preparing. Events were moving to a climax; the Conqueror would not have dared to order Height's death and Poland's death unless he was prepared to move in and take charge!

Time moved on leaden feet through a half hour of waiting. Wentworth played out the part of Case Brent, muttering threats, for he knew he was probably under surveillance here. He moved about in the darkness and, suddenly, was aware of faint voices like a wordless murmur of wind. He crossed toward the sound and discovered that, through an apparent oversight, he was able to hear the Conqueror's voice.

Wentworth's eyes narrowed and he altered his thought. The Conqueror would make no oversight in closing the circuit of his speaking hookup. That was not in character. The opening of the switch, even partially, was deliberate. Wentworth was supposed to overhear what was going on in the other chamber of the Conqueror where, apparently, he was talking to one of his gangster underlings.

"Case Brent is still useful to me," he said, "therefore, there will be no punishment, except a fine. When he is no longer useful, I will let you know. Go."

Wentworth tipped back his head as with narrowed eyes he considered what he had heard—plus the fact that he was supposed to hear it. It was a curious thing for the Conqueror to place in Case Brent's way unless he wanted to force a showdown. That was possible, of course. According to Wentworth's original conception of the part of Case Brent, the big shot would plan to take over the whole thing by destroying the Conqueror, but would give the impression of being unable to fulfill his plot. That meant, clearly, that the Conqueror was calling for a showdown.

The *Spider* shook his head. He did not understand clearly why a showdown should be forced at this time, but he continued to wait by the speaker unit and listen to the faint sounds which trickled into his ear. There had been a silent pause, and now the Conqueror was speaking again:

"You have the propaganda distribution system fully prepared," he stated, rather than asked. "You have the list of rumors you are to spread. You will start at once, spreading among the members of Dutton's organization the fact that their leader has been framed by dirty politics—among Height's that Dutton had him killed. You will spread among people, generally, the idea that no one is safe. Dutton's mob is planning to take over the city, and the first thing they're going to do is to murder a lot of important citizens, so their rulership will not be questioned. You will spread also the story that Height's men are on a killing spree and are looting stores and killing people they think are aligned with Dutton. You will tell how they stopped an automobile with a woman and a man. They killed the man and carried off the woman."

Wentworth could not hear the response, but his fists were hard knots at his sides, and his jaw ached with tension. The Conqueror was going to provoke mob rule in the city, divide the people into two warring camps. Such rumors would do the job, provided that a few chosen gangs of criminals provided incidents to support the tales.

"Yes, that is the pattern." The Conqueror apparently was answering a question. "Feature injuries to women and children. They will not be lies. The radio will soon be helping to stir them up. Go."

Brushing aside the anger, the apprehension that the Conqueror's words brought to him, Wentworth considered anew why the man should want Case Brent to hear such plans. The answer was that the Conqueror would not deliberately inform Case Brent in this way. There would be no purpose in it. There was an inference to be drawn from that fact. Wentworth's mind pushed and pulsed at it—and then the Conqueror was speaking again.

"Each of you," he said, "has charge of a group of men. I have given each of you his mission. In every case, you will assemble a group of people who will follow you. Use rumors, lies, anything. Encourage them with stories of loot. Then you will trap the man you are supposed to kill. Let it seem like mob violence, but make sure the man dies. I don't care what happens to any women who are with him. Leave that to the mob. Hang the men, shoot them—burn them in their cars—but destroy them. When they are out of the way, there will be no one to dispute our rulership over the city! We shall be absolute, and there will be rich loot! Go!"

Wentworth left the loudspeaker. He had heard enough. He headed for the door of the room, his movements were soundless. His hand closed on the knob, turned it softly. It was locked. His hand flicked to his revolver—and at that moment, his name was spoken in the room.

Wentworth wheeled, shoulders to the wall, gun in his hand. He was taut with the necessity to get out of this place, to slash out and destroy this organization at its roots. He had thought to enter it early in its development and trace out the tentacles, destroy the roots. The plot was completely formed, and he had come in barely in time to anticipate the kill.

"Case Brent," said the Conqueror. "I want you! Come!"

The door beside him opened and the messenger who had escorted him before was waiting there. The man looked just the same. There was no suspicion in his eyes, no mockery. He, apparently, knew nothing strange about Case Brent, had not learned yet that he was to be destroyed, a fall guy, at the appropriate moment.

Wentworth holstered the revolver and followed, not forgetting to swagger, to boast in the Case Brent manner. "The boss always sends for me," he declared, "when he's got a tough job to do. I'm the lad for that! Me, Case Brent!"

But under that swagger, his mind raced with plans. He had been foolish to think that he could reconstruct a strong authority here and could wait to destroy the Conqueror. The man should have been killed on sight. One thing, Wentworth knew: the Conqueror's sands had run out, his hour had struck. Now, within a few moments, the Spider would take vengeance.

He had only one revolver, for that had been Case Brent's customary armament, which he had picked up from the cache at which he had changed his identity from Wentworth to Case Brent. Plenty of ammunition, but still six shots before reloading. He could destroy the Conqueror, but after that he would have to fight his way out of the headquarters, destroying as he went.

Ram Singh was here somewhere, but wounded; he would scarcely be able to contribute to the battle. Thank the heavens that Nita van Sloan was safe in jail, he thought. It was the safest place. The door opened and closed behind him, shutting him into a dark room. He waited for the lights to blaze behind the silhouette of the Conqueror. It was while he stood there, waiting to make the Spider's kill, that a buried thought gnawed its way into his consciousness.

It had been his premise when first he had heard the words over the loudspeaker that the Conqueror's character was such that he could not have allowed eavesdropping except by intent.

What could be the reason for allowing Case Brent to hear his plans? Wentworth shook his head slowly. There could be only one explanation as to why Case Brent had been allowed to hear the interview with the men who were being thrown out to disorganize the city, to lead mobs in murder and looting, to seize brutal control over the city.

That explanation was that *the Conqueror knew that Case Brent really was Richard Wentworth!*

Even as the thought struck across Wentworth's mind, the conviction that this was the truth, the lights blazed out across the room and silhouetted the arrogant head and shoulders that Wentworth was accustomed to identify with the Conqueror. Wentworth did not tense arm or hand for the draw of his gun. He had no need for preparatory tension. When he was ready, he would draw and fire in a flash of time. His reflexes were conditioned for such action.

The Conqueror's voice swelled mockingly into the room. "I understand, Case Brent, that you are dissatisfied with my treatment of you!"

Mockery, challenge, taunt on top of that broadcast. The Conqueror was not asking for a showdown, but for death. Well, the Spider would oblige him, and gladly.

Abruptly, the Spider whipped out his revolver and fired three crashing shots. He leaped across the room and seized the figure under the blaze of lights. As he seized it, the figure toppled forward, and a mask, a shroud of clothing, tore loose in his hands! And now he knew the blighting answer.

On the floor sprawled, not of the Conqueror—but the body of Nita van Sloan!

CHAPTER THIRTEEN
Disaster!

RICHARD WENTWORTH dropped down on his knees beside the fallen body of the woman he loved. The gun fell from limp fingers. He bent over her and the sounds that came from him were like moans. Across the room, a door opened without sound and five men came in. They held their guns ready in their hands, but Wentworth did not appear to know of their presence.

On the floor sprawled— not The Conqueror—but the body of Nita van Sloan!

They closed in slowly upon the kneeling figure of the *Spider*. Before they reached him, he pushed to his feet and turned his back upon them. It did not seem a deliberate thing. His face was buried in his hands, and his shoulders jerked. He did not hold a gun. The faces of the five gunmen were sneering, triumphant. This would be an easy capture. They closed in. One of them pocketed his gun, hefted a blackjack.

The *Spider* whipped about and went into action.

It was as sudden as a bullet in the night, and as deadly. He drove between two of the men. He seized the gunhand of one, knocked the feet out from under another. He dragged the man's gunarm over his shoulder, elbow down, and heaved on it. There was a crack, a scream—and the gun was in his hand.

The man's body arched over his shoulder and slammed into a third figure, carried him to the floor. All of this came before the first gunblast, and three of the five men were out of the fight, at least temporarily! The *Spider* squeezed off two bullets from the captured gun, and two more men went down. He reached the door in a long bound, jerked it open, and vanished into blackness.

Two of the killers picked themselves off the floor. They dashed for the black doorway, guns ready in their fists. They were kicked back into the room by the impact of deathly lead. They sprawled across the sill, impotent as dummies. Inside the silent room the man with the broken arm cursed hoarsely and cowered to the floor.

His back was turned to Nita van Sloan and he did not see her rise silently from the floor, dropping off her rope bonds, nor see her reach out with the gun that Wentworth had given her. She struck the killer across the nape of the neck and went past him swiftly just as the *Spider* stood in the doorway. She ran into his arms, pressed her head down hard upon his shoulder. Her breath came raggedly. She tugged off the gag that had been squeezed between her jaws.

"Oh, Dick!" she whispered. "Oh, Dick!"

"Where is Ram Singh?" Wentworth's voice was cold, driving. His eyes swept the room. His ears kept watch on the corridor.

"Below, two floors," Nita gasped. "He's wounded."

Wentworth swept her out of the room and went along the corridor swiftly. "You will try to find a way out," he ordered, "while I go for Ram Singh. Get to the mayor and tell him all that the Conqueror said in this room. He must ask the Governor to ask for federal troops before the mobs get out of hand. Rioting must have already started."

Nita nodded her head and Wentworth seemed to know her assent, though they moved through darkness. "I—I thought I was dead when you shot," she whispered.

Wentworth's lips brushed her hair. "It was too obvious," he said. "He let me overhear certain things which clearly meant he knew, or guessed, my identity. Then he goaded me to shoot. He wouldn't have done that had he actually been in the room with me, therefore I suspected a trap of some sort. I just appeared to do what he wanted, in order to spring the trap." He laughed lightly. "There are those who would call it intuition, and there are those who would say it was logic. It doesn't matter, so long as it works."

Death was all about them, but Wentworth kept talking softly to restore Nita's morale. She had been badly shaken. Wentworth would not confess how severely he himself had been unnerved—nor how close he had been to plunging his bullets into the breast of that figure in the light which seemed, truly enough, to be the Conqueror.

Nita was better now. She explained swiftly what had happened at Dutton's home, and how she had been captured. Wentworth listened, narrowly, without comment. They had descended one flight of stairs, were moving toward the last descent that would take them to Ram Singh's place of captivity—and suddenly the hall blazed with lights!

Wentworth heaved Nita over the railing of the stairs toward the lower floor and dropped her. He flung himself aside just as the hidden guns of the Conqueror's assassins crashed out.

The eyes of gunflame winked out of the darkness behind the lights, and Wentworth threaded those eyes with his own bullets.

Two guns were silenced, but the *Spider* was not for one instant motionless. He leaped toward the lights, and he was now crouched low, now bounding to the left, now leaping high into the air.

It was incredible that one man could be in so many places at one time, could move so swiftly, and yet with such paced ease that he covered the distance to the lights in a flicker of time. He bounded high into the air, went in above the blazing eyes of the lights. A gun crashed at him, but his own shot had been an instant sooner. He rode the corpse of his assailant to the floor.

NO MORE guns now at this end of the hall, though they still crashed out behind him. Wentworth flung himself flat behind the bulwark of dead flesh his bullets had built for him in advance. He held his fire and deliberately picked up weapons and fished bullets out of the pockets of the slain criminals. He slipped a gleaming pencil from his pocket and reached out to press its butt against the forehead of a killer. When he pocketed the pencil, he left a signature that would put terror into the hearts of those who opposed his crusade—*The Seal of the Spider!*

The guns had ceased to fire now. Men's voices called out cautiously—and there were answers from below, from above. The entire house was an armed camp. Wentworth nodded to himself. This time, the Conqueror had not been overconfident. He had taken all possible precautions against a miscarriage of his plans. Over the city, his killer-led mobs were being organized. Wanton murder and crime were to be loosed, might already have been unleashed upon the helpless city, in which the police force was disorganized and the populace split into warring camps. He had to fight his way out of this trap.

Men were coming up the stairs now, on heavy, cautious feet. Their guns were wary as snakes. They carried Nita before them, writhing, fighting their grip, but forced inexorably ahead. A thin smile stretched the *Spider's* lips.

There were seven men bunched on the steps. He rose to his feet, hidden in the glare of the lights that focused in the eyes of the killers. He heaved up a body from the floor and gripped the man's coat by the collar. By bracing his elbow against his chest, he could hold the man upright before him. He sucked in a quick breath and charged to meet the men on the stairs.

In an instant, their guns crashed, slamming lead at him. Nita wrenched and managed to throw herself flat and, from the head of the stairs, Wentworth hurled the body into the faces of the seven men. They shouted and the tempo of their guns increased. Wentworth leaped in, feet-first, and the impact of his jump caught the corpse in the back, drove it like a projectile upon the climbing men.

There was a wild scramble on the steps. Men turned and leaped downward. Others were driven from their feet and, in a tangle, fell and thumped downward. Wentworth snagged the bannister with his left hand, landed lightly on his feet. His gun was ready in that same instant, and he threw his bullets with the careless precision that came from months and years of daily practice.

Nita twisted over and, flat on her back on the steps, added her fire to the solid wall of lead that was sweeping the stairs clean of killers. Wentworth reached out for her hand. They went down together. Nita pointed to a door and the *Spider's* bullets searched out the lock before they reached it. The crash of his shoulder sent it slamming inward and they ducked inside.

Instantly, Nita was beside the bed where Ram Singh lay, spread-eagled by ropes that bound his limbs to the four corner posts.

"Ha, Sahib!" he cried. His voice was a roar. "Free me, and then leave to my wrath these fools who have dared to dishonor the turban of a Singh!" This was not the careless, happy warrior—this was a man mortally injured in his pride!

Nita slashed at the ropes while Wentworth snapped bullets at every target that offered. There was a window in the room, he had seen, and now he made his swift and bitter plans. The men who had fallen before their guns did not seem to have weakened the attacking force, nor hurt their morale. They were cautious, but they were viciously determined. They came from every side except the window, and their lead searched through the doorway and made a cone of fire through which it was difficult to shoot.

Wentworth spoke quietly, using Ram Singh's native Punjabi, which both the Sikh and Nita van Sloan understood.

"There are too many of them for us to escape through the house," he said. "The window is undoubtedly a trap. They can pen us here indefinitely, even if they cannot kill us. If they delay us many hours, both we and the city are doomed."

Ram Singh rasped out again, "Leave them to me, sahib! I will destroy them all!"

Wentworth knew the Sikh's courage and anger, but he was not bulletproof. "You two will keep the door," he said. "I will spring the window-trap and force a way out there. If I find I can escape but cannot clear the way for you, I will escape. If we are separated, go to the police and tell them the whole story. They will have to act. If you're trapped, you two, defend this room, hold them off for a considerable while. I will try to return and free you."

Nita van Sloan moved to his side while Ram Singh pushed himself up drunkenly from the bed. His feet and hands were numb and he worked on them with savage anger, restoring circulation. From his pockets, Wentworth took captured guns and ammunition. There were four guns and many cartridges. This, too, the *Spider* had foreseen.

Nita did not question his decision, nor did Ram Singh. There was a violence held down beneath the calm words of the *Spider* that told more than any mere explanation how he hated the decision he was forced to make. These two, Nita and Ram Singh, he held most dear in all the world, but service to the cause demanded now that he perhaps sacrifice them in order to save a city. He would not swerve from his decision—but he would carry the torment of it like hot iron in his breast.

Ram Singh moved to his side, accepted guns. Nita already had hers. "Remember," Wentworth's voice was cold, "this is for defense only. You are to hold out as long as possible if I fail to clear a way for you to escape!"

Ram Singh slid into Wentworth's place as he stepped back and the *Spider*'s hand rested for an instant on his shoulder. Then Wentworth swept Nita into his arms.

Nita grinned at him like a gamin. "You do pick the darnedest times to make love!" she said, and her voice scarcely faltered.

Wentworth smiled down at her, and moved toward the window. He did not wait to ease it upward. He gauged the distance to the earth, then with a flat slam of his hat, he drove the pane outward and went through in a headlong dive that turned into a tumbler's roll.

In that instant, the narrow alleyway below was deluged with screaming lead.

CHAPTER FOURTEEN
King Mob

IN America today, one thing always stills voices and commands attention wherever it is heard—a news broadcast. The beery arguments of saloons will cease while men turn their heads to hear an announcer's voice glibly recite totals of war slaughter or casually mention the destruction of a city with "heavy civilian casualties."

In America, these are still only words untranslated into emotion and visualization by events. In America, war still is largely vicarious, save where a blue star upon a service flag has been changed to gold—and a woman's clothing has been changed to black.

But people listen and, tonight in Garago, the people were listening to lies.

There was no question that the Conqueror had planned well and organized even better. At key points, what seemed to be ordinary radios were that only for music and sketches. When the time signal for the news period had sounded, someone pressed a switch and what came out, as legitimate news, was delivered soapily from a recording in a hidden room of the place.

News—

"Morris Dutton, arrested for the murder of his political rival, Alexander Height, shot his way to freedom tonight when he was being taken to police headquarters. He killed one of the officers by putting his gun muzzle against the man's skull and pulling the trigger. In the gunfight that followed, Dutton deliberately shot down a woman who was in his path. Height's followers, organized as the Civic League, are said to be threatening to take the law into their own hands unless Dutton is promptly arrested. Five of Height's men tonight attacked three policemen, beat them up severely, accusing them of protecting Dutton."

The men, listening in the saloon called Jim's

Place, looked at each other after that broadcast. One man stood with his fists clenched angrily upon the bar.

"That's a lie!" he said violently. "Dutton never did a thing like that!"

There were forty people in that bar room, mostly men. Two or three stood up and looked toward the man who was shouting—who now leaned across the bar and said, "Turn off that damned radio!"

The barkeeper looked at him stolidly.

Other men yelled to leave the radio on.

Someone tapped the shouter on the shoulder. "Dutton is a damned murderer," he said, harshly. "He invited Height to come and see him, and then shot him dead on his doorstep! My wife saw it happen!"

"You're a liar!"

The blow was sudden, vicious. "You can't call my wife a liar!" The impact of the fist bent the man backward over the bar. His clawing hand found the neck of a bottle, and he used it. The place suddenly disrupted into violence. Forty men split into opposing camps. The instigator slipped toward the door, his work done, and went on to spread his poison gas of rumors.

"Dutton's Law-and-Orderers are taking over the city. Dutton ain't his real name. He's a German, and the Nazis pay him—"

"Dutton's Law and Orderers looted a meat store over in Green Street. The butcher's wife tried to stop them, and they—"

Always, the story ran like that. Women and children beaten, killed. Stories to stir the most primitive emotions, and a leader or two scattered in every crowd to start them rioting and killing through the streets. Two groups of looters, meeting head-on, would start shooting before they were even aware of the identity of the others. Once lawlessness started, it spread like wildfire.

And there were other rumors: "Dutton and Height are both crooks. They're rich, and they're planning to grab the city and run it to suit themselves. We won't stand a chance, us poor people. They'll grab all the meat, all the food—"

"It's all the rich guys getting together, that's what it is. We don't stand a chance. They get all the gas; we get rations. They get all the meat—and we eat beans—"

Slander, vicious stuff, setting man against man—rich against poor—capital against labor. The kind of stuff that German agents spread through countries before they invade, making men distrust their government, making men hate their neighbors, spreading fear and doubt and dissension. And it was being larded on with a lavish hand tonight. Tempers were explosive. The radio squawked its falsity into brains already simmering with rumors. There was always a man to start a fight. When the pot was boiling, they took other steps.

A crook, looking just like any other man, turns to his neighbor at the bar. "Look," he demands, "there's a grocery around the corner. If we all go at it together, the cops can't do anything. They can't arrest half the city!"

And a mob presently troops around the corner toward a store. The glass is smashed with a brick, and violence begets violence. A cop comes on the run. A brick catches him in the head and knocks him to the pavement. His gun crashes, and that's a signal for murder—and that mob is primed. A limousine slides down a dimmed out street, stops for a traffic light. Inside, a man and woman in evening dress—

A howl from the mob, and the chauffeur starts too late. He is hauled out, clubbed. The man in the evening clothes tries to interpose, and a dozen hands tear at him, hurl him to the earth. Feet kick and stamp on him, and then the girl—

Screams in the night and presently the whine of a police siren, and scattering men who flee into the night like wolves to assemble presently in some other spot and carry on their depredations—on the ground, the battered torn bodies of three harmless people who "just happened by."

THE Conqueror had planned well, and his myrmidons carried out his orders faithfully, their egos exalted by the havoc they wrought. There were plenty of those mobs about the city pillaging, destroying, spreading disorder while the rumors grew fiercer, wilder, and violence fattened on savagery.

Then there were the Conqueror's deliberate killers, each assigned to his separate task of murder. They needed no mobs to supplement their ferocity, only to give them a protective screen against the already helpless and stricken police.

A mob clamored at the door of Charles F. Strycker, the banker. Strycker phones for the police, and can't even get through to headquarters. He arms his chauffeur and his butler and the three men stand just inside the door, waiting. He tries to get his wife and daughter out the back door, but the mob is there, too. It is a well organized mob, like an army raiding party.

Strycker is an important man who swings a good deal of influence in the civic affairs of Garago. He is a doggedly honest man who has avoided publicity, but who has been fighting, undercover, for a cleanup of the police department. He is a man the governor would listen to. He is a man dangerous to the Conqueror. So the mob howls at his door.

A brick crashes through the glass door, strikes the butler in the stomach. He doubles over, slips to his knees and is ghastly sick. Strycker, angrily, jerks open the door and points his gun.

"The police are on the way!" he shouts at the mob that stands in the darkness, sullen and threatening as wild dogs. "Criminals are stirring you up! You'll be ashamed of all this tomorrow! What will your wives say to you when you get home?"

"They'll ask us for meat!" a voice yells back at him, bitterly, taunting.

Strycker flushes. "I have the same ration you have," he says, "and no more. This is nonsense, and criminals—"

A brick flies from the darkness and strikes him in the head. His head jerks over on his shoulder, and he wheels, falling to his knees. The gun goes off spasmodically in his hand, and a man in the mob screams. Violence is suddenly loosed. Men rush on the sagging banker and beat at him. The chauffeur dashes out and fires the gun once before a bullet smashes through his chest. These are not a mob—these are the organized killers of the Conqueror!

A rope is tossed about the banker's neck, and the loose end is tossed over the flagpole that projects above the porch entrance. A moment, and Charles F. Strycker, the banker, is hanged at his own front door. The rope, knotted about the column, is taut, and the body presently hangs quietly, only turning its toes first this way and then that, as the body seeks rest and finds none.

And the mob of people, fringing the efficient killers of the Conqueror, storms through the house and destroys and loots. The captain of the killers moves quietly away with his men. Their cars are parked nearby.

"Mayor's next on the list. No use trying his home. He'll be at the office. We're supposed to hang him, if we can. That makes it look like lynch law. All right, Mr. Mayor, here comes death!"

The Conqueror was not in his sanctum. The messages that were phoned in from time to time came by a roundabout way. He did nothing as careless as checking off a penciled list as the men he needed to destroy were reported dead by his underlings. He knew them well, and the list was engraved in his brain—the superior dogs who had refused either his bribes or his coercion with their pompous assumptions of honesty. And as the reports trickled in, his triumphant move swelled. Already, half of them had been wiped out. Another few hours, and the city would be completely in his control. Then he would order the police to put down the mobs ruthlessly, restore order... and be solidly in the saddle.

From this spot of utter security, amid the protection of a group of remorseless killers who were his slaves, he would spread out cautiously. First the state, and then the nation. The Conqueror's lips smiled contemptuously. His eyes blazed with the lust to rule.

The phone rang, and another man reported: "Strike off Strycker!"

The Conqueror's lips became more inexorable, and the blaze in his eyes mounted. It was almost in his hands. Almost…

CHAPTER FIFTEEN
Death, Mr. Mayor!

MAYOR KIRSTON was a stubborn man. He had already "taken under advisement" a half dozen phone calls from men whom the mayor thought needlessly alarmed and timid. They wanted him to ask for federal troops. Mayor Kirston felt stubborn about that. He didn't even want to call in Governor Mason.

He phoned police headquarters again and, after a wait, got hold of Deputy Craig, who had replaced the murdered chief, Poland.

"We have hopes of getting things in hand overnight, Mayor," Craig's voice was aggressive, confident. "We have established a curfew as you suggested and announced that anyone on the streets after that hour will be arrested—and if they resist arrest, shoot."

Mayor Kirston said, "Now, Craig, that makes ugly talk. We're not going to shoot our citizens."

Craig's voice rose a pitch. "Citizens who commit murder are criminals, by police law. I've got to at least threaten force, or it won't do any good."

Kirston said, "Well, be careful. Are there plenty of guards around my offices?" He hung up to Craig's assurances that there were, and nervously selected a cigar from a desk humidor. He winced at the sound of a shot, remembering a message he had had from poor Height, only a few hours before he had been murdered. Something about a lot of graft in the police department, and the necessity of the party cleaning it out.

But the police would be loyal and efficient in this major crisis. No amount of graft could make them turn their backs on murderers and looters. Mayor Kirston's thoughts slowed down and stopped. He twisted toward the window, but he had drawn the blackout curtains when he first came to the office. It sounded as if a mob were coming this way.

He pulled aside the curtain and peered out, was reassured by the sight of policemen, placed a few yards apart, all around the building. On those police, his life might depend. He drew out his handkerchief to mop his forehead.

Abruptly, the door of the office was batted open, and Mayor Kirston twisted about and reached awkwardly toward his desk for the gun that lay in an open drawer. Then he saw the identity of the new arrival.

"Governor Mason!" he said stiffly. "I had no idea you were in town."

"Kirston," the governor said shortly, "I'm going to call for federal troops!"

The Mayor's mouth shut stubbornly. "I haven't even asked for state aid," he said, "and I'm not going to. My police will have the situation entirely in hand by morning."

Governor Mason said, "Look, Kirston, I know we're on opposite sides of the fence, but this is a serious crisis. If it gets out of hand, we'll both lose our scalps in the next election. You've got to ask for state aid so that I can call in federal troops or, by the heavens, I'll remove you and take over!"

Kirston smiled imperturbably, "You would be within your rights, Governor, if the situation were out of hand. But if it appears, next election, that you were merely trying to build yourself up and discredit me, it won't help your plurality!"

The mob howl, pushed out of Kirston's thoughts by the arrival of Governor Mason, was definitely nearer now, and unmistakably headed for the City Hall. Once more, Kirston thought uneasily about the police.

Floodlights suddenly blazed outside of the City Hall, drenching the advancing horde in light. A louder swell of sound answered that defense. Governor Mason came around the desk and both men were peering toward the window. Mayor Kirston moved the blackout curtains a little timidly and peered out. He sucked in a quick breath.

"There must be a thousand of them!" Governor Mason said. "Damn it, Kirston, I don't want to go over your head, but it's time to act. We can have federal troops here in a matter of hours!"

A policeman fired a shot over the heads of the advancing people, and three cops on the portico of the City Hall elaborately uncovered a machine gun.

"They'll break up," Kirston muttered.

There were banners carried by this crowds, crudely lettered:

DUTTON WAS FRAMED!
DOWN WITH KIRSTON AND HEIGHT!
WE WANT OUR RIGHTS!

Governor Mason said, suddenly, "I'll go out and address them!"

Kirston swung about like an angry bull. "I cannot permit you to expose yourself to danger, Governor," he said. "This is my bailiwick, and you're my responsibility!"

Suddenly, from the back of the building, there was a crash of concerted gunfire and the shattering, frightening sound of broken glass. A man screamed. Kirston's face was suddenly shaken, pale. He swung toward Mason and then slowly, stiffly, he nodded his head.

"I guess we'll have to call out troops," he said angrily. "Damn it, what's got into the people?"

Governor Mason scooped up the telephone. His face, too, was frightened. He jiggled the hook, called for the operator, jiggled and then shouted. He set the phone down presently.

"The wire's been cut!" he said. His voice was dull.

Mayor Kirston reached into the drawer of his desk and took out his revolver. He was worried. "I don't understand this," he said, slowly. "I can't imagine a disorganized mob doing a thing like that. Some bright youngster might cut the wires, of course, but this wire goes underground directly to the telephone exchange. The phones must be out all over the city. Seizing the phone exchange is the sort of thing that rebels do—or fifth columnists."

The words shook the two men. A stone crashed through the window into the room. Suddenly, there was a rising murmur of sound—and it was inside the building! Mayor Kirston turned out the office lights, moved to the window. There were only two or three police left. The machine gun had been captured without a shot being fired. Most of the cops had broken and run.

THE two men, executives of a city and of a great state, looked at each other. Kirston's words were indignant, vituperative against the police. His voice was loud and angry, the more so because in his innermost being he knew the reason they had fled. They had run away because they had been encouraged to think that loyalty to their jobs was unimportant. They had been allowed to accept graft; political offenders had been allowed to go scot free. In the end, all of this was laid directly at Kirston's own doorstep. He had been the one responsible; he had known, and failed to act. And now his careful policy was paying off!

Kirston's anger faded. "This is it," he said thickly. "Are you armed, Governor?"

Mason said, "Of course not."

There was a thunderous pounding at the door, and the angry lift of voices... and then, suddenly, there was another sound. It was frail beside the roar of the angry mob, but it had a piercing quality, and after it sounded, there was an abrupt cessation of all sound.

It was laughter, flat, sibilant, mocking! It cut like a bugle call through the furor. It was the laughter of the *Spider*!

The *Spider* was in plain sight, and in direct range, of the guns of the mob that was storming the doors of the Mayor's office. At the challenge of the *Spider's* laugh, seven men among the mob suddenly dodged back among the ranks—and Wentworth knew that they had recognized him, and that they feared him. He had learned more than that. He knew that those seven who sought protection were the agents of the Conqueror. Only criminals would react so promptly to the challenge of the *Spider*, whose only real foe was the Underworld.

It was a time for boldness, and the *Spider* knew it. He moved with a seeming leisureliness of stride, straight toward the mob. His guns were not in sight. His cape swung splendidly from his shoulders. Bullets lashed out at him. Twice his advance checked almost imperceptibly, but he continued to near the mob.

There was something supernatural about his imperviousness to death. One of the criminals broke and ran, trying to put the mob between himself and his nemesis. He ran, unhindered, for perhaps thirty feet. Then, he was in the clear.

The *Spider's* right hand lifted. There was no violent contortion of his body to gain speed. He simply moved his right hand, drew his gun and fired, all in one swift, effortless movement... and the criminal plunged, head-first, to the hard floor of the corridor.

The *Spider* re-holstered his gun, and continued his deliberate, stately advance.

Now his voice came, quietly, with crisp authority.

"You citizens of Garago," he said, "have been tricked and misled by criminals. I just killed one of them. There are six more among you. They know me. They know that I exact vengeance only upon criminals. That is why they are trying to hide, and trying to kill me. They cannot kill me, anymore than men can destroy justice. I will kill them all presently."

A flurry of gunfire interrupted the *Spider*. He leaned forward as if he walked into a gale. Twice, his head jarred back a fraction. He kept coming. His voice lifted, slashed through the racket of the guns.

"These criminals," he said, "have lied to you and stirred you up so that they can commit many murders. They have already killed many of your leading citizens, the men who uphold the government. They are needling you now to kill the mayor. When the mayor is dead, the government of the city will collapse, and you will all be at the mercy of the criminals. Do you want your wives and sisters, your money and your homes at the mercy of criminals? Are you armed to protect them? What is happening to them while you let these criminals lie to you?"

He was almost on the fringes of the mob now, and men shrank back from the bitter accusation of

The Spider began to pump out bullets. The first caught the slayer of Governer Mason...

his gray-blue eyes. A lane opened and, though the criminals tried to cringe back into the ranks, those men who surrounded them were suddenly unmoving, rigid. They made a wall, and out of that wall, three of the criminals were squeezed. They turned, in rage, against the men about them, lifting their guns.

The weapons of the *Spider* leaped to his hands and three shots ripped from them so swiftly that the sound seemed continuous. The gunmen were heaped, motionless, upon the floor at the feet of the mob. There were only three others among the crowd now.

"They are using you to cover up their crimes!"

Wentworth lashed the mob with words. "When they have killed, they will run away. They have protection. But you will remain. You are the ones who will be arrested. You are the ones who will be sent to the chair for murder. They are crooks, fifth columnists of crime. They are traitors—murderers! They rob you and kill, and you take the blame. Destroy them. Root them out. Knock them down before they kill you. Destroy them!"

The men were hypnotized by the beat of the *Spider*'s words, by the dominance of him who was known as the Master of Men. His steady advance into the swathe of bullets awed them. His will and the authority of his voice hammered at them. They knew the accent of truth, of indignation in his voice. They heeded it, and the fear of the three criminals who remained confirmed it.

With a sudden shout, the mob turned upon the three men who were in their midst and beat at them with their fists and feet, with clubs and stones. They wrenched the guns from their hands and struck with them.

The *Spider* moved past the fringes of the attack toward the door of the Mayor's office and, as he reached it, he could hear the sounds that came through its thickness. There was another fight going on inside. There was a mob howl in there, and the crash of guns. Wentworth's twin guns somersaulted into his palms and he smacked lead into the lock of the door, shattered it and hit the barrier with a strong thrust of his heel. The door swung open, and the *Spider* went through the barrier—a blazing gun in each fist.

In a flash, he took in the whole scene. A half dozen men had swarmed through the window! Behind the desk, the Mayor crouched and fired at them with a badly aimed revolver. On the floor lay the body of Governor Mason.

CHAPTER SIXTEEN
A Slim Chance

WENTWORTH kicked the door shut behind him and, shoulders against that barrier, he began to pump out bullets. His first caught the slayer of Governor Mason and blew him, lifeless, against the wall. His second caught a gunman, straddling the windowsill, who had drawn a bead on the Mayor. One other man stayed to challenge the *Spider*'s dominion. He had a gun in each fist and he pointed both of them, at arm's length, at the *Spider*'s chest, and squeezed the triggers.

The *Spider* held his fire and, as an echo of that double blast, he laughed.

The man fired twice more, frantically. Then his face loosened, and terror dazed him. He turned to run, and the *Spider* whipped up a chair and hurled it. The edge of the seat caught the man across the base of the skull and hurled him, unconscious, to the floor. That was the end of the attack and, in a space of seconds, the remaining men scrambled out of the window and fled.

Two strides took the *Spider* to Governor Mason's side. At the window, Mayor Kirston was snapping an empty pistol at the flanks of the fugitives. Wentworth turned Mason over and saw at once that he was dead. He got to his feet.

"Have federal troops been called out?" he demanded, harshly.

Mayor Kirston pivoted about, seeming to see the *Spider* for the first time. He pointed the empty revolver and squeezed the trigger. The empty click of the weapon startled him and he looked down at it. Only then did he speak, and it was nonsense—curses against the mob.

Wentworth saw that he was hysterical. He stepped over and brought his palm heavily across the Mayor's face. "Have federal troops been called?" he demanded again.

Kirston said, thickly, "Phone wires cut. Fifth columnists got the exchange."

The *Spider* studied the man before him for a moment, then began to lash him with burning words. Presently Kirston's anger mounted to burn through the fog of terror and shock that had beclouded his mind. Then intelligence came back to his eyes and, bare-handed, he started toward Wentworth.

The *Spider* laughed at him then and moved out of his reach. "That's better," he said, "now we can plan. Since the phone exchange is in the hands of criminals, we will have to go to the central radio station here—not the police shortwave, but the major broadcast studio. You can make your appeal to the people there. The fact that the governor has been killed will shock them and make them listen. You can ask for federal troops."

Mayor Kirston said, "The radio—but we'd have to travel through the streets!" The *Spider* shrugged. "I'll protect you," he said, quietly.

Before Kirston could formulate further protest, Wentworth was hurrying him toward the door. There was a mob still outside and the mayor shrank back from them. Wentworth struck out with words.

"The mob, or rather the criminals with it, have killed Governor Mason," he said. "There's going to be trouble about that, serious trouble. Federal troops are coming, and the men who participated in it will be found and punished. It will be the death penalty."

White faces became whiter still. Men around the fringes of the mob turned and crept away. Suddenly, the whole mob was streaming down the corridors toward the exits. They would spread the terror, and in a few moments the way around the City Hall would be clear—except for the criminals whom the Conqueror had sent to kill the Mayor!

Wentworth gave the Mayor no opportunity to think about that fact. Instead, he pumped into his ears all the facts of the situation: how the Conqueror had organized rumor squads and looters, murderers and agitators, to spread turmoil through the city so that he could destroy all who would oppose him.

"He plans to seize control of the city and rule it for himself," he said. "He will pose as a hero, and the people will accept him. Once he is in the saddle, with all the city's leaders destroyed, he will be almost impossible to remove. He plans to use this place as a center for further operations. But you won't be here to oppose him, if he has his way. You are to die, too!"

Kirston said, "That's fantastic. You don't expect me to swallow that? This is just a breakout as the result of war tension. That's all. The people are all right. They'll come to their senses when they hear my speech. I'm afraid I'll have to ask for federal troops, but that will end the thing."

Wentworth did not attempt to persuade him. But he knew that unless he moved swiftly, the federal troops would come too late. The last opposition to the Conqueror would be wiped out, and the Conqueror himself would be consolidated in power by the federal troops. They would come to uphold constituted authority, and by the time they arrived, the Conqueror himself expected to be that authority.

THE *Spider* had laid his own plans to defeat that plot. He had hoped to win the mayor's cooperation. He would have to operate without that. But he had to have one man on whom he could rely—one man in authority. Wentworth swore under his breath. There was no one on whom he could rely. Dutton was under suspicion, because of Nita's experience in his house. The same applied to Schnieder, who would lack authority in any case. Deputy Craig, of the police? Reluctantly, Wentworth shook his head. The police were never prone to follow the advice of the *Spider*. And Mayor Kirston was obdurate.

Desperation pumped into the *Spider's* breast. He had accomplished nothing except to save the life of a man who was of no value to him, to the salvation of the city. The mob howl echoed down the streets as they moved toward the *Spider's* parked car. There were screams and a scattering of shots.

Unless he moved swiftly, efficiently, and with complete success, the Conqueror would rule, supported by federal troops. If he waited for the Conqueror to reveal himself, under the protection of the United States flag, it would be too late to destroy him. Besides that, the Conqueror might well only put forward a front man and himself remain hidden.

The thought of Nita van Sloan and Ram Singh, left behind in the midst of murderers because, alone, the *Spider* had barely managed to wriggle and shoot his way through the cordons of killers, was a torment to Wentworth.

He hurled his car forward with a violent speed that was the direct response to his inner desperation. And the hammer of the motor, the wind of his passage, even the shouted protests of Mayor Kirston seemed to blend into a repetitive chant of defeat: The Conqueror is winning! The Conqueror is *winning*!

NITA VAN SLOAN counted, once more, their dwindling store of ammunition. There were a dozen more rounds in their guns, and a single reload... eighteen shots in all. She stood against the wall by the window and Ram Singh was across the room by the door. She turned toward him and, in Punjabi, told him the situation.

Ram Singh grunted and swayed out from the wall. Instantly, guns blasted outside in the hall. The lead whined close, and he was forced to shrink back against the wall. He cursed in slow, bitter tones. This was not his kind of battle, cringing for protection while the enemy hurled death at him!

"*Wah, missie sahib*," he growled. "Better to die fighting than to crawl like rabbits into this hole! Let thy servant—"

Nita said, "We obey orders!"

Out of her eye corners, she saw something leap in through the smashed window. It was a little larger than a baseball and ovoid in shape, and recognition of it broke a cry from her lips. It was a grenade!

Desperately, she leaped from her protective spot and snatched the thing in midair. She hurled it instantly back out the window. Gunshots slackened about her for the moment she was exposed. A bullet cut her hair above the temple. Then, with shouts, men scrambled out of the path of the grenade she had tossed back.

She darted toward the wall's protection, and the grenade let go. Red-and-white fire slashed in through the window. There was a humming of torn steel, the impact of murderous fragments against the wall near Ram Singh. Before the stunning force of the blast was expended, another of the grenades was rolled in through the door. With a grunt, Ram Singh leaped for it, shied it back out into the hallway in the same gesture—and another one was tumbling toward him!

This one Nita caught and hurled also into the corridor. And she knew their tenure of this hideout was finished. She gasped to Ram Singh: "When they explode, *charge!*"

Ram Singh's frown vanished at her words and his teeth flashed whitely amid his beard. But the triumphant acknowledgment of the order was lost in the furious, double blast of the grenades. A portion of the wall was blown in. The concussion shook them and Nita reeled dizzily, thrust out a hand toward Ram Singh for support. He stood on braced legs, but the shock made his head wobble loosely. He was almost out on his feet.

Nevertheless, he hurled himself straight at the door. And, as he went, a great roar of triumph burst from his swelling throat. Nita, guns in her fists, went right behind him, stumbling, dazed, but set for battle. There was fire in the hallway, crawling along the floor where a great gap had been torn. The walls were a heap of rubble, and the torn bodies of two men lay amid them.

Ram Singh went over the gap in the floor, over the rubble in a gigantic leap. It was from the opposite direction that a gun spoke. Its very crash seemed hesitant, dazed. It made a small sound after the titan blast of the grenades in this enclosed space. Nita heard the shot, pivoted and fired twice with the right-hand gun. Beyond the gap, Ram Singh whipped around a corner of the hall, and once more his shout of triumph lifted.

THERE were other cries, puny beside the battle-rage that flowed, like sound, out of Ram Singh. Nita crept past the gap in the floor, and there was another shot from behind her. She kept on, made solid flooring beyond and, flattened against the wall, turned to wait for more shooting. It came in a furious blast that seemed to fill the hallway with fire. There were at least four gunmen behind her, slamming death at her. Nita lifted her gun deliberately and used the target that the powder flame illumined. She fired twice—and the answering fusillade was weaker. A man was swearing, in a hoarse, pained voice.

Nita dove for the corner of the wall, sent one more bullet searching for the killers behind her. She turned, then, toward Ram Singh. He filled the corridor. Two men were down, and his foot was set upon the throat of one of them. He had seized another man in his hands and seemed to be trying to tear him apart. From beyond came the belch of guns. Their sound was louder, now that the sound of the grenade blast was fading.

Ram Singh roared and hurled the man from him. Nita went down on one knee and through a narrow space between the Sikh and the wall, sent two more bullets seeking for their enemy. She was rewarded with a scream. Then Ram Singh once more filled the hallway in a charge. He went in with the blundering immensity of a tank, with the same devastating effect. But he wasn't bulletproof.

Nita saw him falter, then slash on. He reached the gunmen and trampled them under like pygmies. His great fist, lashing out, wrenched a man's head about and broke his neck. His left hand seized a man's arm and the man was pulled off his feet and slammed bodily against the wall.

When Ram Singh fought, every object about him was a weapon against which to batter his enemies. He plunged forward again, stooped, and came up with a wriggling killer in his two hands. When he threw him, he bent forward violently from the waist, and all his power went into the cast.

There was a rising scream, a crash—and silence. From behind came a single shot. Nita twisted, and the two guns in her hands rocked against the stiffness of her wrists. She slammed out lead and the killer who took it was pinned against the wall. He wavered there, on rubbery legs, and pitched straight forward. His fall was suddenly loud in the silence.

Nita whirled toward Ram Singh. He stood with drooping head, knees bending. His great beam of an arm was braced rigidly against the wall. "The way is clear, *missie sahib*," he said, thickly.

His knees gave, but still he held his trunk stubbornly erect. His head rolled as he lifted it, and his teeth flashed white in his beard.

"*Wah,*" he said, "it was scarcely worth the effort. These were not men, but—" Blood showed on his lips. He spat it out contemptuously. "They were jackals!" He pitched forward on his face.

Nita dropped on her knees beside him and rapidly tore his shirt to find the wounds. He had been shot through the back, high up on the right. His lung had been hit. She rapidly contrived a bandage and then, with the skill of training, heaved him over on his back. He had been shot in the left side also. While she worked at it, Nita became conscious of a heavy thud, repeated at regular intervals.

She lifted her head, listened a moment, then rapidly completed the bandage. She got to her feet and replaced as many cartridges as she could in her revolvers. She went slowly toward the sound, her eyes tightened in thought.

If it was a trap, it was a poorly contrived one. Nita was quite sure that Ram Singh had spoken truly when he said that the way was clear. She went slowly up a flight of stairs and there was a thick, closed door. It was against this that the slow, regular thud sounded, as if a man beat on it with both feet at once. Some other prisoner?

Nita needed help to take Ram Singh to a hospital. Moreover, she could not leave any person helpless in the Conqueror's hands. But she was very cautious and wary as she sent her bullets crashing into the lock, until at last she could heave the door open.

On the floor lay two men, bound hand and foot and gagged. They were Morris Dutton and his secretary, John Schneider.

For moments, Nita stood motionless on the threshhold while her thoughts ranged over her suspicions of these two men. Wentworth had taught her to think logically and that, when once she had accepted a thing as true, it was best to change opinion slowly. Therefore, she continued to assume that these men were guilty, or at least under suspicion. As she weighed that, her heart gave a great leap of exultation. If these two were guilty—if they chose to attempt to deceive her by this stratagem— it meant Dick Wentworth was safe.

They would submit in this way, building an alibi, only if the Conqueror's men had been routed. Only the *Spider* could accomplish that—therefore the *Spider* was safe and triumphant!

Nita looked at the men coldly, kept a gun pointed at them. "I'll free you," she said quietly, "then you must help me carry a wounded man to the hospital, where we will surrender to the police. There are many people seeking your life, Mr. Dutton. I think you will be safer with the police."

CHAPTER SEVENTEEN
The Spider Strikes

THE man whom the manager of the radio station addressed as Mayor Kirston was dynamic and forceful with anger. "—tried to kill me in my own office!" he stormed. "Did kill the governor of this state! You'll put me on the air at once. At once, do you hear? Sweep everything else off the air. Meantime, prepare a recording studio for me to use afterward; also make a record of my speech. You will keep repeating that, and alternating it with the record I will make. Understand?"

The radio manager was overawed. He had never known that Mayor Kirston had such piercing gray-blue eyes. He had always thought of the man as a figurehead, a puppet of powerful political forces. But this man had authority and strength of purpose. Actually, the radio manager never thought of opposing him.

Programs were interrupted and the announcer said, "We bring you a special broadcast by Mayor Kirston!"

The man with the gray-blue eyes stepped to the microphone. His voice was the voice of Mayor Kirston, but there was a drive and a force to his tones, an authority that was new.

"Attention, citizens of Garago," he said sharply. "I speak to you in the name of your government. Criminals have seized control of most of the facilities of the city. Actually, I had to fight my way into the radio studio. These criminals attacked me in my office, and tried to kill me.

"Governor Mason had come to consult with me about what to do in this emergency. The mob killed Governor Mason and I barely escaped with my life. I address this appeal to the President of the United States. I am unable to reach you, sir, by telephone, because criminals have seized control of the exchange. I ask you, sir, to do what I asked the governor of the state to do before he was killed: to send federal troops to put down mob violence which threatens to assume the proportions of rebellion against organized government!"

The radio men who had crowded to the studio to hear the speech looked at each other and then toward the glass walls which surrounded them. They were frightened. The speech went on.

"I ask every citizen who hears me to turn his radio on full strength, and to contact friends and ask them to do the same thing. I ask those who have radios in their cars to drive them out into the streets and to turn the radios on at full strength. We must reach every citizen in this great city of ours. I appeal to your civic pride, to your decency as citizens of the United States. If these will not touch you, think of your own safety, and security, of your wives and your children and your property! When law breaks down, no man is safe. Do as I ask you so that everyone may hear the broadcast which is to follow!

"I have been informed that a single man, a criminal of utter ruthlessness, is seeking to gain control over the city by murdering public officials and men of importance who oppose him. He is doing this under the cover of mob violence. You will find this hard to believe, I know, but I have become convinced, and I am going to let you hear the conversation that convinced me.

"Certain private investigators, hired by me, managed to install a dictagraph in the headquarters of this criminal, and to make a recording of some of the things that went on there. This is the transcription you will hear in a few minutes. Please do as I have asked you about your radios and your car radios. This speech of mine will be repeated at intervals of every fifteen minutes. At the end of that time, you will hear this exposure of criminal methods which will reveal to you how you have been victimized, and how this criminal has sought to overturn your government, seize control and exploit the wealth and the citizens of this city for his own profit and greed."

He turned away from the microphone and signaled imperatively to the radio manager. "Get the recording of this speech going now, and repeat it at intervals, until I can get that transcription ready for presentation. It has to be remade because of certain things which must be kept secret for a while. Take me to the studio, at once."

There was a mob outside the radio building. They smashed the glass doors and made for the elevators, but they were all stopped at the top floors. They rushed for the stairways that led upward and the doors there were locked. They seemed to be prepared for that. The mob carried axes and crowbars. Finally, they forced the door at the foot of the stairs and rushed upward. At the top of the first flight, there was another door. That, too, was locked. They set to work upon it.

There was a purpose and a drive about this mob that had no connection with the disorganized fury of most mass violence. They were cold and efficient. They accepted orders readily from the man who was in charge.

While they worked, radio sound echoed and slammed through the corridors of the building. The entire place was a broadcasting unit, and from its windows blared the many times multiplied voice that called on the President to send federal troops, which promised an expose of criminal methods, which asked the citizens to turn on their radios full strength so that the truth might be known to all.

It got on the nerves of the men who, successively, forced doors that gave them access to only one flight more of steps. They glanced about them furtively as they worked, and there were some who stood guard with guns in their fists.

The tenor of the broadcast changed abruptly. It was, first, the voice they had learned to identify with Mayor Kirston.

"I promised you evidence which would prove that a single criminal overlord was planning to dominate the city. You have all heard of the *Spider*. The first voice you hear, when this transcription starts, is the voice of the *Spider*. The second is the voice of the criminal who is trying to rule this city!"

LAUGHTER came, and at the echo of it, the men on the stairway stopped their work. They stiffened and, though they knew it was merely a radio broadcast, the gun-guards glanced uneasily about them and their hands tensed about their gun butts. It was laughter they had learned to fear—the laughter of the *Spider*.

"I give you full credit," the *Spider* was saying. "You have a perfect, an unbeatable plan. I thought I could defeat it. I find I can't. I have no recourse except to throw in with you."

At the accent of the second voice, the gunmob shivered and their eyes, regarding each other, became full of apprehension. It was cold with contempt and arrogance. Cruelty and utter ruthlessness were its keynotes.

"You're a fool, *Spider*," it said. "I have no need of you. At a movement of my finger, you will be blown to bits."

"I said that you planned well!"

The Conqueror sounded faintly amused, "And so you want to muscle in on my game? Even you can't be as stupid as to think I would accept you."

The *Spider* said, "There is the little item of your plans, all known to me. And not alone to me—unless you listen to reason."

There was no response and the men who knew the Conqueror, the men who crouched, frightened on the stairs, could visualize his cold anger, could feel the positive menace of his magnetic presence.

"No—don't move, Conqueror!" The *Spider*'s voice slashed out. *"You would die first!"*

The Conqueror's voice came out, raspingly. "You are threatening to expose my plans to officials of the city or the state. They would not believe you. They are greater fools than you. I rule the police department. I have divided the city into warring camps, so that no man trusts his neighbor. I have made the followers of Height believe that Dutton killed him. I have made the followers of Dutton believe that he was framed. Everywhere, my men stir the people to mob violence and rebellion against their government." The Conqueror's voice rang with triumph. "It is already too late, *Spider*, for your threat to have any effect. By this time, my men, moving under the protection of mob violence, have killed every man in the city who might have listened to you. They have destroyed every man of influence or authority!"

The *Spider*'s voice was soft as a whisper, and as menacing. "One thing can defeat you," he said.

"Nothing can defeat me!"

The *Spider* laughed. "Death can defeat you," he said.

The broadcast ended abruptly. The men on the stairs moved stiffly. They tried to smile. They looked at the door they had been forcing, and one of them prodded ineffectually at it with a crowbar. Suddenly, the door was thrust open.

On the threshold crouched a figure in a flowing black cape, and his fists cradled the butts of forty-five calibre automatics. He laughed a flat, sinister sound, laden with death!

The gun-guards shouted hoarse warnings and their guns began to spit flame. In the doorway, the *Spider* answered their fire. The lead that struck him seemed to have no effect. The steel vest he wore and the steel mask that covered his face turned aside the flying bullets. The exchange of bullets lasted only a moment, then those men who were left on their feet fled in terror down the stairs.

The *Spider*'s appearance meant to them that the Conqueror had failed, for they had heard the *Spider* threaten the Conqueror's death—and here was the *Spider*, alive!

For seconds after the killers had fled, the *Spider* stood motionless in the doorway. Then, a little stiffly, he stripped off the cape and the black hat. He tossed them aside and stooped to press a death-seal upon the forehead of a man he had slain. Afterward, he removed his steel mask—and it was the face of Mayor Kirston that was revealed.

Weariness beat upon Wentworth. He was feeling the drain of the long hours of battle. But he could not relent now, could not relax. His thoughts flashed to Nita van Sloan, to the valiant Ram Singh. He had hoped to return to them an hour ago, but that battle, he knew, had long ago been resolved, either in death or safety. He must press through.

He went back up to the next floor above. "I have driven off the criminals," he said pompously. "If your guards are reasonably alert from now on, there should be no interruption of the programs. Have you arranged a broadcast for me on the police wavelength? Excellent. I'll take it here."

Into the microphone, Wentworth made a last broadcast, directed this time to Deputy Craig of the police. Presently Craig's voice came back to him over the air hookup that had been arranged.

"Report, please," Wentworth ordered, in Kirston's pompous tones. "Have your men made any arrests?"

Craig's aggressive voice came back, sharply. "We have picked up Dutton and his secretary. We also have a woman named Nita van Sloan, who probably is implicated in Height's murder. We have not yet been able to find the man, Wentworth."

Wentworth smiled faintly, but his voice remained solid, solemn. "Excellent work!" he said. "Bring them all to Dutton's home. I have a witness who will solve that Height murder once and for all. It will help to quiet the people. You understand me, Craig? At once!"

CHAPTER EIGHTEEN
Death's Witness

RICHARD WENTWORTH, speeding through the streets of Garago in a commandeered car, deliberately took the direct route to Morris Dutton's home. The police force, he knew, was honeycombed with the spies of the Conqueror. His broadcasts had told the Conqueror where to look for "Mayor Kirston." Therefore, he might reasonably expect to be intercepted by the killers of the Conqueror.

Wentworth knew that, and ignored it. There was a hard and driving anger within him, a desperate need for speed, that made him look forward almost eagerly to attempts to stop and kill him. Yet he knew that any men who came between him and his goal would be underlings. Victory would not come through their destruction, but now only through the elimination of the Conqueror. And time was pressed because he knew the Conqueror's plan was to be confirmed in power by the federal troops.

That, in itself, would not be difficult. That civil authority which was in control when the troops arrived would be automatically confirmed and supported. Plainly the man whom Wentworth knew as the Conqueror had another and reputable identity. It would be in this guise that he would appear to the troops and, if the *Spider* were removed, would be accepted.

Two blocks ahead of Wentworth a mob streamed out into the street. Some of them carried torches and others waved clubs and guns. The *Spider* smiled thinly and stepped down hard on the accelerator. The car leaped forward, the motor roaring. He did not press the horn, nor did he seek to avoid the mob. Instead, he turned his headlights on full and drove directly toward them.

Guns cracked, but their aim was wild and, long before he was within reach, the mob scattered from his path. In the immemorial way of mobs, they were looking for easy victims. A resolute and fearless stand disrupted their cohesion, broke their purpose into blind, insensate animal fear.

The *Spider* roared on, but his anger was increased. How many human beings had been sacrificed this night upon the altar of the Conqueror's greed?

Wentworth, swinging into Elm Avenue a few blocks from Dutton's home, permitted himself to cast over the odds in the battle ahead. He had gambled upon his clear reasoning in ordering Deputy Craig to expose his prisoners to transport through the morbid streets. It all hinged on the fact that the Conqueror wanted to destroy Mayor Kirston, and would prefer to trap him in such a position that he could, at the same time, eliminate Dutton and the rest. If he struck at Craig's party, before it arrived at Dutton's home, then Kirston might become frightened off and take to cover.

Nevertheless, entering Dutton's home with the pompous strut of Mayor Kirston, Wentworth was sharply relieved to find police guards at the door and, inside, to see Dutton and Schneider under Craig's watchful eye—and Nita van Sloan!

Wentworth, as Kirston, looked her over with a predatory and appreciative eye, and Nita haughtily turned away her head. Wentworth chuckled inwardly, and his tension relaxed. He felt an upsurge of confidence, a keener alertness.

He took up his position in front of the fireplace, and let his eyes sweep the room. "Craig, the blackout curtains!" he ordered, pompously.

Deputy Craig stiffened, then moved with an obvious condescension to obey. The room became more intimate and less safe except from outside attack. The curtains were dark red, lined with heavy black. They seemed to move the walls inches closer.

Wentworth let the tension build while he looked over the men in the room. Dutton and Schneider were not handcuffed and their eyes met his challengingly. Dutton was plainly ruffled and disturbed. His eyes had lost any humor they ever held. Schneider was bleak-faced, darkly angry. Deputy Craig stood behind them, and all of them watched Kirston directly—except Nita. And Wentworth knew that her eyes were on him, too. He gave her no signal whatever.

Wentworth spoke mildly. "The Conqueror, who set out to rule this city, knows that we are here," he said. "He will undoubtedly attempt to kill us. First, he will probably send a mob spearpointed by some of his killers. When we drive them off, he will be forced to show himself, and then we will kill him. That will end the whole insurrection against constituted authority."

Deputy Craig smiled faintly, a little contemptuously. "You seem very sure that such a person exists, Mr. Mayor. How can you be so positive?"

Wentworth nodded his head. "I have seen him," he said.

Craig shrugged. "Oh, in that case—"

Schneider leaned sharply forward. "You lie!" he said, excitedly.

"I have seen him, and I can identify him," Wentworth declared, emphatically. He lifted his head, listened, and smiled. "You see, I made an accurate forecast of what would occur. The mob is on the way. No, Craig, I will issue the orders to the policemen."

Wentworth strode to the front door of the house and opened it, closed it again while remaining inside. He heard the reluctant, slow voice of Morris Dutton. "I never thought Kirston had so much energy or force," he said. "He acts as if he were very sure of himself."

Craig snapped, "Never mind the talk."

Schneider's voice lifted, "This is America, not Germany! You cannot stop us from talking!"

CRAIG'S voice became angry, and Wentworth silently went outside on the porch. He gestured to the sergeant in charge of the detail. "The moment the mob shows itself, open fire," he ordered. "Get your men out of sight, and tell them that they will not be shooting at citizens at all. This so-called mob will be made up of criminals who are out to seize control of the city. Therefore, you will be perfectly justified in shooting to kill any man who uses a gun against you."

Wentworth's words had the force of blows. His eyes rested calmly on those of the sergeant of police. The man stiffened under the authority of words and voice and eyes. He saluted crisply.

"Remember," Wentworth said, raspingly, "I hold you personally responsible for the repulse of this mob. Our lives, and yours, are at stake. I will keep an eye on you all, and I will personally shoot the first man who fails to perform his full duty."

He turned and strode back inside the house. He said, importantly, "I have arranged for the repulse of the mob." Was that a faint, mocking smile in the eyes of Schneider?

Wentworth turned sharply toward Nita. "Miss van Sloan, you have seen the Conqueror?"

Nita's eyes blanked and she turned a widely innocent look on Wentworth, met his blue-gray gaze. For an instant, she held it, and then a small and secret smile of recognition stirred her mouth corners. "Oh, Dick!" her heart cried. "Oh, Dick, how you fooled us all, even me!"

She said, in a subdued voice. "Yes, I have."

"Tell me about it."

Nita looked at him for guidance and received none. She said, "Well, I was seized by certain criminals and carried, blindfolded, to a house. There I saw this man, who had a very strong light behind him, so that it made it very hard to see his face. He burned me on the shoulder, as a threat, he said."

"Did he know you then as Nita van Sloan?"

Nita shook her head. "No, he didn't. He thought I was the moll of a criminal known as Case Brent."

Deputy Craig uttered a short exclamation. "Oh, that's the picture! Then Dutton and this man you call the Conqueror are tied up together! We have proof that Case Brent acted as an agent for Dutton when he killed Height!"

"That's a lie," Dutton said wearily. "I've told you so, many times."

"It is a lie!" Schneider said furiously.

The mob howl was much closer now. It swelled to sudden intensity and, outside, guns crashed out. The fire was slow and deliberate, and there were shouts of defiance, but none of pain. Wentworth darted from the room to the porch. He had a gun in his right hand as he stepped out.

"I said, shoot to kill!" he snapped. "I'll kill the first man who fails to carry out my orders to the letter!"

A few faces turned toward him palely and Wentworth saw one of the policemen furtively bring his revolver about so that it pointed at Wentworth's breast. The gun in Wentworth's hand kicked against his stiff wrist, and the policeman's cap jarred back on his head.

"I could easily have placed that bullet two inches lower," he said. The edge of his voice was like a knife.

The policeman shook. He turned his face toward the mob. Wentworth returned inside, and there was a curious gleam in his eyes. He had a smile when he faced the group in the living room again.

"The case is solved," he said softly, and he scarcely troubled to disguise his voice.

Dutton was suddenly fierce. "You're not going to railroad me on phony charges concerning Height. I hated the man's guts. He was a stuffed shirt and a special pleader. But nothing is gained by killing his sort. There are too many others to take their places."

Wentworth smiled at him, and turned back to Nita. "Now tell us what happened when you were here in this house earlier tonight—not about Height's murder. There are records of that testimony. What happened to you personally after Dutton excluded you from his office in order to make a telephone call to the police?"

Craig said, in a strange voice, "I didn't know you had read that evidence, Mr. Mayor." His eyes were suspicious, but Wentworth was careless now about his finding out that he was not really the Mayor. The more strains he set up among these men the sooner he would arrive at the truth.

Nita was talking: "...and the lights were turned out, and a man seized me and kissed me. He tore my dress on the shoulder, and deliberately hunted for the burn which the Conqueror had inflicted and pressed on it. Then he pushed me away, and disappeared."

Craig, Dutton and Schneider looked at her, and bewilderment was on their faces. "Here in this house?" Dutton asked. "Then—I see. You wanted to see whether there was lipstick on my handkerchief. That was why you wanted me to show it." His face looked relieved. "But there wasn't any lipstick on that handkerchief."

"NOT on that handkerchief," Wentworth interposed softly, "but it is obvious that you and Schneider were separated. It could have been either of you. It proves one thing, conclusively. The man who did that to Miss van Sloan either is the Conqueror himself, or he is the Conqueror's servant!"

"Her testimony wouldn't be worth a damn in law court," Dutton said angrily. He started to reach into his pocket, and Craig lifted his revolver.

"None of that!" Craig ordered. His eyes were excited.

"We are not a court of law," Wentworth said. "I said we would kill the Conqueror."

The shooting outside was spasmodic, but now suddenly it was violent. There were hoarse shouts and the sound of charging feet coming toward the house. Craig twisted about toward the window, but Wentworth's voice lifted, authoritatively. "Never mind that!" he said.

He turned to Nita. "I want you to enter this room again and, as nearly as possible, stand in exactly the position resulting from this attack in the dark."

Nita rose steadily to her feet. When she passed between Wentworth and the others, it was deftly, quickly. She had learned to keep out of the line of gunfire when the *Spider* closed in on his prey. She went into the hallway and returned, frowning with concentration. She was suddenly bending sharply backward, her pretty face turned up. She laughed at him. "He almost lifted me off my feet," she said. "He bent down toward me—"

Wentworth said drily, "A very nice performance, Miss van Sloan. You would say, then, that your attacker was a tall man."

Nita nodded quickly, her eyes reaching toward Dutton and Schneider. They were both tall.

Wentworth said, softly, "Our field is narrowing down. You are rather tall yourself, Miss van Sloan." His voice cracked. "Dutton, stand up!"

Dutton said, "Go to hell! I'm not going to be framed."

Craig leaned over and jammed a gun against Dutton's side. "Stand up!" he ordered.

Wentworth gestured to Nita and pointed toward a leather-covered hassock which stood in the shadow of a table near the wall. For a moment, Nita did not understand, and then she looked toward the hassock and Wentworth nodded and indicated she was to bring it forward.

"Yes," Wentworth said softly. "Dutton is tall, but he is not tall enough to lift Miss van Sloan off her feet. *And the Conqueror is not tall.*"

Craig said, "What goes on? You're contradicting yourself. It sounds silly."

Wentworth's voice rang with sudden contempt, with scorn, with ridicule. "Not half as silly as a small man who tries to be tall, Deputy Craig. Miss van Sloan, show him the hassock, and show him how even brilliant minds overlook little things—such as the fact that a man entering a house secretly, by a window, almost inevitably steps in muddy, soft, flowerbeds. And that, when he steps upon a hassock afterward, in an effort to appear tall, he inevitably leaves a clear imprint of his feet!"

Nita tipped over the hassock to the light, and here was the clear imprint of two feet, side by side, upon the top of the hassock.

Craig's voice was incisive. "What are you implying?"

Wentworth laughed, shortly, "That it is easy for a man to enter a house, leave it, and then reenter—and thus make it seem that he had not entered before. It's a very flimsy alibi, and the product of an inferior and stupid mentality."

Craig's face whitened, his lips shut thinly.

"And even more gross stupidity to leave footprints which match his shoes in the flower bed and on top of the hassock."

Craig said, with cold venom, "You planted that evidence."

Outside, the mob attack was suddenly quieter. There was no shooting, only the wild rush of feet toward the house. A rock crashed through the glass of a window.

"How do you know?" Wentworth asked casually.

Craig laughed, "Obviously, because I'm innocent."

"Or is it," Wentworth asked, "because you did remember to clean your feet before standing on the hassocks?"

Dutton was on his feet, glaring narroweyed at Craig. "By the heavens," he said, "it had to be you. You are the only other man who was here, and Miss van Sloan was wrong in her evidence. *Schneider and I were in sight of each other the whole time!*"

The glass of the front door crashed in and Schneider cringed a little. This mob violence was an old and fearful story to him, like a nightmare out of the past. Men were climbing in through the door now, and those men were police, supported by criminals. They had guns in their hands and, from the entrance to the living room, they commanded the whole situation.

Deputy Craig moved away from the others, and his gun was conspicuous at his side. His voice rang with sudden incisive contempt.

"It was a feeble attempt of feeble brains," he said, coldly. "Did you think you could trap me by any such petty device? Kirston, if you are Kirston and not, as I suspect, my friend the *Spider*, you were a fool to come here this way. Did you think I would fail to bring *men I could trust?*"

WENTWORTH smiled, "Yes, the device would have been feeble against anyone of real intelligence, Craig—or Conqueror as you call yourself. But it worked against you. It has forced you out into the open. You have confessed your identity. I admit planting the evidence, which means, doesn't it, that I was here before?"

Craig's face became lined with rage. "What do you mean?" he demanded.

Wentworth laughed. "I was here before, and you should by now be familiar with my technique. Your plan was that at the head of the police force, having established order, you would be confirmed in power by the federal troops when they arrived. It is your plan now to kill us all, isn't it, Craig?"

Craig said, flatly, "I will kill you in a very few seconds. You are only stalling for time."

Wentworth shook his head, and his brows were quizzical. He had dropped all pretense of being Mayor Kirston. "Not at all, my dear Craig," he said. "I have no need to stall for time, because you are finished. I call your attention to several things. One, I have been here before. Two, my technique is to broadcast to all the people the facts that they ought to have, and not alone to the people, but to the authorities who are on their way here. The whole nation is listening to the broadcasts which were sent out earlier in the night. Three, I consider that what has taken place here is in the public interest. Four, therefore I arranged a broadcast, and the world has heard you, Deputy Craig, confess that you are the Conqueror!"

Craig shrieked out a curse, jerked up his revolver. He did not wait to issue an order to his men and his men had been trained to act only on his orders. The *Spider* went into action and the *Spider*'s mate did her share.

She leaped quickly sideways. Her hand flashed to the light switch. The *Spider*'s guns somersaulted into his palms and their two convergent lances of flame met in the center of the Conqueror's face. The effect of two forty-five caliber bullets entering his skull was catastrophic. He was picked up and hurled backward upon the men who were his servants and his slaves. They stood in the light of the hallway, and from the darkness, bullets continued to strike into the inert and quivering body of their slain leader. No bullets touched them, but their leader was destroyed.

"You are beaten," the voice of Wentworth cut coldly into their ears. "Your master is destroyed. Your only hope is to flee, to run fast, and hide. You are beaten, defeated. The federal troops are coming, and they will destroy you!"

The voice ceased abruptly. The bullets stopped. The police stood uncertainly and then a beam of light from the flash of one of them cut across the room from which voice and death had issued—and that room was empty. It was empty save for a single, whispering mocking sound—the laughter of the *Spider*!

They turned and fled.

IN THE car in which they raced toward the environs of the city, Wentworth stripped off the disguise of Mayor Kirston with slow and suddenly leaden hands. The reaction had set in now that the battle was over. Wentworth's face was the face of the *Spider* now. Under the guise of removing the mask of Kirston, he had applied that of the *Spider*. He turned to Nita. "Miss van Sloan," he said, "I think you will be safer if I carry you away from this area until Mr. Dutton can get things in hand, and a reputable city government is established."

Dutton grunted, "I'll say so!"

Wentworth leaned over and flicked on the radio. "Perhaps the troops have arrived," he said. "We ought to know soon. I hope I can get you out of here before that. Military government inclines to shoot first and ask questions afterward." He broke off, then, because there was a familiar voice on the air, the voice of Mayor Kirston.

"I have been tricked and humiliated," he said. "After pretending to be my friend, the *Spider* knocked me unconscious and, disguised as myself, did things in my name. He is a trickster and a murderer. He is a thief and a cheat! He must be apprehended at all costs. You all have heard, over the air, how he bargained with the criminals who tried to take over the city. He was in league with them when he kidnapped me and took my place. Only the vigilance of the police prevented him from achieving his ends. I have just been informed that he brutally, and deliberately, murdered Deputy Craig, of the police, in order to escape. He—"

Dutton said, furiously, "He is an idiot!" He wrenched the car around a corner as a police car showed ahead, and a few moments later changed direction again. They were drawing near the point where the *Spider* had parked an escape car.

Ram Singh, in the hospital, would not be disturbed for a while. By the time it was possible for police to question him, there would be a sound city government here. Dutton would see to that—Dutton and the men who had survived the Conqueror's massacre.

Dutton's voice was slow. "I hadn't realized until now what a courageous thing you did, *Spider*. You deliberately labeled yourself a criminal, knowing what use Kirston would make of that fact, in order to arouse the people. You have a name which people fear. The Conqueror was unknown to them. But by labeling yourself a criminal, you have terrified them into consistent strong action!"

Wentworth shrugged. "It was the only way. If you will turn the next corner and stop, we will avoid the police who will probably cut across to intercept us."

Dutton whipped the car around the corner, stopped and shut off the engine. The radio still squawked for a moment. "...That arch-criminal, that false leader, that murderer and assassin, the *Spider*—"

"We'd better take cover," the *Spider* said, and he and Nita stepped to the darkness of a doorway across the sidewalk.

Dutton cut off the radio and followed them across

the walk. "I want you to know, *Spider*," he said. "that I think you did the bravest thing any man could do. You have deliberately blackened your name in order that the people might be saved from their own folly. There is no greater sacrifice. I'd be proud to shake the hand of the man who did it, and I'll tell the world, always, you're a gentleman and a man."

He thrust out his hand toward the dark shadow into which the *Spider* had stepped and after a moment he felt a little foolish. His hand was not grasped, and there was no answer from the dark. He said, "*Spider?*"

He groped into the darkness—and it was empty. The Spider had vanished! The *Spider* had no use for the praise of men, nor for their blame. He followed his own heart, his own conscience to whatever end it led him, and Nita van Sloan followed, too, because she loved him. They were two of the secret great of the world. There are many such.

Morris Dutton took off his hat, as if he stood at an altar, as indeed he did. "*Spider*," he said to the empty night, "you are —"

And his voice trailed off. There were no words to describe what Morris Dutton felt about the sacrifice and the service of the *Spider*. He turned away toward his car, feeling his burden of responsibility a little more heavily, but more steadfast in his determination to carry out the ideal in service which had been acted out before his eyes.

A police car zipped around the corner. Its radio was blaring with the voice of Mayor Kirston. Three blocks away, Wentworth got behind the wheel of an inconspicuous coupé and Nita van Sloan slipped in beside him. Her head fell naturally to his shoulder, and his arm went about her. They looked at each other, and they smiled. He kissed her, tenderly, and Nita sighed.

"I could do with a night's sleep," she said.

THE END

MY DINNER WITH NITA
REMEMBERING IRIS MEREDITH
by Ed Hulse

In the summer of 1976, I had an experience most serial fans could only dream of. I actually met, interviewed, and broke bread with the Spider's paramour, Nita Van Sloan!

Not the *real* Nita, of course. That would have been impossible, because there wasn't any real Nita. No, I attended a dinner with the *reel* Nita, the beautiful actress who played opposite Warren Hull in *The Spider's Web* (1938), first of two fast-action Spider chapter plays made and released by Columbia Pictures.

Her name was Iris Meredith, and she had come to Nashville, Tennessee as a guest of the Fifth Annual Western Film Fair, a movie-buff confab sponsored by *Western Film Collector* magazine. Over the course of this four-day convention, some 160 feature-length films and a couple dozen serials— including *The Spider's Web*— unspooled in six makeshift screening rooms outfitted with

16mm projectors manned by bleary-eyed collectors. Movie showings began at 10 a.m. every day and continued until the wee hours of the next morning. The hucksters room included well over a hundred tables, some of them covered with boxes full of vintage-movie memorabilia, others sagging beneath the weight of film cans containing 16mm prints. Film Fair attendees could either screen themselves blind or spend themselves poor. Some did both.

Much-needed diversions were provided by panel discussions (in which the many guest stars reminisced about filmmaking in the Good Old Days) and the Saturday-night awards banquet, when actors long forgotten by the public at large accepted handsome plaques and standing ovations from True Believers who still cherished the Saturday-matinee movies of their youth.

I had already attended several such events and would likely have returned to

Nashville even if Iris Meredith *hadn't* been among the dozen or so performers invited to this year's convention. But her presence was the icing on the cake for me. To think I'd be meeting Iris Meredith— the silver screen's one true Nita Van Sloan! (Those of us who had seen both Spider serials rarely spoke of The Other, that garish, brassy floozy so obviously miscast in the 1941 sequel, *The Spider Returns*. As far as we were concerned, Iris Meredith *was* Nita. Period.)

Born on June 3, 1915 in Sioux City, Iowa, Iris Shunn didn't have an easy childhood. By the time she was ten, her family had moved twice, first to Minnesota and then to southern California. By the time she was 13, both parents had died, leaving her to support three younger siblings with a Depression on the way. She attended school in the morning and toiled as a theater cashier in the afternoon and evening. Legend has it that Iris was discovered by a talent scout while working at the Loew's theater in downtown Los Angeles. Still just a teenager—albeit a beautiful one—she briefly joined the fabled Goldwyn Girls and first appeared on screen with them in a 1933 Eddie Cantor vehicle, *Roman Scandals*.

Iris worked as a chorus girl in several movie musicals before landing her first substantial part: an ingénue role in *The Cowboy Star* (1936), a better-than-average "B" Western in which she played opposite Charles Starrett for the first time. (This film was the first in which she received on-screen billing, and for it she assumed the Meredith surname.) Starrett, scion of a wealthy northeastern family, had taken up acting while attending Dartmouth College. In the early Thirties he appeared in numerous major-studio productions, among them M-G-M's *The Mask of Fu Manchu*, which starred Boris Karloff and Myrna Loy. But Starrett never really caught on with adult moviegoers and in 1935 began starring in low-budget horse operas released by Columbia. He spent 17 consecutive years making Westerns for that studio, appearing exclusively as The Durango Kid from 1944 to 1952.

When Iris landed a Columbia contract, she was initially assigned to the unit cranking out Charlie's pictures, and she co-starred with him in some 19 Westerns released between 1937 and 1940. The Starrett vehicles of this period maintained a fairly high standard, but their strict adherence to formula made one virtually indistinguishable from another. The Sons of the Pioneers, a Western-music group to which Roy Rogers once belonged, worked with Charlie and Iris in every picture. The supporting casts nearly always included Dick Curtis as the principal heavy and silent-screen veteran Edward Le Saint as either Starrett's or Meredith's father. Even the bit players were the same from picture to picture, and they almost always wore the same clothes. For that matter, so did Iris: She generally showed up in an ensemble consisting of plaid shirt with vest and split skirt.

Iris pressed for parts in better movies but rarely escaped the Western and serial unit headed by producer Jack Fier. And when she did, it was only temporarily and usually in a thankless role. In late 1940, after appearing in 22 Westerns and three serials, she left Columbia. For the next couple years Iris freelanced, finding it difficult to land roles outside of Hollywood's Poverty Row. By 1943 she had married director Abby Berlin, himself a Columbia contractee, and shortly thereafter she had a daughter and settled into domestic life.

Unlike some of her contemporaries, Iris never attempted a comeback when television series production created new opportunities for technicians and performers used to working at top speed on short budgets. She never dreamed that people still remembered her fondly, or that she had won new fans thanks to TV reruns of her old movies and the proliferation of 16mm dupe prints of the old Westerns. By the mid Seventies, however, the word was out. The "B"-Western stars, starlets, and supporting players were very much in demand at nostalgia-oriented film festivals, and Iris eventually accepted an invitation to appear at one such event.

Of course, those of us who attended that 1976 Western Film Fair had no way of knowing what hell Iris Meredith had been through. Some ten years earlier she had been diagnosed with oral cancer. She endured 14 operations, surrendering part of jaw and tongue in her fight against the disease. None of us expects our film favorites to withstand indefinitely the ravages of time, but we weren't fully prepared for the severely disfigured, prematurely aged woman who courageously greeted her fans.

However shocked Film Fair attendees may have been, they never let on. Iris bravely met and talked with her fans, laboring mightily to make herself understood. Losing part of her tongue made it impossible to clearly articulate certain words, and her slurred speech was reminiscent of someone who'd had way too much to drink.

But ultimately this didn't matter to us, and our outpouring of love plainly lifted her spirits. As the convention progressed, Iris seemed demonstrably happier; by the second or third day one could see a twinkle in her rheumy eyes. Initially reluctant to speak, she pushed herself to engage fully with fans who approached her with questions, often bearing stills and lobby cards for her to sign.

She was accompanied by her grown daughter, who occasionally sat with her mom when Iris elected to watch one of her old movies. About half-way through a screening of The Spider's Web—all fifteen chapters in one marathon session, interrupted only by the projectionist's reel changes—the daughter excused herself, leaving Iris all alone. The screening rooms were sparsely attended at that moment; my recollection is that another guest-star panel was just getting underway. Only a dozen or so people remained to see the Spider battle his arch-foe, the Octopus, to a standstill.

A few rows behind and to the right of Iris, I stared at her as the next episode began. She sat very still and very straight, apparently transfixed by the flickering image of a younger, beautiful version of herself. I couldn't help but wonder what might be going through her mind. Having already seen the serial several times, I left the room after one more chapter to attend another screening. As I eased through the door, I shot a glance back at Iris. She was still riveted by the adventures of Dick, Nita, and the others.

On the third day of the convention, I persuaded Iris to sit for an interview. She briefly stiffened when I brought out my portable cassette recorder, but after a few seconds—just as I was about to stuff it back into my briefcase—she relaxed again. "What would you like to know?" she asked.

Naturally, I was most eager to hear whatever she had to say about The Spider's Web. "You know," she said, "a year ago I couldn't have told you anything about it. But now that I've seen it again, little things come back to me.

"Those serials were very hard to do. With the Westerns, you worked for a week or two and then you had time off. But those damn serials went for four, or five, or six weeks at a time. And we worked very long days, sometimes 12 or 14 hours. So every night you came home exhausted. It was all we could do to remember our lines the next day. The directors had it bad because they had to keep track of everything, all those little things that happened in the chapters."

I asked her what she remembered about her castmates.

"Well, of course, I knew Richard Fiske already. We worked together on some of the pictures I did with Charlie [Starrett]. Warren Hull was a dear. Between takes he was a great kidder. And he loved to sing. He had a lovely voice. But then we would get in front of the camera and he would get so serious and squint, you know, and starting shooting at people.

"I remember we all thought it was funny that

Kenny Duncan was playing this Hindu [Ram Singh]. He was Canadian! And they gave him some of the craziest lines to say." (I imagined Iris referred to Ram Singh's snarling threats, like my favorite: "Dog with a pig's face! If I had my knife, I'd carve my name in your heart!")

"The other thing I enjoyed was that I got to wear nice clothes. I only had a few changes of wardrobe, but it was so much fun to wear nice dresses after doing all those Westerns in that damn split skirt. And of course, in the *Spider* film I didn't have to deal with horses."

Iris insisted, as had so many serial actors before and since, that she barely remembered making the chapter plays. "Really, we were rushing around so much we didn't know half the time whether we were coming or going. The scripts were as thick as telephone books and every night I only memorized as many lines as I needed for the next day. We didn't shoot the chapters separately, it was all done according to where on the back lot we were scheduled to be on any given day. Or on which set; we did many scenes on sets that had been built for other movies. I still wonder how the production managers kept things straight [during the making of a serial]."

She did, however, have specific memories of *Overland with Kit Carson,* the 1939 serial she did with newly minted cowboy star "Wild Bill" Elliott. "We went to Utah to shoot most of it," she told me. Then she tried to pronounce the name of the town where the company stayed while on location, but I couldn't understand what she was trying to say. Finally she scribbled the name on my notepad: "Kanab." Several Westerns were made in and around that community, which the town fathers hoped would attract Hollywood producers in greater numbers. A Western street was built in the area to make Kanab a more appealing location for filmmakers; *Overland with Kit Carson* was the first production to utilize it.

Iris was fond of her *Kit Carson* co-star, with whom she also made three feature films. "Bill Elliott took his work very seriously," she said. "The first picture I made with him, he wasn't much of a rider yet. But he always practiced between takes. He got to be very good at it. And you know how he wore his guns, backward in the holsters? Well, he spent *hours* practicing a quick draw with those guns. I really admired him for working so hard to be convincing."

She also had kind words for Ed Le Saint, another member of the Starrett stock company. "He was such a dear man. Very kind to me. But, you know, he was so *old!* I could never understand why they cast such an old man to play my father. Really, he was old enough to be my grandfather."

By this time Iris seemed to be enjoying herself. She was no longer self conscious about the tape recorder, or about the effort it took to pronounce certain words. But I inadvertently brought our chat to an awkward halt with my next question:

"In 1940 you did your last serial, *The Green Archer,* for one of your *Spider's Web* directors, James W. Horne. What do you remember about that film?"

Her face clouded and the spark went out of her eyes. She seemed more than a little sad as she quietly replied: "I don't want to talk about that film. Please don't ask me about it."

I was stunned. What on earth could have happened during the making of that serial to elicit such a reaction? Fortunately, *Green Archer* was the last film about which I'd wanted to ask, and with nothing else to say I cleared my throat nervously and mumbled, "Well, I think we're pretty much covered everything."

That night at the banquet, following the typical rubber-chicken dinner, Iris Meredith was one of a dozen people presented with the inscribed plaque traditionally given to Western Film Fair guest stars. As she made her way to the podium, every person in the ballroom rose to give her a lengthy standing ovation. It was our way of honoring her for the courage and grace she had exhibited during the show. The room fairly crackled with electricity. Even from where I was, some ten feet from the dais, I could see her eyes welling up with tears. When the applause died down, she said just two words: "Thank you." Then, as it swelled again, she took her seat and stared intently at her award.

Subsequently Iris Meredith attended another film-fan convention, but she never became a regular on the "nostalgia circuit," as did some of her contemporaries. She continued her struggle with cancer, but the disease eventually overtook her. Not yet 65 years old, Iris died on January 22, 1980.

In 40 years of convention-going, I have met dozens of the actors, writers, directors, and stuntmen who worked on my favorite serials, Westerns, and "B" movies. I've enjoyed my encounters with all but two or three of them. But none ever affected me quite the way Iris Meredith did. It's difficult to explain, but even now, decades later, I get a little thrill whenever I run individual chapters of *The Spider's Web* and view the optical player credits—you know, those brief shots of the principal actors with their names across the bottom of the frame. Iris always stands there, clad in Nita Van Sloan's flying togs, smiling sweetly and placidly even though she will shortly find herself menaced yet again by the minions of the Octopus.

In those moments, I like to pretend she's smiling at me. •